Ruins

And

Shadows

MaryseMarullo

Copyright © 2024 Maryse Marullo-Paquette
Editor: Courtney Blackburn courtneylb1991@gmail.com
All rights reserved. No part of this publication may be reproduced, distributed, or transmitted in any form or by any means, including photocopying, recording, or other electronic or mechanical methods, without the prior written consent of Maryse Marullo, except in the case of brief quotation embodied in critical reviews and certain other noncommercial uses permitted by copyright law.
ISBN: 978-1-7383004-6-4

Dedication

For those who would like to start all over again.
For those who have a sad past but keep hope.
For those who love a morally gray man with a tragic backstory.

Acknowledgments

A heartfelt thank you to Courtney Blackburn for her exceptional editorial prowess. Her insights and meticulous attention to detail transformed this manuscript into its polished final version. I am deeply grateful for her expertise and collaborative spirit, which greatly enriched the overall quality of this book.

Also, a big thank you to my beta readers. Lauren MacIsaac, Rosalyn Butler, and Tara MacNeil. You always boost my confidence and I love you for that.

Content Warning

For adults only

The content of this book may be triggering and disturbing to some readers. This is a dark fantasy romance. Please read the trigger warnings on the next pages.

Several sexual topics and tropes of this book may be disturbing for some readers. The subjects include the following:

Abandonment

Age difference

Amnesia romance

Confinement

Dark creatures

Death of a loved one

Decapitation

Depression

Forbidden romance

Forced proximity

Forced marriage

Fighting

Gore

Hate/love relationship

Immortality

Kidnapping

Manipulation

Medieval setting

Murder

Mature language

Orphaned protagonist

Paranormal romance

Revenge plot

Secrets and revelations

Shadows manipulations

Stabbing

Slow burn

Torture

Villain

War

This story takes inspiration from the real-life story of Grand Duchess Anastasia Nikolaevna. While rooted in historical threads, it's <u>important</u> to note that this narrative has been <u>wildly modified</u> to weave a unique and captivating story. The characters, events, and settings have been crafted with imagination, giving them a distinct identity within the realms of fiction. Enjoy the journey through this re-imagined narrative, where the essence of history blends with the magic of storytelling. This work is a creative endeavor and should be interpreted as such.

Playlist

Again – Noah Cyrus ft. XXXtentation
Darkside – Bring Me the Horizon
Work Song- Hozier
Tears of Gold - Faouzia
Questions - System of a Down
Born to Die - Lana del Rey
Frozen - Madonna ft. Sickick
Demons – PLAZA
Fill the Void – The Weeknd

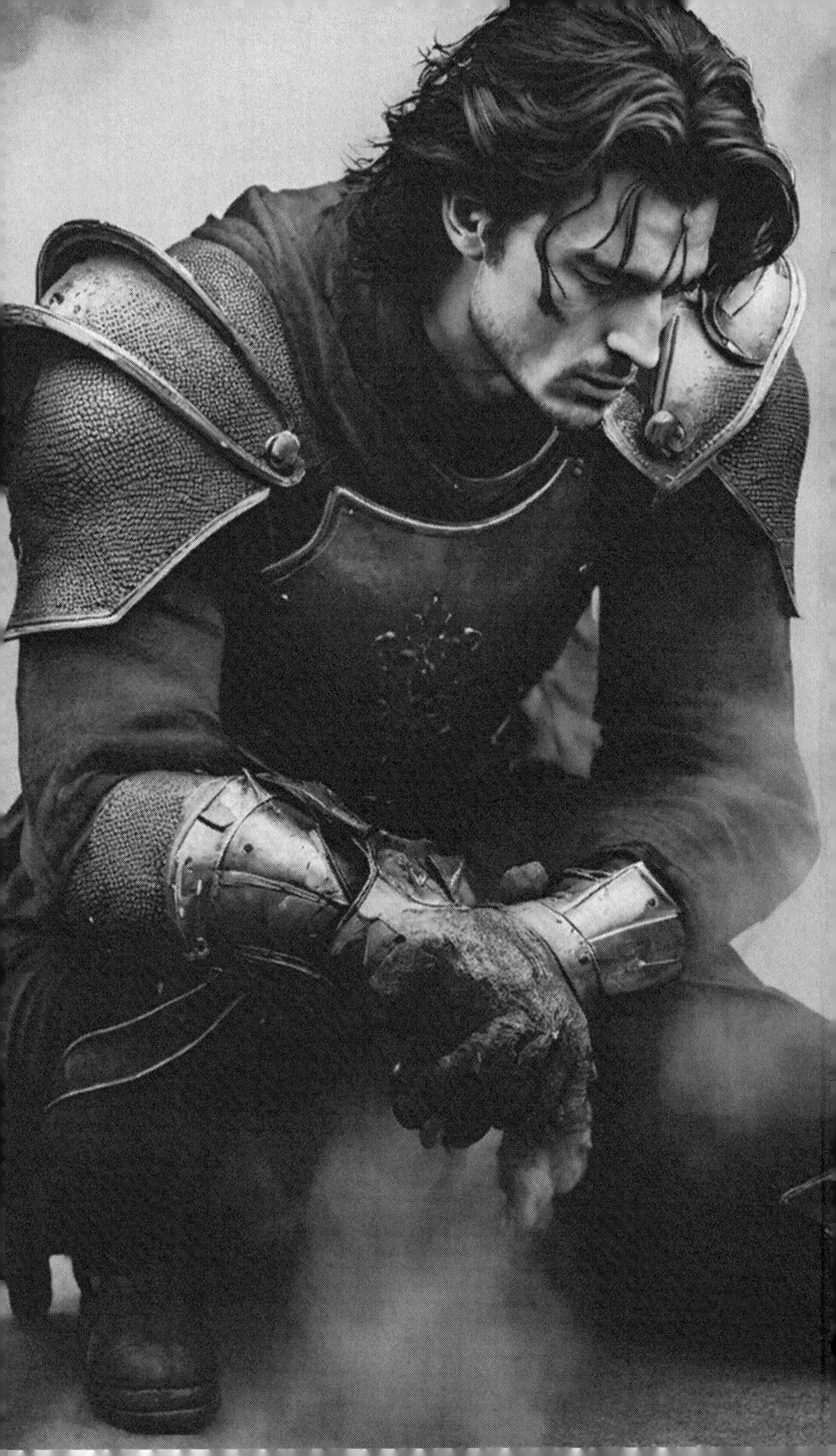

Chapter 1
Rory

400 years before Anastasia's birth

Life as a twenty-five-year-old man living with his family in the woods is simple. Our little cottage is tucked away so far in the mountains ass that no one would find it unless you knew exactly where to look. It's here that I've spent every day of my life with my ma and pa, and my younger brother and sister.

They are my world, my people, the ones who get my jokes, and the ones whose laughter fills our home. We're happy. We're a team. We're the kind of family that has each other's backs through thick and thin.

As for the woods surrounding our cottage, they're magical. Maybe not in the 'spells and incantations' way, but in the way that every bird song feels like it's singing just for us. The trees are our neighbors, and the brooks and streams have heard more of our secrets than the pages any diary could hold. We work hard—farming, hunting, and ensuring that when the winter snow blankets our world, we have enough to stay warm and fed.

It's not always easy, but at the end of the day, when we're all sitting around the fire, in our cozy cottage, it feels like we've got everything we need. But deep down, I sometimes wonder if this is all there is for me.

I love my family, I really do, but there's this little voice in my head that whispers to me about what possibilities lie beyond the tree line. What adventures could be waiting out there that I haven't even dreamed of yet?

I shove those thoughts away most times because I know my duty is here, helping my family. Yet, as I lie in bed each night, listening to the crickets perform their lullabies, that tiny voice becomes a little louder and more insistent. And I can't help but feel like something else is calling me beyond the comforting embrace of the woods. Something... thrilling.

But for now, I keep those dreams locked away. "Race you to the big rock, Rory!" Lily's challenge was half-gurgle, half-glee as she kicked up a froth. "You're on, little fish!" I let her get a head start—she's got the heart of a dolphin, that one—but even then, I'm pulling through the water with easy, practiced strokes.

It's our thing, Lily and me, teammates in our own little water world. Afternoons like this are when pa's magical stories come to life.

As we haul ourselves onto the sun-warmed rock at the edge of the creek, I can almost hear his voice mingling with the lull of the waves, telling tales of monsters and mermaids, his hands swirling and shaping the air into great, shadowy beasts.

Lily's eyes widen as she clings to my side. "Do you think the lake monster is watching us, Rory?" I scoop her into a one-armed hug before diving back into the tale. "Oh, absolutely. But you know he's just a big ol' softie deep down. He wouldn't dare disturb a swim with the legendary

Rory and his fearless sister, would he?" Her laughter rings clear across the water, and I can't help but join in.

That sound is my anchor; as long as it rings true, I know that my world is just as it should be. I'm not as good as Pa is for tales and legends; that's his job, not for me. Cause I'm Rory, the lake-swimming, monster-laughing, sister-protecting guy.

But sometimes, when the stars come out to play and the night cloaks the forest in its mysterious veil, I can't help but let my imagination run wild.

With Lily snuggled in the crook of my neck, having fallen asleep with the setting sun, I gaze up at the cosmos and let pa's fables and legends mold into dreams of my own making.

Adventures of distant lands, cities gleaming with lights and colors I've never seen, ships sailing across vast, uncharted oceans, and beings with powers that could change the course of history.

Pa's stories have a way of stitching themselves into the fabric of my mind, and I find myself yearning to be the hero of his tales and weave it into my own, to explore. It's a longing I can barely contain, a restive spirit that no stretch of serene water or whisper of the woods can soothe completely.

Dreams, once dreamed, have a curious way of not letting go. They linger, waiting for the day they might be blessed with wings. I can't shake the feeling that they will insist on being heard one day. And so, one day, I might answer their call.

Carefully taking my sister's little body, I lift her up and make our way back to our wooden house. She stirs a little, and when I look down, all I can see is her pretty brown eyes. "Seriously, Rory, are the monsters real?" She looks afraid, and I'm not in the mood to put her to sleep with that thought. "No, Lily, of course not. They're just tales from long ago, told to entertain people is all. Magic doesn't exist, nor do monsters."

But Lily isn't quite convinced by my words. She clings a little tighter around my neck as we step inside our cozy home, the flickering light from the fireplace dancing across her face. "But what if they are real, Rory?" she whispers, her young mind wrestling with the unknown.

I crouch down to her level, balancing her on my knee, and with the warmth of the hearth brushing against us, I embark on a mission to ease her worries. "Listen, Lily," I begin, my voice a mix of gentle tones and brotherly reassurance. "I'll let you in on a little secret." I say in a whisper for only her to hear. "Our imagination is a powerful thing—it can create whole entire worlds and paint monsters and heroes. But just remember, it is all within our heads. The monsters and magic are just that, stories. They can't hurt us." I say with conviction, hoping to ease her little mind.

Her eyes widen with a mix of curiosity and a touch of lingering fear. I reach out to tuck a stray lock of hair behind her ear, smiling to reassure her. "And even if, by some strange twist, they were real," I continue, my tone light and playful, "then they haven't met the fierce Lily and her brave brother, Rory. We'd protect our family, wouldn't we?" Ma approaches us, her long black hair, the same color as mine, cascading down her shoulders as she smiles her beautiful smile and gives me a kiss on the crown of my head.

"Not me! You silly, I'm too little. But you are our hero." Lily exclaims, throwing her little arms around my neck. Ma laughs at Lily's statement and adds. "Don't forget your other brother and of course your father, little girl."

She nods, her small face beaming with pride at the mention of our tight-knit family. "Of course! How could I forget the strongest men in all the woods?" Her innocence reminds me of the world we've managed to carve out here, away from the chaos of city life. We have built our own sanctuary, a place where the imaginary creatures of pa's tales are the most fearsome things we face.

Not the barbary of the King's army on the peasant or the public execution. Our days are structured yet free, dictated by the sun's rise and fall rather than the relentless work in filth that the poor people of the Lyskva kingdom must do to please the ruthless king.

Although we may seem isolated, our lives are full. We are connected to the land, to each other, and to the lineage of stories that have been handed down from generation to generation.

In this place, away from the world's sharp edges, our family's love is the most potent magic of all. "We'd be the best monster hunters!" Lily declares, her fear eclipsed by a big yawn. "That's the spirit!" I chuckle, lifting her into the air for a moment, eliciting a delighted squeal from her. "Now, how about I tuck you into bed and tell you a story? One without monsters—just heroes and wild adventures."

Her nod is vigorous this time, excitement bubbling within her. As I carry her to her room, the shadows of the woods outside seem to retreat, the essence of our shared courage proving mightier than the darkness.

And as Lily drifts off to sleep, her fears forgotten, I can't help but wonder what stories we might tell in times to come. Stories where perhaps, just maybe, a little bit of that long-ago magic does exist, within us all.

Lily's soft breathing becomes a rhythm, a peaceful lullaby for the night, and I promise myself to always be the keeper of her dreams—monsters or no monsters.

The last breath of summer has blown, and now winter's whisper flirts with the trees. My brother Andrei and I are outside with Pa, working up a sweat chopping firewood.

We need a good stock to keep the chill from biting too hard when the cold fully takes over. Ma and Lily are out front playing, making the most of the waning warmth, giggling, while chasing the last blooms of the season before the frost claims them.

Pa straightens up, wiping his brow with a calloused hand. "Rory," he says, "would you mind fetching us a couple buckets of water? Gotta store some in the house for the night."

"Sure thing, Pa," I say, setting down my ax, I grab two buckets from beside the woodshed and start heading for the stream.

My boots crunch through the fallen leaves, a steady rhythm that calms my mind. But then, I feel a shift in the atmosphere, one that is not so calming. There's a strange prickling at the back of my neck. The forest, usually so full of sounds, goes as silent as a grave. Something isn't right. I feel it, deep in my bones.

I'm knee-deep in the stream, water gushing into the buckets, when I hear it – bloodcurdling screams, slicing through the silence like a scythe through wheat. My heart leaps into my throat, and I drop the buckets, the water forgotten.

I take off towards the house, legs pumping, breath coming out in harsh puffs. I'm lightning on two feet, never in my life have I run this fast. The fear is like a wild horse galloping in my chest, and I'm not the best rider. The edge of the forest is a blur, the cottage coming into view. I skid to stop in the clearing, my chest heaving, and legs aching.

But the pain from running is nothing compared to what I see before me.

Ma, pa, Lily, and my brother – all strewn across the ground, their bodies twisted in angles nature never intended. Blood is everywhere, painting the grass, the walls, our door. The sight of it, the smell, it robs the air straight from my lungs.

And there, standing amongst the ruins of my world, is a Domovoi. An immortal creature of legend, one of pa's stories come to life, a nightmare I cannot seem to wake from. "No!" I cry, my eyes flitting from one massacred body to the next. "Bring them back!" I plead, my voice cracking like the dry wood we'd been chopping only minutes before. "Please, bring them back!" I cry as I crumble to my knees. The weight of what I'm seeing is too much.

Pa has told us stories about these old men. Saying that the Domovoi are a household spirit or guardian. They tend to be helpful and protective of the household. But others?

Pa would say others are mischievous or even malevolent in nature and will demand outrageous things and make bargains resulting in a cursed immortality and ridiculous favors.

I didn't think it could be true, but here, right before my eyes, is a small, silver-bearded, old man wearing simple tattered peasant clothing, his eyes white, and the blood of my precious family, my entire existence, all over his pale, wrinkled skin.

His eyes, eyes that must have seen centuries, look at me. "Okay," he says, his voice like the rustling of dead leaves. "But" he pauses, and his eyes narrow into a glare so sinister, I feel it deep in my core. "If I return your family to you, you will belong *to me eternally,*" he says, enunciating his last three words with conviction. My eyes widen, and I realize I'm holding my breath. "And" he continues. "When the time comes, you *will obey me.*" What choice do I have? I nod, swallowing down the sob that threatens to escape. "Yes" I whisper. "Yes, I'll do it. Please, just bring them back."

And that's the deal I make, under the setting sun, sealing my fate to a creature of old, to a legend I have never believed... until now.

I'm not sure how it happened, how I got so lost in the hopeful desperation of thinking we could escape the inevitable. But here I am, standing among the stillness of what should be, of what used to be our sanctuary, my heart pounding so hard it drowns out the silence.

Ma, Pa, Lily, my little brother—they are all lying there, motionless, but breathing. Resurrected. Or so I thought. It's anything but the relief I expected to feel. I try speaking to them, to get some kind of response. But it's like they aren't even here, like someone has snatched their minds right out from their bodies.

They stare blankly, their eyes so hollow that it sends shivers down my spine. I've always been the one to believe in the best of things, especially in a not-so- great situation, to cling to the hope that there's more to this world than meets the eye. But this is not one of those times.

I begged a Domovoi, a creature from the stories Pa would tell, to bring my family back from the bloodbath that he created. But now, standing in the wreckage of my foolishness, I realize that wishful thinking has a price. The

Domovoi is gone, vanished into whatever realm or dark crevice it crawled out from.

And I am left with the shell of my family, bound by a deal I'm now cursed with and the terrible weight of what I've done. Mortality has always been straightforward for me; you live, and then you die. But what is this?

This isn't living. This is an echo, a cruel imitation. I can't let them be like this. Trapped. It's all my fault, and now I've got to fix it. I've got to do the one thing I never thought I could. It's a twisted mercy, but it's the only escape from a lifetime—or rather, an eternity—of empty stares and silence.

I can feel my own mind scrambling to cope, to understand the enormity of the task ahead. In gaining my immortality from the Domovoi, I've now found myself trapped in a nightmare. I can never join my family in death. And that means that what I must do next... it's on me, and me alone.

My hands are shaky, my insides cold, but I need to be strong. One last act of protection, as a big brother, and as a son. I love them too much not to free them from this half-life.

I need to spare them a fate worse than death. It's not the end I had envisioned; it's not the peace I sought to preserve. But here, as I look upon my beloved family, I know that as impossible as this task is, and it will not bring peace to my existence, it will to their resting souls.

But as I prepare to do the unthinkable, I falter in my heartbreak, and I need to take a deep breath. This next moment is going to change everything. But it needs to be done.

For ma, and pa, for Andrei and Lily. I look at their faces, my mother and her timeless beauty, my father, aged yet handsome and comforting, my little brother, sure to look just like pa, and little sweet Lily, I commit them to memory knowing that this is the last time I will ever see them.

My breath comes out ragged, tears stream down my face as I stand over the bodies of my family. That old bastard, he fucking tricked me!

He disappeared, leaving behind a curse instead of a blessing. I clench my fists, anger boiling up inside me. With a primal anger surging through my veins, staring up at the sky, I let out a loud yell, like that of a feral animal. The sound tears from my throat, raw, deep, and powerful and it echoes through the forest.

As I scream, it's like I'm releasing some unknown dark power I didn't know that I had. Shadows swirl around and escape from my skin, surrounding me in a coil of darkness, listening to my raw fury. Then, in a single, swift motion, I'm moving faster than I ever thought possible.

Suddenly, I'm beside them and before I realize it, my hands are doing the unspeakable. Their necks... within seconds, they're free.

Free from the half-life that wasn't life at all. The shadows retreat into my skin, leaving me feeling hollow, completely broken.

Lily's little body lies there, so still now that her chest is no longer breathing. I gently pick her up, cradling her in my arms, she's so light that if I closed my eyes, I wouldn't know that I held her tiny frame. With the last bits of shadow seeping away, I am left alone with my grief.

Tears fall like raindrops onto her pale face. I sob, I scream, I whisper apologies into her hair, but it's too late.

I'm holding her tight, as if I could somehow protect her still, as if I could take back my choice, take back the last twenty minutes and be here to die with them! "Forgive me, Lily," I whisper, my voice choking on each word. "Forgive your foolish brother who thought he could be your hero."

There in the clearing, where our cottage stands, a silent witness to my family's end, I rock back and forth, holding what was once my heart, against my chest, and cry.

I cry until there are no more tears left, until the sky turns dark, and the stars dare to peek through the canopy of leaves.

But the night brings no solace, only the cold touch of immortality, and the incessant whispers of my shattered soul, screaming for the redemption I don't deserve.

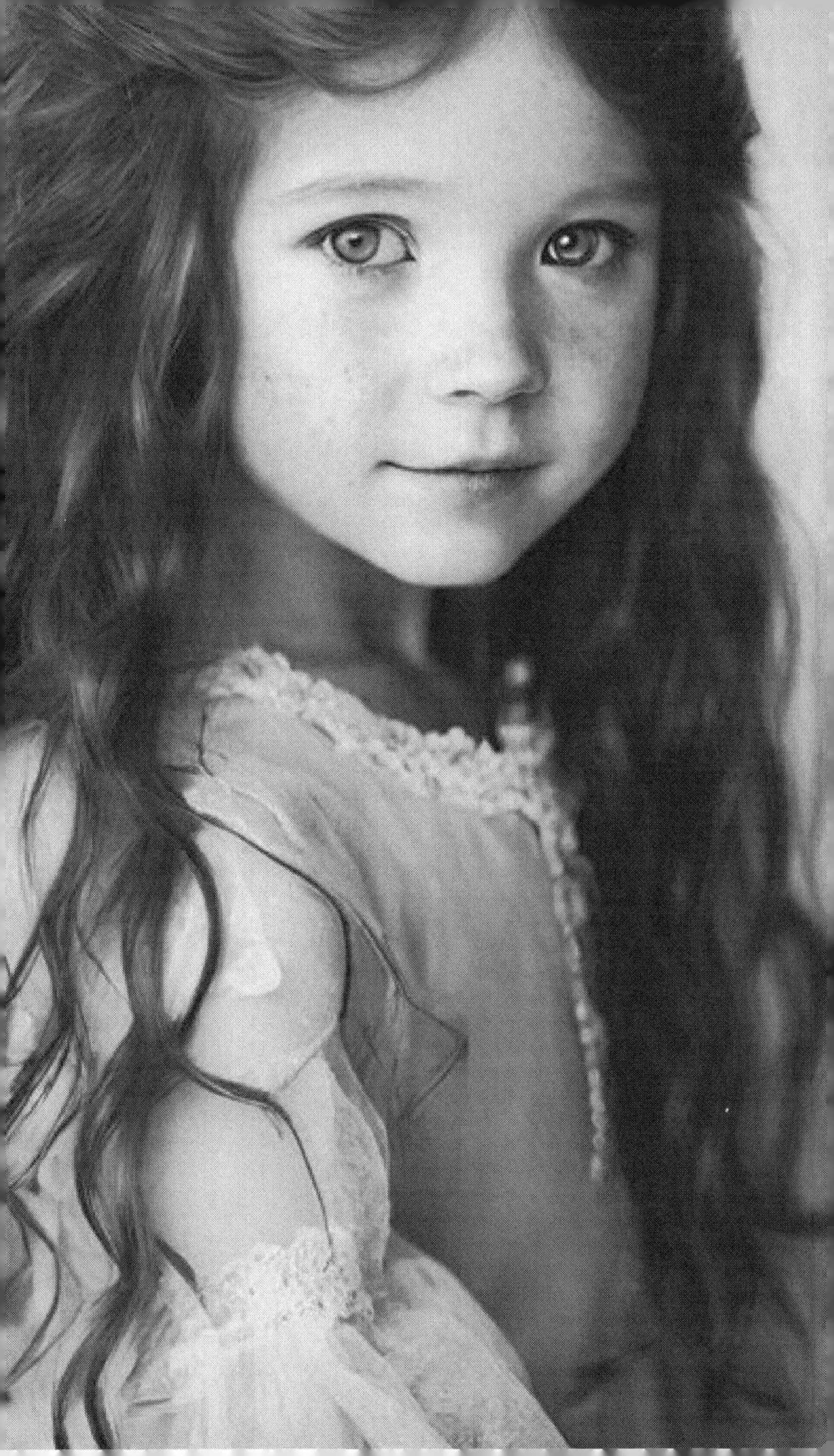

Chapter 2

Anastasia

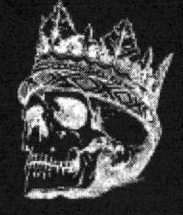

Anastasia's 5th anniversary

      The air is alive with laughter, the kind that twinkles like the chandeliers hanging high above the ballroom where I stand, my eyes wide with delight. Today marks my 5th anniversary, and the Romanov castle, my home, is dressed in its finest splendor for the celebration. It's a swirling sea of colors and melodies, a tapestry of joy just for me. As I skip through the grand ballroom, adorned in a dress as blue as the summer sky, I'm swept up in the festivity. Musicians play with fervor, their notes rising to kiss murals painted on the ceilings. Servant's glide across the marble floors, trays of pastries and sweets in hand. The scent of sugar and spice mingles with the floral perfume of nobility, gathering in a cloud of pure happiness around me.

My sisters, three visions of beauty and mischief, join me in a dance, twirling around the floor with giddy excitement. "Faster, Ana!" they coax, their laughter harmonizing with the music. And so, we spin, our smiles as bright as the candles that light the room, lost in a moment as perfect as any I've ever experienced.

Amid the revelry, I spot my brother, Alexei, seated off to the side from where guests are dancing, a gentle smile on his lips.

My heart squeezes with love but, also a touch of sorrow, for hidden beneath his finery is the truth of his frailty—illness, a storm cloud that lingers over our happiness, threatening to drench our family in grief at any moment. I break away from my sisters and approach him, careful not to startle. "Alexei," I say gently, "you must enjoy the party too!" His smile widens, and he reaches out, his fragile fingers caress the white ribbon in my hair as if it's the most precious thing he's ever seen. "I am, little sister," he says softly, his voice a tender melody amidst the clamor.

"Seeing you so happy, so alive—it's the best gift I could ask for." My heart swells, my affection for him blooming like the roses in our palace gardens. I love my big brother, and I don't know what would become of us if he weren't with us anymore.

So, I make a vow, right there, surrounded by the pomp and circumstance of my birthday—an unspoken promise to bring as much light into his life as he brings into mine.

As the evening wanes, the adults drift into their boring conversations of politics, war and power, their words falling like whispered rain upon my youthful and completely uninterested ears. They speak of alliances, of lands far beyond our walls, but all I can think of is the here and now. My family, my castle, my world—it's all I need.

I dance until my feet ache, until I'm dizzy with the sheer joy of being alive, of being loved. Father's proud gaze from his throne is a beacon guiding me through the throngs of people. I reach my parents and my mother's gentle caress on my cheek is the soft whisper of a lullaby, even amid the celebration's roar. As I lay my head down tonight, the echoes of the day's jubilation will lull me to sleep. I'll dream of laughter and light, of futures bright with promise.

My footsteps echo as I wander through the empty corridors of our castle. The noise of panic woke me tonight. The sound of muffled voices and rushed footsteps lures me to Alexei's bed chamber. The doctors swarm like bees around his bedside, their faces etched with concern deeper than any of the lines of worry that crease my parents' brows.

Their conversations are a blend of medical jargon and grim prognoses I don't understand, of failed remedies and fading hope. I stand at the doorway, unseen, a silent witness to the heartbreaking scene. They don't notice me; they see only the heir's failing strength, the fading pulse of our family's future.

Alexei coughs, his body wracked with a pain that I can only imagine, the sound makes me wince with empathy.

The doctors exchange hushed words, and helpless looks. They've exhausted their knowledge, their potions, and prayers. They are powerless in the face of his suffering, and so am I. Yet, Alexei still smiles—brave, beautiful, unbowed.

His eyes find mine, and there's an unspoken connection, an understanding that needs no words. He's tired, so terribly tired, and still his spirit fights on. I feel as though I'm drowning but the strength that he has is the only thing that gives me any courage in this.

I slip into the room, my presence finally registering to the healers. Their apologies are a murmur lost to the sweeping silence that has settled over us. I sit in the armchair next to his bedside. Mother sits here, on days when Alexei is very unwell. I take his hand in mine. His grip is weak but determined, a lifeline for us both; his resilience is unwavering it seems. My brother, the heir to the throne, the boy who should be laughing and playing, is instead fighting a battle that no royal command or decree can win and he's fighting harder than soldiers in father's military. "Mama and Papa are worried sick," I whisper, "you must get better soon, Alexei. The kingdom is not the same without your mischief," I say trying to interject some lightness into the heavy air. His lips curl into a half-smile, his voice a mere wisp of sound. "I am trying, Ana. For them. For you."

A glimpse of his playfulness tickles his words, and for a moment, I allow myself to believe in miracles, for his sake.

But reality claws back with a vengeance as I look around the room, at the faces marked with sorrow and the boundless stretches of uncertainty ahead. My heart is a pendulum, swinging between hope and despair, and I am left wondering which side will claim me.

The doctors eventually recede, their treatments offering no reprieve. The room empties, leaving just Alexei and me, siblings wrapped in the silence of impending loss. My heart clenches as I hold his hand, savoring the warmth that still lingers on his fingers. "I will stay with you," I say, my voice hardly more than a breath in the air. "Until the sun comes up, until you're better or... or whatever may come. I'll be here, Alexei. Always by your side." His eyelids flutter, a silent thank you, an acknowledgement of the unbreakable bond we share. I find myself praying to anyone or anything that might be listening.

Let him live. Let him be the exception. Let my brother, the heir to our future, survive this.

The candle by his bed flickers, casting dancing lights that play across his closed eyes—the same eyes that once sparkled with mischief and joy. I don't know what tomorrow will bring, but I know that tonight, as I watch over him while he falls into a restless sleep, my heart whispers a single, fervent wish: please, let him wake.

The early morning air nips at my cheeks as the castle begins to stir from its slumber, the sky painted in soft hues of dawn. The unexpected sound of the castle's front gate creaking open sends a shiver down my spine. Visitors at this hour are uncommon, and I can't help but feel a twinge of apprehension.

My heart quickens as I make my way to the foyer, the ornate floorboards whispering under my tentative steps. Standing boldly in the entryway with my parents, is a man shrouded in mystery, a stranger to our household. His presence carries a weight that commands the room, despite his unfamiliarity.

I can just make out his words from where I stand at the top of the stairs, his voice a blend of urgency and confidence. "I am a magician," he proclaims, "one of true power, capable of healing your son." What did he just say? I must have let out a gasp at his words because his eyes, a vibrant green that seem to capture the very vitality of nature, move to meet mine, and for a moment, I'm entranced.

There's a gentleness to his gaze, a sweetness that belies the boldness of his entrance. As if to prove his claims ring true, he extends his hands, and swirling shadows begin to dance around him, dancing in an elegant yet eerie display of his abilities.

I giggle when one of his shadows comes to tickle me on the ribs as I reach the bottom step. His smile is infectious. It spreads warmth throughout the room, and it's as if he is showering us with a kindness reserved for cherished friends rather than strangers.

I watch as mother and father fall under his charm. There's a genuineness to his demeanor, a sincerity that seems to reach far beyond the surface. He speaks of his travels, of the people he's cured, and of the hope he brings.

It's a desperate sort of hope, the kind that clings to the heart and whispers assurances. "You must be weary from your long journey," Mother says, her voice a tender lilt of hospitality. "Please, rest, and we shall discuss your offer to heal Alexei."

The magician, with a gracious nod, accepts her invitation. I'm left pondering his magic, the possibility that Alexei could be saved by this stranger's hand. And on his departure from the foyer, a single thought takes root in my mind: Could this be the miracle we've been waiting for? The miracle I just prayed for.

I've never seen someone quite like him. He stands with an air of mystery that somehow feels both frightening and thrilling. The shadows that follow in his steps seem like living, breathing things, whispering secrets that only he understands.

I'm just a child, but not too young to sense that there's something different about him. He's not like the hordes of doctors who have come and gone, leaving behind only the scent of medicinal plants and the echo of heavy sighs. This man, he's like a character from one of the fairy tales my nurses used to whisper to me at bedtime.

My heart thumps wildly in my chest, skipping like a rabbit caught in a snare. Part of me wants to hide behind the towering curtains of the drawing room, to peek out just enough to keep him in view.

But another part, a much bolder part, wants to stand right next to him, to see the magic up close, to understand the power he claims to wield. I catch his eye for a moment, and he smiles at me—his grin is like a secret handshake, an invitation to a club of wonders. Is he a friend? Or is he a storm dressed as a savior, with his green tunic and silver armor.

Hugging myself, arms tightly wrapped around my middle, I try to still the fluttering in my belly. It's a mix of fear and fascination. He moves with such grace, and it's an elegance that doesn't quite belong in our world of stiff, royal decorum. Why is he here? I want to ask, my lips tingling with the question that hangs back, shy on my tongue. Can he really do what he says? Can he take the pain away?

When he speaks to my parents, there's a hum in the air, a vibration that tells me things are changing, shifting in ways that might never shift back. Mama is laughing at him, and papa seems interested in his war tactic.

They both listen intently, my mother with hope blooming in her eyes, my father with a stern focus that hints at the desperate wish hidden behind his royal mask. I watch the magician. "Ana stop listening." Olga murmurs in my ears, making me jump.

I didn't even hear her approach me. "I want to know who our guest is." I reply, looking back at the mysterious stranger. "His name is Rory Rasputin." She whispers, and I look at her shocked. "How do you know?"

She smiles at me, and then she takes my hand to lead me in the direction of the big door leading outside. "Your mama told me." I roll my eyes, always privileged when you're older it seems.

The doctors would bring all sorts of remedies and bottles on their rare visits here. Those little vials filled with bitter liquids that failed to cure Alexei.

Today, I don't see any of that, no jars of medicinal herbs or various colored potions. Rory's hands dance in the air, and he whispers a language that speaks only to the disease ailing my brother's body. I'm mesmerized, and I feel blessed to witness this dance of shadows.

Each day, Alexei's cheeks seem less like the winter's snow and more like the flush of spring's first bloom. His laughter, once a rare treasure, becomes a melody that plays more and more through the halls of our home. The magician, the shadow weaver, Rory – he's changing the tune of our lives, note by whispered note. I tiptoe into Alexei's room sometimes, just to see the miracle for myself.

Rory catches my eye, he winks, and it's a secret only we share. It makes me giggle because I remember the tales of brave heroes embarking on daring quests, and here, right in the heart of my family, a real-life one unfolds. But with each passing day, I start to feel a tickle of uncertainty regarding the hero of our life. Even in all the joy and happiness that is the miracle of what he's given back to my family, I sense a sadness in him. The way Rory's brow furrows when he thinks no one's looking; the way his eyes hold stories he's not ready to tell.

Papa and Rory became friends, sharing laughs and secrets. Mama has been including him in our family gatherings at the lake for picnics, as well as all our formal parties for birthdays and other celebrations. Rory seems happy to be a part of our family. I see it in the way he smiles at us, plays with us.

Though, sometimes I catch him at a time when he thinks he's alone, and I see it. Is it guilt? He's a portrait of bravery and burden. He's battling more than just Alexei's illness; he's standing on the edge of a precipice, arms outstretched, trying to keep the darkness at bay.

And as much as I want to help him, all I can do is watch, and hope, and wish on every shining star that he finds peace.

For several months now, Dad has become stricter with me. He says I don't behave lady-like enough, I'm too noisy and agitated. According to him, I need to be quiet. He took away my toys, leaving me only a small porcelain tea set. But I don't feel like playing house.

I walk down one of the corridors farthest from Dad's office, hoping to avoid another lecture. I kick a small ball, making it bounce off the walls when a sound at the end of the hallway catches my attention —a soft, gentle melody that fills the palace, sweet and clear. It's Alexei, my dear brother, playing his violin. The music is pure and strong, a song of triumph, of life reclaimed. I rush to his room, my heart a pounding drum in my chest. There he stands, the magician at his side, both bathed in the soft glow of candlelight.

Alexei's fingers dance across the strings, his eyes alight with the fire of a spirit reborn. And Rory—our savior, our shadow weaver—stands tall, even as I see the weight of a thousand unspoken battles etched into his face. He's done it; he's brought my brother back from the edge of a cliff we dared not look over.

But as our family rejoices, as the castle breathes a sigh of relief, I can't shake the feeling that this is not the end. Rory's work is done, but this tale, *our story*, is just beginning.

And as I hug Alexei close, whispering words of love and relief, the magician's eyes meet mine. They hold an ocean of secrets, and a flicker of something like sorrow, or maybe it's resignation. In that gaze, I understand. We've been given a gift, a miracle—even if only for a moment.

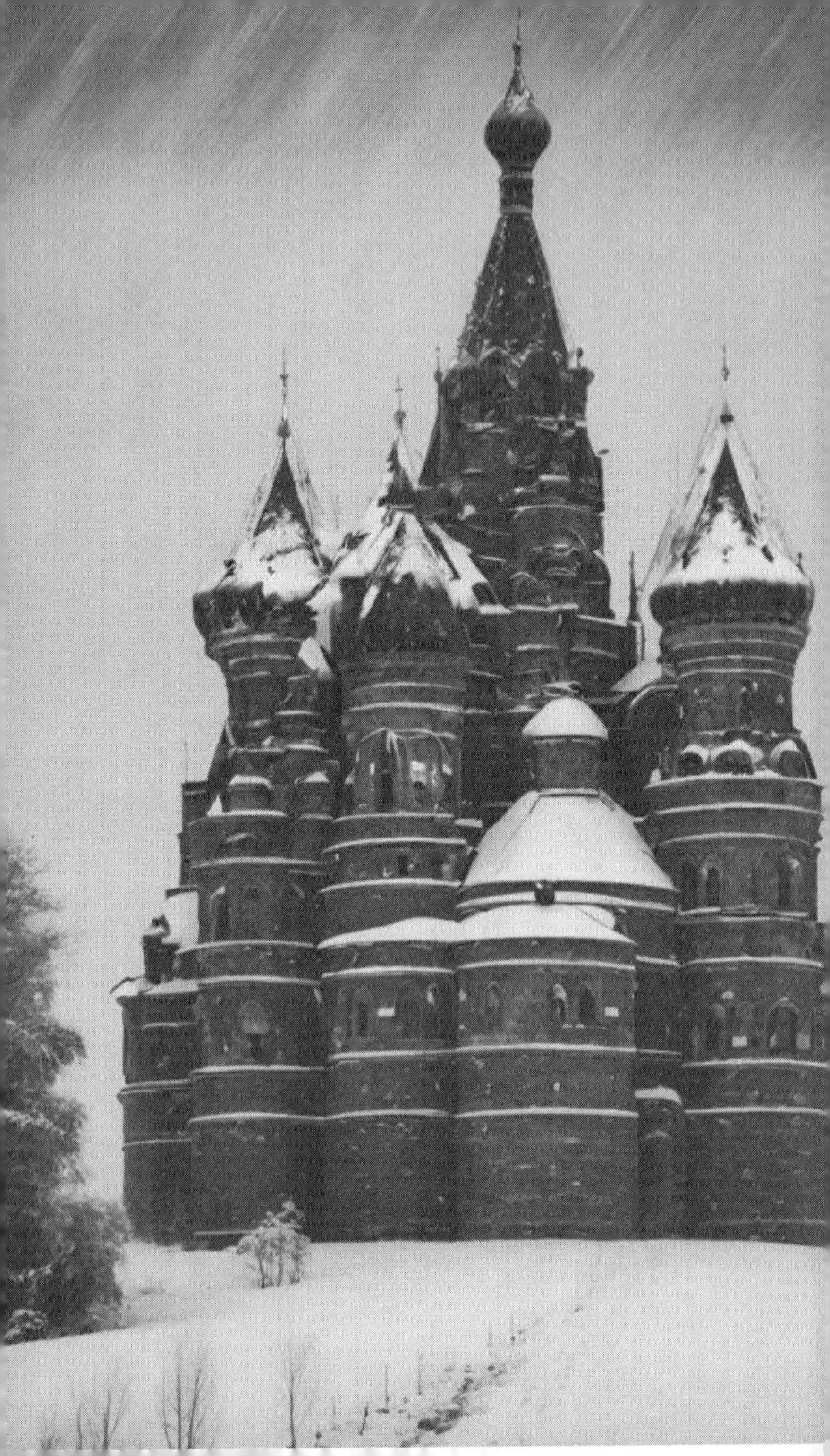

Chapter 3

Anastasia

Anastasia's 10th Christmas

Five years have passed since Rory came to us, yet I remember it as if it were yesterday. The way he walked in, shadows trailing behind him, a magician with the promise of healing. He's become a part of the castle now, a respected figure whose magic whispered hope into Alexei's pale cheeks.

My parents thank the stars for Rory's mysterious gifts, his art of healing that no doctor could match. He's a hero in their eyes, and mine. His influence is like vines, steadily growing up the castle walls, wrapping around everything with strength that's both comforting and suffocating. I notice things, though, the way only a child who's seen too much too soon can. Yes, there's wealth in our walls, gold and silks and laughter at banquets, but just beyond the gates, our people suffer.

They're like ghosts in rags, haunting the kingdom's edges while we dine on feasts that could feed them for weeks. It twists something in my chest, this divide between our splendor and their squalor. My father sends them to war on horseback, but they return broken, scarred, sometimes missing limbs, and other times they don't return at all.

I hate him for that. I hate him for the way he's started treating me. Our relationship is not what it once was. He keeps me locked away, sometimes for days in my room. Saying my spirit is too wild, too impolite for the throne. I feel more like a prisoner than a princess, isolated in my private quarters.

Alexei is the golden thread, my once sickly brother whose eyes now sparkle, thanks to Rory Rasputin, is the miracle heir and is treated as such. I watch them sometimes when they're together, and I can see the cost of this wonder. Rory's eyes are heavy with unspoken stories, and I understand that his battles are not just with the frailties of the flesh but with something deeper, something darker.

This evening, as the sun dips below the horizon, I find myself alone in my room as is the norm lately, the usual guard is absent from the door. A melody reaches my ears, gentle and pure, the sound of a violin playing with a joy that seems to chase away the shadows creeping in the corners of every room.

It's Alexei's music; I'd recognize it anywhere. I slip down the corridor, my dressing gown a whisp of silence in my wake and follow the notes that dance in the air like fireflies. I reach Alexei's doorway a peek inside. Rory stands beside him, a smile on his lips, but his eyes—there's a wariness there as there always seems to be, a tiredness that speaks to me.

Alexei's fingers dance on the violin strings, his face alive with a vibrancy I had feared we'd lost. The moment is a slice of happiness, a sliver of normal, a piece of what our family once was before.

Rory slips out of the room, passing by me. He is no longer a stranger or just a friend now; he's found his way into the very essence of our family unit, our dwelling, our existence.

Over these past five years, he's endeared himself to us all. His sorcery, once a spectacle that captured my juvenile wonder, has become an integral part of our home's daily rhythm.

Rory catches my eye and inquires, "Are you doing okay, Anastasia?" I nod, and we fall into an easy conversation. "Yes, thank you. You always seem to know when there's something on my mind," I confide. He settles beside me standing in the doorway as Alexei continues his beautiful song, an assuring presence. "It's a gift, and a curse sometimes, to notice the unspoken," Rory remarks, half-smiling.

I share with him my concerns, pouring out thoughts of my father, whose regal burdens seem to grow with each passing day. Rory is all ears, his expression soft with empathy. "Heavy is the head that wears the crown," he muses softly, a sympathetic note in his voice. Somehow, his compassion shrinks these vast hallways, making the stone enclosures feel just a bit cozier.

An insatiable curiosity takes hold, prompting me to venture a question I've always wanted to ask, "Rory, will you tell me about your past?" His smile wanes, he seems to shrink back from my question, like he's been stung.

It's evident—there's secrets buried deep within him. He averts his gaze, a silent declaration that some narratives are too dark for sharing. "Some pasts are best left undisturbed, Your Highness," he deflects solemnly.

I perceive then that all warriors harbor their silent skirmishes, Rory included. Perhaps his magic brought us deliverance, but at what cost to him?

Does he bear wounds as deep as the aged tree bark framing my chamber's view? "You are part of this family now after all, and I feel like I know nothing about you, please Rory?" I say, my voice barely above a whisper.

He stops breathing for a second, and then he looks at me like a lost little boy. After a moment, he lets out a long sigh. "Ok Anastasia. I'm really old." He responds with a shoulder shrug, and I giggle. He's so handsome, not more than twenty-eight years old, I'm sure. I know better than to press for more answers, so I change the subject.

"I don't want to sleep." I say, my voice small in the vastness of the room. He turns, his eyes finding mine. "Why is that little princess?" His voice is soft as feathers, but I can hear the edge to it, like he's carrying a heavy bag on his back.

"I keep having bad dreams," I admit, my heart heavy like it's been dipped in lead. His face changes, shadows seem to gather around him. "Me too, Anastasia," he says, looking away again. "Yours?" I ask, curious. "What are they about?" Rory hesitates, there's a world of wonders in his eyes, and for a moment, I see him—not the healer, not the shadow weaver, but just Rory. "Every time I close my eyes, I see her. A woman. I never catch her face, but I feel joy, and love. Like sunshine after a storm."

I pull my arms around myself. "Who is she?" He shakes his head, the lines in his face deepening. "I don't know. I've tried to find her, tried to know more, I've travelled all around the world and still she is lost to me. No trail to follow. So, sleeping..." He trails off, his hands clenching into fists. "Sleeping feels like being haunted by a ghost that warms my soul."

I reach out, touch his hand. It's big, rough—the protective hands of a troubled man. "Rory, that sounds so sad." I whisper. "But you have us now."

He looks at me, and I see it—that flicker of pain, quickly hidden behind a smile. "It is what it is, Anastasia. Now, no more talk of dreams. It's late, if you are caught out of bed you know your father will be upset."

He walked with me back to my bed chamber after we said goodnight to Alexei. I'm tucked in my bed and he's retreating from the room.

"But—" I start, wanting to say more, to find a way to help him. He walks to the door, his magical shadows falling back as he moves. "Shh, little princess," he presses his fingers to his lips in a hushing motion. "And remember the night is for sleep, even if dreams can be...troublesome." He whispers something I can't quite catch, and the room fills with a gentle glow. It brings me warmth and comfort.

I can feel sleep tugging at my eyelids, but I fight it. "Will you be okay, Rory?" He doesn't answer, just gives me another of those smiles—brave, sad, and full of secrets. And as he retreats down the corridor to his private chambers, I wonder about the woman in his dreams, about the love that haunts him, and I hope... I hope one day he finds her.

57 - *Ruins and Shadows*

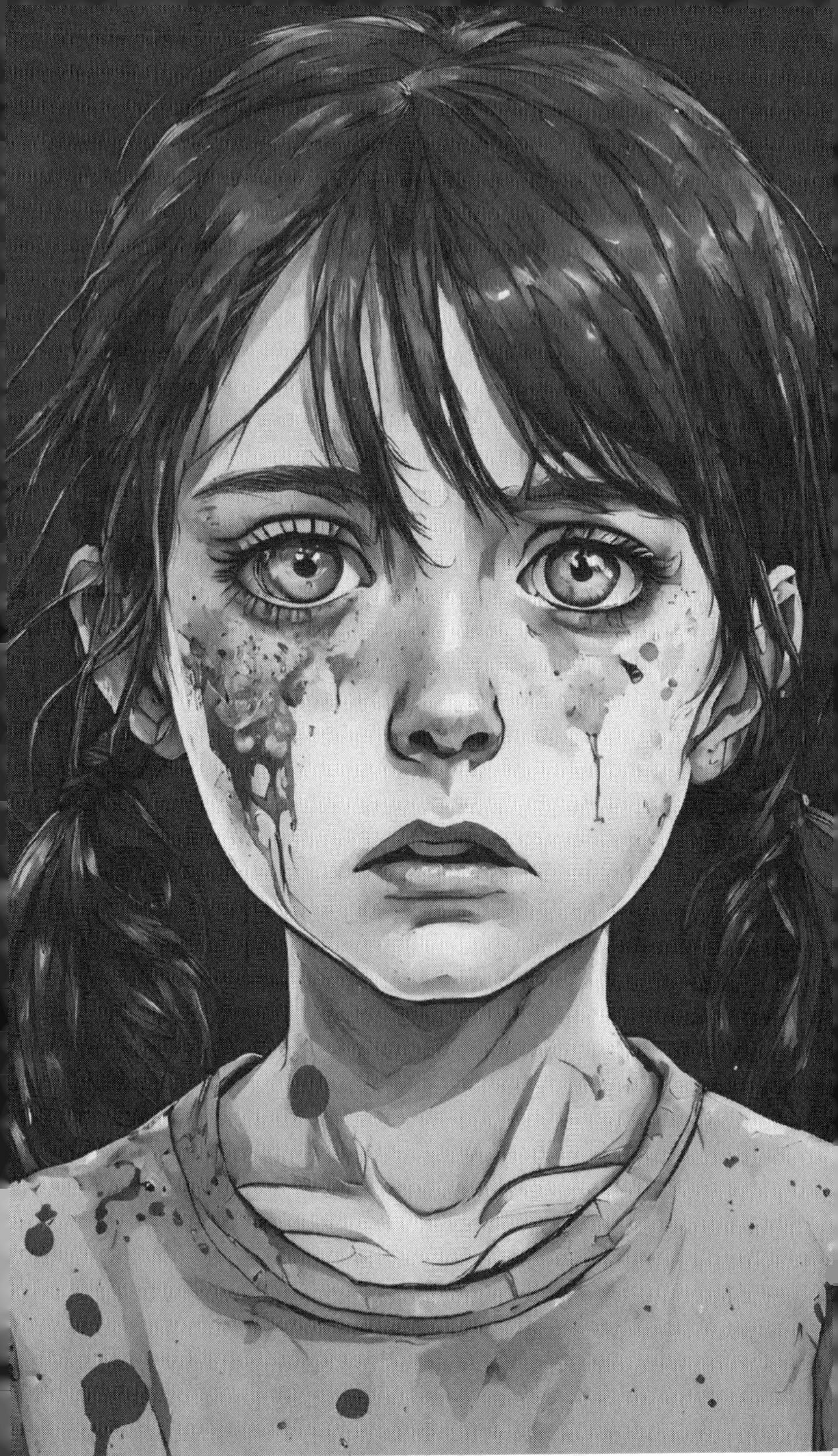

Chapter 4

Anastasia

The world outside, now blanketed in snow, is calling for us to come out and play. My siblings and I are in the courtyard laughing and having fun, our breaths coming out in white puffs of air, it's cold today.

We're making a house out of snow, shaping the walls with our mittened hands. It feels like we can build anything, do anything when we're together like this. I love it; it's my favorite thing about winter.

Out of nowhere, a snowball flies past my head! I duck and giggle, spinning around to see Vitriev, my closest friend from the village, grinning mischievously. He's the same age as me and we've been friends forever. He throws another snowball at us, and my sisters and I squeal with delight as we scramble to make our own snowballs to throw back at him. It's the best kind of battle, the kind where everyone is laughing so hard that your sides ache.

His papa died in a far-off war, fighting for my father, who wanted to conquer new lands in the south. I heard many men died during that battle, and now Vitriev's mama, who has always been so kind to me, is forced to sell her soul and body to make enough money to feed him. It hurts my heart, but even today, Vitriev is smiling and laughing as if everything is right in the world.

I wish I could do more for him. Sometimes, when our family chefs aren't looking, I grab some extra bread or pastries to sneak for him. I hate seeing him so sad, and if a little stolen food can bring him a smile, then I'll be a thief every day.

Sometimes it seems like there is a pane of glass between us and them. They can see us, but they cannot touch us. At times it feels smothering, the constant reminder that here we are, the royal family literally living like kings while my dear friend and his mother fight to make it another day.

I want to help more, do something big for Vitriev and all the other kids just like him. I'm just a little princess though and can barely convince the kitchen staff to give me an extra cookie.

Still, I must try something, right? Because if Rory can do magic and heal my brother, maybe there's magic out there to help Vitriev too.

Our fun is cut short when father appears. His face is like a thunderwcloud, all dark and scary. He doesn't say a word at first; he just stares at me, and I can tell he's angry.

My smile immediately faulters and my heart rate increases tenfold. I'm about to get in trouble. Without warning, my father grabs me by my hair and drags me towards the castle. I cry out, his grip is so tight I can feel little hairs pulling from my scalp. It hurts and I'm terrified. What did I do? I don't understand why he's so angry. I try to pull away, but he's too strong for me. I'm crying now, big, hot tears that make my face all wet. "Father, please!" I cry out, but he must not hear me in his blinding rage.

He drags me all the way to my room, and he tosses me inside like I'm some criminal being locked away in a dungeon. I'm so upset I can barely make out the words he's yelling at me. Something about Vitriev. He's a peasant and a boy, that I'm a princess and should know how to behave around such people. Vitriev is my dearest friend, how could father say such horrible things about him? We grew up together!

I can't stop crying, and I feel so confused and hurt. Why can't I play with my friend? Why does it matter that I'm a girl? None of it makes any sense to me, and I feel so alone even more so now.

Father finally leaves, slamming the door behind him. He leaves me with my eyes burning with tears that won't seem to cease, and my mind is firing off a million questions about what just happened. I feel trapped, not just in my room, but by all these rules that don't make sense to me.

Rory, where is he? Would he understand? Would he help me? But he's not here now, and I'm just a little girl who's been told she can't be herself. It's like there's a big, heavy lid on all the fun and freedom I felt just a moment ago. I press my face to the window, looking out at the snowy courtyard that's now empty and quiet.

My breath fogs up the glass, and I draw a little heart with my finger, wishing more than anything that tomorrow could be a day for play, for being just Anastasia, with no rules telling me who to play with or how to be.

For now, though, I'm in my room, the door closed, the laughter outside silenced by my father's scolding. As I look outside through the center of the heart I drew, I see droplets of condensation drip down the pane of glass, causing the heart to be severed in two, just like mine.

The castle buzzes with life, the kind of lively hum that can only mean one thing—a grand celebration. We're throwing a massive ball to celebrate my brother's miraculous recovery and the Christmas holiday.

The castle is practically dancing with energy. Everywhere I look, faces shine with excitement under the golden glow of countless candles. The sumptuous tapestries on the walls seem to dance to the music that fills the air, melodies twirling up to the highest towers of the castle.

The scents of pine and cinnamon and sweet treats mingle together, drifting through the grand halls like an enchanting spell, promising a night of pure magic. I'm wearing my favorite dress, the blue one with the ribbons and soft lace.

The ballroom is swimming in a sea of colors, swirling with the beautiful gowns and the crisp clean fabrics of the nobility in attendance. My sisters are already inside the ballroom, their laughter floating above the crowd like music.

They beckon me over, and I can't help but skip a little as I join them. I want to drink in every moment, to remember this night forever. We dance and spin, the whole world blurring into a dream of light and sound. My heart aches with love when I see Alexei, watching us with a gentle smile.

He's propped up on his special chair, looking stronger than he has in months. I sidle up to him, careful not to jolt his fragile body. "You should be dancing too," I tell him, taking his hand.

He squeezes back, his grip tender but firm. "I am, in my own way, little Ana," he replies, his voice barely above the noise, but it sounds like a song to me. He's here, he's smiling, and that's all that matters tonight.

I vowed once to be his light, and I'll shine for him as long as I can. As I stand next to my brother and we watch the guests dance and have fun, I realize that I don't see Rory anywhere.

The adults are immersed in their talks of war, wealth, and alliances. Their words are a distant drizzle to my ears, a soft background to the evening's delight. I don't care for their stories of battles and politics; my world is here with my family.

I twirl until my feet are sore, and my head spins with the intoxicating thrill of being alive. Right as I'm spinning, I catch a glimpse out a window, and I see the snow swirling like angry bees.

It's a big snowstorm, removing all color from our world and coating everything in sparkling white. Down below, I see the people on the streets. They look mad, cold, and hungry. Their faces are pinched, their hands empty.

The winter is really rough this year, and my heart feels heavy. I heard Papa say that he won't help them. They asked him for food and warmth, but Papa said no. And now they're out there, looking at us, having this grand party while they're left to freeze outside in a blizzard.

It makes me feel weird, like I've eaten too much candy and now my tummy is telling me that was not a good idea.

Staring down at them from the warmth of this huge castle, I see them huddled together trying to keep the wind from biting their thin frames. I don't understand why Papa won't help them. Isn't a king supposed to take care of his people?

Their King is not doing anything for them. From the looks on their faces, it's very clear they don't enjoy watching us celebrate with full bellies, surrounded by love and warmth, while they try to survive off nothing.

In this moment, something in me changes. I may be the youngest Romanov princess, but now with the growing knot in my chest, a determination takes root. These are my people too and I want to help them.

As I return to the festivities, I think of the future and the princess I hope to become for my people. But it's hard. I'm only ten, but even I know that it's not right to have so much when others have so little. And looking at my family, dancing and laughing, I wonder if they see what I see. Do they feel it too? This twisty feeling inside that tells me that something is wrong. Do they see the same angry faces when they look out of the castle windows? Do they hear the quiet cries of the people over the music?

I suddenly remember that I have a secret mission. I've been sneaking little bits of food for Vitriev. I look around to make sure no one is paying me any mind and run through the kitchen, and out the door leading to the courtyard.

The cold air pinches my cheeks, but seeing Vitriev's happy face is worth it. His eyes light up when I give him the little bag full of cakes, meat, and treats. "Happy Christmas, Vitriev!" I say in a singsong.

His smile is the best gift I could ask for. But when it's time to go back into the castle, something isn't right.

The music has stopped. I push open the door, and my heart drops into my shoes. Guests that were just happily celebrating are now lying in large pools of blood, not a breath of movement to be seen. It's like a bad dream, but I can't wake up. I run and run, frantically looking around for my family, hoping they're okay. But once I emerge into the big sitting room, I halt my steps so fast I nearly lose my balance.

They're all here—my sisters, my brother, father, and mother. They're not dancing or laughing anymore.

There's so much blood. Their faces frozen in expressions of pure terror. Fear roots me to the floor. Rory! His eyes, illuminated by festive candles hung on the chandelier, glowing a shade of green I'm sure I've never seen before, stare off in a daze, as if looking into another world.

His usually playful shadows now violently swirl around him, mimicking the blizzard outside.

I want to run, to scream, and cry but I'm too scared to do anything.

He walks toward me, and I see a tear slide down his cheek. It makes me want to cry too. His face is so full of sorrow, of grief and something I don't quite understand. This is Rory, he's one of us, part of our family. What is happening?

He stops a few feet from me, just looking at me, and for a second, there's a flash of something across his face, like recognition.

And then, he's gone. I'm left alone with the lifeless bodies of everyone I love dearly. I collapse to my knees, holding my head in my hands, I sob, and I don't stop until my throat grows raw, my voice grows silent and the only sound that can be heard are the yells from the angry villagers outside the castle, mixing with the howling winds of the storm.

71 - *Ruins and Shadows*

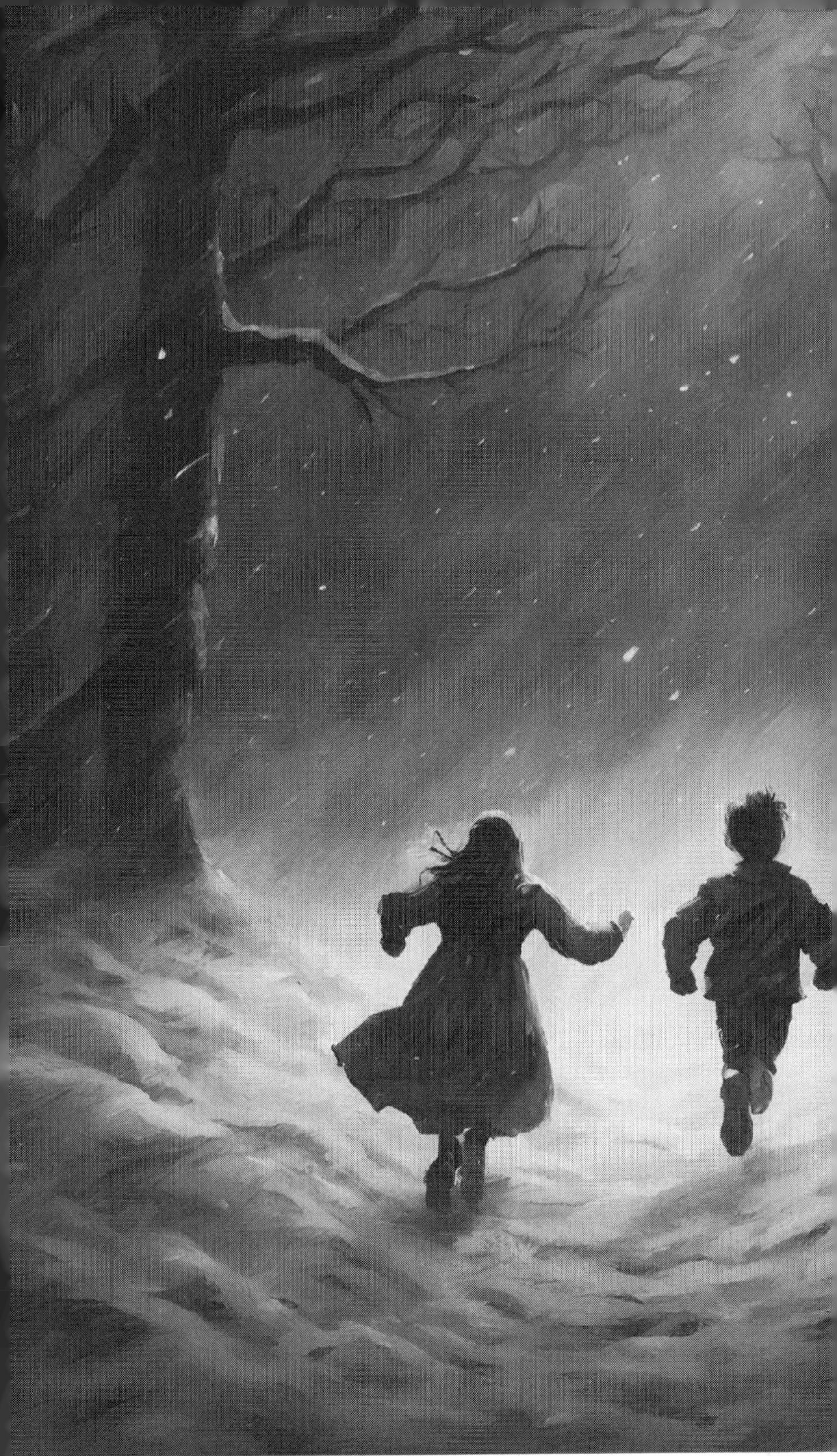

Chapter 5
Anastasia

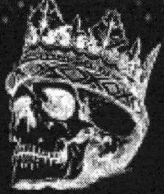

They're coming, I know it—the villagers, failed by their king, who've been suffering for so long while we dined and danced in the warmth behind these castle walls. They're not far now.

Vitriev bursts into the room, his face panic stricken. "Anastasia! The people are coming!" He says, his voice sharp with urgency. "We need to run Ana!" He looks back at the doorway where the yells from the villagers can be heard louder than before. They're closer now.

"Ana! Run, now!" He turns his face back to mine, his eyes wide with concern, but if it were possible, they grow even wider when his gaze finally falls upon what remains of my family.

I'm still frozen from the horrors I've seen, the blood of my family staining the floor, Vitriev's eyes meet mine from where I've collapsed on the floor. Shock registers on his face when he sees Alexei's lifeless body clutched tightly in my arms. I hadn't even realized I reached for him when I fell, wrecked from my grief.

A vision of Rory—a trusted friend, —turning into something unrecognizable, a whirlwind of dark shadow magic and sorrow flashes in my mind and I let out another sob.

My cry of betrayal snaps Vitriev into action and suddenly he's in my face.

"Ana," he says, calm but firm. "The people are storming the castle. They want justice from your family, we can't be here when they arrive."

He grabs one of my hands, tightly wrapped around my dear brother, trying to loosen my hold on him.

"I love you." I whisper as I look down at Alexei's face, a tear falls free and lands on his cheek, one final goodbye to my family. I kiss him on the forehead one last time, and then Vitriev's steel grip on my hand is whisking me away.

Vitriev tugs me along the corridors, his familiar face—once the source of childhood laughter and spontaneous snowball fights—is now etched with the determination of a soldier heading into battle.

"Hurry!" He gasps as we dash around fallen tapestries and shattered bits of furniture.

We reach one of the servant's doors that lead outside. I pause and look back just once at my childhood home, my feet now stumbling through chaos, have danced along these halls many times—but never like this, never fleeing from an invisible yet deadly threat. I don't want to remember my family or my home this way, but I'm terrified the image will stay with me always.

Vitriev pushes the door open, and the chill of the crisp, cold air hits me like a slap across the face. The snow has stopped falling, but it coats everything, making it hard to keep up with Vitriev's fast pace.

"Anastasia," He implores, his hand gripping mine like a lifeline. "We need to keep moving." But where can we go? The world outside the castle has always been a distant thought, a landscape I've only seen from high windows and heard about in tales told by visiting travelers.

"The forest Ana, we need to get to the forest! There's a cavern in the mountain just a little ways in. I'm going to leave you there, and I'll find my mother, she'll know how to help." The grip he has on my hand tightens in his determination.

After what seems like forever, we make it to the cavern entrance and my legs are so tired I need to crawl my way in.

The stone floor of the cavern is cold against my skin. In our haste to escape, there was no time to grab my coat. I'm freezing and it's dark in here, but at least I'm hidden, even if just for a moment.

"Stay here." He crouches in the cave entrance. "I'll be back as soon as I can." He doesn't give me a chance to respond before he's turning and fading off into the darkness.

Alone again, my mind recalls the horrible images of my family, eyes unseeing, skin covered in red and then, Rory. I can't unsee his face, shadows so dark, his clothing covered in blood, and looking nothing like himself. What happened to him? Why did he change? Just a while ago we were celebrating, laughing, and dancing.

I hug my knees, trying to keep as warm as I can. There's no way of knowing how long it will be before

Vitriev returns with his mother, or before Rory finds me. I try not to cry, but tears come anyway, hot, and fast.

Ahead of me lies a path unscripted, terrifying, and real, with Vitriev by my side and the specter of a broken kingdom in my wake. I don't understand. Why did Rory do this? Tears threaten to take over again, but I manage to keep them at bay.

I wipe my face and inhale a long, slow breathe, deep into my lungs. I must be brave, like the hero tales say. For Alexei, for my family...for myself.

When Vitriev returns, with his mother or not, I'll be ready to face whatever comes next. I must be. I need to take this time to rest and wait for help.

I lean back against the cool stone wall of the cavern and let my eyes wonder around, taking in my surroundings, searching for anything that can be of use. My eyes sweep over what I can see of the walls and floor in the dark of night—there's nothing here.

I close my eyes—not to sleep, just to try and calm my mind enough to make sense of the chaos that played out this evening, but my thoughts are disjointed and confusing. I can't focus.

I feel myself fading into unconsciousness when I hear it—the echo of footsteps approaching.

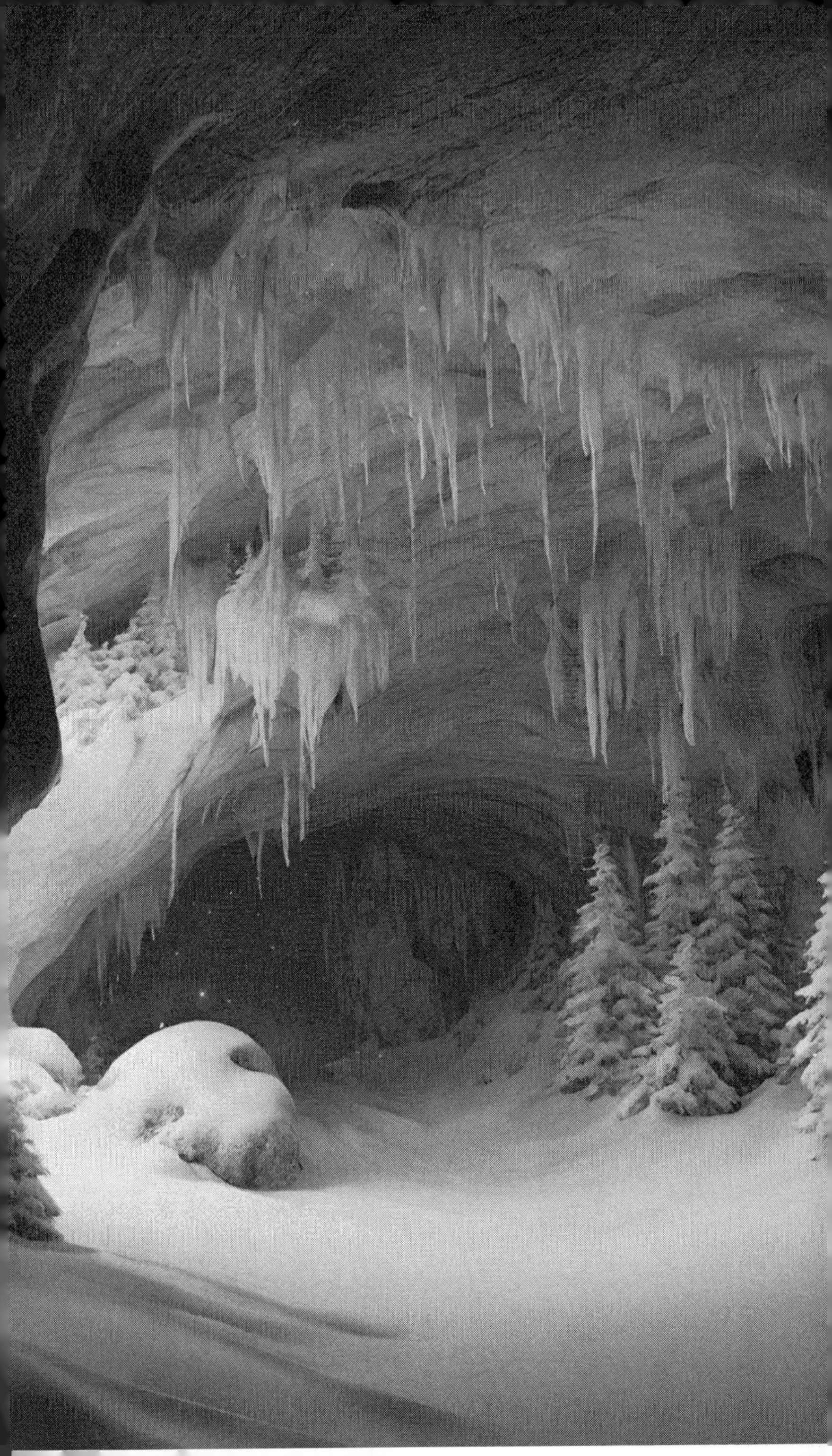

Chapter 6
Anastasia

The sound sends a fresh jolt of adrenaline through me. My eyes snap open, the brief respite gone.

I scramble to press myself to the wall of the cavern, trying to make myself small, to blend into the shadows. Holding my breath, I wait, my hands clenched into fists. The footsteps grow louder, more distinct, and I brace myself. Friend or foe, I'm ready to face what's coming. This cavern has been a brief refuge, but now it's time to confront the reality outside its walls.

I can only hope that it's Vitriev returning with reinforcements, and not Rory trying to finish what he has started. The silhouette of my best friend appears, cloaked in a heavy coat, a sword now sheathed at his side.

His eyes widen when he sees me, and a whisper of relief washes over his features. "Anastasia," he breathes, rushing to my side. Before I can respond, another shape emerges, his mother.

Wrapped in a worn shawl, her face is a mixture of concern and worry, but there's support and love in her eyes. She doesn't hesitate; she rushes to me, and she pulls me into a hug so tight I can barely breathe, but it's comforting, grounding. "You're both here," I manage, my voice quivering.

Miss Ivanov puts a large fur coat around me as I pull back, her gaze intense when she looks at me. "We saw the commotion at the castle, the people... They're saying terrible things, Anastasia. They won't let you live if they find you." My throat tightens as the memories flood back.

Rory's face, the blood... my family. "Rory... he killed them all." A sharp gasp escapes Vitriev's mother, her hand flying to her mouth. "Sweet girl," she murmurs, her eyes brimming with tears. She's silent for a moment, her eyes boring into mine. "You both must go," she says at last. "To the city of Zyvoz. My mother lives there. She will take care of you, keep you safe." Vitriev nods, a determined set to his jaw. "Will you come with us?" He speaks.

His mother shakes her head, a sad smile on her lips. "No, my place is here. I have to stay, help in any way I can." We share a moment, the three of us, understanding the weight of what's to come.

Then, Vitriev turns to his mother, their farewell silent but filled with a thousand unspoken words. I can see the bond they share, the love that will stretch across the miles between us.

"I love you, mother," Vitriev says, his voice thick with emotion. "And I you, my son. Always," she replies, pulling him into one final, fierce embrace. Then they part and she envelop me in another hug before we step into a future filled with shadows.

At least I won't be alone. I'll have my best friend by my side, we will have each other, and the hope of sanctuary in Zyvoz.

The people my father should have cared for won't give up easily, and it is certain this journey will be fraught with danger at every turn. As we turn to leave the cavern, I can't shake the feeling of piercing eyes watching us—a hawk hunting its prey. I see no one though, just the winter darkness.

In the distance, the castle fades into a mere speck, a remnant of a life forever changed. We press forward, the crunch of snow beneath our boots marking the rhythm of our escape. Each mile adds to our distance away from a past thick with tragedy, and every step taken is a hesitant tiptoe into the unknown.

Vitriev's presence beside me is steadfast—an anchor. Together, we traverse the icy terrain, the silence between us filled with the unspoken promise to protect each other. The weight of our journey is heavy upon our shoulders but hope refuses to die within our hearts.

The path to Zyvoz is long and perilous, and as night hits us with its cold, we find solace in the stars that guide us. They, too, have witnessed the fall of empires and the plight of lovers; they whisper tales of endurance and rebirth.

As I walk, each step feels like I'm moving through a dream. The castle is lost to me now.

Vitriev walks beside me, his little sword so out of place in his hand. It's his protection, he says, against the dangers of the road. I still remember the way he found me in the castle, I wouldn't have left that sitting room if he hadn't come for me. He saved my life.

We've been on the move for days, walking under a sky that's too big and too open, I don't think I realized just how big this world is. Day turns to night, and night turns into day, and my thoughts are wild things I can't tame.

It's cold, so cold that it seeps into my bones. Each breath is a cloud of white, and each mile blurs into the next. The cold is a living thing, a beast that nips at our heels and tries to crawl under our skin. My fingers and toes are numb, and I barely feel the ground beneath me, my legs are so tired from taking step after step.

But I keep walking. Vitriev is here, his breaths puffing out in little determined gasps, his eyes always scanning the road ahead and the scenery around us.

He doesn't complain, and that makes me hold my own complaints at bay. Vitriev's sword is always at the ready, his grip tight around the hilt. It's a futile gesture, maybe, against the vast uncaring wilds, but it gives him courage, and I envy his strength.

I wish I had a sword too, not to fight, but to have something to hold on to, a piece of steel to anchor my spinning thoughts.

As the night creeps in and the temperature drops further, we find ourselves huddled together under a patch of trees, seeking some respite from the wind that cuts through our clothing like knives.

Our breaths mingle in the freezing air, and we don't speak much. Talking seems to take too much energy, energy we need to keep moving, to stay alive. I keep thinking about Rory, about how he left me alone, surrounded by the aftermath of his massacre. The shadows that had clung to him. The love that haunted his dreams.

Vitriev shifts beside me, his sword clinking softly. He murmurs something, maybe a prayer, maybe a curse. I don't ask. We each have our way of dealing with the fear that stalks us, as pervasive as the cold. The nights are the hardest part.

There's nothing to do but try to sleep and sleeping means dreaming. My dreams are jumbled flashes of the castle, of my family, of Rory's tormented eyes. There's no peace in rest, only a different kind of exhaustion.

Vitriev seems to sense my unease. He keeps watch as I drift in and out of a fitful slumber, his eyes ever-open, his sword ever-ready.

As the first light of dawn breaks the hold of night, we rise, stiff and aching. The road stretches on, endless and unforgiving. But we continue walking. We need to keep moving.

Ahead is the unknown, and as we march into it with a little sword and a silent prayer. Vitriev's hand finds mine in the dim morning light, and threading out fingers together is a reassurance that we are not alone.

89 - *Ruins and Shadows*

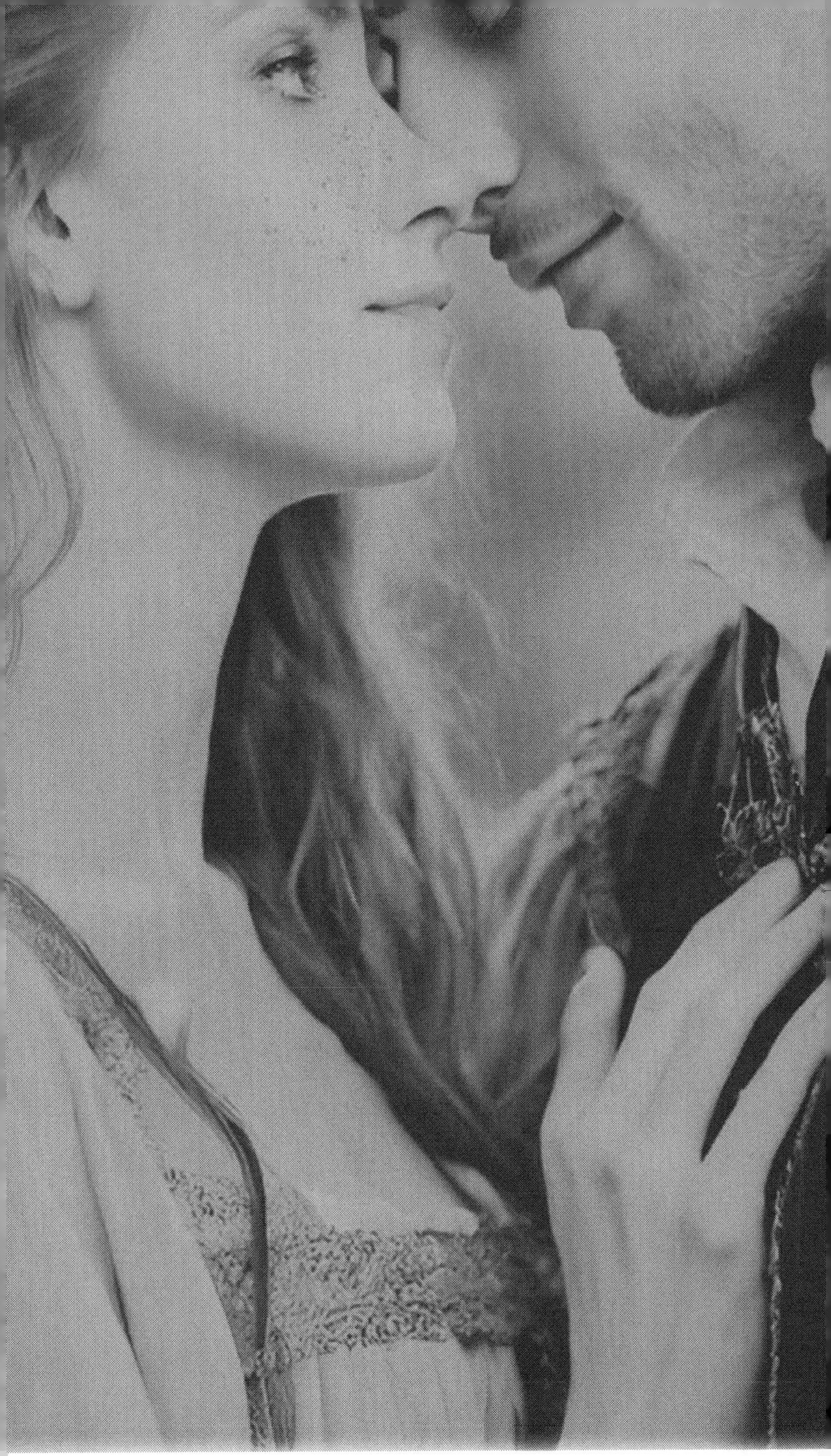

Chapter 7
Anastasia

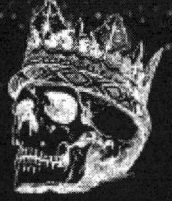

14 years later

I feel strong arms wrap around me from behind, and I almost jump out of my skin. Then I hear his voice, a low chuckle right by my ear, and I relax into his embrace.

"Well, hey there Natalia," he says, a hint of amusement in his tone. I lean back into his chest, feeling the solidity of him.

"You know I hate it when you call me that," I reply, but there's no bite to my words. I can't pretend to be annoyed with him, not when he's here, holding me like this.

It's a beautiful summer day, and I've been out working in the garden. The sun is warm on my skin, and the air smells like fresh hay and blooming flowers. It's a perfect day, and I'm feeling good, trying not to think too hard about the future or the past.

He spins me around to face him, and my world tilts for a moment. His eyes are bright, and his smile is one I've come to love more than I ever thought possible. "I know, but I just love the way it sounds," he says, a gentle smile on his lips. I roll my eyes despite the blush that heats my cheeks.

Living in on the outskirts of the city, I'm as alive as I've ever been. But here, I'm Natalia Ivanov. It's been over a decade since we arrived in the dead of night in the city of Zyvoz. Vitriev's grandmother has a small farm near a little village outside the city, and she welcomed us into her home without judgment, no explanation needed, just arms wide open with love.

Anastasia died fourteen years ago with the rest of the Romanov family, according to the help of rumors encouraged by the mouth of Vitriev's mother.

So, while the rest of the world believes me to be long dead, this village, and this farm life, about as ordinary as it gets, is safe and comforting. And sometimes when sleep is lost to me in the dark of night, I look at the stars and I can't help but think—maybe this is exactly where I'm supposed to be. Just focusing on the now and the earth beneath my hands.

"What brings you out here?" I ask, a slight playfulness to my tone. He doesn't usually spend time in the garden, preferring to leave that to his grandmother and I while he handles the more difficult farm chores. I suppose it will be left to me alone now since the passing of his grandmother last summer.

He grins, a spirited light in his eyes. "I just wanted to see you. To be with you." His hands slip around my waist, pulling me closer. "Is that so wrong?" I laugh, feeling light and free. "Never," I say, and I stand on my tiptoes to kiss him, he tastes just like sunshine.

We've been a couple for a while now, ever since we realized that being best friends was just the beginning of our story. It's strange, this life we lead, just the two of us in this big wood farmhouse.

But it's ours, and we're building something together, something real and strong.

The kingdom thinks I'm gone, dead. But here I am, working the earth and living a life I never would have imagined, all those years ago in that castle of stone and secrets.

I was Anastasia Romanov—princess of the Romanov Kingdom. My thoughts turn back to that time, remembering that awful nightmare of heartbreaking betrayal brought onto me by someone I never thought could ever do something so... *sinister.* Rory.

King Rory Rasputin.

The downfall of the Romanov family, disguised as our savior. The man came into our lives, gave my brother Alexei the gift of his life back, became a member of our hearts, only to turn on us and snuff us all out for his own personal gain.

Rory, *murderous bastard.*

I wonder where he is. I wonder if he ever thinks about me. Does he doubt the validity of the rumor of my death? I grow tense with those thoughts.

Vitriev senses the shift in my mood, like he always does. "Hey," he says softly, drawing me back to him. "Don't do that. Don't go to that dark place. You're here with me, you're alive, and that's what matters." I nod, knowing he's right. "I know. It's just... hard, sometimes."

I swallow the lump in my throat. "He just disappeared." I say, recalling the moment Rory's intense green eyes bore into me before he vanished after the slaughter. He kisses my forehead, a gentle promise. "I know, love, come let's get inside," he takes my hand and leads me back to the farmhouse.

We settle in for the evening, the fireplace crackling and the smell of freshly baked bread enveloping us, I'm filled with a profound sense of peace. I know the world out there is still turning without me, and there are moments when the shadows of my past life creep up on me, but they are quickly dispelled by the light of my present. For now, though, I am content, maybe even happy.

I've shed the skin of Princess Anastasia, but in her place, Natalia Ivanov has found a different kind of royalty – one of the heart.

Vitriev and I have built our own kingdom here among the crops and livestock, a kingdom where trust and affection reign supreme.

I've learned that you don't need a crown to find happiness, nor do you need the world's recognition to live a life of significance. Rory may be a king in his own right, but I, too, have risen—risen to a place of love, purpose, and belonging. And maybe, just maybe, that's the truest form of ascension there is.

97 - *Ruins and Shadows*

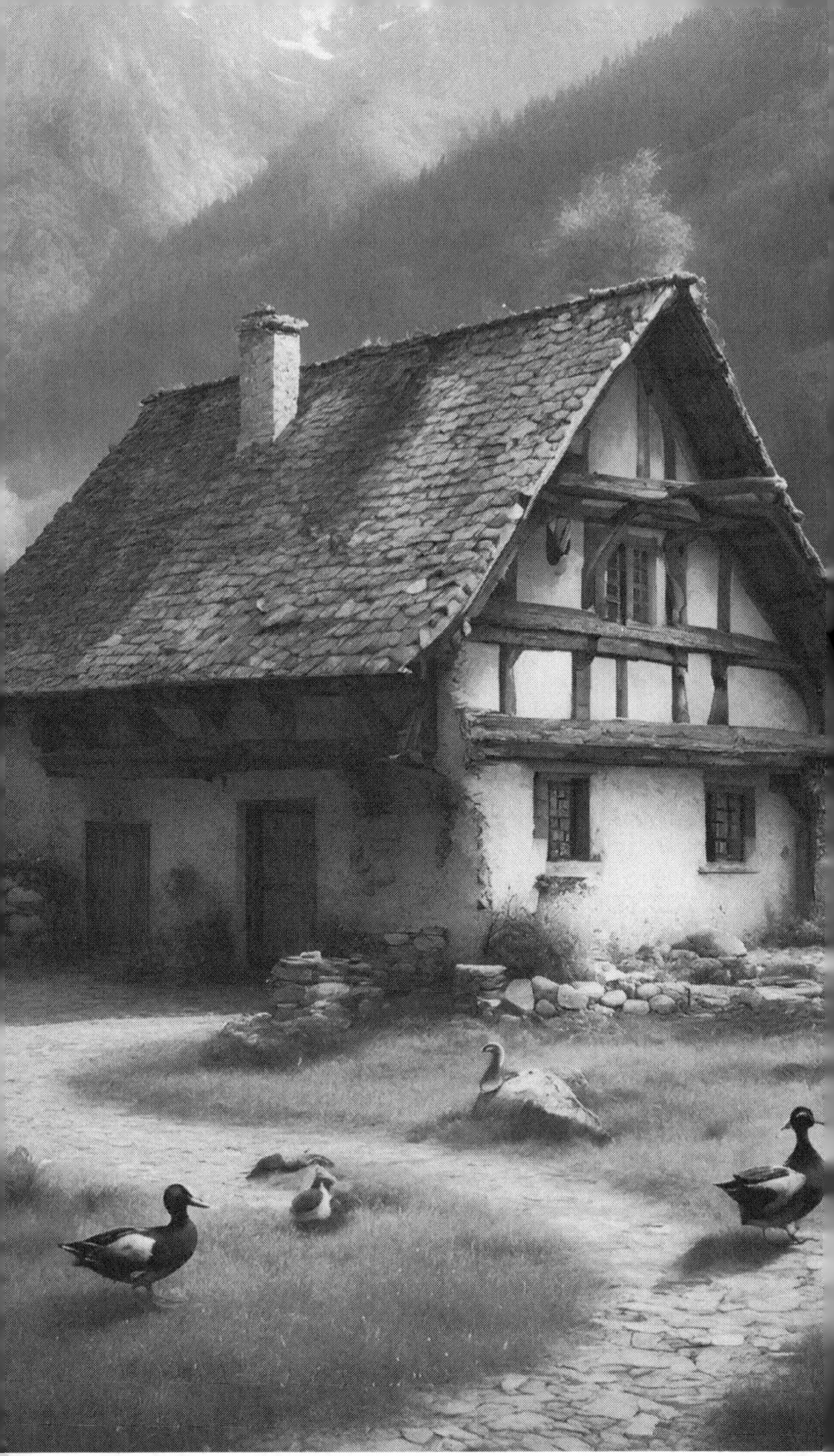

Chapter 8
Anastasia

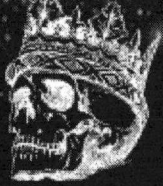

The mountain air slices through my lungs as I swing my sword with a grunt, the cold steel glinting in the sporadic sunlight that pierces through the dense canopy overhead. I can't afford to tire—not now, not with Vitriev pushing me to my limits, not when my life—and his—depends on our ability to fight, to survive.

The weight of the sword in my hand is foreign and familiar. I remember watching father's royal guards training from the windows of my childhood home, the dance of their blades always seemed so elegant, so controlled.

Now, as I face Vitriev, sword in hand, I understand the raw power, the deadly grace required to wield such a weapon. "Focus, Anastasia!" Vitriev's voice cuts through my thoughts as he advances, his sword a silver arc headed straight for me.

I parry, the clash of our swords ringing out through the trees, startling a group of crows into flight. My muscles scream in protest, but there's a fire igniting within me.

He's taught me well in these past years, turning the once dancing princess into a warrior poised for battle.

My nights are almost sleepless. The image of Rory haunts me—the way he looked covered in the blood of my family, the way he healed my dear Alexei, only to tear him away from me again. A friend turned foe; a healer turned harbinger of doom.

How do you mourn a man you thought you knew, a man who was part of your heart's very tapestry?

Vengeance whispers to me, a constant companion in my mind. I plot and I plan, turning over scenarios in my mind like stones in a river, each one polished by the flow of my hatred. However, Vitriev never encourages these thoughts. So, we train.

The rage within me begs for release, a torrent that cannot be contained by the decorum of royalty or the expectations of a long-lost innocence. The world has forgotten Anastasia, the little princess, the girl with a heart unburdened by the weight of a kingdom.

They remember only the tragedy, the bloodstained snow, the wails of a dynasty extinguished. But beneath the veils of death rumors and the silent watch of my guardians, I grow stronger, training almost every day, learning combat skills, and sword maneuvers.

The man who brought ruin upon the Romanovs must be brought to justice, must feel the sting of the same pain he inflicted upon us all. All I need is time.

Vitriev feints left, and I take the bait, leaving my right side exposed. His sword comes at me, but at the last second, I duck, feeling the rush of air as the blade narrowly misses my shoulder.

My heart pounds with the close call, and adrenaline floods my veins, lending strength to my weary limbs. "Good! Now attack!" Vitriev commands, and I launch forward with a cry, swinging my sword with both precision and desperation. Our swords meet again and again, singing a discordant duet that echoes through the mountains. He's a formidable opponent, but I'm learning to adapt to his rhythm.

The mountain's rocky terrain forces me to work to keep my balance, each stone and crevice a potential ally or enemy to our dance. The elevation weaves its difficulty into our training, but it's a challenge I accept wholeheartedly.

If I'm to face Rory, I'll need every advantage, and drop of skill I can muster. Sweat forms on my skin, but I push on, parrying Vitriev's strikes, and countering with my own.

He's relentless, but there's pride in his eyes I can't help but cling to. With each swing, each step, I'm proving to him—and to myself—that I am more than just a ghost princess. The legend of Anastasia will be rewritten, not with the ink of sorrow, but with the blood of vengeance.

Vitriev lowers his sword, a nod of approval etched in the lines of his face. "We're done for today," he says. We're both panting from the long training session as the sun dips below the rugged peaks of the mountains, it casts long shadows across the land, cooling the patches of sun-warmed earth. It's refreshing after all that exercise.

Our shadows stretch out before us as we make our way back to the farmhouse. My muscles ache, although not unpleasantly, from the clash of swords, from the push and pull of our bodies moving in harmony as we sparred.

We reach our simple home, and as I step inside, I can feel Vitreiv's gaze on me, hot and unwavering. The air is charged, the space between us humming with an energy that's both electric and intimate.

I begin to remove my armor and the tension in the air thickens. My movements are deliberate, sensual in their suggestion, each buckle and strap undone feels like an unwrapping of the trust and desire that exists between us. My tunic follows, then the rest of my clothes, discarded thoughtlessly as I stand bare before him.

The heat from the fireplace competes with the heat from his stare, and in that moment, I am both woman and weapon, soft flesh and honed steel.

He's close, but the space between us remains untouched, as delicate and tense as a drawn bowstring. As I stand before him, the air is thick with my arousal.

There's an intensity in his gaze that strips away the layers of my being, leaving me unshielded. "Anastasia," he breathes my name like a prayer, an incantation that hums through my veins.

With each step he takes towards me, the distance between us diminishes until it's nothing but a whisper of space. I am vulnerable under his touch, as his fingers trace the contours of my body, mapping out territories that belong only to him. His caress is a language of its own—a dialect of desire that speaks directly to my soul.

The connection of our lips is full of passion and tenderness. It's hungry, fervent, it represents the ache that pulses just beneath our surfaces. Vitriev speaks, his words weaving through the fabric of our embrace, "You are the most beautiful woman I have ever seen." And then I am lost in the timbre of his voice.

Swept up in the moment, he lifts me effortlessly into his muscular arms, my peaceful sanctuary. He moves towards our bed.

And there, amidst the tangled sheets, he settles himself on top of me and his brown eyes find mine, burning with love. Our bodies entwine. The arch of my back, the curve of his shoulders, the meeting of flesh—these are the brushstrokes of our masterpiece, painted in the hues of passion and tenderness. And ss we find our release; he kisses me tenderly and whispers sweet nothings in my ear.

With only the sounds of our relaxed breathing and the crickets singing outside, I curl into Vitriev's embrace as he folds himself around me, his chest to my back.

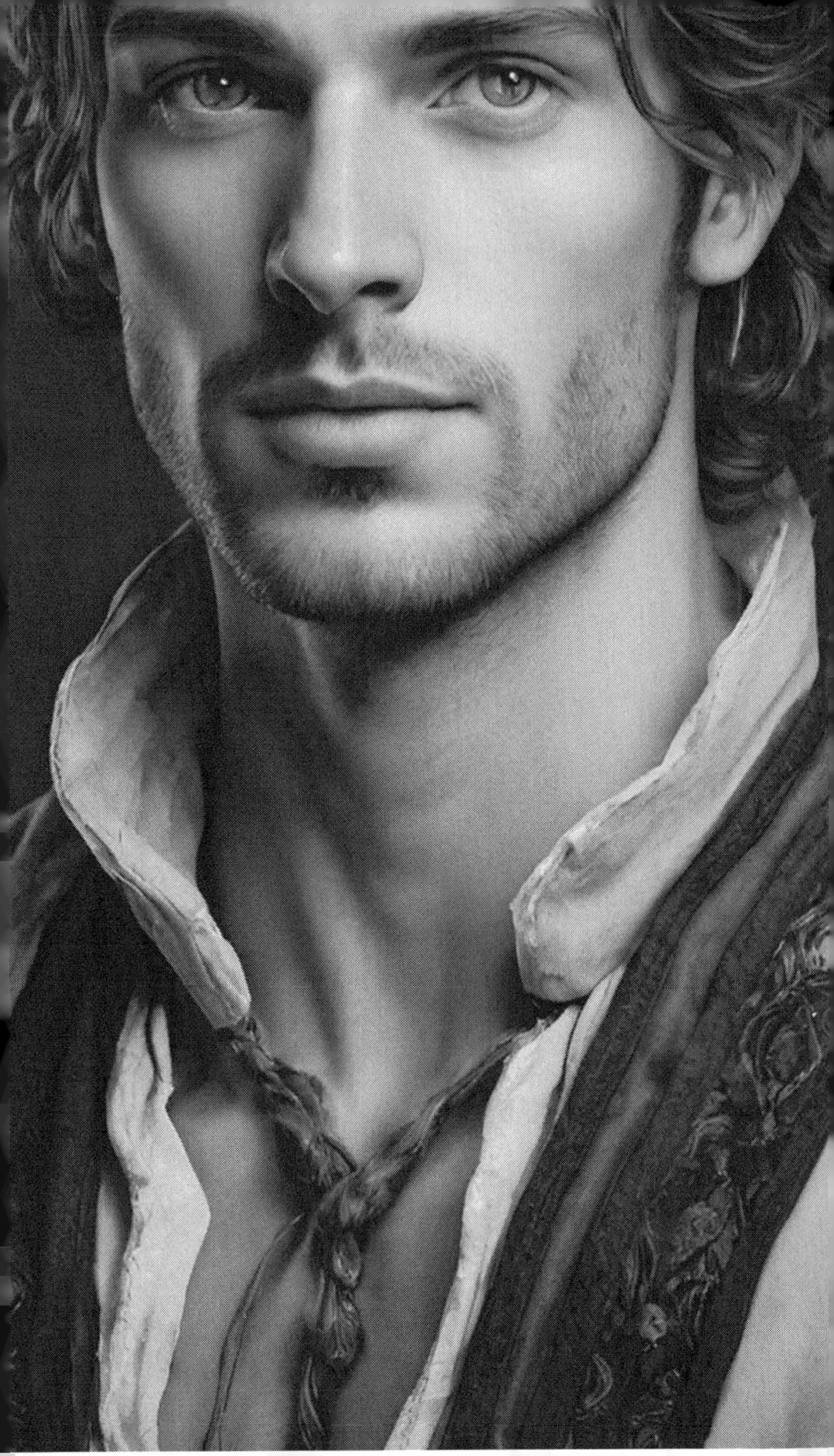

Chapter 9

Anastasia

"Take care, Anastasia," Vitriev says as he helps me put the last of our wares in the wagon harnessed to our stallion.

"Always," I say, then I kiss him softly on the lips before mounting the horse.

One of the farm ducks lets out a loud quack before flapping its wings and waddling off into the field nearby. "Seems like I'm not the only one going to miss you today," Vitriev chuckles, and it makes my heart thump with excitement at the sound. I need to make him laugh more often.

"I'll be back before you know it," I reply, giving him a smile and a small wave before setting off to sell our goods at the market in the city of Oleksandr.

It's an important city for trade and travelers, sitting prettily on the coast. Once a month, the docks bustle with more life than usual, when ships dock, making their own deliveries and stocking up on goods to survive life at sea.

But I don't make this trip once a month for the sight of the beautiful coast or the big ships. I sell our chicken eggs and the pelts of the animals Vitriev and I hunt at the market. I don't just go for that though. The market in Oleksandr is much larger than the one here in Zyvoz.

I love wandering the market under the stars, when the air is cooler, and the evening flower blooms mixed with the sultry spices from the different merchants blend in the air with the salty sea mist, creating the most beautiful aroma.

I look forward to this monthly trek, even if I don't like travelling much. I need time, alone, with my thoughts and my feelings. So, I make the two-hour journey to the night market.

It's a beautiful day overall, but I find the weather a bit gray. The clouds don't seem to want to make way for the sun.

With the leisurely trot of my horse, my mind wonders as it normally does on this ride. Lately, the wind seems to whisper in my ear, and I've been having this strange feeling that my every move is being watched.

The journey's mostly quiet, just the sound of horse hooves crunching on the ground and the occasional bird's song. But something stands out from the calm and familiar sounds. Something odd— strange to hear in a forest.

I halt my horse's pace, listening hard. It's like a whisper, or maybe a hiss, coming from the woods. My hand instinctively goes to the knife I keep at my belt.

Then I see it. A shadow slipping between the trees. It's big, too big to be any normal animal, and it sends a shiver down my spine.

"Who's there?" I call out, trying to sound braver than I feel. My heart's racing, the stallion starting to be agitated.

It could be a lost traveler, could be something worse. The shadow stops, like it's caught off-guard, then it vanishes as if it were never there.

I'm still listening for a little while longer, but nothing more happens. Shaking off the uneasy feeling, I give a slight tug on the reins, and the cart begins to move again. The noise and the shadow niggling in the back of my mind.

The rest of the way is uneventful, but that encounter sticks with me. As night falls and I reach the city, ready to trade and barter, I can't help wondering what that shadow was—a trick of the light, or something watching from the woods.

For now, I've got work to do, eggs to sell, and fur to trade. I need to focus on the night ahead and the promise I made to Vitriev—I'll be home before he knows it.

I'm sitting by my cart, arranging the fur pelts with care. But I can't concentrate. There's a feeling, like prickles on the back of my neck, someone has their gaze on me, I can feel it.

I try to shake the discomfort, but it clings stubborn. My eyes dart around, scanning the crowds, looking for the eyes I feel knitted to my back. It's odd, like being tracked but not attacked, and it's giving me the jitters.

My hands tremble ever so lightly as I touch the soft fur. The sounds of the market ebb and flow around me. Lute music tickles my ears, a far-off bard strumming some melody. I should feel alive, full of that market rush, but instead, I'm caught in the web of someone's unwanted attention.

"Miss, how much for this fine piece?" A voice slices through my unease, and I'm pulled back, masking my feelings with a smile as bright as the lanterns above. The customer, a burly man with a beard like a bear, points at a mink pelt.

"For you, sir," I say, slipping into the familiar rhythm of haggling, "a price that'll warm your heart as much as it will your shoulders come winter."

He laughs, and we barter a bit, as he saunters off, with his coin in my hand and a satisfied grin on his face, the sensation returns. With unknown eyes on me, I slide my hand into the elastic waist of my long skirt to feel my knife strapped to my thigh. Good, it's there, just wanted to make sure.

I draw a deep breath, trying to focus on the customers who come and go, their words a soothing balm to my unsettled nerves. But it's a mere distraction. As time goes on, I want to leave more and more, but we need the money.

The night grows colder, the crowds thinner, and as I pack my cart, ready to call it a night, there's a taste of dread in my mouth. It's not the dark that scares me. It's the unknown, the unseen watcher who's marked me tonight.

I clutch my leather coin purse tightly, a small comfort against the early morning chill. I make my way through the thinning crowd, trying to catch glimpses of their faces as I pass by.

Someone is watching me, and I will find them. In this city, whispers travel faster than ships sail across the sea, no secret stays hidden for long.

Light is starting to kiss the horizon, morning has come. Vitriev, will be waiting for me back home, but I can't go just yet. Pushing a stray lock of auburn hair behind my ear, I continue to wander through the market streets. Maybe I'll spot my stalker.

The hustle and bustle is steady as the morning market begins. I slowly walk, smiling at people as I stride past them.

I catch the movement of a shadow in the corner of my eye. Like the shadow I saw in the woods lining the path to the city. It's a strange movement.

I snap my head around completely to see, but it disappears. My eyebrows furrow in confusion. "What the...?" I mutter under my breath. It's impossible for that shadow to have been cast by a person. The shape wasn't right. Curiosity grips me, and I start running in the direction it vanished, chasing the unknown darkness.

I push through the crowd, heart hammering like the hooves of a wild horse. The stones of Oleksandr's streets are now a blur under my hurried steps.

What is this? Questions race through my mind while I track the fleeting shadows that mock me from the edges of my vision.

My rushed pace earns me strange looks from the people I scramble past, but I pay no mind to them. I've got to find out what's happening.

During my sparring sessions with Vitriev over the years, I've developed confidence and an assured bravery within myself, but this...this is different. This has me spooked. It feels like some sort of wicked magic, and that thought has Rory's face flitting to the forefront of my mind. What if this is him?

No, I can't think like that now, it could be any number of things, right? I need to focus.

I round another corner, breathing hard from the running, and stop dead in my tracks.

The alley is empty, save for some old crates and bits of forgotten trash strewn about. There is no movement except for the gentle sway of the lanterns overhead. The shadow is gone, as if it were never haunting me.

My chest heaves as I catch my breath. Was it even real? Or just a trick of my mind?

I lean against the cool stone wall, pressing my hand to my racing heart and my other to my forehead, I try to calm myself. "Get it together, Anastasia," I scold myself quietly. "You're better than this." I just need to go home and sleep, it's been a long night. Despite these small reassurances, deep down, I can't shake the feeling that something isn't right.

I reckon I should head back now. Vitriev's waiting, and I need to stop chasing shadows that nobody else seems to pay any mind to.

I start walking back, the first rays of the morning sun peek over the rooftops, cutting through the remnants of night. I keep an eye out, watching for any more strange sights, but it's just me and the morning now.

If there is something out there, I'll be ready for it. I'm a survivor and warrior, and a shadow is certainly not going to get the best of me. However, I can't help worrying, will the shadows keep following me?

I sigh a long stressful sound. Feeling a mix of unease and determination, I jump on my cart and pat softly the rear thigh of Romy, my strong, trustful horse. "We're going home Romy. Let's go." He starts trotting along the stone path that leads out of the city, and I'm lost in my mind. Could it really be him?

Later that night

I'm certain I heard an unfamiliar sound outside the cottage. With Vitriev in a deep slumber next to me, I rise from our bed, slip my dressing gown over my shoulders and quietly tiptoe to the window.

My eyes scan the landscape, sweeping and squinting in search of the source of the strange noise, but there is nothing, no one.

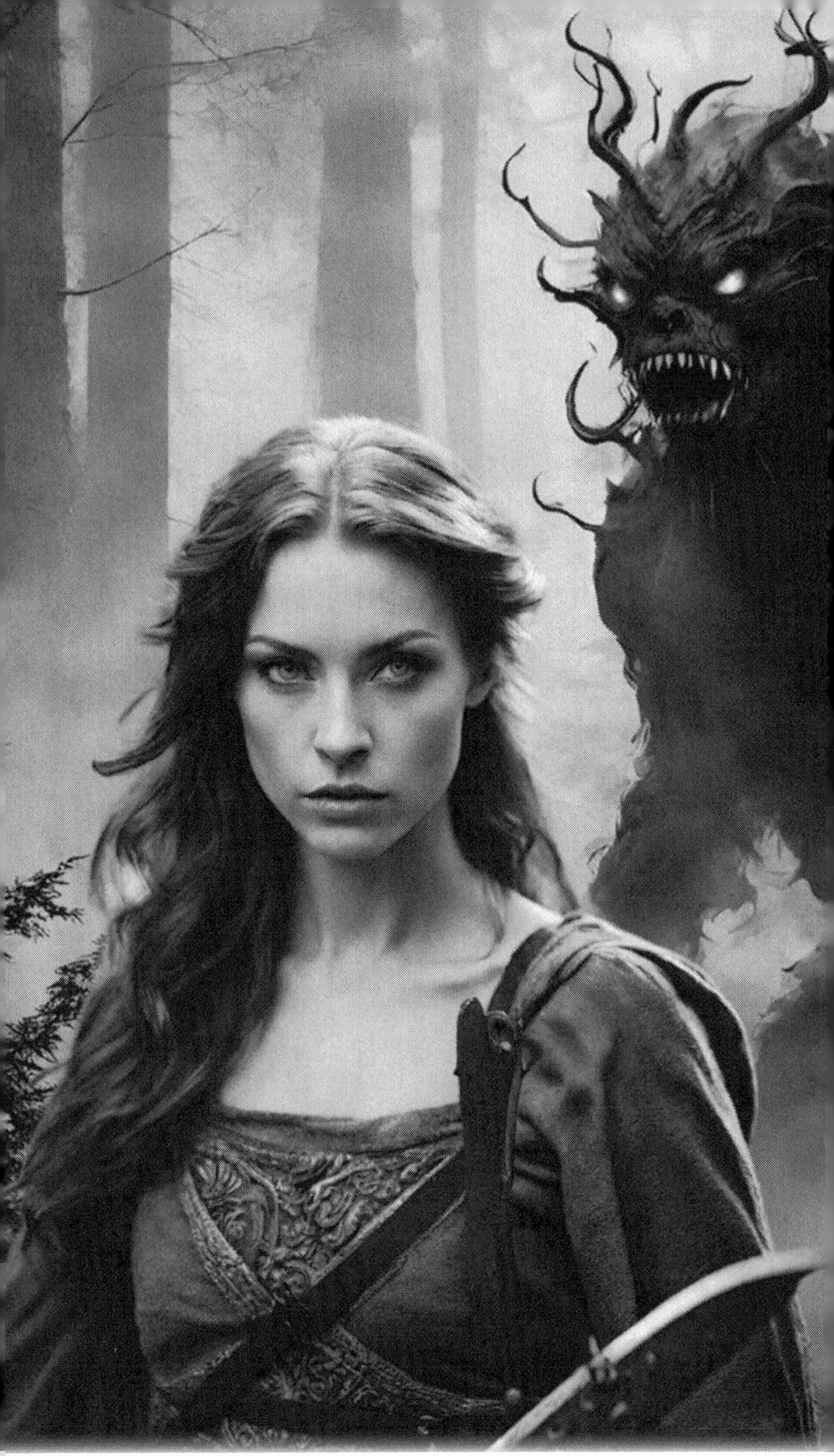

Chapter 10

Anastasia

I scatter a handful of grain before the chickens and ducks, watching them peck at it greedily, their soft quacks a reassuring sound on the edge of the Zyvoz forest. The coop is small and rickety, a far cry from the grandeur of the one we had for the chickens that lived on the castle grounds growing up, but it's warm and safe, a haven for these feathery wards of mine.

I catch a glimpse of Vitriev, from the corner of my eye, his muscular form outlined against the farmhouse. He's chopping wood, shirtless, always a pleasure to witness. The sheen of sweat on his skin and his pale brown hair shine in the sunlight as he swings his axe with a steady rhythm.

As much as I appreciate the view, I can't let myself get too distracted; the strange, unfathomable sound I heard in the early hours this morning, still lingers in my thoughts.

Quack.

The birds are busy with their meal, oblivious to the world beyond their coop.

Whoosh; Another swing of the axe. *Quack.*

Clunk; the wood falls to the ground, split right through its core.

And then...

There! There it is again, the sound that doesn't belong. It's like the earth itself is groaning, a series of heavy footsteps accompanied by labored breathing that sends a prickle of unease down my spine.

I pause, my heart thrumming in my chest as I listen intently.

What could it be? A lost traveler? Or something far more sinister? My young mind understood that the woods have always been a place of mystery and danger, and now that old fear creeps in, wrapping its cold fingers around my heart.

The birds, sensing the shift in the air, retreat to the safety of their coop, their instincts sharp. I should probably do the same, but curiosity and a stubborn streak of bravery propel me forward. I need to know what's out there, to face it head-on.

I leave the coop, making my way to the cover of the bushes and trees, each step cautious and calculated.

Vitriev, noticing my departure, calls out, "Where are you going?" His voice is a mix of concern and confusion. "One of the ducks just wandered into the forest I'll get her," I reply over my shoulder. I feel a small sting from the white lie.

The underbrush crackles beneath my boots, the forest's eyes—both animal and, perhaps, not—watching me tread into the unknown.

As the distance between me and Vitriev grows, the sounds become clearer. I press on, determined to find the source, to unravel this mystery.

Deeper still, the canopy above blankets me in dappled shadows, the cool darkness a stark contrast to the sunny field I've left behind. Then I see it—something large and unsettlingly out of place. My breath catches at the sight, the answers to my questions hanging just out of reach.

My hand steady upon the hilt of the blade strapped to my thigh. The forest's breath brushes against my cheeks, carrying the musky scent of earth and the lingering fragrance of pine. I'm still as can be, while my eyes take in the horrid thing before me, I don't think I'm breathing.

A creature of black shadows so dense they seem to drink in the light, horns crown its amorphous silhouette, and its eyes—green, almost fluorescent—pierce the darkness, seeking, searching, haunting.

Fuck, it'll know I'm here.

The breeze picks up and my red hair whirls around my face, the beast sniffs the air, its sinister gaze locking on to me, recognizing perhaps the animosity that I carry like a banner into battle. Yet I do not cower.

I run towards the monster; blade ready. The beast roars, a sound that echoes through the trees and into the marrow of the earth. We collide, claws meet steel; my blade sings as it slices through the air. "Come then, you vile creature," I taunt.

The shadow beast, an aberration birthed from the darkest corners of magic, lunges with a guttural growl that seems to vibrate the very air around us. Its shape is elusive, with edges that dance like a candle flame battling against the wind. It embodies both emptiness and entirety, resembling a black void armed with teeth and claws.

As I deflect its initial strike, my blade collides with the shadow.

Each step, each swing, is a deliberate choice—chaos molded into strategy.

I pivot, avoiding the snapping jaws that seek to tear into my flesh and bone, my counterstrike a silver flash cutting through the morning haze. The beast recedes like smoke under the sun's scrutiny, reforming to attack anew.

As I've learned to anticipate the moves of an unpredictable enemy, I'm one step ahead. I feint left, exploiting a weakness only I can see, the culmination of hours upon hours of dedicated preparation.

My blade cuts through the shadow with a decisive slash, the enemy's anguished cry a fading whisper as its form dissipates, surrendering to the daybreak's embrace.

Chest heaving, I stand victorious, my dagger lowered but not sheathed, ever ready for the next challenge. The forest is once again tranquil, the only evidence of the confrontation are the lines of exertion etched upon my skin and the intensity that still lingers in my gaze.

Fuck, fuck...FUCK!

I need to tell Vitriev. The shadow beast may have been vanquished, but I know Rory has found me. I know it with such overwhelming certainty that Rory is the culprit behind the conjuring of that abomination.

As I approach the farm, the sight of Vitriev waiting for me, concern etching his brow, offers a momentary balm to my frayed nerves.

His eyes meet mine and immediately his worry crystallizes into action, his strong legs closing the distance with an urgency that mirrors my own racing thoughts.

"Anastasia," his voice thick with alarm as he takes in my disheveled appearance, the cuts and the blood marring my skin, setting his face into deep lines of pure alarm. "What happened to you?" I find myself engulfed in his arms, his warmth a sharp contrast to the chill that clings to my bones, a remnant of the beast's breath.

"Rory," I begin, my voice barely above a whisper, "he sent a creature after me, a beast made of shadows and fucking horns."

Vitriev's hold on me tightens, protective and filled with unspoken vows of retribution. "Tell me everything," he demands, his voice a commanding rumble that I've come to only hear during his rare bouts of anger.

I recount the attack, describing the encounter that nearly resulted in my *actual* demise.

I faced a creature, a perplexing blend of emptiness and form, summoned by a once-trusted friend now turned enemy king.

Vitriev listens, his eyes darkening like a stormy sky. "I should have been there," he mutters, the guilt evident in the set of his jaw, the clench of his fists.

"Fuck off, you cannot shadow my steps every moment. Besides, I am not a damsel. I can handle a shadow or two." I laugh. But there's no amusement in Vitriev's gaze, only a fierce determination. "You said you were bringing one of the ducks back to the coop, Ana." His glare is serious, it sets me on edge.

"I'm sorry, I thought I saw something, so I wanted to go see for myself," I say, hoping my apologetic tone eases some of the tension in the air.

"This isn't a game, Anastasia. If Rory's sending beasts of shadows after you, this is war," he says with a look of dread on his face.

Indeed, it stands as an undeniable, chilling reality. Rory, once a name that warmed my heart with a gentle smile, now summons a creature from the depths, intent on snuffing out the spark of my existence, just like he did the rest of my family.

"I know," I reply, my grip on Vitriev's arms a plea for grounding. "I know and I'm ready. Today was a warning—a prelude to the battle that awaits us."

Vitriev pulls back to look me in the eye, his gaze fierce yet filled with a tenderness that is uniquely ours.

"Then we face it together." His resolve is a fortress, his presence my stronghold.

The farm is quiet as we sit in the dim light of the kitchen, maps and old tomes spread before us on the table. We need to move, as well as formulate a plan.

After helping to treat and dress my wounds from my unexpected battle, Vitriev insisted we begin our preparations immediately.

Sensing my unease, he slides his hand across the table to grasp mine. The unspoken words in his eyes, a silent promise that I am not alone in this darkening world.

He squeezes my hand before his eyes return to scanning the pages, his mind racing.

"We must find allies," he insists with a decisiveness that is born of necessity. "The Smithson's to the north, if we can..." His voice trails off, our planning is interrupted by a soft tapping at the window—a messenger bird, recognizable by its gray feathers and the faint glow of enchantment about its beak.

I rise to receive it, my fingers gentle as I untie the message from its leg. The script is familiar, urgent, and as I read, my breath catches. "It's from Lysandra," I divulge, the name of a good friend and spy for us in the village just outside my childhood castle. "She says Rory is never seen among the people, that they are doubting he is even there in the kingdom."

I look up from the parchment, my eyes locked with Vitriev's from where I stand at the window, unblinking. "He's probably close now." Vitriev declares, his voice a low murmur that doesn't need volume to carry its conviction. "I know," I reply, my voice almost non-existent.

The candle flames dim, succumbing to the relentless flow of melted wax. Vitriev stands and walks to my side. Though our bodies may be fatigued, our spirits remain awake.

"We must prepare our things for the move so we can be ready to depart the day after, Ana." With his words echoing in the silence, I feel the truth of them.

I pull on my armor, and its weight is strangely comforting. The days of silk dresses seem like a lifetime ago. Now, leather and steel are my preferred garb. It's a tangible reminder that life has changed, that I have changed.

The wooden wagon is packed with supplies needed for the move and it's hitched up to Romy. Vitriev secures his own armor, glancing up every now and then, his eyes scanning the forest tree line.

We're almost ready for our departure, when the forest erupts with a sound so gutturally deep it could be the earth itself bellowing, followed by what sounds like very large footsteps, crushing and stomping.

Birds are scared into flight, Vitriev freezes, our eyes locking in silent communication.

Springing into action, I climb into the cart, Vitriev leaping in beside me as he whips the reins, urging Romy into a frantic gallop.

I dare a glance back, towards the tree line now obscured by the dust kicked up by our desperate escape. The sound—it's growing distant, and yet I can't shake the feeling of eyes on us, watching, waiting.

Riding hard and fast with the village as our destination, I don't speak, and neither does Vitriev. We know the stakes; we've played this game before. And as the cart rattles beneath us, my mind races—green eyes, black hair. Rory.

The faces of my family—my mother, father, and siblings—flash before me in a cruel parody of reality, their smiles warped into expressions of horror. It's the same every time I'm reminded of my nightmares.

There's Rory, his hands dripping with shadows and blood. The remnants of my dreams, echoing the desperate pleas of my family as they beg for compassion from a foe bearing a hauntingly familiar smile. In the quiet of the night, I am just a girl haunted by dreams twisted from memories that refuse to be buried. The dreams are relentless, they're monstrous echoes of a past I can never return to.

These nightmares, they're not just figments of my imagination. They're messages—a reality that Rory, once my confidante, now my nightmare, has found me.

Fucker! It took him fourteen years to find me, and it shakes me, because that means he won't give up.

Never.

He has taken everything from me, and these nightmares are an unwavering connection to a life that was stolen from me.

They speak of debts unpaid and a vengeance that simmers like a slow-burning flame within me. One day, Rory will know that the true nightmare is not the one that haunts *my* sleep, but the one that awaits *him* when I awaken.

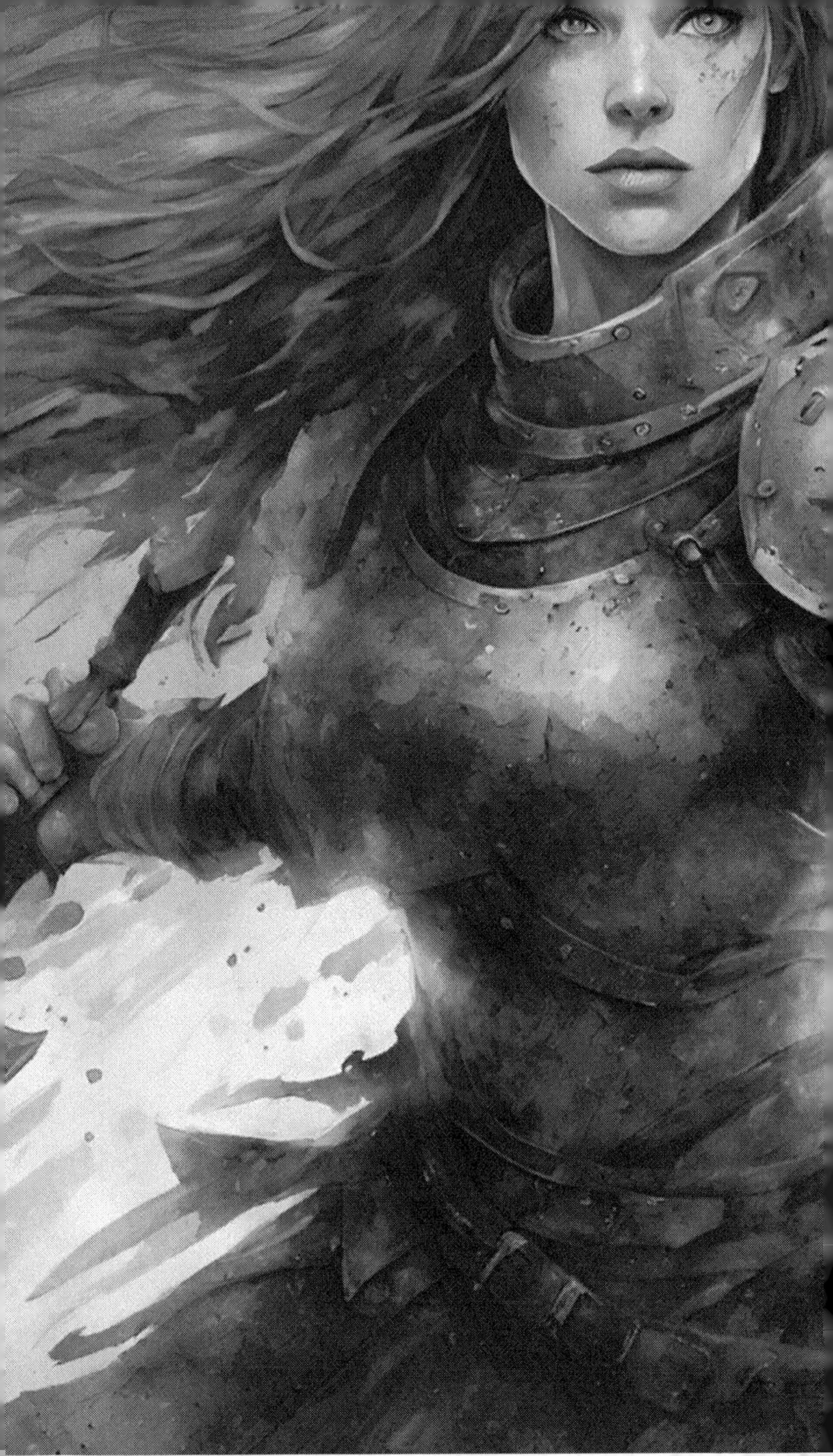

Chapter 11

Anastasia

We enter the inn located in the village, eyes cautiously scanning the room. I feel a small tinge of relief being behind a closed door, even if this hostel isn't much of a shelter against the evil out there.

Carefully approaching the innkeeper, Vitriev grabs my hand in his, his grip is a welcome addition to that small relief. "Just one room, if you have it," he tells the innkeeper, his voice pitched low.

The innkeeper nods, a flicker of recognition passing over his face before he masks it with a businesslike smile, his eyes glancing at our locked hands.

The room is a simple space consisting of a bed, a table with two chairs, and a small chest of drawers.

There's a heavy sense of weariness that seems to permeate the air, as if the walls themselves are tired of standing. But for us, it's a haven—a place to rest and, more importantly, to prepare.

We don't bother to unpack; our bags stay closed, our weapons within reach, our wagon and horse with our supplies are in the barn outside the inn.

Vitriev's moves are efficient, securing the door and windows, while I carry a chair to wedge below the doorknob. "Just in case," I murmur, and Vitriev nods.

We're a team, moving in synchronization born from years of looking over our shoulders. We're hunched over the small table in our room, an old map scattered like fallen leaves in autumn.

We're supposed to be figuring out where to go next, to stay out of Rory's reach, but my mind, it's stuck on him – on what he did, on what he's become.

Vitriev's eyes are on the map, tracing routes with his finger, his brow furrowed with concentration. I break the silence, telling him about my craving for justice, for confronting Rory. I need to fuck him up, I need to kill him. It's like a fire inside me that won't go out, no matter how much time passes. "Anastasia, this isn't just about what you want," Vitriev snaps, his voice sharp like he's trying to cut through my stubbornness.

He's mad, I can tell, mad that I won't let go, that I'm still clinging to a past that's out to get us. But I can't help it. Rory's betrayal, it's a wound that won't heal, and the only medicine I can think of is facing him, looking him in the eyes, and asking him that one question – why? "I don't understand, Vitriev," I say, the shadows from the flickering flames of the lit candle on the table playing across my face. "How can we just keep running? There has to be a way to fight back, to get justice for what Rory has done."

Vitriev looks up from the map, his expression etched with concern. "We have to be smart about this," he urges, his fingers paused from tracing invisible paths.

"We need to stay alive." He speaks.

"But it's more than that Vitriev! Don't you see? He's taken everything from us." My voice hitched as I lean in. "I *need* to face him—to ask him why he ripped our lives apart!" He shakes his head, frustration clouding his voice. "It's not that simple. Confronting Rory could mean the end for us."

The world outside changes drastically, the sun disappearing behind thick grey clouds, the wind rattling on the windows.

Goosebumps make their way along my spine when I hear the footsteps, the same I heard in the woods the other day, but now, it's like they're a hundred. I run to the window and look outside, everything spins.

The shadows spill out like ink, roaming the village streets—they creep, and they crawl, and they bring death with them. The shadow beast, gnashing and clawing through the village, and my heart bursts with a terror that sparks my blood to fire.

I'm no longer Natalia Ivanov, the farm girl; I am Anastasia Romanov, and my people are dying. "Beware!" I scream, my voice drowning in the chaos, But the village is already a nightmare come alive, with bodies falling and the wretched sounds of sorrow.

I need to fight. "No, Anastasia!" Vitriev's grip is iron around my arm, holding me back. "It's suicide!"

"Let me go!" I retort. My eyes are fiery comets, my hands bawled into fists. "They're my people! I can't just—"

"Listen!" he insists, desperation etching his face. "We have a plan. We'll head north, find the Smithson's." He is reason, he is sense. "And what of these people, Vitriev? Will you turn your back on their screams?" I feel it.

The urge to rush into the fray, sword in hand. "No," I hiss, a serpent ready to strike. "No, we must—" I hear it all—the chaos, the cries for help, the sound of a world being torn apart.

I can't just stand by. My hand clenches around the hilt of my sword, the one I've kept on my side. Vitriev eyes widen, knowing what's coming. There, I see it—a sight that chills me to my core.

Through the inn's dusty window, a beast looms over a man, towering and terrifying. It's easily nine feet tall, its muscles rippling shadows and death.

The poor farmer doesn't stand a chance.

The monster tears him in two, blood spraying like red rain over his family, who scream and scatter, trying to escape the nightmare before them. I turn my face away, bile rising in my throat, my heart aching for the lives being shattered.

I'm no stranger to monsters, to horrors that slip through the night, but this—this is a cruelness that reaches deep into the marrow. It's a wake-up call, a scream that cuts through the numbness we've wrapped ourselves in.

This fight isn't just about hiding and running. There are people out here, innocent lives being snuffed out by the shadows that Rory, that fucking traitor, sends to hunt me down. Suddenly, the air itself seems to crack, the bass of a shout—Rory's voice, a thunderous call. "PRINCESS!" His voice finds me, and I am lightning.

I am wrath and fury. With a roar, I strike, my fist colliding with Vitriev's jaw—he staggers, and I bolt. Out the door, into the carnage.

Rory's voice coils around my heart, a clarion call that cannot be ignored. My feet pound the earth, my breathing ragged, my eyes wildly searching.

I see them, the villagers, my people—slashed, and shredded.

Their life's blood paints a grotesque tapestry on the cobblestones. Panic sets my skin to prickle, and horror claws at my throat. "COME BASTARD!" I scream, tears and fury blurring my vision.

I barrel through the madness, the faces of the dead etched into my soul. Another roar, another call—my name on Rory's lips. Running, desperation is my cruel companion.

I see a little boy, no older than five, his chest open—this cannot be. "Rory! You fucking coward!" I cry out, my voice tearing at the edges. "Show yourself!" My heart pounds like a drum, the rhythm of fear and urgency driving me forward.

With every step, I push harder, ignoring the burn in my chest. The evening sky is a canvas painted with the dark strokes of winged beasts—creatures of nightmare that swoop and dive, menacing the innocent below.

My sword, an extension of my body, is drawn and ready. I'm no damsel in distress; I am a storm, a force to be reckoned with.

Appearing in front of me—two monstrous forms, born from dark magic, blocking my path.

Their eyes, glowing with malevolence, fix on a young woman who's frozen in terror, a rabbit caught in the gaze of wolves.

Not on my watch.

I let out a fierce cry and charge, my blade slicing through the air with precision. The first beast meets my wrath, an eruption of shadows clashing against steel. My blade finds its mark again and again. The second beast joins the combat, "You want to dance motherfucker?" Its form is a swirling mass of darkness and fangs.

I am fury, and I will not fall today. My blade sings a final, triumphant note as the creatures dissolve into nothingness.

I stand over the young woman. "Go," I tell her, my voice a low command. "Find safety." She nods, scrambling to her feet and disappearing into the shadows from whence our attackers came.

Turning, I sprint once more, the urgency of finding Rory consuming my thoughts. The air shudders with the cries of the villagers and the roars of monsters not yet slain.

This battle is far from over, and I am far from done. As I near the inn, there's no sign of Rory, but there's destruction.

My pulse thunders in my temples. Rory, where are you? The doors to the inn hang off their hinges. I enter, every sense on alert. The air is thick with smoke and the metallic tang of blood.

I call his name, my voice a beacon cutting through the darkness. "Rory!" My call is answered by silence and the soft echo of my desperation.

Debris and bodies line the floor, a macabre view. I stumble through the wreckage, each step a mixture of hope and fear. And then I see Vitriev, his strong form crumpled against a wall, eyes closed, his chest barely rising and falling. I kneel by his side, calling his name, shaking him gently. "Vitriev, wake up. Please, you have to wake up." His eyelids flutter, and he groans, a sign of life amidst so much death. "Anastasia," he rasps, his hand reaching out to grasp mine.

His touch is weak but determined. "The beasts... they came out of nowhere." I help him sit up, my eyes scanning the room for more survivors, for any sign of Rory.

The fight has taken its toll on Vitriev, but I know he's strong, stronger than most. "We have to find Rory," I say, urgency sharpening my voice. "He's out there, somewhere."

We step back into the chaos of the village, I look left and right, trying to find a safe place to sit with Vitriev.

The day is not done with its horrors, nor am I done with this fight.

The village burns around us, but my spirits, tempered in the flames of adversity, burn brighter. "I'M HERE COWARD." My yell is full of hate, rage and the need to slice his fucking throat.

145 - *Ruins and Shadows*

Fire crackles, eating up homes, and the sky is painted orange, black and red. I find a spot behind a house to hide Vitriev, my hands shaking but my voice steady as steel. "Stay here," I command, pushing him down. He looks at me, his eyes wide with fear and something else pleading. "Don't go, Anastasia," Vitriev's voice breaks as he grabs my arm. "Take a horse, leave with me. We can survive, start over." He doesn't get it.

Not yet.

I can't run, not when every fiber of my being screams to face my enemy head-on.

There are people here, people who need help fighting off these monsters. I can't leave them behind. I won't. I yank my arm free, meeting his gaze. "I need to do this, Vitriev. They need me." My words are like a promise etched in stone.

He tries again, desperation leaking into his voice. "Anastasia, please!" But I'm already gone, my feet carrying me towards the danger with each growl of the monstrous creatures echoing inside my skull.

I unsheathe my blade, the metal cold and comforting in my hand. One of the shadow lunges at me, its claws aiming for my heart, but I'm faster, and it cuts my arms just under my shoulder instead.

I hiss in pain and dodge with a strike, my blade slices through the dark flesh. I've killed monsters before, and I'll kill them again.

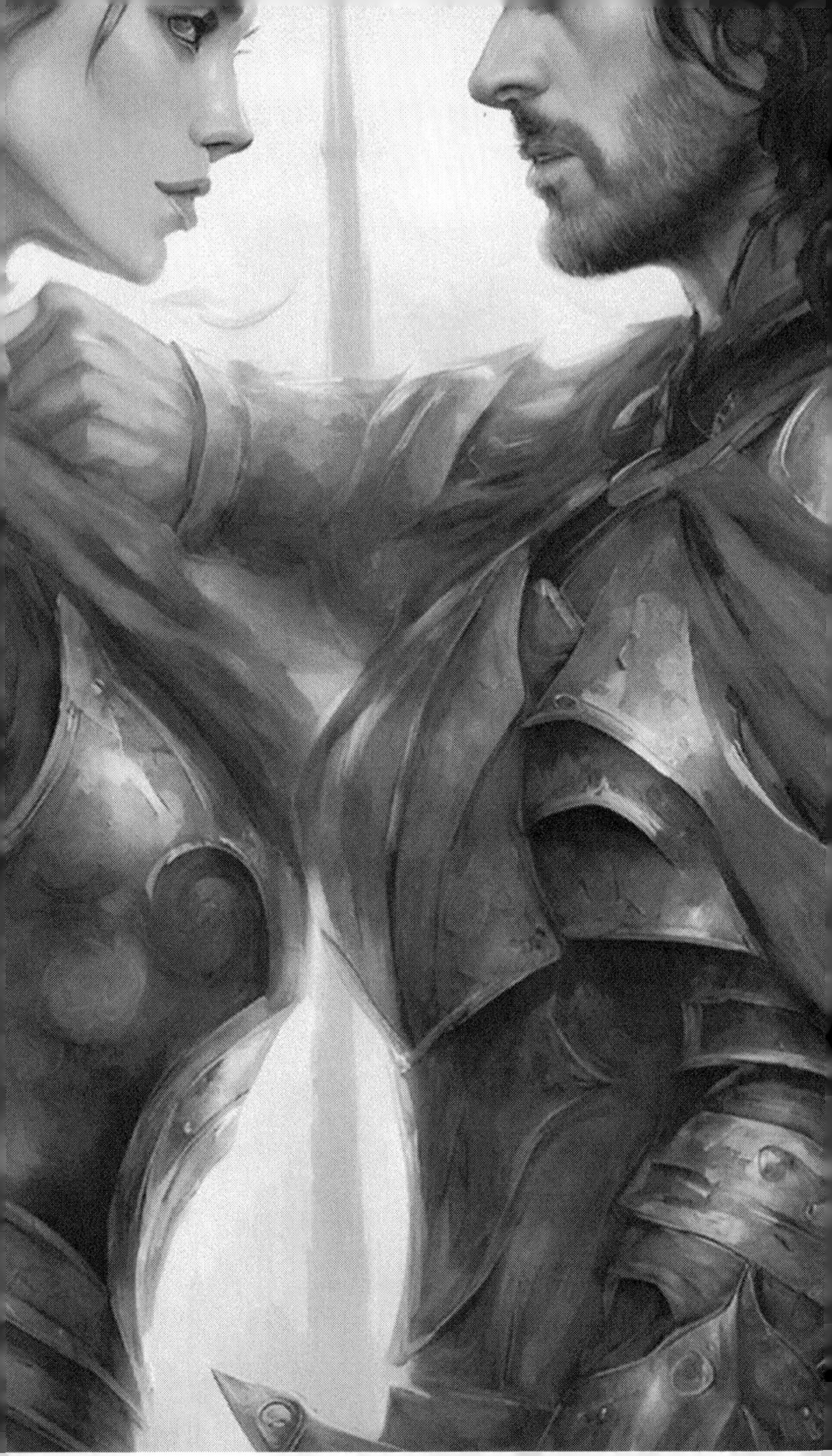

Chapter 12

Anastasia

Each slaughter by my hand is like a stroke against the canvas of my vengeance, painting a picture only I understand—a picture streaked in darkness and the resolve of a woman scorned. The more I kill, the more I feel like I lost myself, despite the evil actions my foes intend.

Pulling my sword from another dead creature, I quickly scan my surroundings. The hairs on the back of my neck stand on end, he's here, I can feel his eyes on me. My heartrate increases as my eyes are darting left and right. Where is he?

"Princess..." I almost didn't hear it in the chaos of the battle playing out between us. Rory, my eyes snap to his when I hear that familiar word fall from his lips.

My heart starts pounding in my ears, my breathing is heavy and shallow as my vision darkens at the edges. It's as if everything else has evaporated and it's just us two alone in this world.

Facing him is like looking in a distorted mirror of my past, and staring back at me is a familiar face engraved with all the pain and betrayal.

As if in slow motion, anger fueled by revenge takes over and I'm slicing through the space between us, my every move set ablaze with a flame of deadly intent.

I come to a halt a few feet from him, breathing heavy, my sword arm relaxed but ready. Rory's gaze doesn't waver, green grass eyes that remind me of the fields surrounding the home I just fled.

"Princess," Rory's voice cuts through the muted sounds of war.

I take notice that the waves of shadows seem to be retreating, crawling back into his skin, under his armor.

I'm frozen, watching him, shocked to see he hasn't changed in all these years, except for his eyes, looking sadder. Anger flares within me, a fire that has been stoked for far too long. "Monster." I say, voice steady despite the tumult in my heart.

He takes a step closer, hands empty, a gesture of peace in the middle of chaos. "I chose what I thought was right. But I was wrong. I was wrong about so many things." The air crackles between us, charged with a dangerous energy that only those about to clash can truly understand.

I stand face to face with Rory, a cruel smirk emerges on my lips. My heart beats rapidly; a drumroll preceding the storm of violence we're about to unleash.

Without warning, I lunge. My hands grasp the little dagger hidden against my thigh. I strike swiftly, the blade slicing through the air, aiming for his throat. Rory jerks back, but not fast enough. The dagger nicks him, a shallow cut. Blood, dark and damning, seeps from the wound, a reminder that I am not a girl to be trifled with.

I stand immobile for a mere second, a statue with the ghost of a smile tracing my lips. Rory staggers, regaining his balance, his own lips curling up in a smile that mirrors mine. "You really are a beautiful killer" he says, his voice a velvety caress that does nothing to soothe the spike of anger within me. "I've missed those freckles, Anastasia."

"Fuck off, you're the only killer here" I hiss back, venom lacing my words as I launch myself at him once more.

We battle fiercely, our movements a blend of grace and savagery. My hands and dagger are a blur, meeting Rory's fists with equal ferocity. "Always so spirited," Rory chuckles, evading my thrusts with a dancer's finesse. "It's one of the many things I admired about you."

His words are meant to disarm, to distract, but I see through his guise. "Admire this, asshole" I snarl, as I feint and strike, my dagger a silver flash in the fading light. Rory conjures shadows that slither and snap at my heels. I bob and weave, my own sword a streak of silver against the dark.

The clash of our blades sounds like a wicked kind of music. "Come on, Princess, is that all you've got?" he taunts, and a snarky grin splits my face. I can't help it. I'm in my element – a badass with a blade.

I can tell he's holding back, fucking bastard. Even so, I'm all in, giving as good as I'm getting. My blade nicks him again, and there's a hiss of magic in the air.

A drop of blood, dark as the shadows he wields, beads on his skin. He throws back his head and laughs, a sound that's all ice and fire. "Not bad, Princess," he says, that smirk still playing on his lips. From head to toe, I'm pure focus, pure will.

I'm not just fighting for myself—I'm fighting for every ghost that haunts me, for Vitriev, for... well, for a whole damned lot of things.

The ground beneath us rumbles, breathes like a beast waking up hungry.

It's the forest, alive and kicking. And for a second, just a heartbeat really, I see it in Rory's eyes—he's connected to this place, to the power here.

It's like the land's singing through him, and that voice is something fierce. "There's more at play here, Anastasia," he growls, and the words are a red flag waving in my face.

Yeah, no kidding, Rory. He's close now, close enough to hear the battle-rage breaths sawing in and out of my lungs.

My next move's a feint – a trick Vitriev taught me. Rory's defense is wide open, just a sliver of a second, but it's all I need. I press my advantage, my sword a silver flash aiming straight for his throat.

A touch, a whisper of steel against skin, and the fight's mine.

Only I hesitate. Rory sees it, the flicker of doubt, and he capitalizes on it like the sneaky bastard he is. Shadows wrap around my blade, tugging it from my grasp.

It's a standoff now, me unarmed, him all cocky with shadows coiling around his fingers. "What now, Princess?" he asks, and I can hear the honest curiosity in his voice. Like he's genuinely wondering what I'll do next. So, I straighten up, square my shoulders, and meet Rory's gaze with a glare that could cut obsidian. "You and me, we're not done here," I say, voice low and full of that Romanov fire. "Not by a long shot."

His laughter echoes in the clearing, a challenge and a promise all rolled into one. And me? I take it as an invitation.

The blood from Rory's cut drips down his neck, staining the collar of his shirt. It's a small victory, but a victory, nonetheless. Fingers tight around the hilt of my dagger, panting. "I'm glad you're entertained. Just know that next time, I won't miss."

Rory steps closer, undeterred by my threat, his green eyes alight with a fire that matches my own. "I wouldn't expect anything less from you, Princess."

"Don't call me that," I growl. Rory's smile softens, just a fraction, as if he's seeing not the enemy before him, but the girl he once knew.

With a roar, I surge forward, my dagger poised to end this, to end him. But as I move to strike, the world blurs, and suddenly, we're not in the village square anymore.

We're back at the palace, I'm young and reckless, trading blows not with fists and knives, but with words and laughter. I'm running through the corridors, hiding from tutors and castle guards, alive with the thrill of stolen moments.

But the illusion shatters as quickly as it formed, leaving me back in the present and I stop moving, trying to find my balance back. "I am not that girl anymore, Rory. And you... you're nothing to me now," I spit out, each word a slap to his face, a declaration of war.

He looks at me, really looks at me, and I see the conflict in his eyes. But the moment passes, and the mask of the King slips back on. "Then let us finish this," he says, his voice steady once again. We circle each other, wary and wounded, each waiting for an opening.

And as we stand there, poised on the precipice of violence, I realize that this is it – the point of no return.

"Come on, then," I taunt, daring him to make the next move. "Show me what you've got, your Majesty."

Rory lunges. The darkness swallows the whole village. I'm out in the open, weapon in hand, each muscle coiled tight and ready. Despite every instinct screaming at me to take cover, to run, to live to fight another day, I can't pull my eyes away from him. It's like the darkness listens to his command, the air teeming with his sinister energy.

Shadows circling me, making it impossible to see beyond this dark wind. "Rory!" I scream into the night, but my voice is just a whisper against the roar of his shadows.

He's changing, transforming before my eyes into something terrible, a dark figure clad in a shroud woven from the abyss itself.

Arms raised, he beckons the darkness closer, and it responds eagerly, encircling him like armor, his features now obscured by the encroaching gloom. There's a moment, just a heartbeat in time, where I see him clearly amidst the shadows.

His lips curve into a smile, a taunting, cruel twist that chills me to the bone. It's a smile that says I'm no match for him, that my efforts are futile against the breadth of his power. But I can't—won't—back down.

I charge forward, my battle cry tearing from my throat, a wordless defiance that echoes around the empty houses. But it's too late. The shadows respond to Rory's silent command, surging forward to engulf me, pulling me into their cold embrace.

I fight against the tidal wave of darkness, my every move desperate and fierce. "Not like this!" I snarl, my voice barely heard over the din of the encroaching void.

But the shadows are relentless, drawing me deeper and deeper into their realm.

As my strength wanes, the edges of my vision blur, and the world tilts dangerously.

The shadows twist and writhe, a living entity that seeks to squeeze the life from my lungs, the fight from my spirit.

Rory's face hovers above me, a faint silhouette in a sea of black. The last thing I feel is the cold grip of unconsciousness clawing at my senses, and the last thing I see is him—Rory Rasputin, smiling among the shadows.

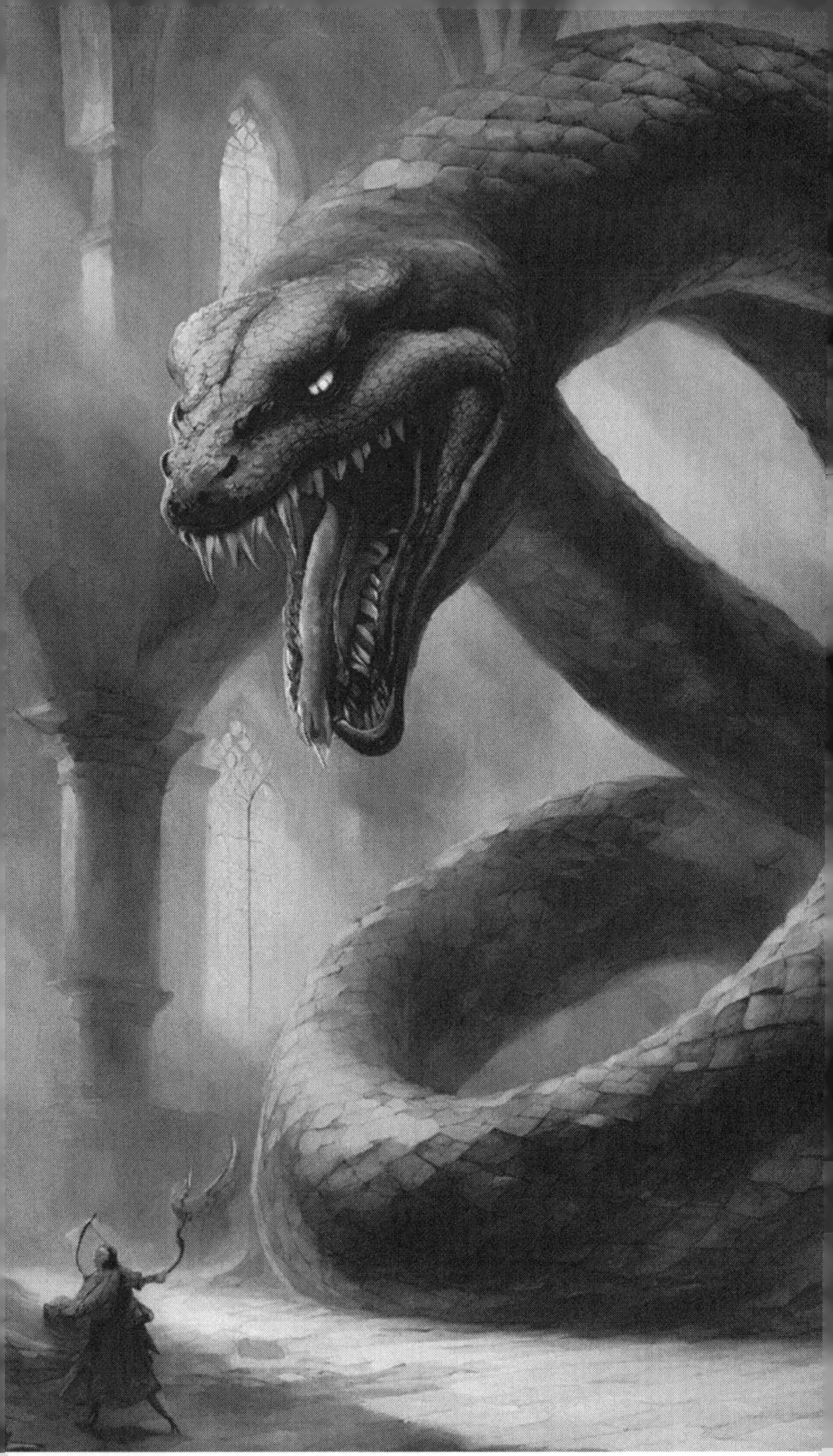

Chapter 13

Rory

The castle looms over me, its stone walls cold and unwelcoming, but I'm not swayed. Even now, Anastasia's tenacious form lies unconscious in my arms, a prisoner of circumstances and my own unwillingness to let her go. There's a numbness in my actions, a detachment that's settled into my bones.

I'm not sure when I became this hollow, when I started to view people as pieces on a chessboard rather than lives to be cherished. Maybe it was the first time I killed, or maybe it was when the centuries started to blend into one endless march of solitude and power plays.

I carry her through the corridors, the walls seem to lean in, curious about the girl in my arms. Anastasia's fiery spirit, her relentless drive to kill me, it's fucking impressive.

It's a mirror of her ancestor's perseverance, the very ones that I've had a hand in silencing. I can't kill her, though. There's something about seeing her now, helpless and fierce even in unconsciousness, that holds me back.

What it is, I can't quite pinpoint.

As I lay her down on the bottom of a large metal cell, her new chamber, I can't help but admire her. She's pure strength, righteousness and stunningly beautiful.

Her freckles, like a constellation of stars painted across her cheeks, remind me of a night sky that I've not truly seen in centuries.

I lock her away in a cage. The metal clangs with finality, a sound that should assure me of security. Instead, it's a dull thud against the numbness.

I know this won't hold her—not her body, and certainly not her resolve. Even chained, she will come for me, relentless as the tide.

My fearless Princess. The emptiness of this place echoes around me, this bedroom abandoned years ago now has a new occupant.

I lift my right arm, sending shadows to the candles in the rooms, lighting them. It's starting to darken outside, and I have a lot to do now that I'm back in the kingdom. I glance at her one last time, wondering why the fuck I wasn't able to kill her, again, and then I walk out of the room.

I'm sitting down to eat in my professional chambers. Taking in the quiet around me around me, when one of the castle servants bursts in, out of breath and wide-eyed.

Before I can ask what's got her all worked up, her words tumble out in a rush. "The girl, in the new cell—she's yelling up a storm!"

I sigh, rubbing at my temples, feeling the weight of the day just getting heavier. With the last bite of my sandwich, I toss the napkin aside and stand with a groan. It's off to deal with Anastasia then.

I make my way through the castle halls, the sound of her yelling growing louder with every step closer I get to her room.

My hands ball into fists at my sides; anger simmers in my chest. Why does she need to make things so complicated?

Stepping into her room, I can see her shaking the bars of her cage like a furious little beast trying to break free. I can't help but feel a twinge. No, pushing that aside, it's time to lay down the law.

"Enough!" I bark, and my voice cuts through her rage like a knife. She stops yelling, but those defiant eyes of hers are searing into my flesh, accusing and ablaze.

"Princess," I sneer, advancing toward the cage. "What is it? Miss me?"

Anastasia jerks to her feet, her eyes flashing with shards of ice. "Go to hell, Rory," she snaps.

I laugh, harsh and loud. "Looks like you're already there, aren't you?" I lean in close to the bars, my face inches from hers. "You're going to break soon enough. They all do."

She spits in my face, a desperate act of rebellion. I don't even flinch. Instead, I lift my finger, scooping up her spit, and lick it off slow, my eyes never leaving hers. Then I spit right back at her. "Tastes like defeat," I say, grinning cruelly.

Anastasia recoils, her disgust writing plain as day. I don't care. It's about power, about showing her who's boss.

I have her life in my hands, and I aim to squeeze every remaining bit of fight out of her.

"You can't keep me in here forever," she says, but her voice cracks. She knows she's trapped.

"We'll see about that," I retort. I still have plans for her, plans that'll twist her up inside. But for now, I'll settle for watching her squirm.

"Your time will come, Rory," she warns me, but her words fall flat.

I turn away, feeling the thrill of our bitter dance. "Keep dreaming, Princess. In the meantime, enjoy your cage." As I leave her there, rattling the bars in her rage, I can't shake the unrest bubbling within me.

Advisors gather in the throne room at my summons, the air of the castle shifting from one of oppressive silence to the murmur of voices.

I've been gone for far too long, having spent what felt like an endless amount of time tracking down that pretty, soon to be dead princess.

They sit before me, faces drawn, eyes wary. We have politics to speak of and decisions to make. The people are restless, dissatisfied with a king they believe absent.

I can't seem to focus my thoughts; my mind keeps drifting to the cage and the woman bound within it. The clatter of chains is a distant song accompanying our discussion.

Every sentence, every debate about the kingdom, it's all underscored by the knowledge that soon, very soon, those chains will rattle with her anger and her undying will to fight.

I raise my hand in silence, commanding silence.

I scan the dozens of pairs of eyes fixated on me. I see expectation, wariness, and even a hint of fear. I steel myself; they see a King, they see danger.

"At this very moment," I begin, my voice deep and firm, "our enemy readies her forces just beyond our lands." My eyes sweep their faces, expressions of concern form on them, I have their attention. "However, within these walls, we hold a potential catalyst—a Romanov whose very bloodline could end us or save us."

A ripple of uneasy curiosity passes over the council. Some shift uncomfortably in their seats, others lean forward, eager for me to say more. "We must decide our course of action. I saw their army. It's impressive, I can take a lot of them down, but we must assemble our own forces." I say, with finality.

The debate is intense. Voices rise and fall, passion and reason clashing like swords on a battlefield.

One of the council members speaks up, "Respectfully, King Rasputin, the people. They are angry.

They believe they have no king, you disappeared for years." His voice, fucking annoying, is full of judgment.

My eyes are drawn to the window and the endless stretch of grey sky.

The numbness within me is a constant companion, as familiar as my own pulse. "Your Majesty, this has raised questions among the court, and it is doubtful the people will put their lives on the line for you willingly," the advisor finally says, breaking through my fog of indifference.

I look at him, really look at him for the first time during this tedious meeting.

His eyes are full of something that could be concern or barely concealed ambition; it's hard to tell with these courtiers.

Rage flares up in me, quick and hot like a bushfire. My gaze turns sharp, slicing through him. Silence falls, heavy and thick. His face blanches, a drop of sweat trailing down his temple.

He doesn't understand, can't possibly comprehend the battles I've fought, the blood I've spilled, and the love I've twisted and broken. He could never understand the pain, no one can.

A thick shadow coils around my feet, unnoticed by the man across from me. It rises, swelling into a sinister form.

A giant snake, manifested from the darkness of my soul, towers behind the advisor. Its eyes gleam with feral anticipation, reflecting my inner turmoil. With a sudden strike, faster than the man could scream, the shadow snake sinks enormous, ethereal teeth into his chest.

He levitates, suspended in dark magic as it tears him open. His chest splits grotesquely in two, blood and viscera sliding down and spilling across the polished table.

The other advisors in the room recoil in horror at the display, frozen, eyes wide with fear. "I guess we'll need to find a way to ensure their willingness then, won't we?" It's a show of power, a warning—cross me, and this is what awaits. I watch impassively, my chest hollow. There's no pleasure in this display, no satisfaction.

There's only the cold, callous hand of duty guiding my actions. What am I becoming? The question lingers, but I shove it aside. The giant snake vanishes as quickly as it appeared, leaving only death and terror in its wake.

I rise from my throne, my movements deliberate as I step around the carnage, my boots avoiding the blood soaking into the cracks of the wooden floor. "Your personal opinions don't matter to me. I'm the King." The room is silent but for the soft whimpers of the man clinging to life—a life I could spare or snuff out with a thought. I leave him there, a reminder to all who remain.

Let them whisper about my cruelty, about the heart of darkness beating within me. Let them fear me, for fear is the leash that will keep them at bay. And somewhere, in a place I've buried deep within me, a fragment of the man I once was screams in silent rage at this necessary evil. But he's weak, a ghost of the past who has no place in this world of shadows and power. "It won't be long before our enemy attacks. Spread the news of my arrival at the castle. Start to plant this fucking idea in their head, I'll come with up with a plan for them to join in the meantime." I stride out of the room, leaving them to stew in their fear and tension.

As the echo of my steps fades into the silence of the castle's cold stone halls, I know that fear alone won't inspire loyalty—not the kind that we need to face the impending war.

I walk back into the room where Anastasia is. I sit in a chair, the wooden legs groaning under the weight of a man who has lived for far too long.

My eyes, green like the depths of the forest, find hers, still closed from the charm I cast to her. I need her to sleep for another day, to think clearly.

"Wine," I murmur, my voice void of the weight it carries.

The servant changing the sheets on the lonely bed nods, disappearing quickly. My gaze settles on Anastasia, her features softened by slumber.

A lock of auburn hair falls across her face, and I'm struck by the urge to brush it away. But I restrain myself. She will die by my hands, the least I can do for her is to not touch her before.

The servant returns, a glass of deep red liquid in hand. I take the goblet, the cool touch of the stem against my calloused fingers a stark reminder of the blood that has stained my hands over my immortal lifetime.

I take a sip; the richness of the wine is a welcome contrast to the numbness that envelops my heart.

As I drink, my mind begins to craft a plan, a strategy. I need soldiers, followers, people who believe in the crown, or at least fear me enough to obey. The world outside these walls is changing, and I must adapt, must gather strength for what is to come.

Anastasia stirs, a small frown creasing her forehead, and I can't help but wonder what she dreams of.

Does she still have nightmares? Does she still see the faces of her family or is it my face that haunts her the darkness behind her closed eyes? I take another sip of wine, the bitter taste barely registering.

I need to be cunning, ruthless even, if I am to see through the vision that has propelled me forward through the centuries. Yet as I sit here, in the quiet before dawn breaks, with Anastasia lying before me, I find myself longing for something I cannot name.

175 - *Ruins and Shadows*

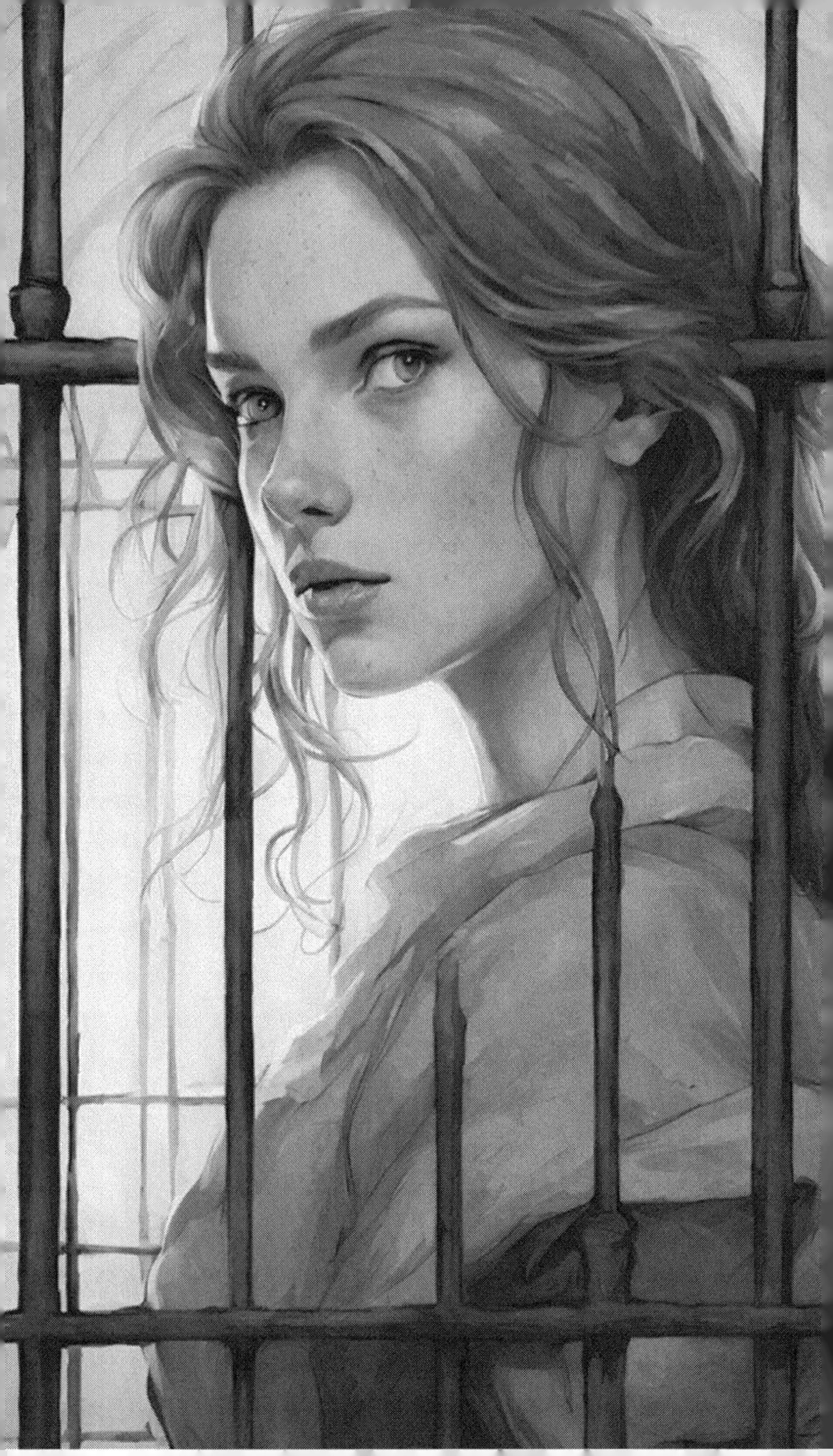

Chapter 14

Anastasia

I blink my eyes a few times to try to clear away the fogginess clouding my vision. The room slowly starts to come into focus as I roll to my stomach and rise to my hands and knees.

Feeling the cold steel beneath me, I look around, I seem to be locked in some cage like a wild animal.

As I take in my surroundings, I feel a tinge of recognition, these walls are familiar to me. I stand, gripping the cage bars, my sight soaks in the room and I soon realize I am back in my childhood home.

The room comes into focus, and it's like looking at a faded painting of my past. This place was my sanctuary, where I'd curl up with a book and dream of adventures beyond the stone walls. Now, it's my prison, decorated with dust and shadows.

My hands hold the bars, knuckles turning white. I start to panic as I look around the room, there's a small bed, a chair and a window. Nothing of any use to my situation.

Seeing these walls again is a cruel twist of fate. This castle used to shine with laughter and life, now it's just as dark and miserable as its ruler.

The thought of Rory has my mind scrambling to remember the events that led to my capture. My mind races with questions. Where's Vitriev? What does Rory want from me?

Flashes of shadows, so many shadows, spring to the forefront of my memory. Black whisps, wrapping around me like a shroud at the command of their master. I can't suppress the shiver that flutters through me as I think of his twisted smile, the one that used to promise friendly mischief and now foretells only evil.

My eyes drift to the door, sturdy and unyielding. It's quiet out there. Too quiet. It's like the entire castle is holding its breath, waiting for... What? My end? A rescue? I can't hope for the latter. It's likely I'll have to be my own hero.

At this realization Vitriev's face, exhausted and bloodied, comes to mind. Vitriev! Has he been kidnapped as well? Or worse, did he try to fight them off from where I left him, broken and injured?

Images of people being slaughtered like cattle, the village under attack by Rory and his wicked shadows, flash across my vision. My chest tightens at the reminder. We've been through too much for it to end like this.

My eyes scan the room, taking in every detail. There could be something here that I might use to my advantage. I need to get out of this cage, out of this room. My thoughts are interrupted by the sound of the lock turning.

The door opens, revealing nothing but more darkness beyond its threshold. But even without seeing him, I can feel him there—Rory, darkness personified.

I stand straight, defiant despite the shackles of my circumstance. "Come to relish, Rory?" I ask, my voice steady, a touch of mockery coloring the words. The silence that follows is heavy with unspoken truths and questions that ache for answers.

But I stand ready, a warrior queen in a cage, my blue eyes blazing with a challenge. The door creaks closed, and I'm alone once again. Fucker.

As the silence stretches out, I understand that this is more than a momentary incarceration; it's a psychological battle. Rory wants to break me, but he's underestimated the strength that runs through my veins.

I need to focus on what I can control. I'll need to study everything about my surroundings, try and figure out a way to escape this prison and get a message to Vitriev, I need to believe he's still out there.

Daylight comes and goes, punctuating the stillness of my confinement. It's been one day.

The soft morning light makes the little dust particles in the air shine and dance; I wave my hand and the movement sends the little pieces flying off in all directions, sparkling like little crystals, it's beautiful. I never thought of that before, beautiful dust. That just solidifies my boredom.

The sound of footsteps echoing with a dreaded rhythm can be heard ascending down the hallway. Rory, the thief of joy, enters the room and I roll my eyes.

He pauses his steps just a few feet from the cage, his eyes meet mine and my breath catches in my lungs. He's annoyingly handsome, and that just makes me loath him that much more.

His assertive glare is so striking it sends a wave of goosebumps across my flesh.

"Anastasia," he says, his voice far too calm and husky. If he wasn't a murderous bastard, I would wish to hear my name fall from his lips every day of my remaining life. "The people of the kingdom seem to be in need a reminder as to why they must put their faith in me as their King," he continues.

"Hmm, I can't possibly think of a reason why that is," I say dryly. "Maybe it's because you're an evil fucking bastard."

"You and I, Princess, are going to play the greatest of roles," he continues, as if I hadn't spoken a word. "You will put on the best performance of your life," he takes a step towards me, hands casually resting at his sides, "and I know you can do that for me darling, for the last fourteen years you've been living as someone else, so surely this is well within your skill level as an actress." He says, a wicked smile playing on his perfect lips.

Where is he going with this?

"Together we shall bring the people around to my side, with you playing the role of my doting love, and I, the redeemed." His voice, low and husky sends a shiver to my core.

My eyes widen at the realization of what he's saying, "you cannot be serious!" Folding my arms over my chest, I say with conviction, "you're dreaming Rasputin, you can't manipulate me into pretending to love you, never." I set my jaw; my heart encased in frost. "You want to kill me? Then let's get this fight over with!" Rory's laughter, deep and self-assured, sends a shiver down my spine.

"My dear, I hold the subtler hand. No, I will not harm a single hair on your head. Not until I have my army. The people don't realize a war is coming and they don't want to fight for me. Stupid fucks!" His eyes glisten with a cold menace, "they don't realize it's for their benefit, and you must remember Princess, I have ways of persuasion that are far more effective than fear."

Staring into his searing green eyes, my thoughts are racing. Could I outplay him in his own vile theater, turn the charade against him? Reluctantly, I speak, my words dripping with disdain. "What makes you believe I would ever agree to this farce?"

A smirk tugs at the corner of his lips. "Because, Princess, despite your fiery spirit, you long for freedom. And play along with my plans, and I assure you, your chains will not be as tight. Consider it as... a little light in your otherwise darkened cell."

It's a devil's bargain, a sacrifice of my integrity for a sliver of autonomy. "No." I flip him off, offering him my brightest smile. He smiles, and if this man wasn't such an evil monster, I could have fall for him.

He's much taller than me, sculpted by the battles and time. His green eyes glow with his smile, dimples in his cheeks. "We'll talk soon Princess." He says and turns his back to me, walking out of the room.

The cage becomes my world—a small, cold corner of a vast and indifferent universe. Rory's words ring in my head, a twisted lullaby for the long days and nights in this iron embrace.

Days pass, marking their existence with the changing light.

His shadows become my only occasional visitors, bringing me food, water and wine. I eat because I must, drink because it numbs the edges of my solitude. Water, the only respite from the harshness of wine, soothes my parched throat.

But with each day, the shadows grow longer, and I feel a part of me slipping away, the part that fought, that raged against the imposing darkness. Now, there's just a dull acceptance, a realization that I am truly, utterly alone. Except for the visitors.

They don't speak, these silhouetted bearers of sustenance. They move with a quiet efficiency that's almost graceful, leaving behind trays of food that speak of a world beyond these bars—a world filled with flavors and textures now foreign to my tainted tongue.

As the shadows retreat once more, leaving behind the remnants of a meal I have no appetite for, I think of Rory. He sees himself as a puppeteer, the master of this grim theater, but little does he know, every villain has his downfall.

Time trickles past, slow like molasses in winter, and the cage that's become my world feels smaller with each passing moment.

My muscled legs ache for movement, for the stretch and sprint of escape. I'm a wild thing, caged and pacing, and my heart—it beats too fast, too fierce for this trap of iron and despair. Rory returns, his footsteps echoing like the call of a steady drum.

My pulse jumps. It's been days—days of gnawing uncertainty and cold solitude.

He stands there, that familiar silhouette, the magician, the betrayer, the once-dreamed-of friend turned nightmare.

"Have you changed your mind yet princess?" His voice is honey and gravel. I stand straight, my spine a rod of defiance. "You wish," I spit back, sharp as the makeshift knife hidden beneath my blanket, ready to be unsheathed.

One day, while a shadow entered the room with my meal. The little wind she carried with her caused a candle and its holder to fall to the floor. They rolled until they stopped at a sufficient distance for me to grab it.

I spent several hours sharpening the wooden holder against the metal bars of the cage to give it a point.

The silence stretches between us, taut as a bowstring.

We're two predators eyeing each other, calculating, anticipating. His gaze is unreadable, those depths hiding more than I've ever managed to uncover.

Rory walks closer, his steps measured, his face a mask that says nothing and everything all at once. "I'd rather rot in this cage than help you," I lash out, my words laced with venom. He doesn't flinch, damn him.

"Ask your questions, Anastasia. I know you're dying too." He's baiting me, but I bite anyway. Because if there's one thing I need to know, it's this—"Vitriev," I start, the name tasting like blood in my mouth. "Why is it that you're here, breathing and smirking, and he's not? Tell me, Rory. What did you do to him?"

He pauses, and I see something flicker in his eyes—a shadow of guilt? Or maybe it's just my wishful thinking.

"Vitriev is..." He takes a breath, choosing his words with the care of a man disarming a bomb. "He was a casualty, an unfortunate obstacle that stood between us."

My heart clenches, a fist wrapped around it, squeezing tight. "An unfortunate obstacle?" I echo, my heartbeat pounding in my ears. "You make it sound like he was nothing! He was everything, you monster!"

Rory watches me, his expression is masked as a low growl comes from him. "He was in the way, Anastasia. And in war, those that are in the way often find themselves underfoot."

I want to hit him, hurt him, make him feel a fraction of the pain slicing through me. "No." I murmur, tears forming in my eyes. "Yes," he agrees. I don't believe him. I can't. Believing him means giving up on Vitriev, on us, and I'm not ready for that. Not now, not ever.

The tension hangs between us, a noose waiting to tighten. "Let me out of this cage, Rory," I say, my voice low, deadly. "If you're going to kill me, have the guts to do it to my face." He leans in, considering me with those unsettlingly calm eyes. "Not yet, Anastasia. There's still a part for you to play." He turns, the king in his corrupted court, leaving me with nothing but iron bars and the weight of unanswered questions, and my tears.

They come unbidden, slipping down my cheeks like traitorous streams. I haven't cried since... this damn night fourteen years ago.

Vitriev is dead.

He's dead.

I will never see his beautiful face again. Touch him, hold him! *Vitriev is DEAD!*

The words circle my brain like vultures, pecking at the remnants of my heart. I can feel the phantom pressure of his hand in mine, the warmth of his smile, now gone, extinguished by the man who has already taken so much from me.

I've lost track of how much time has passed; my eyes raw with crying. "Rory," I rasp, my voice raw from disuse and sorrow, "why did you have to kill them? My family...Why have you done this to me?" My hands claw at the metal that holds me, as if I could tear it apart with my bare fingers.

Rory stands there, his figure a looming shadow against the dim light filtering in from the small window high above. I didn't hear him return, lost in my sadness. He's silent for a moment, I want to scream, to make him feel a fraction of the pain that tears through me, but I remain silent, waiting. Finally, he speaks, "I won't answer that." It's a simple declaration, almost indifferent, and it ignites a fury within me that burns hotter than any tear I've shed.

I sit on the floor. "You owe me that much," I say, though my voice is steely calm, belying the storm raging inside me. "You owe me an explanation. After all these years, after everything you've taken from me, I deserve to know." Rory joins me on the ground, lowering himself to sit in front of me.

His green eyes locked onto mine, revealing nothing of his thoughts. His refusal is a wall I cannot scale, a mystery I cannot solve. "Why can't you just tell me?!" The desperation creeps into my voice despite my efforts to sound in control.

The silence stretches between us, a widening gap that grows with each moment he refuses to tell me the truth. I want to hate him more than I already do, but there's a part of me, a foolish, hopeful part, that still seeks answers from the man who once brought light into my brother's sickroom. "You will answer me, Rory," I state, my voice breaking through the quiet room like a whip. "Maybe not today, but someday. I will have my answers, and I will have my vengeance."

He looks at me, and there's a flicker of something before it's gone, snuffed out by the coldness that settles back onto his features.

I sit cross-legged on the cold floor. Rory leans against the opposite bars, close enough that I can see the rise and fall of his chest with each breath. He murmurs, his voice a low stream of words meant to coax and manipulate.

Each syllable a needle, each pause a punctuation in his strategy to break me. But I'm not the kind of woman who shatters—I'm the kind who sharpens, like steel on stone. I tighten my grip on the little knife I made under my cover. He speaks but I'm not listening, it's likely just more bullshit anyway. Lies, all lies.

"Anastasia, think of your people," he says, his words a soft plea. His fingers slip between the bars. My fingers, gripping the wooden blade tighter. I wait, the tension in my muscles a prelude to the storm about to break. And break it does, as I launch forward, my hand a streak of vengeance, aiming for his heart. But Rory moves, a swift shift of his body.

The pick sinks into his shoulder instead of the heart, a strike that draws blood but misses the mark. It's a hit, but not a killing blow—a mistake that I won't repeat. Rory recoils, his face contorting in surprise, his hand clutching the wound.

The scent of his blood is sharp, and metallic, a reminder of the line I've just crossed. Missed opportunities swarm my thoughts like hornets, but my focus is unfractured—I've made my stance clear. He leans back, his breaths heavy, eyes locked on mine.

A twisted smile curls his lips, the perfect reflection of his madness. "You never cease to amaze me, princess," he grinds out through clenched teeth. "Stop calling me that," I spit back, hatred coating my words.

He examines the wound, a test of his own mortality. Then, with a pained heave, he stands, distancing himself from my reach but not my fury. "Your spirit is boundless, it seems," Rory concedes. "A lesser man would fear you." A smirk, as cold as the stone surrounding us, slices across my face. "Then it's a good thing you're no man," I retort, my grip on the blade unwavering.

We are locked in this moment, predator and prey, but the roles are interchangeable. This cage may hold me, but my will is free, roaming wild and untamed. Rory retreats, a fading figure nursing his shoulder—a wound that will heal but never erase the fact that I've drawn his blood.

The bite of the dagger in Rory's shoulder is satisfying, but the laughter that follows is like acid on my victory.

There he stands, blood trickling down his arm. He brings his hand slowly to his mouth and the fucker licks the blood while holding my gaze. "You're sick," I snarl, my eyes locked onto his as I grip the bars of the cage.

Rory's smile doesn't fade. Instead, he wipes his bloody hand on his jacket, a dark stain spreading across the fabric. "Oh, Anastasia, don't be so dramatic. You know you'd revel in bathing in my blood soaking the ground," he taunts, stepping closer, the proximity imposing.

His hand shoots through the bars, seizing my throat. I gasp, not from fear, but from the ferocity that kindles within me. "Fine," I choke out, my voice edged with ire. "I'll help you with this damnable project." His fingers loosen.

He gives me a once-over, eyes flashing with the knowledge of his win, and then, as abruptly as he appeared, he's gone, leaving me alone with the sting on my neck and the taste of treachery in my mouth.

The door slams shut, and I am left to simmer in the cauldron of my thoughts.

197 - *Ruins and Shadows*

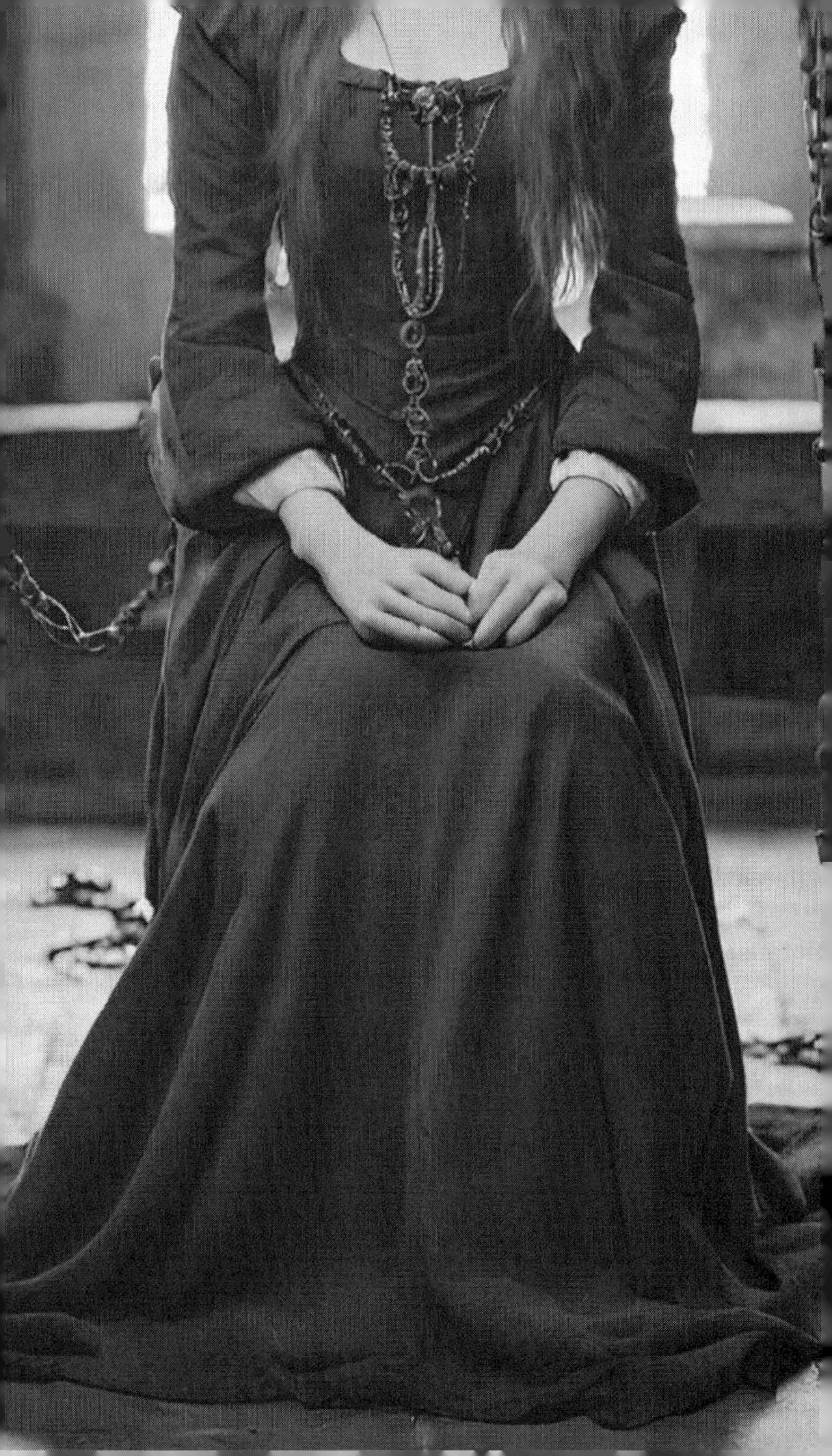

Chapter 15

Anastasia

The room feels like it's breathing – dark, oppressive breaths that match the racing of my pulse. My muscles are tense, I'm on edge, and my mind is swirling with too many questions, too little answers, and more emotions than I ever thought I could feel in one single moment.

Shadows creep into the room like thieves in the night. They circle around the bars of my prison, and then with the silent grace of smoke, the bars disappear, and for a moment, I think I'm free.

Looking around the room, it's then that I realize my cage has vanished only for shadows forming chains to replace them around my waist, dissolving into the darkness of the ceiling above me.

The hairs on my neck stand up. Magic. This is Rory's doing. As I analyze them, my hands go to the cold metal binding my waist, but they're just illusions. I can't grip them, can't rip them away. My fingers go through them like playing in the mist. They are not painful, or even tight. I believe they are only there to follow me in case I try to escape, tightening at that moment.

I sigh. What a nightmare.

I grit my teeth, anger boiling inside me. That fucking bastard is playing with me. Trying to show me the kind of control he thinks he has. But I won't give him the satisfaction of letting him see fear in my eyes.

I will not cower, not in the darkness of shadows, not in the confinement of magic chains, and certainly not in the face of this monster who calls himself a man.

The room is quiet, I take a deep breath, letting the silence wrap around me like a cloak. I will not break.

Using the solitude to study the room more closely for anything to use in my advantage, I pace the room, my hands tracing the contours of furniture I'd once known, the adjacent bath chamber a reminder of luxuries I'd taken for granted.

Exploring the room is like stepping into a memory, images of my siblings and I running down these halls come to mind, and I blink away tears that threaten my eyes. I press my hands against the cool marble, taking solace in the stone's unyielding nature – a trait I recognize in myself.

A moment later, the shadows return, this time with pails of hot water, and I watch them pour it into the tub. It's an act of reluctant kindness, or perhaps another facet of Rory's twisted sense of care.

With a last glance at these silent servants, I shed the remnants of my dignity along with my clothes and slide into the bath. The heat sinks into my skin, searing away the cold touch of the chains and I can't help the whisper of a moan that slides past my lips.

It's odd, the chains disappeared when I submerged into the water, but I can sense them close, in the air. I close my eyes, letting the water wash over me, if only for a moment forgetting the fact that I'm a prisoner of war, and the darkness that has crept into my life.

I allow the warm water to envelop me, a temporary shield from the reality that awaits. My head breaks the surface, and I start crying uncontrollably. My eyes and head burn with the intensity.

I've lost everything. My family murdered, leaving me orphaned. My home, never able to go back. My sweet Vitriev, my love, killed so I could be kidnapped and taken hostage by an evil King.

And the asshole is trying to assert power and control over me by forcing me to participate in a ridiculous charade as his lover to convince his people that he can be redeemed?!

How am I supposed to have the will to live when I feel I have nothing left to live for? How do I find the courage to go on? I place my hands on my face, trying to control my uneven breathing. A strange sensation tickles my face, like a cold wind. When I open my eyes, there's nothing there.

When I emerge from the bath, the chains slither their way into place again. I know it's only a matter of time before Rory makes his next move in this sadistic game.

I wrap myself in a towel left by the shadows, feeling depressed, I walk towards the bed. I am tired, both literally and metaphorically. I can't go on. Every beat of my heart is a fierce drum against the silence.

I lie naked in bed, my eyes feel swollen and irritated, but I've managed to stop crying. I need to kill him, but I want to die with him. I have nothing left in this world; I might as well join my loved ones.

The chill of the room crawls over my skin, a reminder that despite waking up in a bed, I've not truly left my prison. My eyes flutter open, the morning's weak light slipping through the cracks in the curtains covering the small window. The smell of damp stone and disuse hangs heavy in the air; even the sun seems hesitant to enter completely, as if it too fears the man who keeps me here.

Bare and cold, I lie motionless under the thin sheet that barely serves as a blanket. The soft rustling of fabric against skin as I shift alerts me to my nakedness. I'm exposed, vulnerable, a feeling that's become all too familiar.

The sound of a throat clearing jolts me into an upright position, as I clutch the flimsy sheet to my chest. My eyes snap to the figure standing near the door.

Rory lazily leans back against the door, his arms crossed at his chest, staring at me. At my breasts more specifically. His gaze lingers shamelessly over my chest, and a surge of anger chases away the remnants of sleep.

I narrow my eyes at him, tightening my grip on the sheet. "You've got a lot of nerve," I hiss, venom seeping into my words. Rory merely cocks an eyebrow, a smirk playing on his plump lips. "I've seen more than you've yet to show, Princess," he replies, and his casual tone stokes the fire of my rage. "Just get out, if you want to stare, go find your whore," I snap back, forcing a calmness I don't feel.

He chuckles, the sound grating against my already frayed nerves. "As much as I enjoy this delightful view, that's not why I'm here." He steps forward, dropping a bundle of clothes onto the foot of the bed.

They're new, clean, royal, nothing like the tattered dress I had on when he locked me up. I eye the clothes warily, then fix my gaze on him, trying to suppress the shiver his presence brings. "Planning to dress me up for some nefarious purpose? Prance me around in front of your kingdom?" I ask, already imagining the worst. Rory shakes his head, seemingly amused. "Not everything is a conspiracy, Anastasia. Consider it... a necessity for what's to come."

"What's to come?" I echo, dread pooling in my stomach like lead. He crosses the room, settling in a chair that's too ornate for a room as sparse as this. "We have a kingdom to secure, and I need you by my side," he says simply as if this isn't absolutely absurd. I snort. "And why would I ever stand with you?"

"Because, Princess," he says, using that damned title again, "you have no other choice." I study him, this creature of shadows and lies. He seems different today, as if revealing a part of a puzzle he's kept hidden.

A sense of foreboding settles over me, my mind racing with the possibilities his words conjure. "Why didn't you kill me, then?" I demand, my voice a whisper of silk and blades.

His face darkens, the playful facade slipping to reveal the monster beneath. "I don't know," he admits, and though it's barely a murmur, the weight of his confession crashes into the room.

I sit in the bed, processing his words. His eyes meet mine, and for a moment, we are just two broken souls trying to tame the other. Maybe this situation is my best option. Playing by his rules, stabbing him when he's not looking and hopefully it makes him so furious that he kills me in return.

I take a deep breath, the air thick with the scent of morning. The clothes lie untouched, a symbol of the choice I must make. To wear them is to play the part Rory has set for me.

However, as I gaze upon those garments, I know they are more than mere cloth and thread. They are the armor I must wear to achieve my task.

"Together," I finally say, my voice sharpened on the stone of inevitability. "We secure the kingdom." Rory's lips curl into a damn beautiful smile, and he rises from his chair. "And then I'm going to kill you," I add.

He gets up from the chair and walks toward me. Unconsciously, I clutch the sheets tighter around my chest.

He kneels on the bed and moves closer to me, stopping about two feet from my face. The urge to lunge at him is strong, but I haven't got a weapon on me. "I would expect nothing less." He speaks.

As he turns to leave, I hear him mumble something, but I didn't quite catch the words. "What was that?" I question.

He twists around, looking surprised that I heard him. "Those fucking freckles." He smiles but it is nowhere near one of kindness. It is however just enough for me to catch a dimple, goddamn. "That's what I fucking said." He murmurs, turns on his heels and very obviously makes sure to slam the door on his way out.

What the fuck? My brow furrows in confusion.

I reach for the clothes, the fabric cold against my touch. Every fiber is a whisper of luxury and comfort. A beautiful royal blue dress, adorned with golden decorations and a pair of tight black pants.

As I dress, I armor myself in the knowledge that Rory and I are bound by fate—a fate that I will bend to my will. I finish tying the laces of my boot and rise, my muscles protesting the stillness they've been subjected to.

With a deep breath, I decide it's time to test my boundaries, to see just how far I can go before the shadows come slithering back to herd me like some unruly sheep. One step. Then another.

The door to my room creaks its surprise as it swings open under my touch—it's not locked. A small oversight, or perhaps a part of Rory's sick game. Either way, it's an opportunity, and I don't want to waste it. The chains have not reappeared, but I know they are there, a constant reminder that I am still a prisoner.

I step out, beyond the threshold, into the hallway. And there they are—the shadows, alive and moving like living things. They form a little snake that follows me, a slithering tail to my every step. Annoying little buggers. I'm tempted to stomp on them, but I don't. It's their house, their rules, at least for now.

I walk. Walk through the hallways of my once-beloved home, now a carcass of its former glory. Paintings of my family stare down at me, their eyes following me as I pass. Dust blankets everything, like the world here stopped when their hearts did.

I roam without direction, taking in the state of ruin around me, the silence of a heavy cloak draped over the castle's shoulders. It feels like I'm in a mausoleum, a museum exhibit of a life that was—my life. I used to know every corner, every secret passage.

Now, it just feels foreign, like a dream you try to remember but can't quite grasp.

I'm admiring—or perhaps mourning—a particularly old painting, its edges eaten away by time, when I hear a voice, little and feminine, piercing the silence. "Are you hungry?" it asks.

I turn to see a servant, her eyes a mix of curiosity and fear. She's pretty, with blonde hair that falls in waves down her back. Her beauty is almost cliché, like she stepped out of a fairy tale and into my nightmare. "Are you real, or another of Rory's tricks?" I snap, more harshly than I intend. The attitude spills from me like water from a broken vase—uncontrollable, spreading fast.

The servant arches a brow, unfazed by my tone or my stare. "The kitchen is stocked. I could get you something if you'd like," she offers, her voice holding the barest hint of... is that sarcasm? She has guts; I'll give her that. "Hmm, a meal served with a side of attitude. How can I resist?" I retort, but there's a reluctant smirk tugging at my lips.

Her presence—normal, human—breaks through the surreal fog I've been walking in.

As she turns on her heel, the way only someone used to obey orders can do, I follow. Why not? I have nothing to lose except maybe a bit of my sardonic dignity. The shadows slink along.

The servant walks ahead of me, head held high and back straight. "How long have you been working here?" I ask, trying to be less harsh than I was earlier. She stops walking and turns to face me, eyebrows furrowed. "Listen, carrot freckles. I don't need to talk to you. The master told me to bring you to the kitchen to eat. That's it," she snaps at me.

This audacious woman! I move quickly to punch her, but the chains tighten, and the snake hisses at me. "You're a prisoner; you think you can lay a hand on me?"

She laughs in my face, and I boil with rage from within.

After I eat a lavish spread that reminds me of better times, I make my way back to my room.

The little snake of darkness curls around my feet as I sit on the edge of my bed. This castle is a tomb, but it's a familiar one, and I strangely find myself appreciating the company of my little shadow snake.

213 - *Ruins and Shadows*

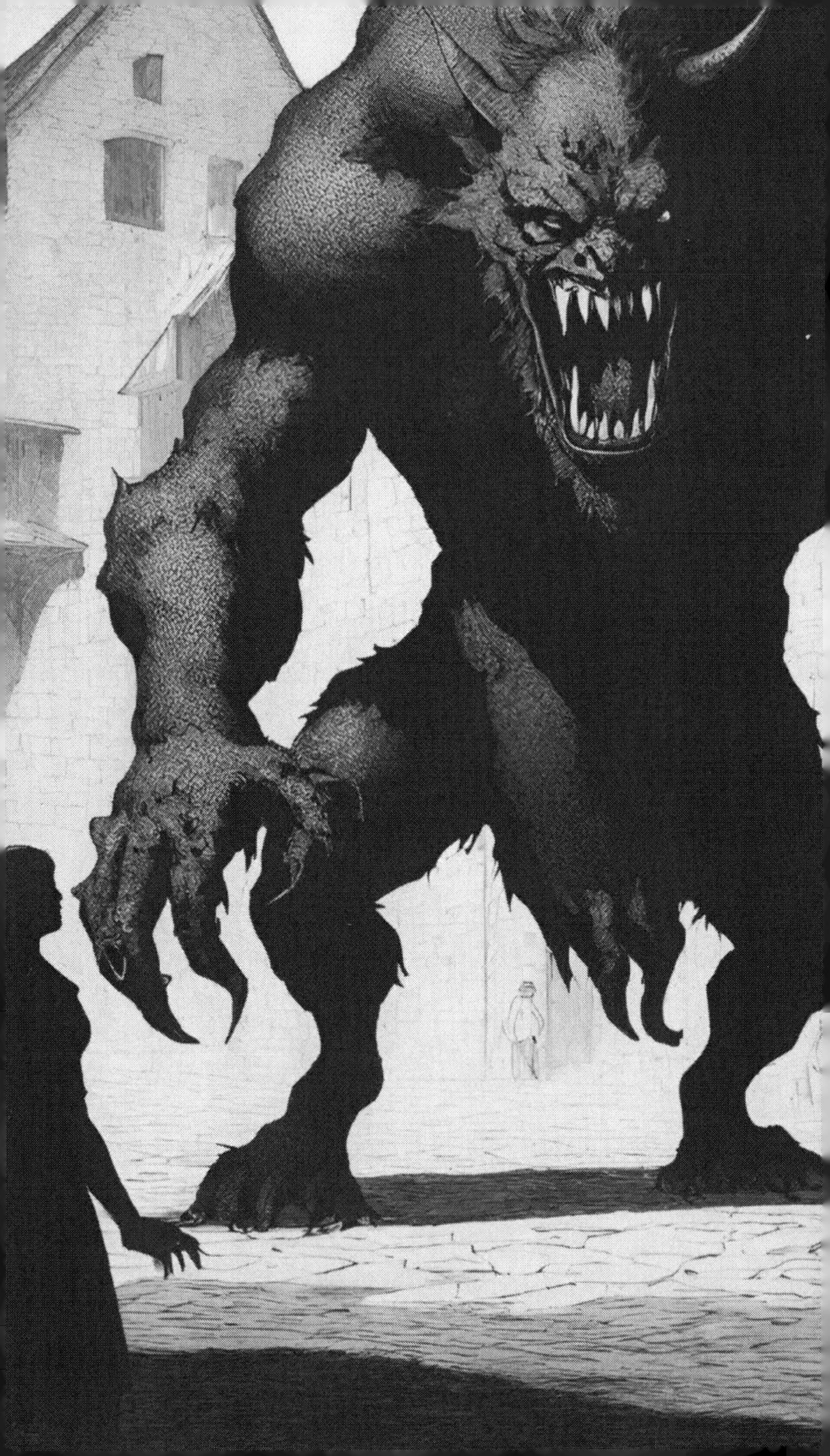

Chapter 16

Rory

I let out a sign before swinging my legs over the side of the bed, the cold floor a welcome shock to my senses. I feel an itch under my skin, and a relentless buzzing in my head, the anticipation of today's events has been a constant annoyance to me.

The people of this kingdom will finally get the shove they need to move their asses and accept the fact that a fucking war is coming, so they better fall in line or die.

I really don't give a shit. I would simply walk away and let them fend for themselves, if it weren't for the orders given to me by that damned Domovoi.

Raking a hand through my hair, I take a breath and rise from my bed to dress for today's public appearance.

I stride toward Anastasia's room, breakfast tray in hand. A courtesy, or maybe a peace offering. Doesn't matter. It's all part of the game. She's just another pawn with a fast-approaching expiration date.

The door creaks open, and I see her there sitting on the bed, looking like a caged beast, all fight and fire.

Placing the tray down on the little table next to the fireplace, I give her my back, "Big day today, you'll need to eat up," I say, the words sliding off my tongue like venom, "you'll need your strength."

She moves toward me, taking slow and calculated steps.

Before she even has the chance to strike, I turn and grab her wrist with ease as she tries to lunge at me, a legacy to centuries of battles hard-won.

The glass shard falls, shattering on the floor. Our eyes meet, and I grab her by her wrists, so small I only need one hand, and push her back forcefully to the wall, she releases a hiss from her lips when her spine collides with the stone.

"Nice try, princess," I chuckle, the edge in my voice betraying my own dangerous excitement.

Her chest heaves, fight and fervor etched into the lines of her face, so close to mine. Again, those fucking freckles. "Anastasia," I drawl as I run my nose along hers in a feather-light whisper, the sound of her name a velvet caress laced with poison. "You're spirited. I'll give you that. But even you can't deny that you're trying to play a game you cannot win." I whisper each word into her ear.

"Go to hell, Rory," she snarls, but her breath hitches, betraying the impact of my closeness. She loathes me, yet that very loathing is what makes this so damn exhilarating.

I press closer, my free hand tracing the contour of her jaw—a delicate line that belies the strength within. "Oh, I've been there and back, princess. The worst one is when I'm with you." I whisper, our lips mere inches apart.

Her breath catches, the softest gasp that speaks volumes more than her biting words ever could. I release her, slamming her once more into the wall and watch as she slides down to floor. "Get dressed princess, for today we tell the people the truth, or some version of it," I say dryly, "Princess Anastasia has returned, and she is betrothed to their King, and surely as the people love their Princess, they will agree to follow me willingly into war."

As I leave the room, I make sure to call out, "Just letting you know. The way you listen to my orders will determine the level of suffering of your death."

The courtyard is filled with a vast assembly of upturned faces. The air is thick with fear and anticipation, these people look at me as they should, an evil monster.

"We face a war, a tide that will wash over our lands unless we rise to meet it," my voice, laden with power, slices through the morning stillness.

The sea of eyes before me flits with uncertainty. "Today," I continue, and glance to where Anastasia exits the castle, her auburn hair ablaze with the light from the morning sun, "you witness the return of this kingdoms *true* Queen, the rebirth of a bloodline thought suppressed."

I track her graceful movements while she steps onto the balcony to join me. She is an absolute vision in the bright blue gown I chose for her, it's her favorite color, matching her exquisite eyes.

She walks into my outstretched hand, and I possessively slide my arm around her waist. Her face is a perfect mask of regal calmness. "Princess Anastasia has returned." I say looking down at the beauty at my side, my voice deep, and sultry.

A ripple of murmurs expands over the crown, and then a wave of shock soon turns to gasps of surprise and then an excited applause breaks out.

I raise a hand to silence their welcoming, and with a slight movement of my hand, shadows slither like smoke around my feet ready to obey.

They quickly take the form of a great beast. A large monster with long horns and cruel eyes that reflect their own terror back at them.

Anastasia's gaze locks onto mine, betrayal written in her stunning blues. The beast roars, a sound that shakes the very earth beneath us, and I feel her shock as if it were my own.

"As your Queen, and my beloved wife, let it be known," I bellow over the over the fading echoes of their fear, "disloyalty, insults or any kind of mistreatment of her will be met with the severest of punishments."

My gaze finds Sylvana, the little thieving bitch. Unfortunately for her, I discovered her mistake of mockery. I cannot, nor will I ever forgive her for scorning my beautiful Anastasia's freckles.

Without a word, the shadow beast strikes, a nightmare kiss, lifting her from the ground, her screams piercing the air around us. Pathetic. I have no pity for her.

She is fortunate that Anastasia's presence has inspired me to become a better man again. Otherwise, I would have severed her head on the spot.

Instead, the shadow beast carries her, eight feet off the ground by the torso, towards the dungeon. She will remain a prisoner down there, until illness or death comes to claim her.

When the beast is gone, out of our view, Anastasia inhales on a sharp gasp, her hands flying to cover her mouth. Some in the crowd look at their feet, others avert their eyes, but all understand.

I am not a ruler forged from mercy.

"Stand for your home, your families," I command, the remaining shadows dissolving into the light, "and your Queen, and we will conquer this enemy." I hold Anastasia's gaze, letting her see the monster she's bound to, yet also the man who could not end her life. The air is heavy with the taste of iron and fear.

But beneath it, beneath the horror and awe, there's a current of assent. They will follow.

I step down, leading Anastasia away as the whispers follow—a symphony of terror and respect.

My shadows curl around me, a cloak that whispers of darkness and power.

Anastasia pushes away from me. "Why?! Why did you do that to her?!" She shrieks at me as we enter the castle.

I stop abruptly in my pace, and she turns to face me. Her face is paler than when I found her. Her cheeks with those glorious freckles are sunken, and she looks empty. She'll be of no use to me if she falls into a depression or if the kingdom sees her as weak and mistreated. "Rory, why?"

Her lashes brush her cheeks as she looks at the floor, her voice barely above a whisper.

I raise a hand to her face, using my index finger to trace her nose with just the lightest touch. "Because she insulted you. She spoke against your freckles. And I, fucking love them." She looks at me with surprised eyes but doesn't pull away from my touch. "Are you fucking mad?! You imprisoned her because she made a ridiculous comment?!" Her voice now well above a whisper.

I grab her and spin her, so her back is to my chest, she lets out a small grunt when she hits my steel body. With her arms pinned behind her back, I face her towards a large obsidian framed mirror hung on the wall in the grand entrance.

I'm much taller than she is and need to bend a fair amount to whisper in her ear. "She was vile, thieving and sneaking about the castle, she deserved it anyway," my voice has grown husky.

This close proximity to her gives me the perfect angle to enjoy her enchanting floral scent. "And these, my feisty new wife," I continue, my fingers teasing the air just above her skin, "are worthy of no offense."

Her breath catches on a small gasp, "I've never liked them." She says defiantly. I stand tall in the foyer, my gaze fixed on her eyes in the mirror. My god, she is a vision with those ginger constellations gracing her face and bright blues I could drown in. My heart is a block of ice, yet her presence is the flame that threatens to melt it.

"You're foolish to dislike these," I murmur, daring to graze the spots she finds so offensive.

I watch her, the way her eyes hold defiance and anger—emotions that fuel me, give me purpose. As her chest rises and falls with each heavy breath, I can feel the tension between us, a living thing with its own breath and fury.

I stand behind her, our battle of wills silent but as violent as clashing swords in our locked eyes, I summon my magic. With a wave of my hand, the brown little flecks she so despises transform.

In their place is a shimmering dusting of gold specks. "Ethereal," I breathe in her ear.

She's stunned, her eyes wide in her delicate face, reflecting the new hue that adorns her skin. It's a small victory, an assertion of my power, my control.

But as our eyes continue to bore into each other, something within me stirs—a longing, a curiosity, a connection I don't fully understand. I need her, more than I've allowed myself to admit.

Not just as a pawn in my grand scheme to win the trust of my people, but as the missing piece of a puzzle I've been trying to solve for centuries.

Her voice cuts through the silence, a blade aimed at my heart. "I'll never be what you want, Rory," she spits out. But I see the doubt in her eyes, the war she fights within herself.

I know this game too well—the push and pull. She hates me, wants to kill me, but part of her yearns for something more, just as part of me does.

I reach out once more, this time allowing my fingers to brush her cheek, a touch as light as a whisper. It's cruel, to give her such attention when I plan to use and then kill her.

Yet, I can't stop myself. The moment is electricity, a spark that ignites the air between us. My magic swirls around us, an invisible force that dances with the charged atmosphere. My jacket tails flapping in the gust like ribbons, her flaming locks whirling around her face.

Immediately I step back, concealing the tumultuous waves of emotion behind a mask of indifference.

We hold each other's gaze while both breathing equally hard by the unexpected excitement, before she says, "I'll be in the garden," her voice steady but infused with a tremor of uncertainty and as she starts walking turning her back to me.

The sunlight streaming through the windows illuminates her silhouette; her long, curly hair gently sways against her hips as she moves, and I watch her.

Her face turns back for a fleeting moment, and my entire being cracks.

Déjà vu.

Impossible.

It's like a tornado in my mind, images, memories that do not yet belong to me. Deep down, I know the truth. I can transform her freckles into gold, bend shadows to my will, chain her up in this castle, but I cannot change what's woven into the fabric of her soul.

She's dying, slowly, falling into despair and sadness. Anastasia Romanov, she should be dead, and still. Now I understand.

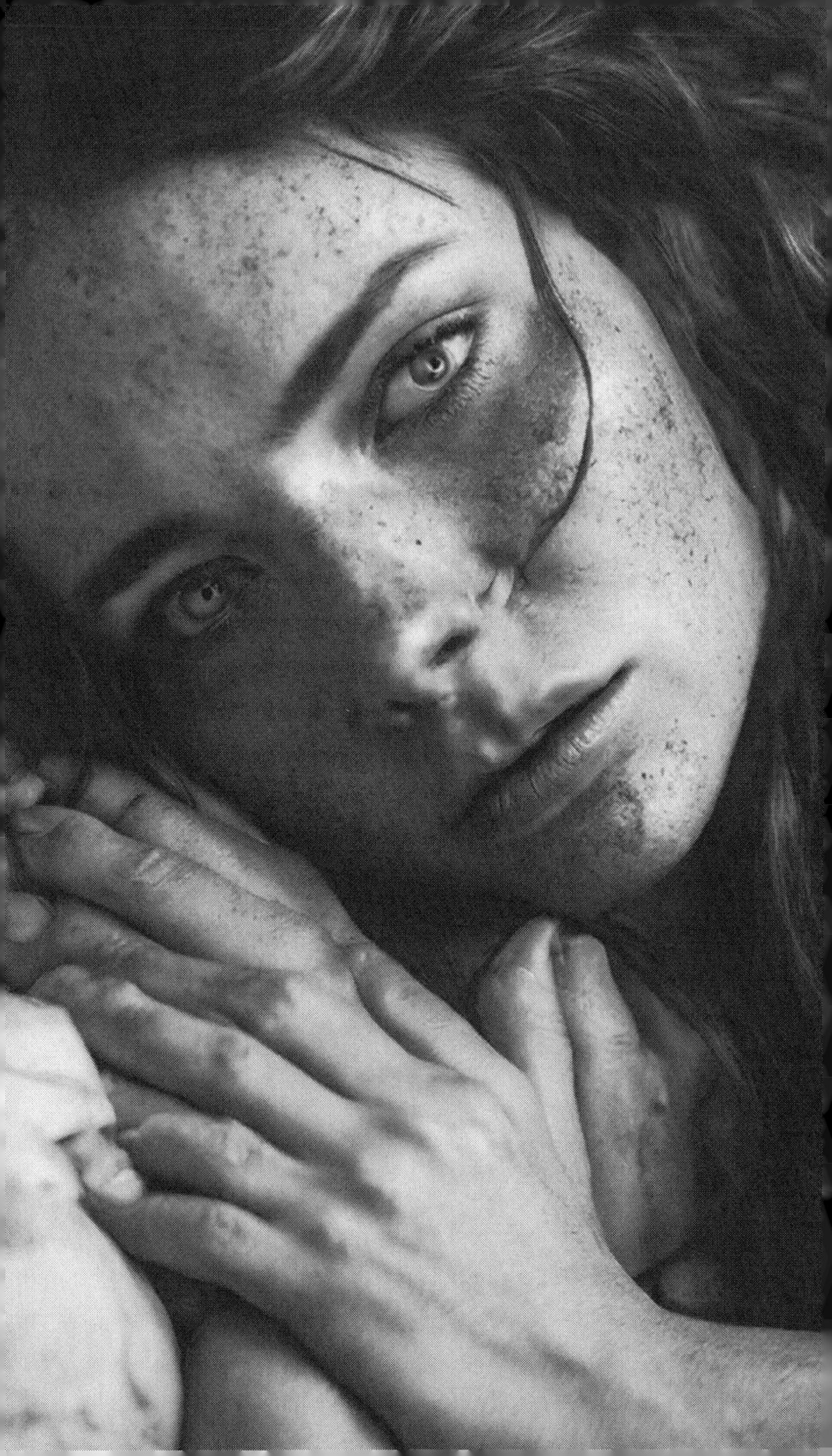

Chapter 17

Anastasia

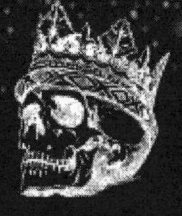

5 months later

I pace along one of the many endless hallways in this castle I once called my home, now known to me only as a prison. The constant restriction of the ghostly shadow chains only serves to further remind me of that.

We must give the illusion that you appear to have freedom, for the benefit of the people. Play my doting wife; I win over the kingdom's adoration. Rory's words echo in my mind as I pause next to a marble pedestal holding a vase with a beautiful arrangement of white flowers.

I reach out and lightly stroke one of the petals. Closing my eyes, I feel the velvety flower between my fingers, and my eyes sting with tears I've tried so hard to keep from falling. Just like the stem of this flower, my heart has been severed.

The salty dam building behind my eyes for the last five months has finally reached its limit.

As the tears fall, so do I, right to the marble floor, taking the flowers with me, and the vase shatters to pieces next to my crumbled frame as sobs wretch from my throat.

The ache in my heart is a constant unwanted companion, a reminder that I'm alone in this vast, silent tomb. Five months, and not a soul has come for me. But why would they? I have no one left. I'm a forgotten relic of a fallen empire, a whisper of a bygone era.

I can't hold back anymore; it's too painful, too many bad memories here, too much hatred for the evil monster keeping me hostage here.

Vitriev is dead! The villagers during the attack, innocent people! Ma and Pa, my sister, Alexei! They are all dead because of that fucking bastard!

Through my uncontrollable sobs, I feel a presence approach. I snap my head up, and blue eyes meet deep green. The devil himself, of course he would show up during my breakdown. His eyes sear into mine, like a mountain lion looking at a dying doe.

Rage ignites within me. "You!" I yell, my voice echoing against the stone walls. I leap to my feet, snatching up a large, jagged piece of broken vase. With all the fury of a storm, I swing it right at his jugular.

He's too quick and manages to easily dodge my arm with a laugh. "Come now, my love," He taunts, his eyes glinting with amusement. "Is that any way to greet your beloved?" I hiss, "Don't call me that and you will never be my beloved anything!" I lunge again, the shard swishing through the air. But he evades easily, and I can't touch him.

He circles me like a wolf pack, his voice smooth as silk, coming to a rest a few feet away, he casually leans against the wall and crosses his arms, eyes burning a hole through my sadness. "Come, Anastasia. Show me that fire I so adore."

His words stoke the embers in my soul. However, it's not just anger Rory sparks in me. There's something else too, something dangerous. I despise this man but, I can't ignore the allure of his strength, the way my pulse pounds at his nearness, and the flutter I feel in my stomach when his intoxicating, manly scent intrudes on my senses. He's large, physically yes, but he himself, his presence is invading. "I hope you're ready," I spit out, gripping the glass harder, feeling tiny slices cut my fingers, "because I'm not stopping until one of us is dead."

He laughs, a sound that's low and seductive, he pushes himself away from the wall and the movement causes a lock of his dark hair to fall over his forehead. If I didn't wish him dead, I would have fainted from how beautiful he looked. "Oh, my fierce warrior queen, what a glorious battle that would be. But perhaps you should ask yourself, would you really kill me?" I pause, and I slightly lower my arm, confusion forming on my face.

Rory's lips curl into a smirk, and he steps closer. "You're the thorn in my side buried so far I can't fucking remove it, a challenge I can't resist." He purrs, his voice low and raspy. "Shut up!" I scream, swinging again. He ducks, and the shard of vase smashes against the stone wall. "Passionate and beautiful," he murmurs, stepping back into the shadows. "But ultimately futile." I'm left panting, the taste of defeat bitter on my tongue. I have no strength left.

I'm becoming so weak; I find myself repulsive. Rory is still there, watching, waiting. "Come on, stab me, fight me, hate me, give it all you've got princess." He looks at me with a smile. I don't have anything left; exhaustion is taking over.

My knees give out and I fall back to the floor, my hands trembling and my heart heavy. I lift my gaze to Rory's; his expression is puzzled. He crouches down, his elbows resting casually on his thighs.

With his eyes holding mine, he tilts his head to the side and says, "what have you become, princess?" A tsking sound slides from his perfect mouth, "must I torture you to bring back that little spitfire?" I don't respond. I look at him, but my eyes are unfocused, my vision empty, lost to nothingness.

Rory releases an irritated sigh. Standing, he combs his fingers through his hair and soon his heavy footsteps fade off into a deafening silence.

I stand and as I do, I glimpse my reflection in the windowpane. The face staring back at me is thin and marred by tears and exhaustion. The visage is not one of the warrior I trained so hard to become. The warrior I became with the guidance of my Vitriev.

You're the thorn in my side buried so far, I can't fucking remove it, a challenge I can't resist.

His statement replays in my head, and it both annoys me and excites me. I despise the part of me that revels in this acknowledgement, that craves his attention like a plant starved of sunlight.

I've desperately wanted him to die all these years. And now, it's me I wish death upon. A tear travels down my cheek, over a patch of glimmering gold freckles, and I see a small glimpse of the little girl that used to live behind these walls, and it brings a small smile to my lips.

I will not grant Rory the satisfaction of seeing me broken and miserable anymore. I straighten my spine and start walking down the hall, leaving the shattered vase and shredded flowers behind me.

Each of my steps is a silent vow to reject Rory's vision of me. I'm more than a pawn in his sadistic games; within me rests the bloodline of a lost empire.

That thought alone musters a fight in me that no number of chains could contain.

I will train in the shadows of my captivity.

I will observe Rory's movements.

I will fortify my mind against his psychological warfare.

I understand now that my escape will not come from brute force—it will come from cunning, and from patience.

Rory has underestimated me, and that will be his downfall. I've seen what Rory is capable of, his cruelty is scarring, and surrender is not an option. If I am to die, let it be as I live, fighting. My future will be forged from victory, not defeat.

237 - *Ruins and Shadows*

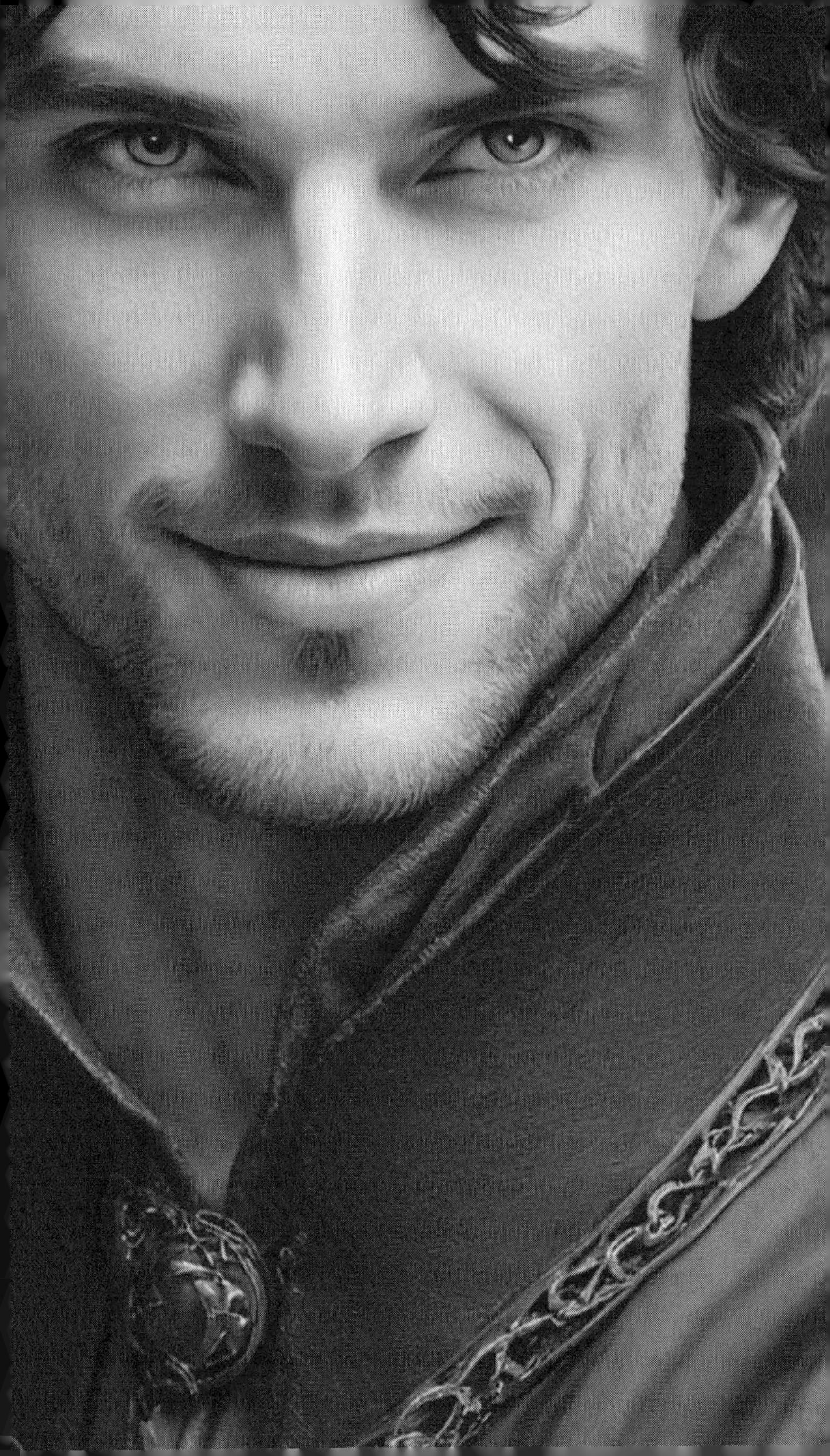

Chapter 18

Anastasia

2 weeks later

The garden, once a riot of colors vibrant and joyful, now whispers a mournful tune as petals fall like tears.

I wander, my fingers trailing over blooms that shiver with the encroaching cold. Winter's breath taunts the once-warm haven, sapping the life from each stem and leaf. I miss my ducks, I miss Vitriev, I miss last summer. I've been spiraling, tumbling down into an abyss that seems to have no end.

The beauty around me feels distant, a faded painting of a time when my heart knew more than just this haunting emptiness. With each step, I feel the ground solid beneath my feet, yet it offers no comfort. It's as if with the coming of the harsh season, the very earth seeks to remind me of the relentless march of time—of lives turned brittle and barren.

The only light in my vision is my now golden freckles, catching each ray of sunshine. I didn't know his magic could do something other than destroy.

The air is crisp, biting at my skin with invisible teeth, and I wrap my arms around myself to defend against the chill. Now, as the leaves rustle their final lullabies, I sink to my knees, the dirt cold against my skin. I clutch at the ground, the little snake shadow always by my side, making room for my hands, seeking an anchor in the storm that ravishes my soul.

My slithery companion weaves in and out of my hands, almost grounding me. Gathering what little strength I can muster; I push back the oppressive cover of sadness and rise.

Each movement is deliberate, a battle against the languor that clings to my limbs. It doesn't seem to matter how strong my will to survive this is.

I feel like I'm growing weaker by the minute, I'm starving but I have no desire to eat. As much as I wish to kill Rory, my wish for my own death is much stronger.

I look at the snake curled around my feet, knowing that through it, Rory can hear me, I say, "Why don't you just kill me already?" The little shadow tilts its head to the side and stares at me; I roll my eyes and sigh. My mind is a haze, and every small victory in pulling myself together feels hollow.

"Excuse me, my Queen."

I'm startled when one of the castle servants approaches from behind. "Sorry to disturb you, your Majesty, but the King wishes to dine with you."

I nod and return to my room to dress.

Inside, something snarls, a part of me that wants to scream and rage against the demand. But it's buried deep, under layers of fatigue and the relentless force of Rory's will.

I retreat into my bath chamber, and the sight that greets me pulls at the seams of my composure. The bath is ready, steam curling from the hot water like wraiths rising into the chilly air. It's an unexpected comfort.

Submerging into the bath, I let the heat strip away the veneer of numbness, if only for a while. The water cradles me, a liquid embrace that I wish could wash away more than just the grime of confinement and the stink of fear.

When I emerge, the world is no less dim, but I am cleaner. The gown laid out on the bed is a beautiful mockery, its fabric rich and color vibrant. I dress with mechanical precision, the jewels and adornments feeling like weights rather than finery.

I paint my face with the colors of life, rouge, and kohl to conceal the pallor that has claimed my features. Every brush stroke is a lie, a façade created to meet the expectations of a man who claims to be king, a man who once meant something more to me.

Primed, painted, and masked, I stand at the precipice of the evening. The servant returns, a silent guide through the castle's corridors. I follow, my mind adrift.

The dining hall is grand, its opulence a ghastly specter of happier times. The table is set for two, and King Rasputin is already there, waiting.

He looks at me, and for a heartbeat, I allow myself to wonder what thoughts lurk behind those calculating eyes. I step into the room, the sheer opulence of the space takes my breath away, I had forgotten it could be so beautiful.

Towering stone walls, adorned with intricate tapestries depicting epic tales of knights and war, surrounded me. The soft glow of flickering candles cast a warm, golden hue upon the room, while the sparkling chandeliers overhead glimmer with a thousand crystals, reflecting light in a mesmerizing dance across the ceiling and walls.

A massive oak table, polished to a shine, stretches the length of the room, adorned with ornate silverware and fine red porcelain dinnerware fit for royalty. The air is filled with the tantalizing aroma of roasted meats, spiced wines, and freshly baked bread.

Gilded mirrors framed in intricate gold patterns hang on the walls, reflecting the grandeur of the room and amplifying the sense of space and majesty.

High-backed chairs upholstered in rich black velvet line the table, each meticulously carved with motifs of the era, inviting guests to indulge in the lavish banquet that awaits.

The dim ambiance mocks the spread of untouched food before me, a feast I cannot stomach. Sadness wraps around my heart, squeezing tight enough to kill my appetite but not the memories.

Rory's gaze is unwavering, his question cuts through the quiet. "What's wrong with you, Anastasia?" He leans in, a playful glint in his eye. "It's been ages since you've tried to kill me—I miss the thrill." I can taste the sarcasm. "Just lost my taste for pointless endeavors," I murmur dryly, my words more for me than for him.

A cruel smirk dances on Rory's lips, a silent command emanating from his eyes. "Eat," he says. And I do, the weirdness of the flavors mingling with the heaviness in my soul. One bite, then another, each mouthful a betrayal to my senses.

Rory chuckles, a sound that grates on my nerves, but also new to my ears as a grown woman. A beautiful laugh "Something funny?" I demand, the question laced with the venom of a heart darkened by too much loss.

His laughter blooms into a full smile. "Oh, it's just—your face!" He points at my contorted grimace. "Do you like your new freckles, princess?" The question seems genuine; he leans back comfortably in his chair, at ease.

Our eyes meet, and I place my fork on the table, unable to continue eating. "I really don't care," I reply. His lips tighten, and he squints as he scrutinizes me. "I hate it," he snaps. "I hate the way your soul just gave up." I struggle to hold back tears, lowering my gaze.

He sighs heavily and leans forward again, resting his face in the palm of one hand above the table. "How do you like the food?"

"It tastes like shit." I say honestly. "Well, that'll be the poison," He bursts into laughter, and I quickly raise my head, eyes wide, utterly speechless. Shock ripples through me, the cold realization that Rory would, that Rory did.

I push the plate away, my mind racing. The taste still lingers, metallic, wrong. I look up, defiance flaring in my eyes. "Is this supposed to unsettle me?" I spit out the words, a challenge thrown across the tablecloth battlefield. Rory leans back, the darkness of his amusement a shadow that threatens to engulf the room. "Not at all. I just miss how lively you are when you're... dying at my hands."

I stare, the silence thick with unspoken curses and a longstanding hatred that weaves through us. As if sensing the battle brewing within me, Rory unfolds from his seat with the grace he doesn't deserve.

He circles the table, the soft sound of his boots against the marble floor echoing in the tense silence. There's a gleam in his eye that I recognize all too well—the thrill of control, the joy of toying with a life. "You know," He coos, his voice smooth as silk yet cold as the winter air outside, "most would cower at the thought of being poisoned. But not you, princess. You've always been... different."

I rise to meet him, every muscle in my body tense. He steps closer, close enough that I can feel the warmth of his breath. "You want me dead. Do it." I reply, my voice steady despite the fear threading through my veins. "Not right now," he replies with a shrug.

Then, his expression shifts, softens almost imperceptibly. "Don't worry though, it won't hurt." I recoil at the word, but Rory's hand shoots out, fingers wrapping around my wrist with an iron grip. He draws me close.

His other hand finds my chin, tilting my face up to look at him, and I can see the madness swirling in his eyes, a storm I've become too familiar with. "You see," he whispers, "it's not enough for me to hold your chains. I want more, Anastasia. I want your spirit to fight, to blaze with the same fire it once had."

I yank my wrist free, my heart hammering against my ribcage. "You won't find it here," I say with quiet defiance. "You've extinguished it." With a soft chuckle, Rory steps back. "We'll see," he murmurs, turning to leave the dining room. The doors close behind him with a resounding thud, and I am left alone with the ghosts of our encounter.

The poison, real or metaphorical, courses through me, a reminder of the twisted bond that ties me to this man. The King who sees me not as a person but as a pawn in his sadistic games.

I return to my bedroom, where the moon casts eerie shadows across the floor. The little snake shadow slithers beside me, a silent companion in the night. The tingling sensation in my body begins to intensify, and I feel increasingly weak.

Using one hand to support myself on the edge of my mattress, I settle into my bed and lie down slowly, trying not to exacerbate the dizziness. A single tear rolls down from my eye, landing on my lips.

This is how I die. Alone, dizzy, and at the mercy of a cruel monster. As if sensing my fear, the small serpent slides onto the bed and nestles against my cheek. I burrow in close.

I let out a sigh; this is it now. I'm so tired.

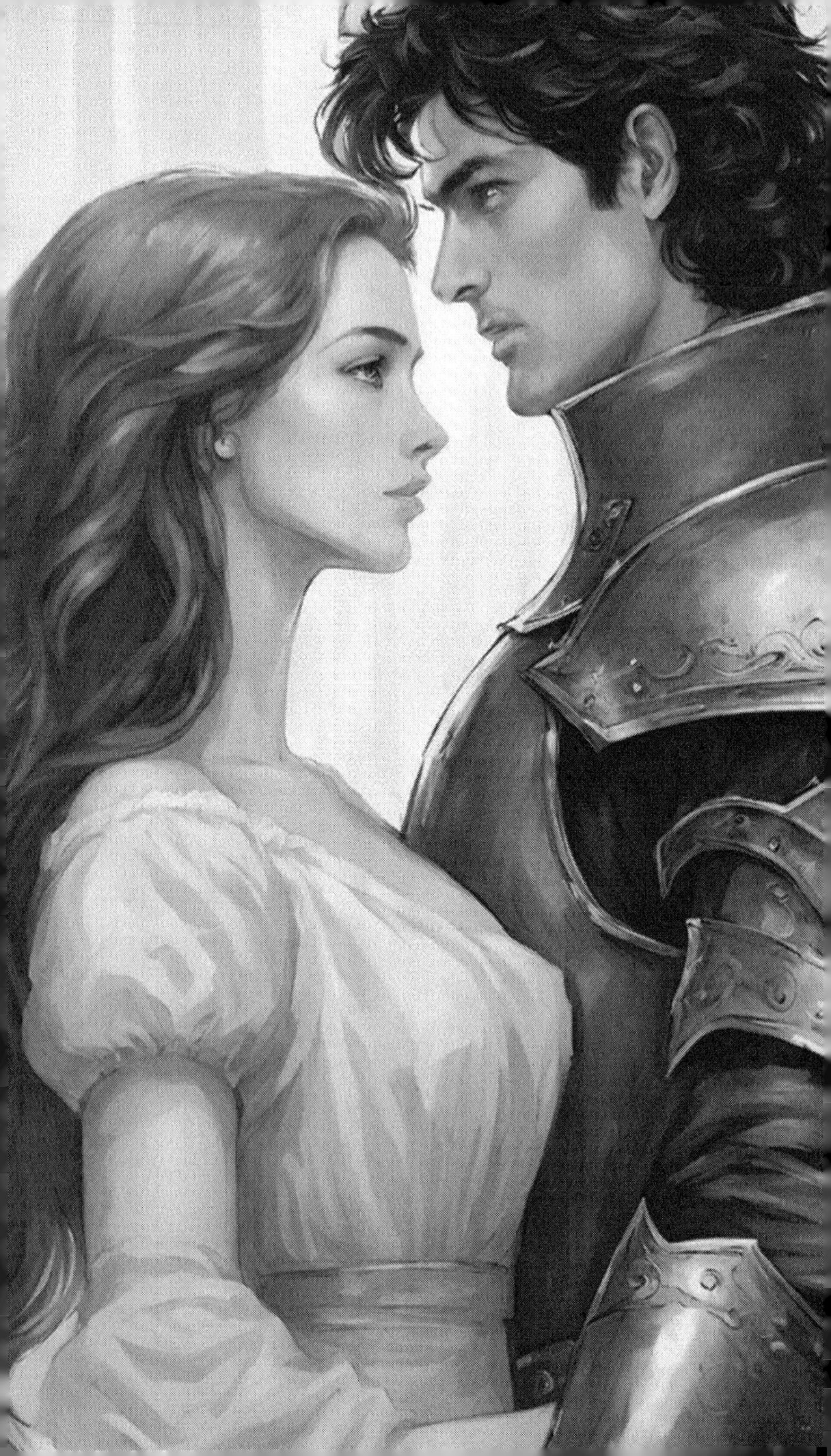

Chapter 19

Anastasia

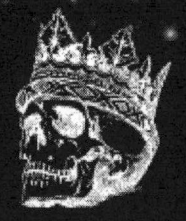

My body aches with a deep soreness that tells me I've been still for too long, like sleeping on a bed of rocks for a hundred years.

Every muscle and joint are screaming at me. I open my eyes, and slowly try to blink away the grogginess.

What the hell happened?

I have no recollection of going to bed, and the more I think on it, I don't seem to have memories of anything.

I sit up in the bed and rub my eyes. When the room finally comes into focus, I survery my surroundings, hoping something will spark recognition. The room is dim, shadows clinging to every corner like cobwebs. Nothing looks familiar to me. The stone walls are bare, and the scent of dust and old parchment lingers in the air.

"Where the hell am I?" The question slides on a whisper from my lips, evaporating into the stillness of the room. The quiet creaks and groans of the structure around me are my only reply.

Rubbing my temples, I squeeze my eyes shut in frustration. There's something... a dull ache, reminding me that something is not right.

My name. Anastasia. Well at least that much I know. It echoes in my head, clear among the fog of lost memories. It's a lifeline, a starting point to pull myself together. Only, as I try to reach beyond it, to pull out more threads of who I am, where I from, why I'm here and where is here even?... there's nothing. And the more I try to grasp onto anything, the more I realize there's a black void where my memories should be.

"I need to get out of this room," I whisper to myself, even though I haven't a clue where *out* will lead me.

I inhale deeply, trying to calm my racing heart.

As I stand from the gold and red satin covered mattress, a new sound punctures the silence—a distant echo of footsteps, heading this way it seems.

Unsure of what to expect, I ready myself for whatever or whoever is approaching by grabbing the hand mirror on the table next to the bed.

As the heavy door creaks open, I smash the mirror on the corner of the nightstand and grab the sharpest piece of glass. Just as I raise my arm to point the weapon at the intruder, I am met with eyes a shade of vivid green I'm unsure if I've ever seen before.

He stops walking and stands about six feet away from me. He has a presence that commands attention, the kind that you couldn't possibly ignore even if you want to.

I examine his face, searching for any clue that will help me determine if I need to attack him or not. He's terrifying and so fucking beautiful it's infuriating. The damn dimples on his face are making me lose focus, my heart is pounding uncontrollably in my chest, and I feel a squeezing flutter in my stomach just looking at this man. How is he affecting me so intensely?

"Who are you?" I say, narrowing my eyes as I tilt my head slightly to the right. My voice came out softer than I intended. He takes a step closer to me, and I hate how my whole body reacts, how there's a part of me that wants to reach out to him, just to see if he's real.

His eyes search mine, and it's alarming how raw and exposed I feel. He hesitates, and there's a flicker of something in his expression. "I'm Rory," his says, and his voice sends a shiver to my core, "I'll be able to help you understand what is going on here."

Cautiously lowering my arm holding the bit of broken mirror, I search his face for honesty. "How am I to know if you can be trusted? That I should believe your words?" Feeling my confidence building, I cross my arms over my bosom and continue, finding strength to cement my voice, "I don't know you."

He takes a few more careful steps, closing the distance between us even further. If I dared to, I could reach out and touch him. I catch a whisper of his scent, a deep, woodsy, masculine scent that sends a rush of heat between my legs.

There's a tense energy forming between us that feels charged, like the calm in the air before a storm. Rory's gaze is unwavering, insistent. I feel so vulnerable under his stare.

"I am all you have left," he says simply, and a small gasp escapes from my lips, dissolving into the space between us. His words spark a sudden confusing anger in me, and my automatic reaction is to yell at him to get the fuck out, but I don't.

I can't bring myself to say a word. What is he talking about?

My face must betray my thoughts because he continues, "your family was killed when you were just a girl. The murderer is still after you," he pauses, when I remain quiet, he lets out a gentle sigh, "Anastasia, I am your husband, and you are safe within these walls." He gestures to the room around us, but I don't follow his movements.

I gape at him, unseeing. The room has started spinning and I feel a heaviness forming on my chest. Husband?

His words cut through the fog of amnesia like a beacon in the dark. A thousand questions bubble up inside me, each one fighting to be the first out. "My family...? I... I don't understand...how?" I whisper, the pain raw and unexpected. "Did you know them?" My grip on the glass loosens slightly, but I don't let it go—not yet.

Rory nods, solemnity etched into his features. "Yes. I worked with your father. He was a good man." His face has softened slightly, seeming to try and deliver this information to me as gently as possible.

"Tell me everything," I demand. The urgency to know, to understand, overshadows my initial distrust of this man. He takes a cautious step forward, eliminating the remainder of distance between us. "It's a long story, Anastasia, and it's dangerous. The less you know, the safer you'll be. But I understand your need for answers. I'll tell you as much as I can," he says, his eyes never wavering from mine.

I sit on the edge of the bed, and gesture for him to continue, the sharp mirror shatter still in my hand, now more a token of my unresolved fears than a real weapon.

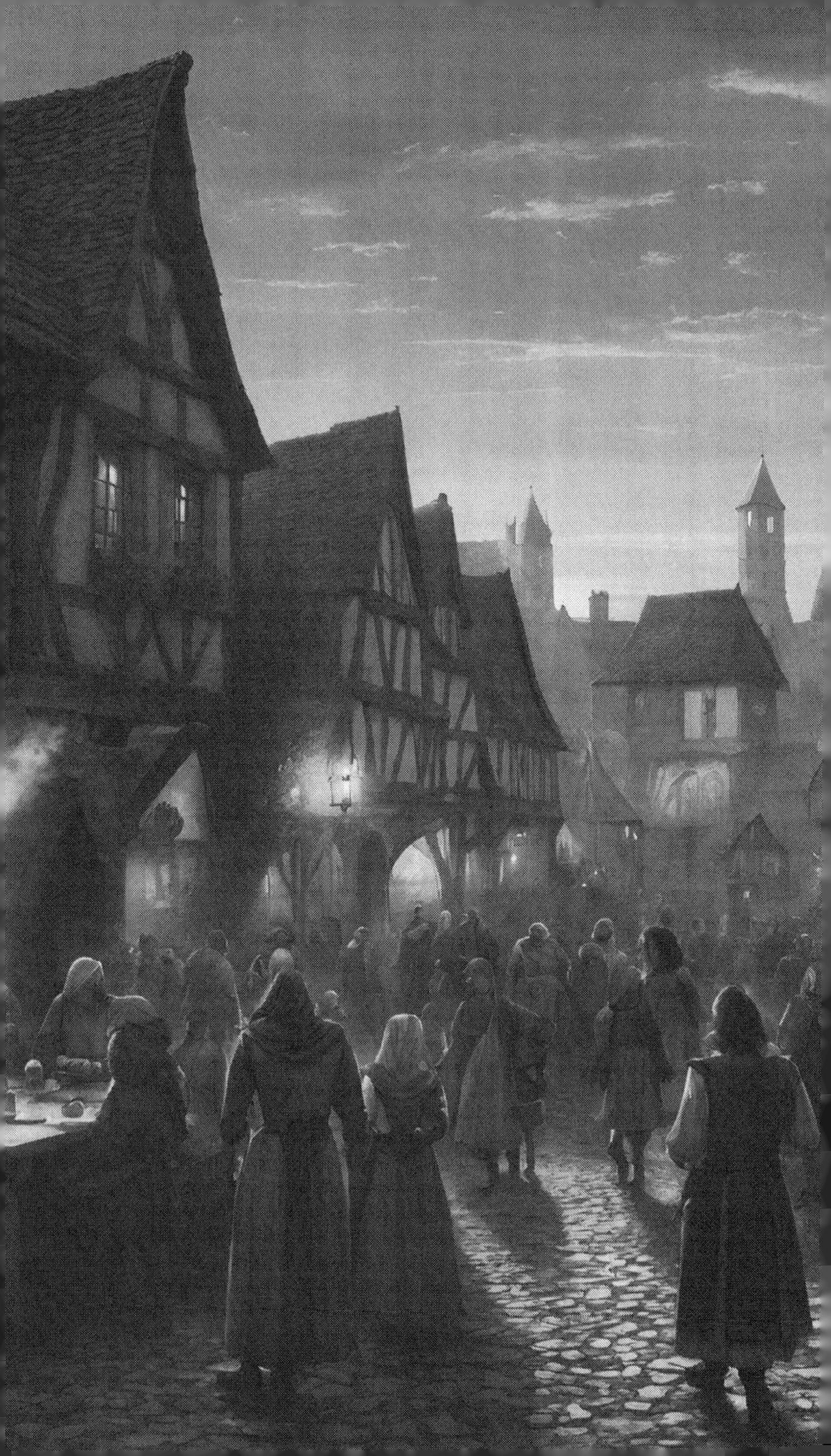

Chapter 20

Anastasia

As I follow Rory outside, the fresh, cool air hits me like a forgotten whisper. I'm not sure why I agreed to his request for a walk, but after he recalled events from my past to me only an hour ago, I thought perhaps the cold breeze from a walk outside would wake up my slumbering memories.

As we pass through the grand entrance and out the heavy, carved doors into the front courtyard, Rory's words play over in my head on a constant loop.

"Your family was killed by a very disturbed man seeking power. He wanted to take the throne. During all the

commotion, you managed to flee the castle, to where I am uncertain. I succeeded in hunting down the traitor and reclaiming the crown for your family, but I failed in his capture. I've spent over a decade searching for you Anastasia, and I found you just months ago, for you to be kidnapped by an unknown party while out on a walk in the city and I rescued you a few days ago, finding you bruised, with a substantial head injury. So, I brought you back here to recover... and, here we are now."

The streets of the kingdom unfold before us, a demonstration of a life that seems both foreign and familiar. My thoughts are racing as I view the villagers going about their daily lives.

My memories are so distant, yet at the same time so close. I feel them scratching at the door of my consciousness. Rory's presence is a constant at my side, a guide through the maze of my fractured mind.

I'm unsure if what Rory has told me is the truth but I do know that something about him, something about all of this does give me a small sense of recognition, I just can't unfold the images.

Despite that little hint of something I feel, he troubles me—the way people look at him with fear in their eyes when we cross paths with them, it's unsettling. Why though?

We pass by bustling markets and quiet alleyways, the contrasting scenes painting a picture I can almost recall.

"You see," he begins, stopping to face me, and I can tell that this walk is about more than just sightseeing. "It's important that you understand everything, Anastasia." I nod, a five-year-old's eagerness mixing with a woman's dread. He tells me of the time when my world was smaller, enclosed within the castle walls, my days a blend of royal duties and my brother's laughter.

Rory Rasputin, the enigmatic magician, had come like a shadow, offering his arcane assistance to keep my ailing brother's health in check.

I stare at Rory, trying to connect the man before me with the healer from my fragmented past. "You helped us," I murmur, a realization that warms and chills me simultaneously. A shadow crosses his face as he confirms, "Yes, I did." His voice cracks a bit, like a mirror threatening to shatter. "If you helped us. If you're a good person, why do these people look at you as if they've just seen their own death?" My question is honest, firm, and his eyebrows are raised in surprise.

With his index finger and thumb, he grips his chin, chuckling softly. "I see you haven't lost your sharp mind, princess." The words ring a bell in my head. "I helped you. But since the royal lineage died, and I had to take the throne, I had to do atrocious things. And now, people are afraid of me."

I gaze into his eyes; beautifully green and hypnotizing, but also, filled with emptiness. His smile doesn't reach his eyes. "What are you looking at, princess?" His voice pulls me out of my trance. "You have beautiful eyes," I blurt unexpectedly, and my cheeks redden.

His smile drops immediately; he takes a few steps back and clears his throat. "Like I was saying." He adds and the story darkens like a storm cloud as we walk on.

He speaks of my tenth year, the year my innocence died, a beautiful Christmas celebration twisted into a nightmare.

My mouth goes dry as I listen, unable to fathom why I was spared from this inexplicable violence. "And now you find me, after all these years," I interject, my voice fraying at the edges. I glance at him out of the corner of my eye. He nods, pain etched in his gaze.

The chill nips at my skin, biting through the layers of my cloak as we make our way through the streets. Winter is whispering its arrival in the faintest of chills and in a way, the sunlight seems thinner, almost fragile.

I can feel it in the way the cobbles beneath my boots grow colder, and how the air carries the scent of impending frost. The brickwork of the structures that line our path, the steeply pitched roofs look aged, and the stones underfoot are worn smooth by countless footsteps.

In the fading light, it feels almost as if the whole city huddles beneath the weight of its own history, much like I carry my own silent burden.

The market square sprawls before us, a scattered puzzle of vendors closing up shop, their stalls groaning with the remnants of the day's trade. The clang of a blacksmith's hammer ceases, replaced by the muted conversations of merchants and the soft rustle of fabric as goods are packed away.

I glance sideways at Rory, catching his gaze for an instant before he looks away, a tortured expression forming on his chiseled jaw. His shoulders are hunched, not against the cold, but something far more burdensome. My heart aches for him.

Our steps slow as we approach the remnants of a fallen statue, a stark reminder of the empire's decay. Its once grand stone face lies half-buried in mud, the crown that adorned its head now tarnished. It's a glimpse of what could befall us—our own potential ruin.

There is a strange sort of beauty in the way the darkness clings to the edges of the streets, to the corners of Rory's troubled eyes.

I wrap my fingers tighter around my cloak, holding onto the fabric as if it might anchor me against the cold air. The evening draws in, the last glimmer of sunlight fades slowly. I draw in a shaky breath, the cold air biting my lungs. "Cold, princess?" Rory stops walking. "Yes." I shiver. Softly, he raises his hand, his long fingers pointing towards my face.

I stare intently at the tip of his index finger when a small tornado of black smoke swirls around it.

Gliding gracefully and spinning on itself to grow larger. In the blink of an eye, thick shadows surround me, and the air feels warmer, more comfortable.

As it retracts and lets my hair fall back onto my shoulders, a thick fur cloak is now upon me. A small gasp gets caught in my throat, I lower my eyes to my new coat; the fur is black, long, shiny, silky, magnificent. "Wow. It's exquisite, thank you," I catch his eyes and quickly lower mine.

With my lashes brushing my cheeks as I watch my fingers glide through the delicate little hairs, I release a sign, reveling in the softness. Rory makes a low groan in his throat, and I look up at him.

I clear my throat before I say, "I didn't know that this magic could do such beautiful things." He runs his finger down the side of my face, so close but not close enough to touch me, I can feel the heat from his skin. "I am capable of many things, princess, has the question of your gold freckles crossed your mind yet?" He asks in a deep, sultry voice I need to clench my thighs against the tickle it causes.

I gasp and touch my face with both hands. "I haven't looked yet. Are my freckles gold?" My voice is panicked.

Rory bursts into laughter, and I step back in astonishment. The sound of his voice is one of the most beautiful laughs I've heard in all my life. "I gave them to you," he tries to say between bursts of laughter.

As Rory's laughter subsides, he takes a step towards me, his eyes twinkling with mischief and a sort of warmth that feels like a soft blanket around my heart. "Your freckles are beautiful, you are fucking perfection," he says, his voice now a gentle murmur, "However, princess, you said you didn't like them," I raise an eyebrow, the confusion evident on my face, my fingers still feeling the spot where the gold dusting decorates my skin. "I can't imagine why; your magic is beautiful." I reply, feeling slightly shy suddenly.

Rory releases a breath, looking up at the first stars piercing the twilight sky. "Anastasia, we have a responsibility to the people of these lands," His words settle upon me, heavier than the finest cloak.

He looks down at me, "war is coming princess, we need to be ready."

I think I've become numb, hearing the words he says invade my senses causing a ripple of ice to coarse through my body. I unexpectedly say, "why do you keep calling me princess, you're my husband, the king, so am I not the Queen?" I stare blankly at him and to my surprise he chuckles again.

"You certainly are Queen, my love, but you will always, be my princess." He says, and the pad of his thumb grazes my lower lip light as a feather. Gently he releases it and I part my lips on a small moan.

269 - *Ruins and Shadows*

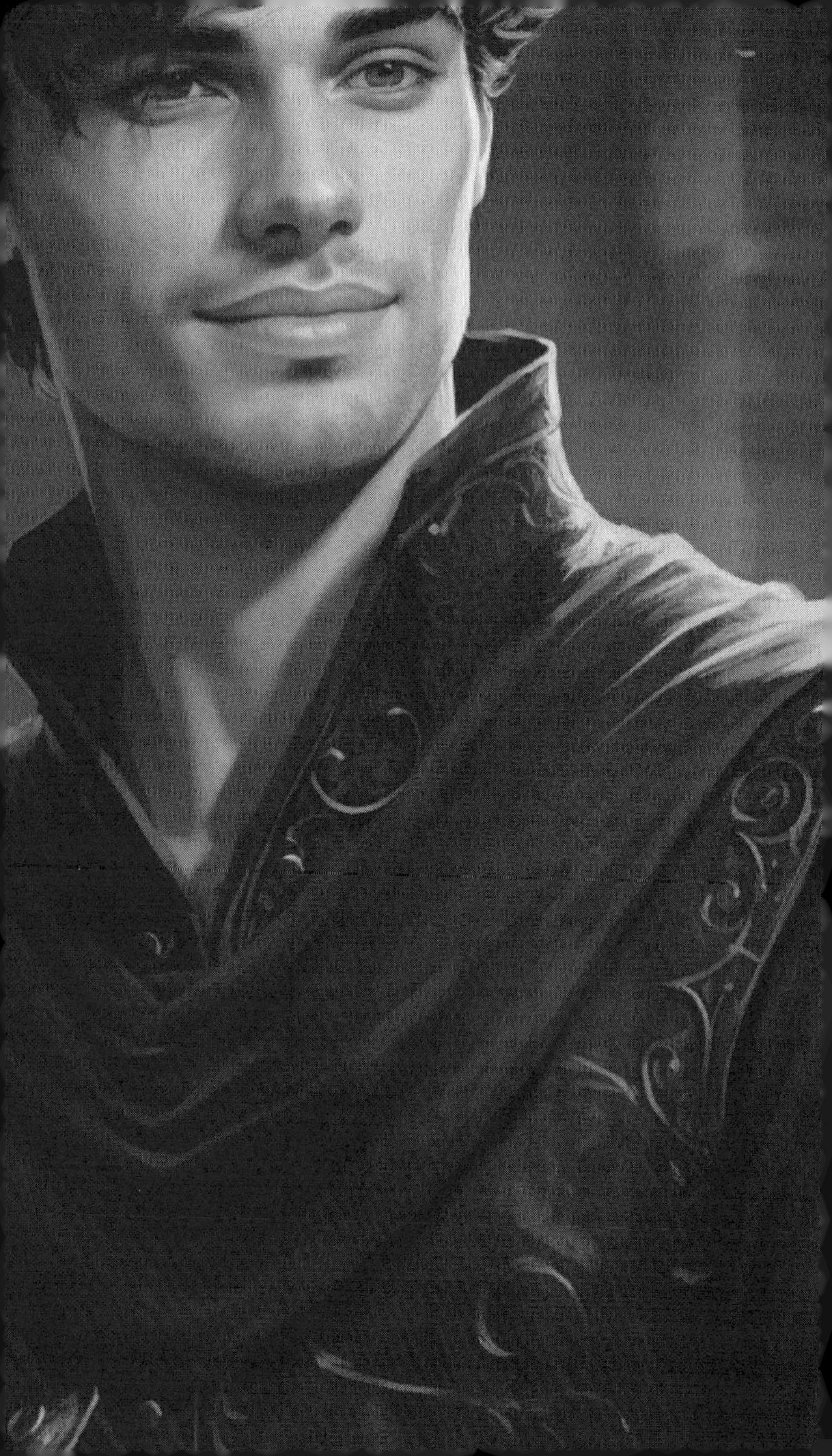

Chapter 21

Rory

We arrive back at the castle grounds, sharing a comfortable silence as we walk. The kind of quiet that speaks volumes without the need for a single word. Thoughts are whirling in my mind. What it is with this woman?

Why the fuck didn't I simply kill her when she was a child? I steal a glance at the beauty beside me, the woman I once thought of as nothing more than a means to an end, as if the answers are written in her face.

Stars twinkle above us as we make our way through the courtyard and up to the castle doors. The blanket of darkness has unfolded over the kingdom and the little gold flecks sprinkled across her dainty nose, glow even more vibrantly, bringing out the intensity of her eyes.

Fucking hell.

but I feel strange. Am I feeling guilty about doing this? Impossible. It's an emotion I haven't felt in hundreds of years.

I intended to lie to her. Manipulate her into believing a picture I painted of myself, one of beauty equal to her own, rather than the dark, misery that is my reality. Only now I wonder what this strange feeling I'm experiencing is... guilt perhaps? No. Impossible. Guilt is an emotion long forgotten to me; it's been hundreds of years.

Tonight, a shift has occurred, and I can sense a change in my view of her. I avert my eyes before she notices I'm staring. I just want to shake off this feeling that gnaws at my insides. It's like a gentle tug, a whisper of something that wasn't there before. I feel a flush of anxiety flow through my body, I think I might be starting to care for her.

Shit.

For me, that is not normal, especially having spent multiple lifetimes pulling on the puppet strings of those around me.

Yet it's undeniably there, making the lines between what is truth, and what is lies, blur in a dangerous way. I cannot lose focus; I can feel it slipping though.

The way she looked at me when she heard me laugh, the sparkle in her eyes I witnessed when I used my magic to conjure a coat for her shivering frame, and her beautiful blues attempting to pierce their way right to my very soul.

These thoughts rattle me to the core, and I don't know what to do with them. Anastasia doesn't seem to notice the turmoil turning over inside me. She's likely lost in her own thoughts, her own struggles, trying to come to terms with the information I have given to her this evening.

A part of me is wondering...is she feeling this too, this strange connection that grows between us? I thought she would ask me a lot more questions, but she's been quiet. I suppose it makes sense, given she's probably battling internally with the question of trusting me. She observes the space around us as we tread up the stairs to the castle entrance, and I've noticed her small retroussé nose slightly scrunches in this cute little wrinkle when she deeps in thought.

Now, her nose is scrunched up and I know her mind is racing. I want to ask her what she's thinking, but I know that I shouldn't.

It's best I don't push, and it's even better for me if she doesn't ask me anything if I'm being honest. Despite that though, I can't help the small smirk that I almost let slip through my mask, at the thought of this stunning vision being my wife.

She's. Fucking. Mine.

And now I'm not sure that I ever want to lose her again.

I'm fucked.

The castle looms ahead, our walk ending just as abruptly as it began, but everything's changed. Or maybe it's just me. I find myself reaching out for her hand. Why? I can't say. Maybe because it solidifies the image I'm trying to portray to the people, doubtful though. With her soft, delicate hand in my much larger one, we step over the threshold into the grand entrance, back into the stone cold of the castle and, I'm hit with a question. What happens when the villain starts caring for the hero? I guess only time will tell.

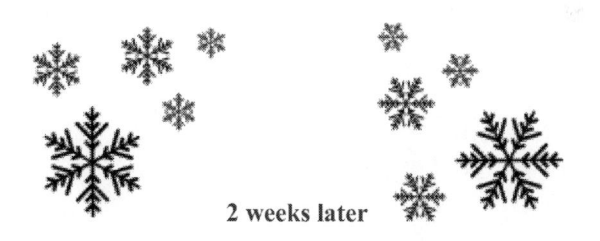

2 weeks later

I lean heavily on my desk, face in hands, a strand of hair on my forehead. Maps and various parchment strewn before me, trying to construct battle plans for the war looming over us.

My mind is a whirling pit, spinning with strategies and allegiances. Exhaustion clings to my bones, a relentless ivy, climbing up the inner walls of my limbs, as the days roll into nights, each indistinguishable from the last. I'm tired, so damn tired.

Since my stroll with Anastasia through the kingdom's streets, I have avoided her like the plague. I was tempted to confine her again to avoid seeing her, but when I saw her spending her days reading books in the grand library, I couldn't bring myself to do it.

Now that she believes I wasn't waiting for an opportunity to kill her, I can no longer use my shadows to watch her. At least not as I did with my snake. They are now much more subtle, hiding in every dark corner wherever she goes.

She has tried to come see me in the past few days, seeking my company. She shouldn't. I've spent several sleepless nights above her bed, watching her sleep.

Ready to finally end her life and my curse, but each time, I was distracted by a stray lock of hair on her face that demanded my attention to be fixed, and once my focus moved from her death to her beauty, the only thing ended up dying was my confidence. I've had to instruct the castle staff not to let her approach me, because I find I'm having more and more difficulty staying away from her.

For now, it has worked.

My office doors burst open, and I lift my eyes, Anastasia, like a gust of wintry air, walks in like she has the right, all vibrant smiles and sparkling eyes, her joy as bright as the snowflakes that cling to her lashes.

"Rory!" she exclaims, a lilt in her voice that sets my nerves on edge. "Anastasia," I acknowledge, my words clipped, my attention not fully diverted from the weight of leadership on my shoulders. "You have to come see!" she hops from one foot to the other, utterly undignified for a woman her age, yet disarmingly adorable. "It's snowing like it never wants to stop! Will you come with me to play, please?"

I look at her, incredulous. "Play in the snow?" The idea is ludicrous. "I'm an adult, as you are. I have a war to plan for." She pouts, a damn irresistible pout with her plump lips, and insists. "Just for a little while. It'll be fun! And you look like you could use some fun." I run a hand over my face and through my hair. "How the fuck did you even get in here, princess?" I will have to dismember some employees for this. "I don't know. I walked through the door," she shrugs and rolls her eyes. "Rory, are you coming or not?"

My resolve wavers against my better judgement. She sees the world with eyes unclouded by the darkness that is my constant companion, and it's... refreshing, in a way that unsettles me.

I scowl, pretending the idea is entirely distasteful. "This is a waste of time," I grumble, even as I find myself rising from the desk, drawn by the sheer force of her will.

Outside, the world is a canvas of white, untouched—a sad contrast to the tainted hands I keep shoved in my coat pockets. She laughs, a sound clear and light, and I watch, transfixed, as she dances in the crystalline downpour. Her blue dress is a perfect complement to her long flame colored hair, flowing around her as she spins under the soft, fat snowflakes. "See? Isn't this better than brooding over maps?"

Anastasia grins up at me, snowflakes in her auburn hair, turning her into a vision of ethereal beauty. I want to disagree, to tell her that my responsibilities can't be set aside for childish games.

But as she grabs my hand and pulls me into a clearing, something in me cracks. We build a snowman, of all the ridiculous things, under her expert direction.

She names him Boris, and I can't help but snort at the absurdity, while trying to mask the smirk threatening to reveal my true feelings about the frosted man.

Boris the snowman, watching over us with coal eyes and a crooked carrot nose. "I didn't take you for a snowman expert," I comment dryly, though the corner of my mouth twitches, betraying my amusement "Did I not make snowmen when I was a child?" she asks me. "No.

Your father... he didn't like seeing you play outside. It wasn't ladylike enough for a princess." She blinks at my words, she looks hurt.

I toss a handful of snow at her, trying to find, if only for a moment, the cheerful woman and her beautiful smile. She takes it right in the chest, looks at me with her mouth wide open, then dashes towards a tree, leans over, grabs some snow, and hurls it back at me.

We dart and weave like children, laughter punctuating the chilly air. She nails me right in my fucking face with a particularly well-aimed snowball, and the shock of cold against my cheek is a startling reminder—I'm alive, here in this moment, with her.

Soon, reality intrudes, as it always does. The knowledge that I shouldn't be enjoying this, that I'm meant to be her captor, her enemy, lingers like a shadow at the edge of this illusion of happiness. I can't afford to forget what I am, what I've done—what I may yet have to do.

"Anastasia," I call, and she pauses, a snowball half-formed in her hand. "We should go back inside." Her smile dims, a sun clouded over, and it tugs at something deep within me—something I thought long dead. "Yes, of course," she says softly. "Duty calls." We trudge back to the castle, the weight of leadership settles back on my shoulders, the brief respite now a memory as fleeting as the winter's sunlight.

I watch her walk ahead of me, her footsteps light upon the snow, and realize with a jolt of terror and wonder—Rory Rasputin, master of manipulation, might just be falling for the very woman he's meant to loath. This can't happen. It's a distraction, a weakness. My heart, I thought long gone, has no place in the plans I've laid.

We're almost inside the castle when Anastasia spots a glistening pond frozen over, to our left. I'm beginning to deduce she enjoys shiny things, but also, that I like that about her, I like her excitement.

Without a moment's hesitation, she glides onto it, using her boots to skate around. Her laugh rings out, pure and carefree, and I can't help but crack a smile. "Anastasia, come on!" I call out, urgency lacing my voice. "It's time to go inside; you're going to catch a cold!" But she's having none of it.

She twirls, a graceful figure against the winter backdrop, and it's that wild spirit of hers that's both infuriating and... captivating.

I take a couple of cautious steps onto the ice. "Seriously, we need to go in," I say as I reach out to her. My touch is meant to ground her, to pull her back to reality, but the moment our fingers brush, I'm the one who's unmoored.

My feet fly from under me, and suddenly I'm flat on my back, the icy cold seeping through my clothes. Anastasia's yelp turns into a surprised squeal as she tumbles down with me, landing on my chest.

Our gazes lock, and for a frozen heartbeat, everything else falls away. I'm aware of every point where her body presses against mine, the warmth of her breath on my face.

She's a vision above me, her hair a fiery cascade that curtains us in a world of our own making. "Rory," she whispers, and there's a question in her eyes I'm not sure I'm ready to answer.

"Princess," I say, my voice rough, barely a whisper. I should be pushing her away, setting boundaries, reestablishing the walls between us.

But instead, my hands find their way to her waist, steadying her, keeping her close. It's madness, but I can't seem to help myself.

Her eyes, wide and searching, meet mine. The air between us is charged, filled with unspoken words and unacknowledged desires. The castle looms, a reminder of the world waiting outside our little bubble.

We should get up, I know that, but I can't seem to move, nor do I find myself wanting to. The heat where our bodies touch is enough to melt the ice beneath us, and yet, the cold has never felt so biting.

Fuck, do I want to kiss her.

That thought, mixed with the feel of her perfect frame, heating my body, sends a pulsing through my cock. Immediately she scrambles to her feet, pulling me up with surprising strength. "Let's go inside," she says, her voice a mix of laughter and something else, something deeper.

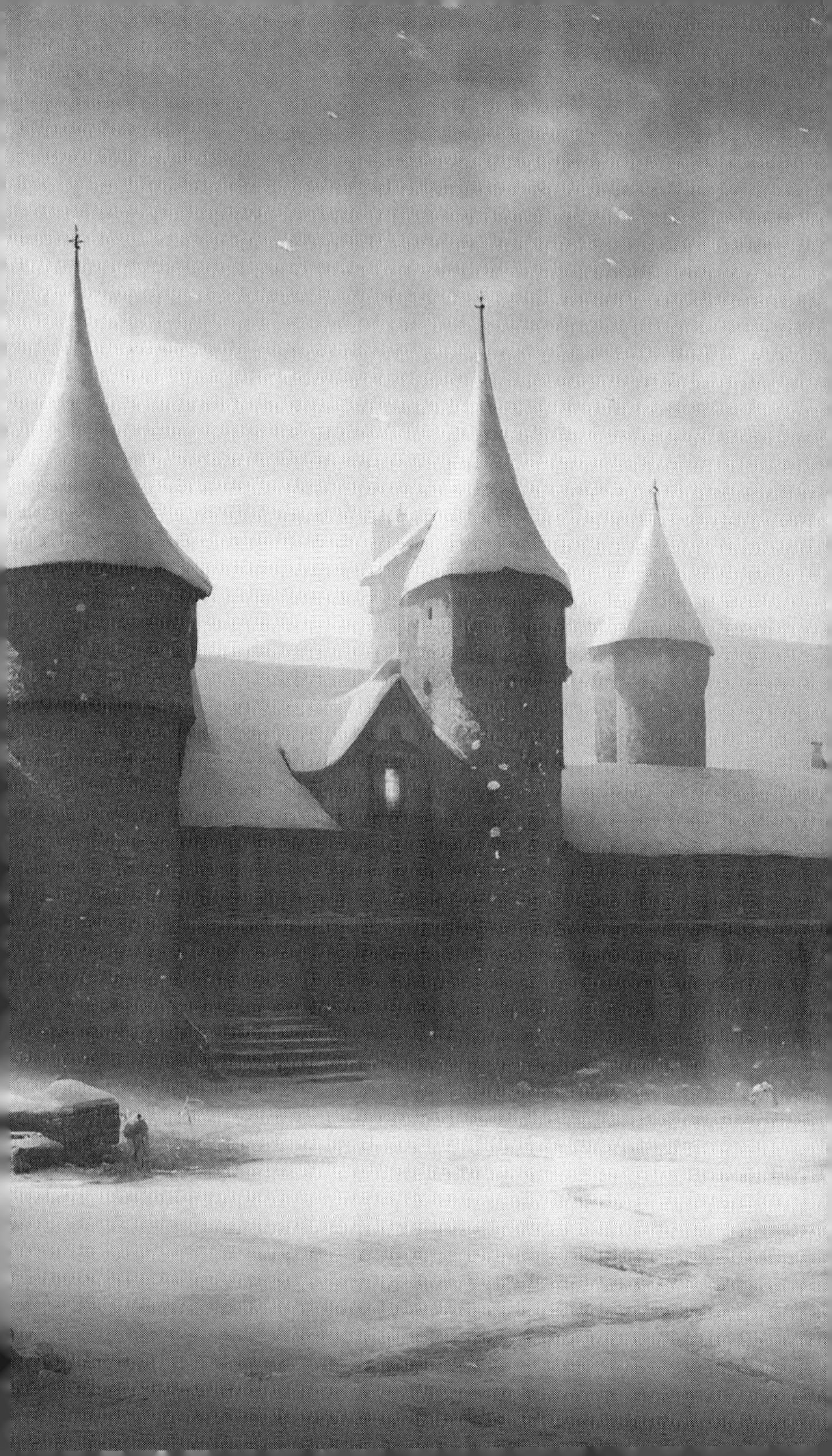

Chapter 22

Anastasia

After shedding our snow-covered coats and boots, I'm standing in front of my reflection in a large mirror hanging in the castle grand entrance.

Staring back at me from the glass framed by obsidian, my face, with its delicately glittering gold dusting across my nose, is very noticeably flushed, and I'm doubtful the frosty winter air is the only cause.

Pressing my hands to my cheeks to bring them warmth, I discover my skin is indeed already heated. I can still feel the way my body reacted to his, how my soft curves melted into his large solid frame, and I need to clench my thighs together at the recollection.

I feel him approach from somewhere behind me, and a current of lightning flows down my spine, leaving me rattled. I feel a hand reach my neck and gently gather all the hair there and brush is over my left shoulder.

I still haven't raised my gaze to his, I just want to enjoy this small gesture. I wasn't expecting him to react in the way he did when we slipped on the ice, and I sure as hell wasn't expecting to feel that he was aroused underneath me, or that I rather enjoyed knowing I affect him just as much he does me.

I finally surrender and raise my eyes to find his in our reflection, but he's not looking at the two people in the mirror. He's hovering over me from behind, one hand resting on my left shoulder while his other hangs at his side, clenched into a tight fist.

He's glaring at the exposed curve of my neck like he wants to bite into the tender flesh.

Slowly, he lowers his head until his nose touches my shoulder. He's then proceeds to glide his stubbled face up the curve of my neck, grazing me with his lips while he inhales through his nose like he needs my scent to survive.

I unintentionally let a small moan escape my lips. His response is a low groan deep in his throat. He slides his free hand around to the front of my waist, flattening his palm and pressing my back further into his chest.

I can't stop myself from carefully turning myself around so that I face him. My eyes lock onto his and then drop to his sensual lips, wondering what's they'd feel like against mine.

My heart's thumping so loud, I swear the guards could march to its beat. He sees it, I know he does—sees the hunger in my eyes as sure as I see it in his. His breath hitches, and oh—there it is, that flicker of something wild and dangerous in his gaze.

My pulse thunders in my ears as I press myself even closer into his firm body, close enough to feel the heat of his breathing on my forehead. He's a statue, a damn beautiful, infuriating work of art that I just want to...touch.

I lift my head, and my eyes find his, I look in one, then the other and finally my gaze stops on his mouth again.

"Princess..." He speaks, a warning in his tone.

I flick my eyes between his and part my lips. He notices and suddenly one of his hands is gripping the back of my neck and his other slides up my front, over my breasts, and up my throat to cup my chin, tilting my face upwards.

His touch is like a spark, igniting a wildfire somewhere deep inside of me. He hasn't taken his eyes off my mouth.

Then, he's devouring my lips like a beast, rabid and starved. It feels so good, like I've been waiting for this moment my whole life without even knowing it.

We're a mess of lips and teeth and urgent need, two forces of nature colliding—wild, savage, and desperate.

The kiss isn't sweet or gentle. It's a battle, a claiming. Rory's mouth is hot against mine.

"Tell me to stop," he says on a groan, it's not a question. It's a dare, one I can't bring myself to accept. I moan into his mouth, and he deepens the kiss, angling my head to better access my lips. "No," barely able to get the word out through his rapid assault on my mouth. I jump, my legs wrapping around his waist, my body seeking him with an urgency that borders on recklessness.

I can feel him, hard against my core, and I grind down, reveling in the groan that rumbles from his chest.

This isn't the tentative touch of a first kiss—this is a storm, a raging tempest of desire that's been waiting to be unleashed. Rory's hands grip my thighs, strong and sure, and I'm certain he can feel how much I want this, want him.

We're teetering on the edge of something wilder than either of us have known, and with every ragged breath, every pulse of our joined bodies, we're slipping further into the unknown.

My fingers tangle in his hair, pulling him closer, if that's even possible. I just can't seem to get enough. I cling to him, lost in the sensation. This is where I'm meant to be—in the fierce embrace of the man who's as much a mystery as he is my salvation.

Suddenly, my legs are being pried off him, he sets me back onto my feet and he takes a few stumbling steps backwards, like he's been shot through with an arrow. Why did he stop this?

"What is it? Don't you want this?" I manage to whisper, suddenly losing all confidence from moments ago. This is unexpected, I'm more hurt than I think I should be. I don't remember this man, and yet, I find myself fighting back tears.

"I will be planning battle tactics with my advisors, you should go back to your room, Anastasia." His words are like a cold shower, dousing the flames that had just started to consume us. The room seems to shift, the high ceilings now echoing with the remnants of our unrestrained passion.

I step back, my legs shaky, unsure if I'm retreating from Rory or the intensity of my own feelings.

"Fine," I say, more to convince myself than him. "I'll leave." I turn on my heel, my heart sinking with every step I take.

The heavy door to the library swings shut behind me. I decided a quiet few hour with a book would do better for my mind than being cooped up in my bedchamber.

Also, oddly enough, I feel a small sense of giddiness at my rebellion to his bossy ass.

Still though, questions pile up, climbing over each other in my head. Why did he push me away? What are we doing? What is this between us?

Then, I'm struck by a sudden resolve.

I refuse to let this be a fleeting moment. I need to understand the man behind our shared kiss, the shadows that lurk in the depths of his eyes.

I open a book, but the words blur before me. I'm not here to read; I'm here to plot. Rory might have sent me away, but I won't be dismissed so easily.

My hot bath at the end of this confusing day is more than deserved. The luxurious bathroom is in complete darkness save for a few glowing candles, and I'm surrounded by the soothing scents of lavender and jasmine.

I sink deeper into the water, feeling the heat seep into my bones. I close my eyes, letting out a sigh as the tension melts away from my body.

This moment of peace is sacred in the madness that has become my life. The air shifts, and I feel a presence behind me.

Without opening my eyes, I know it's him. His energy is unmistakable, a silent force that demands attention. And yet, I don't even bother covering myself. My body, a map of curves and soft skin, remains bare, displayed like a silent act of defiance.

Rory breaks the silence. "Tomorrow, you start training the people for the war," he says, his voice low and carrying a weight of certainty. I open one eye, puzzled. "Why me? I'm not qualified for this," I respond, the confusion evident in my tone.

He's next to the tub, his impressive bulge almost at the same height as my face, and I try my best to avoid staring at it.

He laughs, a sound that resonates with confidence. "There's something you've forgotten, Anastasia," he says. I can't see his face, but I can hear the smile in his voice. "You're an extremely good warrior." His words send a ripple through the water, an echo of a past life where I was capable, strong... lethal.

I'm still uncertain, but his belief in me is almost palpable, wrapping around me like the steam rising from the bath. "How can you be so sure I'll remember everything tomorrow?" I ask, finally meeting his gaze.

In the flickering candlelight, his eyes hold a fierceness that stirs something within me. "Because" he starts, lowering his face closer, his shadow joining mine against the wall, "I've seen it. I've seen your skill, your determination. You were born for this." His assurance is almost intimidating. But at the same time, it's exhilarating.

My heartbeat quickens, and not just from the hot water. Rory is close now, close enough that if I stick out the tip of my tongue; I could lick his lips. I want to. "You have faith in me?" I question him, the words slipping out on a breath. Leaning his face down to my ear, "more than you know," he answers, his voice a soft growl that sends shivers down my spine.

A smirk pulls at the corner of my mouth. "You really think I've got what it takes to lead these people into battle?" His breath ghosting over my skin. "I don't think, princess... I know."

The tension between us crackles, a current of unspoken desire and electric anticipation. It's in the way he looks at me, the raw intensity of his eyes. It's in the way my body responds to his proximity, a mix of wariness and a primal pull.

Without breaking eye contact, he plunges a hand into the warm water of my bath, soaking the entire sleeve of his shirt. I bite my lip as his rough touch connects with the skin of my thigh. He runs his hand slowly up my thigh towards my center, and I can't help the moan that escapes. He stops, his fingers pausing as he seems to remember our surroundings, the candlelight, the soaking wet sleeve, my wet, naked body. The combination makes for a deadly intimate atmosphere, and it seems by his blown pupils and the muscles tensing in his jaw, that he's conflicted, like he's struggling internally with something.

For a moment, we both remain still, caught in the tension of what could and might be. Slowly, he retracts his hand, the trails of water left behind on my skin feeling colder in the absence of his touch.

I clear my throat, my voice steady despite the lingering wanting. "I'll be ready," I affirm, more to convince myself than him.

Rory nods, pressing his lips into a firm line. "I have no doubt." He stands up, his soaked shirt clinging to his arm, water dripping to the floor, a testament to the moment that just passed. As he leaves the room, the air shifts back to solitude.

The room feels larger, emptier. I rise from the bath, water cascading down my body, my determination seeping back into my bones.

I open my eyes; the soft morning light washes over me. Training day. I'm determined to live up to Rory's expectations, but I also feel nervous, what if he's wrong? I don't remember a single thing about training or fighting, which apparently is supposed to be a lot. I run a hand down my face and release a sign. Truthfully, I'm not sure how I'm going to pull this off.

I sit up and, to my surprise, my gaze falls upon a complete set of armor and clothes laid out on the little bench in my room. It's magnificent - silver shining like morning dew, with accents of blue jewels that sparkle even in the soft light.

I can't help but admire the craftsmanship, the way the metal is forged to be both delicate and deadly.

There are daggers with handles wrapped in leather for a firm grip, swords with edges that promise a swift defeat to an enemy, and other bits of gear that leave no doubt—this is the armor of someone who means business.

Dressed in my royal armor, I feel both its weight and power as I run my fingers over the intricate designs. I feel... powerful. I braid my hair tightly, making sure it's out of the way. I'm sure someone well versed in the art of battle and weaponry, would not deem it a smart idea to leave long hair unbound.

When I step outside, the cool air greets me like an old friend. Despite that familiarity, it's the crowd of people waiting for me that takes me by surprise. They're all here, ready to be trained, and I can't help but feel a swell of anxiety mixed with excitement. The rush of emotion coursing through my body boosts my energy, enough to find my voice.

I clear my throat. "Good morning, everyone. I'm Anastasia, and I'll be leading our training today." My heart does a little flip, but it's drowned out by the eager looks on their faces.

We start with the basics, and I move among them, correcting stances and demonstrating techniques. To my own astonishment, I'm good at this—really good.

Swords feel like extensions of my arms, and I find myself lost in the rhythm of combat. It's like something inside me has awakened; this feels like second nature to me. I'm dodging, lunging, and laughing along with the rest as we train.

There's a joy here I didn't expect to find, a camaraderie born from the shared determination to defend our home.

Out of the corner of my eye, I spot Rory watching from a distance. There's something in his gaze that's hard to read—intense, burning. He's trying to mask it, but I can feel the heat from here, and it stirs something wild within me.

As the day goes on, our training is punctuated with playful taunts and challenges. "Is that all you've got?" I tease a burly man who just tried to best me and failed. He grins, wiping sweat from his brow. "You fight like a devil, Your Majesty." I wink at him. "Oh, but sir, you haven't seen anything yet."

I keep stealing glances every now and then and Rory's piercing gaze makes my skin tingle with an awareness that's as new as it is thrilling.

He leans his shoulder against a tree, watching from afar as the clash of the swords rings out like the clang of a blacksmith working their anvil, mimicking the clang of our alliance falling into place, becoming stronger with each smash of steel.

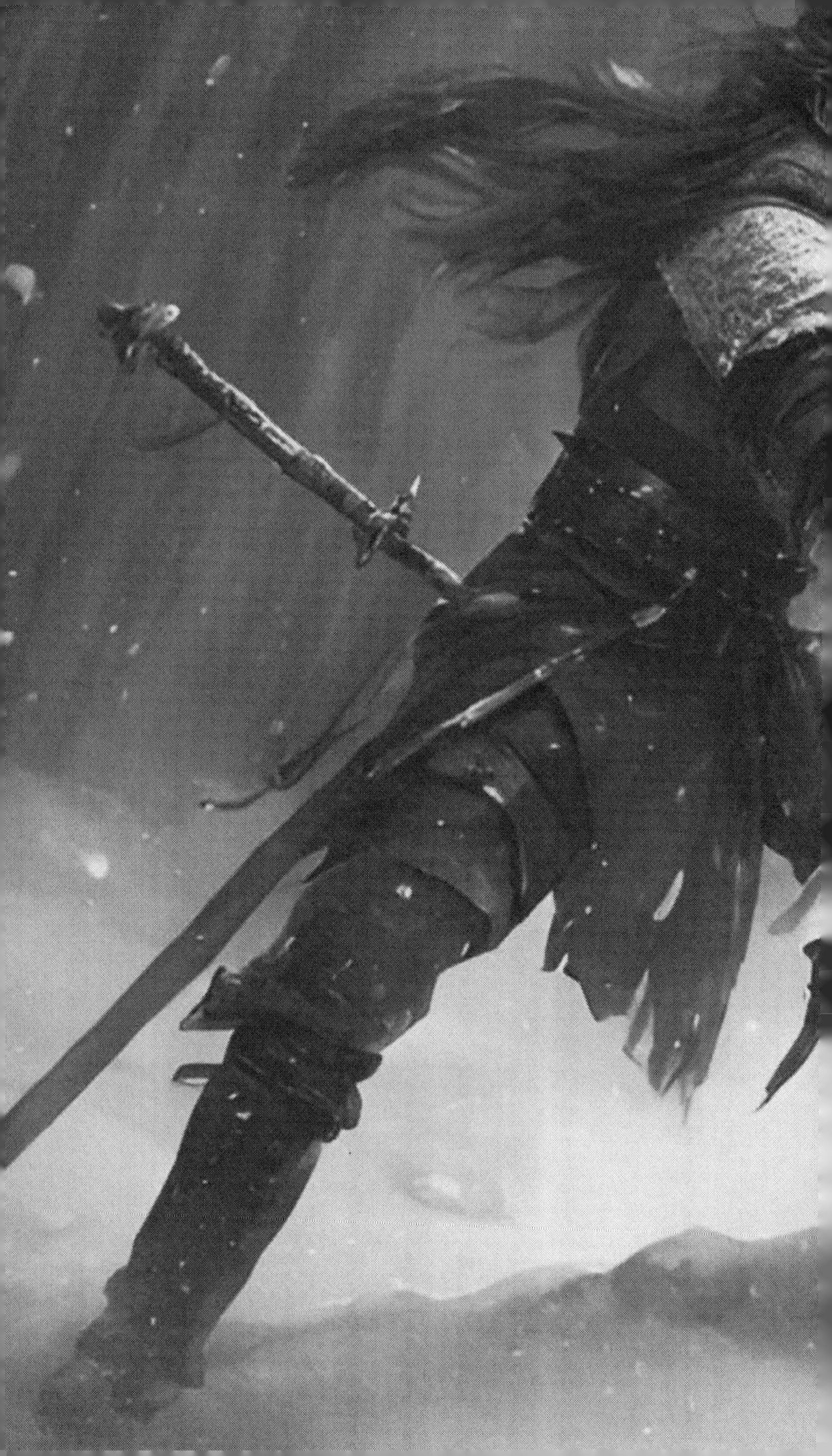

Chapter 23

Rory

The drum of boots against the ground and the chorus of cheers fill the air, igniting this night with an energy that makes my blood sing. It's a training field turned into an arena, and the court habitants circle us, their eager faces a blend of thrill and fear. And there is my princess, my queen.

My Anastasia.

She doesn't deserve any of what I force her to go through, and I know it. I'm repugnant, but too much of a coward to die. I feel like shit about it. I've been a monster for hundreds of years without feeling remorse. I couldn't afford to. An immortal life with emotions is dangerous. Damn, the last thing I wanted was to fall into madness.

Anastasia mirrors me, a smirk playing on those plump lips that have cast fucking charms in my head, haunting my dreams each night, and damn it, I can't help but take note of her perfect figure.

She moves with grace, her breaths moving under the fabric of her clothes. If anything makes me happy in this world, it's seeing her body and face regain their shape.

"Ready to yield, princess?" My voice is a silken taunt, and I feel the air charged with more than just the tension of the coming clash. "In your dreams, Rasputin." She shoots back, the spark in my green eyes challenging her to make the next move.

The first charge is a blur—a clash of limbs and a tangle of breaths. My hands find her wrists, and she jerks away, the warmth of her skin imprinted on my hand. I retort with a swipe aimed at her chest, but she dodges, and our bodies brush.

It's fleeting, but it's enough to send a need down my spine, a whisper of something forbidden and tantalizing. "Is this all you've got?" I mock her, but her breathing has quickened, and I can tell she's as caught up in this moment as I am.

We're locked in this battle, a symphony of moves and countermoves, each parry and thrust brings us closer, and the heat between us builds. The crowd's chant is a distant drum, their voices mingling with the soft groans that slip from our lips as we dodge and weave.

Sexual tension is a tangible thing, a third combatant that fights for dominance over both of us.

I'm so fucked.

My leg hooks around hers, and for a moment, we're pressed together, chest to chest, her breath hot against my chin as she looks up in my eyes. Her scent—a mix of leather and the jasmine from her bath—fills my senses, grasping at the edges of my control. "Getting tired, Anastasia?" I breathe out, my voice a low growl. "Never," She pants, the word more a gasp as she twists away, putting space between us.

I laugh, she's good. Eyes lock, hearts race, and there's a silent acknowledgement that this is more than just a fight. The next exchange is fierce, desperate almost, as we both seek to end this combat that has become far too intimate.

When we break apart again, our chests heave and our gazes seethe with a mixture of emotions.

The crowd erupts as we face off once more, unaware of the undercurrent that flows beneath the spectacle. As our eyes meet again, it's clear the true battle will be fought in the quiet moments after—the moments filled with could-haves and should-nots.

Sweat drips down my face, stings my eyes, my hair clinging to my forehead, but I barely notice. I'm circling Anastasia, every muscle in my body tense, ready to strike.

It feels like we've been at this for hours, trading blows. The court's gaze bears down on us, a ring of expectant faces hungry for a winner. Anastasia's no easy opponent.

She's quick, ruthless, and fuck, it's a turn-on. But enough is enough. I see the flicker of fatigue in her eyes—it's time to end this. I feint left and she follows, just like I want her to.

Then, with all the speed I can muster, I sweep out with my leg and she's down, hitting the ground with a thud that echoes around the courtyard.

Before she can recover, I'm on her, my knee pressed to her chest, pinning her down. I can feel her heart pounding beneath her breastplate, a wild rhythm that matches my own.

Our gazes are locked, both of us breathing hard, and there's a fire between us that has nothing to do with our fight. "Yield," I say, the simple word a growl, more than just a command. It's an invitation, a dare for her to push back, fight harder.

Anastasia's bright eyes burn with the ferocity of the midday sun. "No," she spits back, a smile etched into her pretty mouth.

I lean in closer, our noses nearly touching. "Then let's see how this plays out, shall we?" I whisper, just loud enough for her ears only. With a swift move, I pull out the fake knife I've been hiding up my sleeve, the gleam of its blunt edge catching her eye. I bring it down in a slow, deliberate arc towards her throat, but I stop just a millimeter away from her skin. The point is dull, harmless, but the implication is razor-sharp.

Her breath hitches and there's a moment—just one—where she looks at me with something that's not frustration. It could be fear, it could be surprised, but I like to think it's a flash of desire, quickly smothered. "Trickster," she challenges, her voice steady despite our position. "Did you bring a fake knife to one of the knight trainings?" She laughs.

I can feel the heat from her body, the tension in the air, and it takes everything in me not to close the distance between our lips.

Instead, I lean back, my hand with the fake blade dropping to my side. "I think the court's seen enough," I say, loud enough for all the onlookers. "The lady is bested, but not beaten."

There's a collective exhale from the crowd, a few chuckles and a smatter of applause as I stand and offer Anastasia my hand. She looks at it for a split second before taking it, letting me pull her up to stand beside me. "You'll pay for that, Rory," she murmurs under her breath, but there's a hint of a smile playing at the corner of her mouth. I smirk back. "Looking forward to it, princess."

The sound of the court dissipates as we walk off the training field, leaving the tension of our fight behind us. We stride through the castle halls together; her presence is soothing and a torment all at once.

We're drenched in sweat from our combat, and the drafty corridors send chills, making our bodies quake. "Tell me about your past," Anastasia says, her voice echoing softly in the vast expanse of stone and drapes. "Before all this... immortality."

Her question is a gentle probe, yet it feels like a lance to the heart.

I've lived countless lifetimes, but the memories weigh heavy, like chains I'm forced to drag with each of my steps. "It's a long story," I start, my tone laced with the bitterness of ages past. "Filled with mistakes and misdeeds." She gives me a half smile. "But how does one carry on for an eternity?"

She's truly curious, how can I explain the loneliness, the weight of years that never lead to rest?

We halt before the ornate door to her chambers, a barrier to a realm I both long and fear to enter. "Immortality..." I search for the words. "...is a curse disguised as a gift. Imagine watching the world change while you remain... trapped. Unchanging. Lonely."

Her eyes flicker with the light of understanding, barred by the walls of mortality. "That sounds... heartbreaking." A smirk twitches on my lips. "The only thing keeping me tethered to this wretched existence is a thought...of someone... someone I never knew, yet I feel bound to." Anastasia's gaze clings to mine, a question unvoiced in her depths. "Who is this person?"

I lean closer, our breaths mingling. "A woman. A beacon in the endless darkness that is my life." I can see the puzzle pieces shifting in her eyes, the cogs turning, but I can't—no, I won't—give away the truth.

Not yet. "I didn't know her name," I whisper, the lie bitter on my tongue. "But the thought and dream of her is what kept me from surrendering to death, and I'm too much of a coward to kill myself." I shrug my shoulder and then she's laughing... hard, uncontrollably.

The sound is magical. She's fucking perfect. "Wanting to be loved is the loneliest feeling, princess. So, in my 400 years of immortal life, the mere thought that one day I could feel her lips on mine was enough to keep me going."

She trembles before me; her eyes seem to want to fill with tears. "Rory, I—" Her words catch, suspended in the tension that coils between us. I draw back, and step into the shadows, with the intent to leave the only constant in my eternal life standing at the door to her bedchamber—a door I dare not cross again.

I can't.

Catching me off guard, she grabs the collar of my shirt, sending the lone button of my collar flying to the floor.

With an almost superhuman strength, she walks me backwards and pins me against one of the walls, a growl escaping my throat. She pushes on my chest to keep me still; it's cute but pointless.

If I really wanted to, I would have already slipped out of her grip, but I stay. "What are you doing princess?" I purr, smiling at her. Her braid falling off her shoulder, tangled and halfway undone.

She stares at me, her gaze shifting from one eye to the other, and I swear I see her face inching closer to mine slowly.

To protect myself, and damn it, to protect her. I gently raise my hand, covering her entire mouth and chin with it. Her eyebrows knit together in confusion, and her eyes are full of questions. "Shh, princess." I close the few inches between my mouth and hers—covered by my hand.

I can hear her heart racing, and it turns me on. I bet she can feel me through my pants. I hope she can.

While closing my eyes halfway, I press my mouth against my hand, giving it a kiss. She moans, and damn, my resolve almost cracks. I quickly push past her and walk as fast as my ass can.

War is coming, but the true fight. It's a battle I wage with every step, every breath—a battle against time, against myself.

As I retreat into my office, I can't shake the feeling that my immortality may be my curse, but she—she could be my damnation.

Chapter 24

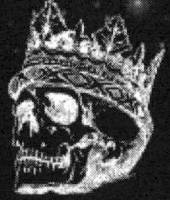

Anastasia

Walking the long stone corridor leading to Rory's office, my mind recalls the feel of our bodies pressed together, the kiss on top of his hand and his hot and cold temperament. He looks at me like I belong to him, and I am his wife, his queen, and yet... why does he acts as if it pains him to touch me? This man is frustrating to say the least.

I wish he'd tell me his secrets.

I arrive at the door, and before I enter, I give my head a few shakes, trying to dispel the thoughts that flicker too brightly against the backdrop of my mind.

I don't bother to knock. I figure as his wife, whether I remember or not, we're beyond formalities now. I push it open and take a step into the large room, making sure to close the door behind me.

Immediately I'm struck by the heaviness in the air. It's like happiness has evaporated and been replaced with anger and impatience.

The source of the negativity sits behind the large wooden desk, topped with scrolls and various maps. He sits rigidly in the chair, a cold statue, with his elbow resting on the armrest, and his left forefinger slowly pacing back and forth on his chin, presumably deep in thought. His eyes, serious and focused, staring unblinking at the parchment scattered before him.

Something is wrong.

"Rory," his gaze flicks to me briefly, before returning to a map he's crumpling in his clenched fist. "Rory, what is it?" I question, my voice carrying a hint of worry.

"They're closer than we anticipated," he replies, his voice tight with anger.

"Who is, and how can you be certain?" I ask, curious despite the tension. "My shadows," he says, the word laced with a darkness that sends a shiver through me. "They're my eyes and ears where I cannot be. What they see, I see, their feelings become my own."

A frisson of unease crawls up my spine, "tell me more." He leans back in the chair, regarding me with a look that's almost predatory. "They are extensions of my being, but they too have their limits," he says, his stare unwavering. It feels as if the room itself is holding its breath, the surrounding atmosphere charged with the same electric heat that sizzled between us during our winter fun, during the training session, in the grand entrance in front of the mirror, and every other damn time we share the same space.

The notion that Rory can be in many places at one time, feeling and experiencing through others, is equally unsettling and fascinating.

I tuck my hair behind my ear and drop my gaze to the floor. "What do they feel now?" I prod, stepping closer, my voice dropping to a whisper, as if the walls themselves are listening.

"Fear," he admits, and his vulnerability in that moment tugs at something deep within me. "The enemy marches to us with a force we might not be able to beat back."

My pulse quickens at the thought. War is upon us, and with it, the risk of losing everything we've fought for. I can see the weight of command pressing down on him, and despite my better judgment, I want to ease it from his shoulders.

I reach across the desk, my fingertips barely brushing the back of his hand. The contact is electric, a spark that ignites my core. "So, what's our strategy?" I ask, my voice low and tinged with a dangerous kind of curiosity.

Rory's eyes darken further. "Fight. Win." There's a quiet intensity in his voice, and I realize this is who he is—

a man of power and shadows, ready to wage a war on multiple fronts.

The distance between us whispers with unspoken desire and the looming shadow of conflict. Yet, as I stand before him, I know that the battle we're about to face together pales in comparison to the war we fight within ourselves—a war where every touch is a battle line drawn and every glance a declaration of a deeper, more perilous venture.

Rory rises slowly, and walks around his desk, the space between us diminishing with each step. "Will you stand with me, Anastasia?" he asks, his voice a low rumble that sends a shudder through my body. "Will you stay with... me?"

I meet his gaze squarely, defiance and desire a potent mix in my veins. "Until the end," I promise, knowing full well that the end might come in more ways than one. I want to be closer; I want to touch him; I want him inside me. But I can see that he's holding back. He's not ready. And I need to respect that. I take a few steps back, smiling at him, and when he returns a smile, I turn around and walk towards the exit.

As I leave his office, his scent lingering on my skin, leather, fire and spice. The shadows are whispering of war, but it's the battle between Rory and I that may prove to be the most devastating of all and I don't know why I feel this way.

I walk quietly through the castle, not ready to retire to my private quarters just yet. My mind is far too occupied; I thought about going to the grand library, but I'm starting to tire of reading the same books repeatedly about ancient wars.

The hem of my dress brushes against the floor, the swishing is strangely comforting, like a soft purr.

My steps lead me through a wide corridor, with white stone walls, the upper half adorned with dark wood. It's stunning and calming; I have no memory of passing through here before, so I continue to move forward.

The farther my steps take me, the more the sound of light laughter reaches my ears.

I place my hand on the large doorframe and lean my body forward to peek into the room from where the sounds emanate.

A kitchen, spacious and bright, filled with the scent of thyme and something else that makes me close my eyes to savor the ambient air. "May we help you, Majesty?"

Startled, I quickly open my eyes. "Oh, sorry, I was walking, and heard laughter, I thought I'd see who it was, but then I caught the scent of something absolutely delightful." My cheeks grow warm with embarrassment, I hadn't meant to eavesdrop on their gossip, and I sure hadn't meant to get caught.

"Nonsense, my Queen, it's no intrusion, would you like a plate? We're making bread." The atmosphere is reassuring, and the ladies give me beautiful smiles that warm my heart. Finding such a light atmosphere here is a surprise. "I have another request. May I join in?"

The two women stop moving and stare at me, their smiles fading. The older of the two wipes her hands on her apron and signals me to come forward.

I'm kneading the dough in the kitchen, my hands moving with a rhythm perfected, as if I had a lot of experience, yet, I've never been in the kitchen, although I don't remember if I have. The aroma of baking bread wraps around me, a warm and comforting embrace. Laughter fills the room as I joke with the castle employees, Melinda and Nana.

Our spirits are high despite the ever-looming shadow of war descending upon these walls. It feels good to be here, to be useful.

Suddenly, a cacophony of sounds pierces our bubble of happiness. Panic grips my chest as screams—a man's screams echo through the stone corridors.

Melinda rolls her eyes and continues chopping up basil. "Are not you concerned?" I ask. "No. It happens quite frequently." She says nonchalantly, but immediately, she straightens up and kneels in front of me, panic on her face. "I'm sorry, Your Majesty, I shouldn't have spoken about your..."

Nana gives her a tap on the back of her head, silencing her, and the woman takes her head in her hands, like a child realizing her mistake. I am completely lost. "What's happening?" I ask, just as more piercing cries of pain invade my ears.

Without thinking, I wipe my flour-covered hands on my apron and dash toward the distress. My heart hammers against my ribs, each beat in sync with the alarming cries growing louder.

I burst into the dining hall, and the sight stops me dead in my tracks. Rory, eyes dark and focused hovers over a man strapped to a chair, magic and opaque shadows swirling around them. Holy shit is he torturing this man?

The man's screams are enough to curdle blood, his body shivering from the pain inflicted upon him by Rory's unforgiving hands. Then he passes out.

My breath catches in my throat. Rory's face is expressionless, his actions methodical, and it chills me to the bone. "What the fuck are you doing?" I yell, advancing closer to Rory. He turns quickly, his orbs a fluorescent green, and my body stiffens. "My shadows caught this man spying on our soldiers for the enemy," his voice, deep and aggressive, there is no mistaking he's pissed. My eyes shift from Rory to the unconscious man several times before I raise a hand towards my dark king.

"We can't afford for him to go back with information, Princess," he adds, his voice hoarse and his gaze empty. "I understand, but is torture necessary? Just kill him!" My tone sounds angrier than I intended. Rory's eyes calm down, returning to a green more like the leaves of tall trees in summer.

He moves towards me slowly, taking my hand in his. "I intended to do just that, until he threatened you, princess." The shadows around us seem to scream, a bloodthirsty cry. My hair catches in their winds, and my heart accelerates at the sight of Rory's enraged face, piercing the man with a glare terrifying enough to scare the bravest of warriors.

"Any threat, assault, any negative word, anyone touches a hair on your head, will exit this place without theirs."

I am frozen, transfixed, completely speechless. It's brutal, cruel, possessive, and sick and yet a part of my heart has warmed at the sound of his words.

The man is a spy, caught infiltrating our ranks, feeding information to the enemy. I feel anger rising within me, my cheeks growing warm once again, only this time I feel no embarrassment. I meet Rory's look with a simple nod.

He smiles, placing his hand on my cheek, and I lean into his touch. His thumb gently strokes my temple. "Stay by my side." I nod again, and then he starts chanting, a dark language I don't understand, and the horror unfolds even further. Magic, dark and ancient wraps around the spy like a sinister serpent.

The man wakes up, and his eyes meet mine, his face portraying the level of fear and pain he's experiencing. Pleading for mercy, he begs me to spare him, but I don't move, I don't say anything. Surprisingly, I don't even tremble at the sight of the horrifying shadow serpent.

The snake tosses the man into the air, then separates into four heads, each latching onto one of his limbs, fangs piercing his flesh, breaking bones, and he continues to scream until he's torn apart limb from limb. Blood is spattered everywhere, splashing across my face and my dress.

The room spins as I watch in a mixture of excitement and disbelief. Rory gestures with his hand, and the creatures hang the man's body from the large chandelier overhead. His torn body is now dangling like he's a grotesque puppet.

Looking at Rory, his handsome face, streaked red with the blood of a man he just brutally murdered in my honor, I realize something, it's ugly, it's brutal, and it's unforgiving, but I think I love an immortal, immoral man.

Rory turns to me, "go, bathe princess," his hand strokes my cheek before falling to his side.

I turn and leave, without saying another word. I'm at a loss, confused by my feelings and reaction to the events I just witnessed.

I stumble out of the room heading for my tub, my legs weak and unsteady, I'm covered in blood, and my mind a maelstrom of conflicting emotions. The laughter from the kitchen feels like a lifetime ago. Now there's only the image of the spy's body, a spectacle of Rory's wrath and power, branded into my memory.

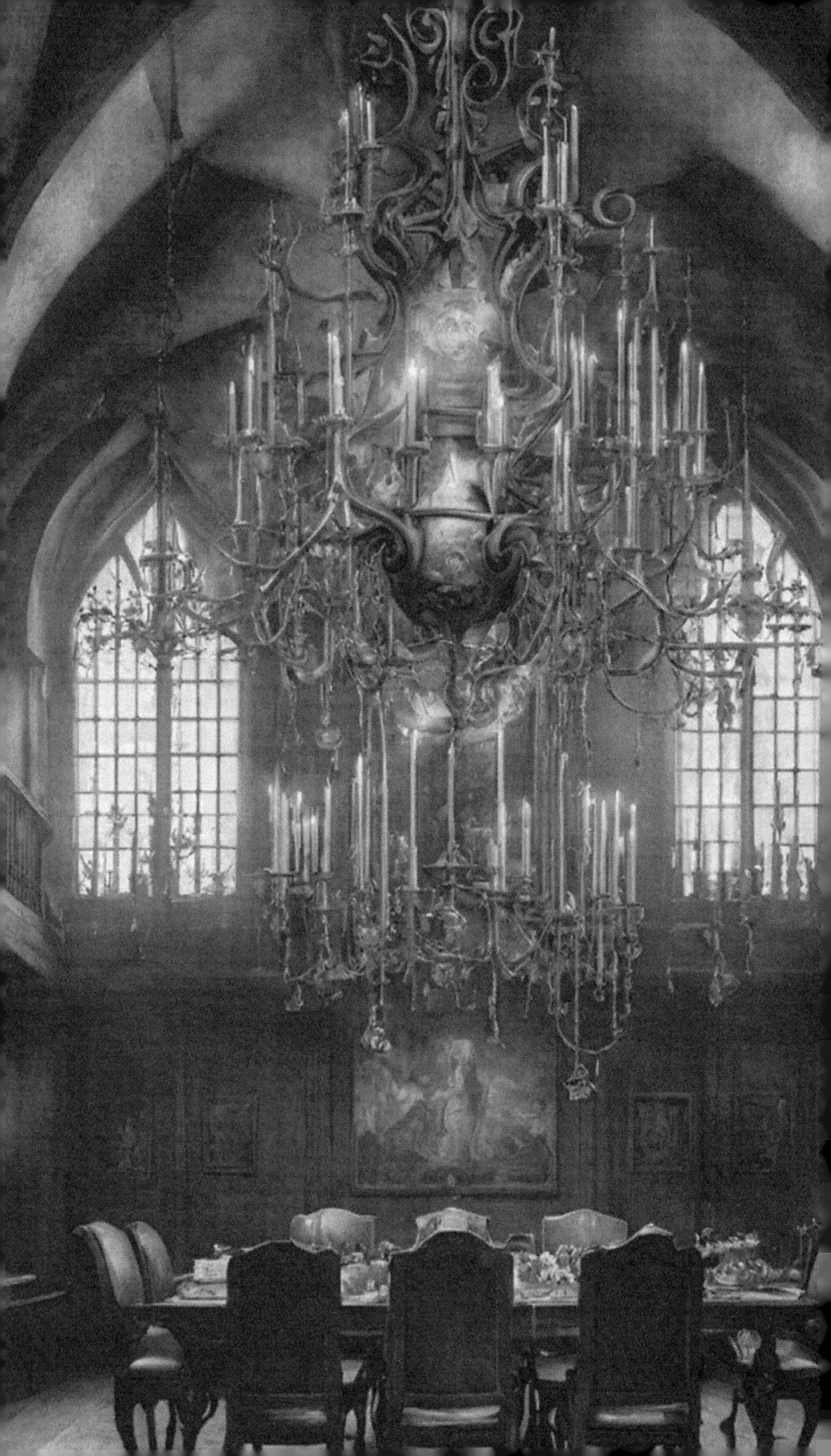

Chapter 25

Anastasia

Rory stands in front of the crackling fire, his head bowed, resting his hand on the stone mantle as he stares into the fire, as if the answers he seeks for his troubles are hidden within the flames.

We're alone, in the large sitting room, in Rory's private wing of the castle, the flickering fire casting dancing shadows across his tormented features. The sight of him, magnificent and broken, stirs a wild ache within me.

"How can you bear it?" My voice is a strained whisper, my own pain lacing the words. I can't shake the horror of it all. The way he made him suffer; the sickening artistry of limbs strung up on the chandelier. It turns something in my stomach, but it's also oddly arousing. Does this make me a bad person? Craving a man that can so easily slaughter another without a second thought? I'm so conflicted.

"I just do," he murmurs, his voice a low rumble that vibrates through the thick air. He drops his hand from the fireplace and turns his body towards me. His eyes searching my features for something...for what? Fear? Disgust by his actions? I feel both, but he won't find that in my face. He'll find only desire.

With a sense of need pushing me forward, one that tears at my senses with sharp teeth, I continue to close the space between us, my body betraying my mind with each step.

There's a magnetic force pulling us into an orbit we can't escape. His eyes are on me, dark and intense, a tempest I'm desperate to lose myself in.

"I need to forget," he breathes, and something snaps. He pushes me down onto the cold, hard floor in front of the fireplace, and I welcome the bite of stone against my back, the heat of the flames on my skin. It's raw, untamed— the kind of passion that consumes everything in its path.

The world narrows down to the heat of his limps and lips on mine. Every touch scorches my skin, branding me. His hands roam with a fervor that mirrors the chaos of his soul, and I match it with my own, relentless in our pursuit of oblivion. We move together in a rhythm as old as time, a primal dance fueled by the kind of lust that borders on violence.

I claw at his back, eliciting a growl that sends shivers down my spine. He responds with a possessive grip on the nape of my neck that speaks of ownership—a claim I both resent and crave.

He presses his hardness between my legs as I welcome his body between them. I let them fall open, exposing myself more to his length, and despite the layers of fabric between our bodies, I can still feel the heavenly sensation of his stiffness against my swollen clit. I move my hips to join his thrusts seeking more friction. I need more of him.

The flickering shadows become our audience, whispering secrets in the language of fire and darkness. I'm lost in the storm of him, the way he makes my body sing and my mind go silent. Our tongues dance, the feeling so intense that I moan into his mouth, and he swallows it with a groan in return.

Abruptly, he pulls back, leaving my lips suddenly cold. Our chests heaving against each other, his pupils, dilated with lust find mine, still panting, he leans his forehead down to rest against mine. I see the flicker of something in his eyes before he shuts it down, buries it beneath layers of self-loathing. "Why?" I ask, the question slipping out between labored breaths.

Rory's eyes hold mine, a haunted depth to them. "I'm sorry, I shouldn't have done that," he confesses, his words loiter in the air, a confession laid bare. I don't understand.

He starts to rise, holding his hand out with the intension to assist me in peeling my body off the floor he just plastered me to. I look away, the hurt of rejection pinching at my heart. I refuse his outstretched arm and find my footing myself.

I pull back immediately once on my feet. His words strike a chord and I find my voice, however small it might feel. "You are full of shit, Rory."

His eyes snap to mine, wider now with surprise. "What?" he says hesitantly, as if he's nervous for me to continue. I see the torment behind his eyes, the way it eats at him, there are things he's not saying, secrets he's determined to hold tight in a death grip.

The fire crackles and pops, a reminder of the world beyond this room, beyond the tangle of our bodies and secrets.

He runs a hand through his hair, gripping the black locks from behind. Why is he so aggravatingly gorgeous?

We stand there just staring at each other. Finally, I relent. "Nothing, I'm caught in a war within myself," I whisper, "I should go now."

I turn to leave, trying to avoid him seeing the tears that are blurring my vision, but he says two words that lock up every muscle in my body, freezing me to the spot. "Please, stay." The words fall from his lips without thought, a raw plea that makes my stomach flip. "Don't go." I turn back to him, and he reaches out into the empty space dividing us. It's the vulnerability in his voice that holds me still, the unspoken longing that we both know is there but have never dared to address. I'm paralyzed by the intensity of the moment, by the sudden shift in power.

He needs me.

Finally, unable to turn him down, I place my hand in his. "Talk to me, Rory," my voice is firmer now, demanding. I need to understand, to sift through the layers of pain and desire that bind us together.

He slowly releases my hand, his own falls to his side but he doesn't break eye contact. "I'm not good for you, Anastasia," he says, but the tremor in his voice betrays him. "But I want you...Fuck, how I want you." His voice grows frustrated, almost desperate as he turns his back to me, to stare into the fire again.

There's nothing left to do for me but take the plunge. "I'm not afraid of your darkness, Rory," I admit, stepping closer and reaching to touch his shoulder, he turns to me, our breaths mix in the charged air. "I have demons just as you do, Rory," I continue finding it harder to keep the words contained, "Maybe..." I step closer, my gaze and lust unwavering, "maybe we don't have to face them alone"

His eyes soften, and for a fleeting second, I see the man he wants to be—the man he can be—if only he allows himself to feel. I want to know everything about him. I want to know his likes, and dislikes, accompany him on long walks outdoors, and I want to feel him holding me safe and warm against his strong frame, in a bed that we share together.

He nods slowly, the beginning of a truce between his heart and his head. "We're both broken," I say, reaching out to touch his face. "But together, we might just fit."

A smile breaks through his brooding demeanor. His arms envelop me, a silent promise in the warmth of his powerful embrace. It's something I really love about him, his body. It's strong, sculpted, and just broad enough. So damn appealing.

With the fire wrapping us in its warm glow, I realize that this is where I belong. Not because it's perfect or easy, but because it's real—because it's us.

"Stay with me tonight," he murmurs against my hair. I nod into his chest, too lost in the feel of him holding me, warm in his arms, to voice my agreement. The fire crackles its approval, the shadows bearing witness to our imperfect, messy, and somehow beautiful beginning.

"I only ask that you do not tempt me, princess. Tonight is not the night." He adds, his voice husky with desire. I nod again, feeling some of the tension release from my shoulders. I want nothing more than to feel him inside me, but I'm just as happy to share his bed, and be in his presence while he's willing to show me this softer more vulnerable side of him.

He takes my hand and leads me across the hall to his room.

Holy fuck. His *private* chamber.

The heavy door creaks as he turns the knob and pushes it open. The sight that greets me is enough to catch a breath in my throat. I release his hand as I step past him into the room and bring it to my lips as a small gasp slips free. My eyes widen at the atmosphere surrounding me.

He leans casually against the doorframe; hands resting comfortably in the pockets of his dark trousers and regards me with hooded green eyes; a sly smirk playing on his lips.

I'm transfixed by the room before me. Slowly taking in the space and I turning in a circle, soaking in as much as my eyes will see. It's like stepping into a dream of dancing shadows.

Different hues of black and grey are mixed around the large room. Floor to ceiling black walls, dark and light grey fabrics blacking out the windows, and a gigantic bed standing in the center of the room; the mattress draped with the richest and reddest silk fabrics with glinting golden embroidery detailed along the edges.

A grand stone fireplace with a grey marble mantel burns violently on one side; a large black velvet armchair angled towards the blaze. I note that the seat cushion has a slight depression, betraying that he must often brood here, lost in the flames, like the mystery he is.

"Wow," I finally whisper, my eyes wide as I take it all in. "It's beautiful."

"Yes, it is," he says, his voice low and raspy. I turn to face him and he's staring at me with the eyes of a predator. I can't help the flush I feel at his insinuation. He closes our distance, and he pulls me to him. "It's yours as much as it is mine," he murmurs, his voice a low rumble that sends a thrill of excitement between my legs.

I am not sure what to say to that, feeling the weight of his gaze on me. I see flickers of uncertainty, the glimpses of the man struggling beneath the surface of the enigmatic figure he presents to the world.

After dressing for bed, in non-negotiable privacy at Rory's insistence, we approach the bed, and I can't help but admire the way the fabric looks under the firelight, like it's lit aflame, the gold gleaming like the burning heat of the flames searing the silk from the edges inward. Rory lets go of my hand and sits on the edge of the bed, patting the spot next to him.

"You must be tired, Anastasia," he says, and I hear the unspoken tension in his voice—the need for some kind of closeness, but he won't admit to it.

I sit beside him, close enough to feel the warmth of his body. Despite the enormity of the room, it feels intimate, like we're the only two people to exist.

Rory lies back, pulling me gently down with him. We curl up under the covers, his arms wrap around me in a way that feels possessive yet protective. I rest my head on his chest, listening to the steady beat of his heart.

I look up at his face in the dim light, and I see the weariness in his eyes. There are so many questions bubbling inside of me—I want to understand him, understand this connection that keeps pulling us together. Tonight is not the night for talking though.

He looks at me, sensing my eyes on him. I can see the unspoken understanding in his expression. He knows I want answers to those questions cycling through my mind.

"I'm not a good man, princess, but at this moment, I'm trying painfully hard to be," he says softly, and I can hear emotion in his voice. "Sleep, my love," he adds while stroking the side of my face gently with his knuckles.

So, I obey.

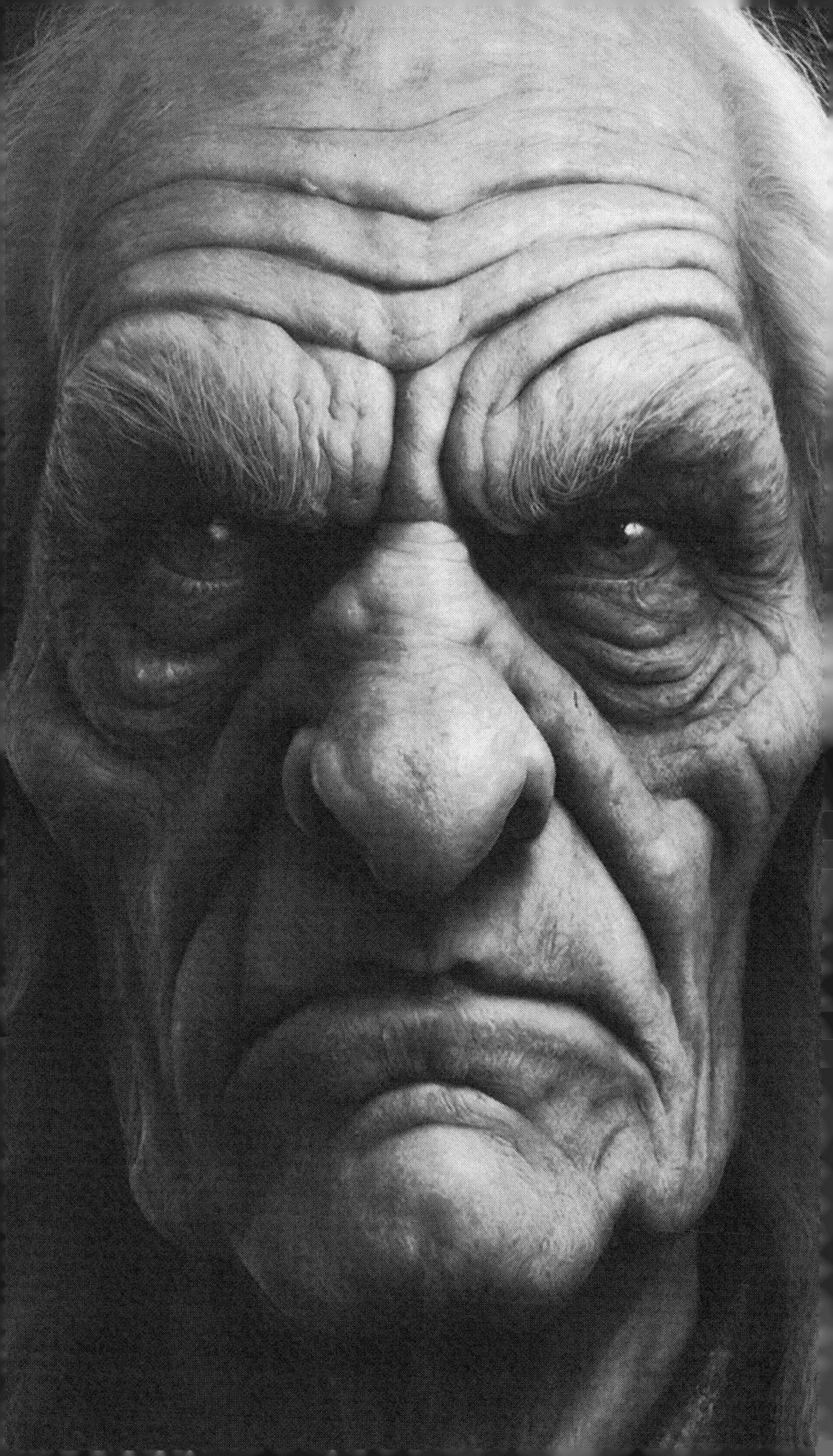

Chapter 26

Rory

Like a colony of ants kicked into overdrive, the castle is alive with the bustle of preparations. Steel clanks against leather as warriors strap on their armor, and the air buzzes with a tense excitement. The enemy will be upon up by this evening.

I can feel it in my bones, the same way I feel the coming of a storm. Every step I take is measured, every piece of gear I lay out a silent promise to those we're about to face.

Like any other morning, I woke, but it couldn't have been a more different experience. I didn't wake to solitude.

Anastasia looked so peaceful sleeping next to me. The morning light creeping across her face setting her golden freckles flickering...absolutely stunning. I didn't want to wake her, so, I slid from the bed quietly, and took my time getting ready for whatever this day would throw at us.

When I eventually returned to her side, there she was, still asleep, her long lashes resting on her soft skin, and somehow even more fucking beautiful in the soft morning glow.

Fuck me.

In that moment, staring down at her enchanting face, I felt something twist inside of me, a mix of unfamiliar emotions I still can't identify. I just *knew* that looking at her like that, peaceful and vulnerable, brought out something in me I'm not ready to face.

Trailing my fingers down her cheek and over her golden freckles, those damn freckles I fucking love so much, I reluctantly, left the room. I needed to clear my head.

My hands work automatically, adjusting straps, checking the sharpness of my blades, but my attempt at distracting is futile, mind is elsewhere. I feel like I'm standing on the edge of a cliff with the wind whispering for me to jump, in my ear. My heart is thundering to an endless drum rhythm, trying to beat its way out of my chest, and I'm half-convinced it's going to succeed.

I'm alone in my office, or so I think, I'm about to reach for my helmet when I feel it—the temperature drops, a chill that slithers up my spine and sets my teeth on edge.

"Show yourself," I growl into the quiet, fingers curling around the hilt of my knife, otherwise I'm unmoving.

The response is a slow, creeping dread that fills the room. A shape coalesces from the corner, darkness upon darkness, and I know who it is before it fully manifests.

The fucking Domovoi. It's been ages since that fateful Christmas night, and still the creature before me is an unforgettable being born of nightmares, eyes like black holes sucking in any light that dares come close.

"Rory," it hisses, with a voice mixed of broken glass and gravel, "you've been delaying the inevitable."

I swallow hard, forcing my body to remain still, to not show the fear that's gnawing at my gut. "I know why you're here," I say, my voice steadier than I feel. "Then you know the price of defiance." The Domovoi's threat hangs heavy in the air.

My grip on the knife tightens. "I won't do it," I spit back, digging my heels into a courage I didn't realize I had.

The Domovoi moves closer, and I feel the malice rolling off him in waves. "Kill Anastasia or suffer consequences far worse than death. You will with for oblivion," it sneers, the words cold and merciless. "I'll let you rot in nothingness—no heaven, no afterlife, endless nothingness. Oh, before that though, I'll torture her, and rape her before your very eyes."

A cold sweat breaks out on my forehead. The threat is as real as the knife in my grip. The Domovoi's power is ancient and undeniable. "Remember this," it adds, its twisted grin showing too many teeth, "I control many involved in this war. All will obey me."

My heart hammers against my ribcage. "If I refuse?" I challenge, even though I can taste the bitterness of defeat on my tongue.

The Domovoi's laugh is like the screech of stone grinding stone. "You already know the answer to that," it sneers.

"I wish to bargain a new deal." I state, sitting on a chair.

"We've already struck a deal, and now it's time for you to complete your part, it's that simple," it responds, the sound of its fucking disgusting toenails dragging on the floor.

"You fucker. You forced me to kill my family." I roar, anger and contempt filling my voice.

"You asked me to bring them back, and I did. Now boy, my patience is limited. I wanted the throne. I wanted the Romanov bloodline dead, only now there's one roaming this castle, and she must die." Its presence lingers even as it fades back into the shadows, leaving me shaken and alone with the echo of its vile promises.

My breath comes in shallow gasps, and I have to lean against the wall for support. This war... it's not just about the clash of swords and shields. It's about the war within me, the battle between what the Domovoi demands and the slice of soul I still call my own.

Anastasia... I can't let her suffer the fate the Domovoi has crafted for her. How the fuck do I protect her from a creature of legends? A force that holds my afterlife captive?

Fuck. FUCK!

The room feels smaller now, claustrophobic. My thoughts are splintered fragments of desperation and anger, and I know I have to make a choice. There's a line in the sand, and it's time to pick a side.

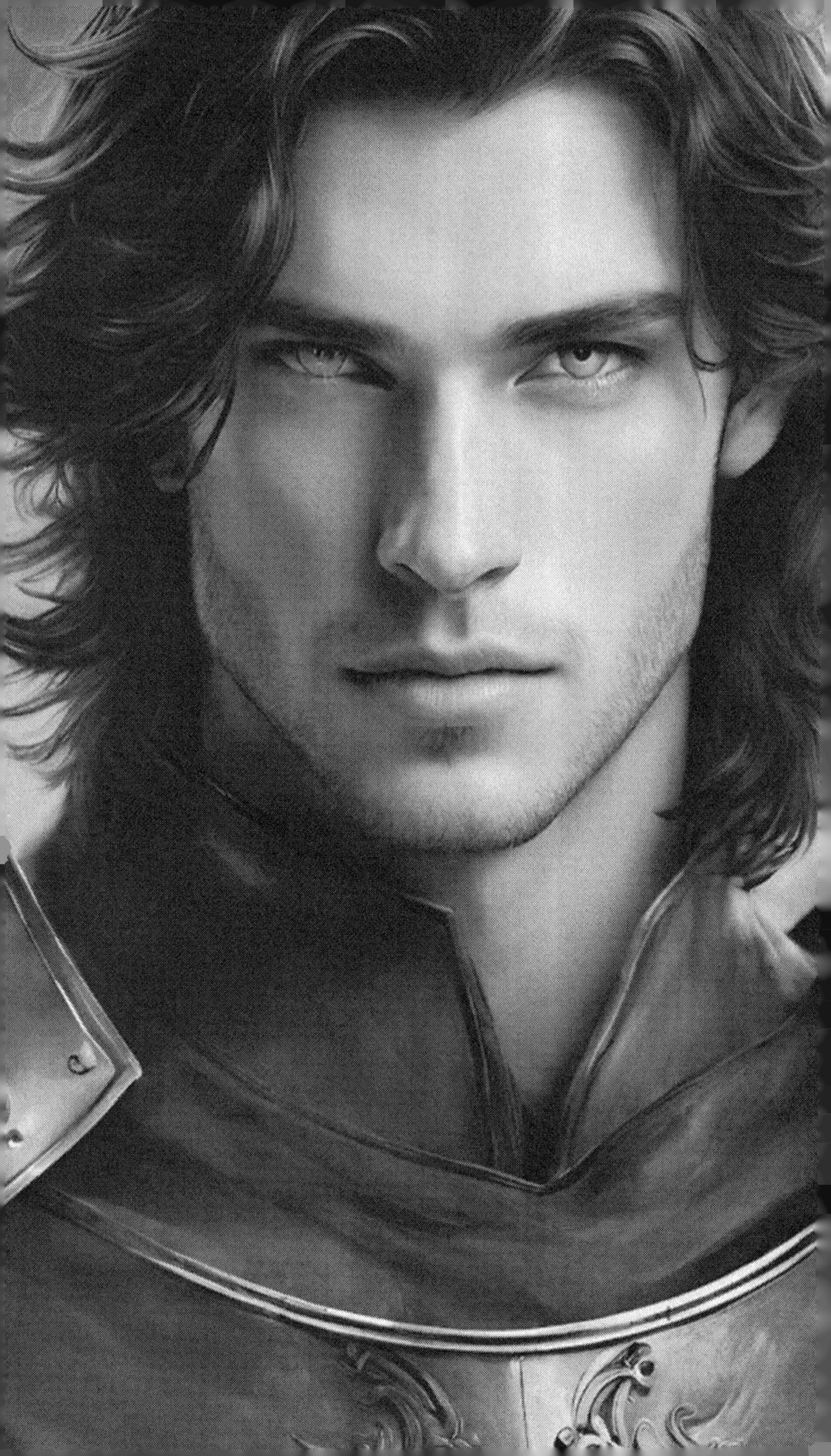

Chapter 27

Anastasia

My breath is coming out in harsh pants, Kicking and punching, I'm feeling every bruise and sore muscle scream at me.

I'm a complete mess, sweat-soaked, and tired but I need to keep at it, despite starting to slightly regret taking advantage of the vacant training room I stumbled upon while exploring the castle.

"Anastasia."

I spin around and find Rory leaning against the doorframe, like he doesn't have a care in the world. His eyes are fixed on me, traveling the length of my body, and I can't help the blush reddening my cheeks, although I'm sure it's not noticeable through the exhaustion already coloring my skin.

"You look like hell," he teases, and I can't stop from laughing because I know he's right. "Yes, well if I look as awful as I feel then I don't know how you can tolerate the sight of me," I reply playfully, trying to stifle a yawn.

"I don't know how I survived without the sight of you for as long as I'd lost you," he says, all traces of the playfulness from his tone a moment ago, gone.

My breath catches in my throat. "I..." I start, but I'm at a loss for what to say, stumbling over my words, and feeling his piercing stare searing into my face.

He swallows and then clears his throat, "come," he reaches his hand out to treat our fingers together. "I wish to show you something," he continues, and I can't read the look on his face.

Exhaustion be damned, I can't say no to his request when he purrs it to me in that deep seductive voice; always sending a wave of pleasure to my center.

We stop at my quarters so I can swap my wet, sweaty attire for a clean, green-colored dress made of light flowy fabric with gold stitching, over a pair light weight leg coverings and brown boots.

I emerge once dressed, ready to see the surprise he has for me, only to find he is the one looking surprised. Stunned, is a more accurate word.

He feasts upon the sight of me, his eyes trailing over every inch of my body.

I do a twirl and curtsy for him. "Does his Majesty approve?" I ask playfully, even though truthfully, I am nervous for his answer. Not because he won't like it, but because I know he will.

He circles me, eyes roving over my frame. "You match my eyes," he says, legitimate surprise painting his perfectly chiseled features. "Yes, it's quickly become my favorite shade," I say, my voice barely audibles over the sizzling fire raging in the empty space between us.

I walk to him, and tenderly place my hand on his cheek and study the mysterious eyes from which my dress was inspired. I had snuck off to the dress shop when we visited the village, and had the seamstress construct it without his knowledge.

I search those eyes as if they hold all his secrets. "I've never seen this shade before, deep and soft, like an evergreen, but wild, beautiful and vibrant like an emerald jewel, and the man they belong to." I say every word a whisper.

Suddenly his brow furrows and a flush of pain or disappointment floods his enchanting orbs, and he removed my hand from his face, and leads me to the stables in silence.

I discover two horses saddled and ready to go. He gestures for me to choose one, so I do. He helps me mount and once he's up on his horse, we ride out of the castle grounds.

If he thinks distraction will make me overlook those rare moments where his walls are down for once, he's very mistaken.

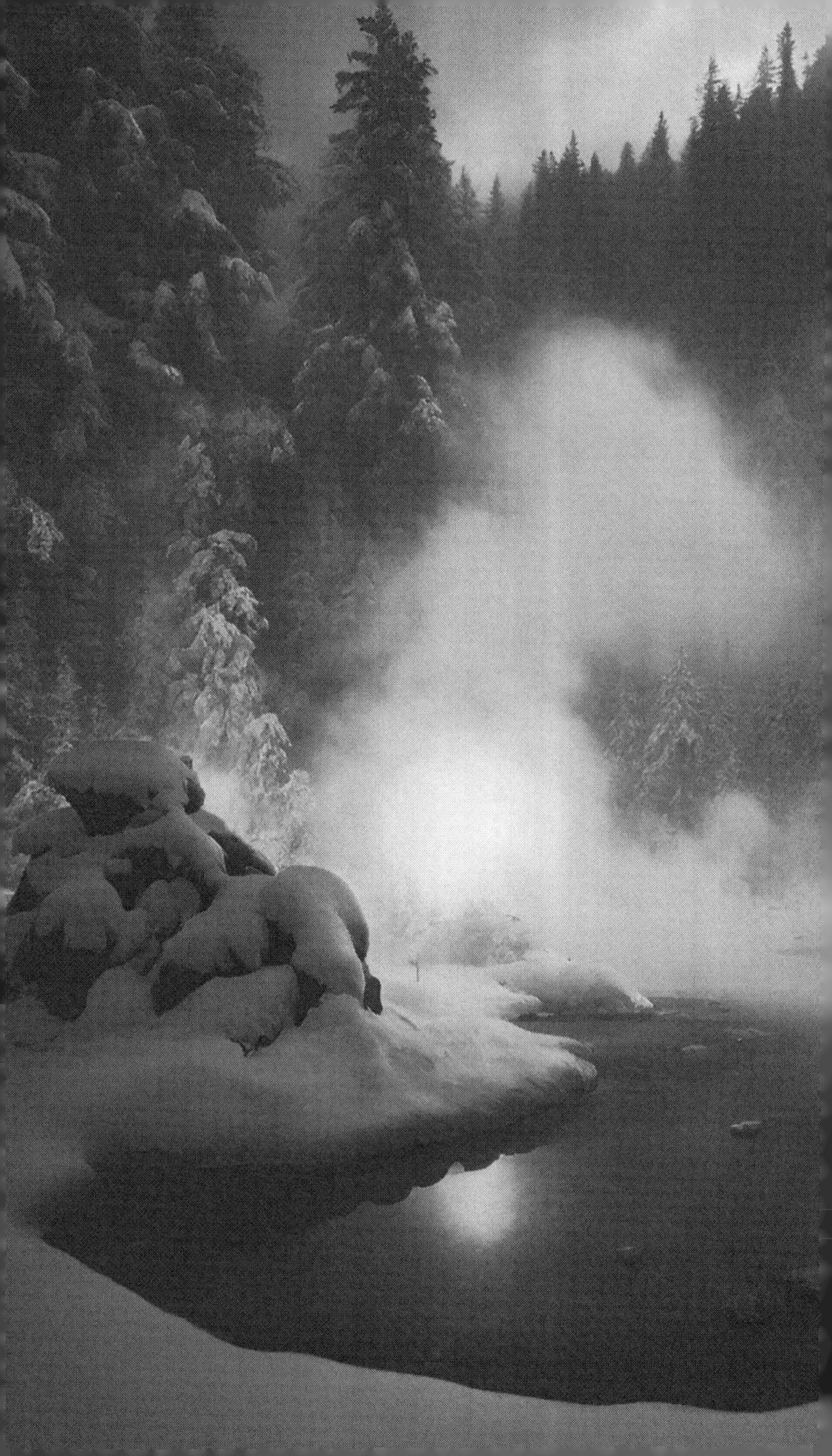

Chapter 28

Anastasia

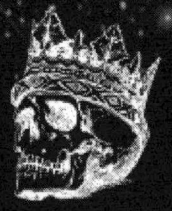

The night air is much colder than I anticipated, and it nips at my skin, making me regret forgoing a thicker coat. I can't stop myself from shivering against the rapidly dropping temperature.

Rory must notice because he then says, "I should have brought you a cloak," his voice tinged with a hint of frustration. With himself? He reaches a hand toward the sky and shadows explode among the twinkling stars above us.

My horse startles at the sudden burst of excitement, but quickly calms once the cloak he conjured for me before settles around my shoulders, enveloping my body in a rush of warmth.

After trotting along the snow-covered terrain for a short while, we cross over the threshold of a large open cavern. I can hear the gentle sound of water, and then I can see the whisps of steam rising from the surface of a large pool of water up to the star speckled sky. A hot spring.

Rory dismounts first, and then helps me get down from my horse.

He leads me to the pool's edge and orders me to get in, already shedding his clothing. I watch as he peels each garment from his sinewy figure, my heart pulsing wildly in my ears.

Holy shit.

I can't move, I can't breathe, I can't do anything except stare open-mouthed at the king before me. The light from the moon bathes his pale skin in soft light and shadows, accentuating all the muscles, contours and scars. His chest is chiseled with the skill of a sculptor, broad shoulders, and defined hip muscles that create the arrow that directs my eyes to the weapon proudly standing between his legs.

I just died.

"You are going to catch a cold if you just stand there," his voice stirs me back to life, bringing me back to the present.

I hesitantly reach up and start to untie the strings of the cloak, I let it drop, pooling around my feet, followed by my dress and then the rest of my clothing. I feel self-conscious but my muscles are begging me to get into the hot steamy water.

We wade hand in hand into the water, the heat like a blessing from heaven, wrapping around me like a blanket, soothing away the ache in my limbs.

We're both quiet, the tension between us far too strong to be fixed with the soothing hot spring. I feel his eyes on me, and it's doing nothing to appease the insecurity I feel being so exposed to him. I'm trying like hell not to look at him, but it's like there's an invisible force pulling my gaze his way.

"Stop." He purrs, his voice husky and low. I jerk my head to meet his gaze, feeling heat on my cheeks. He pauses our slow movement and pins me with his sparkling emeralds, "Anastasia, I cannot put into words worthy of you, but you are mesmerizing. You are so beautiful it pains me to be in your presence because I'm constantly fighting the restraint to prove it to you," his words linger with the steam before evaporating into the night, and he reaches up to press his thumb to my cheek, catching a tear I didn't know was sliding down my face.

Rory moves closer. The water's up to my chest now, and I can't help the way my body reacts to the warmth or the man sharing it with me. "Thank you for bringing me here," I whisper because it feels like words should be spoken softly here, "I'm feeling so relaxed now."

"It's... peaceful," he says, and I nod because it is. He's being oddly quiet, and somehow, it makes him seem more... real.

The steam curls around us, my heart's pounding in my chest, and I'm not quite sure if it's because of the hot water or the man who's observing me like it's for the first time.

His hand brushes mine under the water, and I feel it, a spark of something. I look at him, and he's staring back at me. "I thought the hot, sulfurous water would do good for your body after all that training," he murmurs, the nocturnal sounds of the forest wrapping around his voice. "It's working, just like your shadow magic, cloaking my body in warmth, thank you again, Rory," I wrap my hands around his thumbs under the surface of the water, and gently caress them from pad to palm. He closes his eyes, like the feeling of a tender touch is too much for him.

With his sculpted jaw now facing the stars, and his eyes closed, I take the opportunity to study him further. There is still so much mystery and uncertainty. This man has been through his own battles, ones that have left scars on more than just his body. I want to ask so many things, but I think it's clear he will confide in me on his own terms, in his own time.

His voice severs my thoughts, and my eyes find his mouth as he speaks, "This is where I come when I feel like giving up. For sixteen years, this has been my spot." He straightens up and tries to give me a smile.

I smile in return, squeezing his hands a little tighter. The silence stretches between us again, but it's not unwelcome. It's comfortable, the kind that comes from shared understanding rather than the need for words.

The heat from the springs is working its way deep into our bones, and I know I'll come out stronger because of it.

"Rory," I finally say, my voice echoing softly in the cavern space. "I think I understand why you come here."

He opens his eyes, and they mirror the stars above, deep and fathomless. "Is that so?" he asks, his voice a gentle nudge.

"It's not just the heat or the healing," I explain, looking around at the majestic nature surrounding us. "It's a reminder, isn't it? A reminder that no matter how cold the world gets, there's still warmth to be found."

He considers my words for a moment, a thoughtful look crossing his features. "You're not far off, princess," he admits, and I can tell it's a concession he doesn't make lightly. "Every soul needs a sanctuary. A place to lay down their weapons and just... be..."

"Be human," I add softly, and he nods.

"To be human, to heal, to find strength in stillness and solitude." His gaze drifts back to the sky, and I follow it, taking in the vast tapestry of twinkling lights. "On the battlefield, it's easy to forget that we're not just soldiers. We're people. We bleed, we hurt, and we need moments like these to remember who we are beyond the monsters."

I let that sink in, feeling the weight of his words. I've been so focused on becoming stronger, tougher, more resilient. He's right. We need to hold onto our humanity, to the parts of us that feel and love and seek peace.

"We should get back before it gets too late," Rory says after a while, interrupting the comfortable silence. "Oh," the disappointment evident in my voice. I'm already mourning the loss of our time together, and I'm not ready to return to reality just yet.

Surprising him and myself, I grip his shoulders and swing my leg over his and seat myself directly on his lap, pressing our bodies together.

It's a bold move, one that says more than words ever could.

"Anastasia," he whispers, a warning in his tone, causing shivers to cascade down my spine. I can see the internal battle warring behind his eyes—the struggle between need and the restraint he's been clinging to for so long.

He brings his hand to my face, slowly caressing down my cheek as he peers into my eyes, silently begging me to stop this. His jaw clenched; muscles taut, ready to give in to this overpowering desire that has us both trapped. He grabs my hips, guiding me, and I gasp at the sudden grip.

Breathless, my heart-pounding, the heat of the water only adds fuel to the fire that's been smoldering inside me. I can feel every inch of him, stiff against me, and it sends every nerve in my body singing as I feel his hardness pressed directly on my core—no barriers, no pretense, just the raw, aching need that we've both been fighting against.

Bathed in the light of the moon, the stars blinking above us and the steam rising from the water's surface, everything outside this moment fades away and it's just me and it's just him, skin to skin.

We both know what is about to happen.

I grind my wet slit along his full length, my movements slow and deliberate. The grip he has on my hips is sure to bruise later, and that thought only serves to spur me on. The water ripples around us, echoing the waves of anticipation rolling off us both.

This moment is one out of a forbidden dream—a mingling of heat and water, desire and the inevitable surrender. And as I finally let myself go, letting my body take control, I can feel Rory giving in, too.

My hands griping his broad shoulders, I lean my lips down to his ear, "you belong to me, Rory," the sensual tone of my voice combined with the words elicits a low predatory growl from deep in his chest.

"I've always been yours, even when I didn't want to admit it," he admits, resonance of his voice, rough like sand. "Tell me what you want, Anastasia," he urges, and the words are a challenge I'm eager to meet.

I can't resist the pull between us, and as I slide onto him, the connection we forge is as natural as the surrounding wilderness.

"Fuck..." he hisses, and his head falls back onto the edge of the pool.

"To be yours," I say, my voice transparent, and my breaths are coming out in shallow pants as I work myself to the base of his cock.

We move together in the water, our rhythm as timeless as his immortal life. "You are mine, you will *always* be mind," he purrs. His right hand reaches around and slides up my back to the nape of my neck, tangling his fingers in my hair.

"Kiss me, Rory," and he does, he crashes his lips to mine and my world explodes. He swallows my moans as his tongue fights its way past my lips, licking and sucking, while I continue my movements up and down his hard length. My hands explore his chest, every touch stoking the fire that burns bright within us.

His response is a groan, one that echoes off the water and stone, and I feel his hands grip my flesh harder, my breath hitching as our movements bring us closer and closer to the edge.

The air around us is thick with steam, the heat warming the space surrounding us is not just from the hot springs, it's from this forbidden union that feels as if it were predestined.

"Anastasia," he breathes out, and there's a reverence in his voice that makes my name sound like a sacred mantra.

I meet his gaze, seeing the depth of his surrender, and it's powerful and beautiful. He's laid bare, not just in body, but in soul.

He rises suddenly, water splashing as it rushes off our bodies. He sets me on the edge of the spring, the snow immediately melting away from the heat of my wet skin. Never breaking our connection.

"Do you trust me, princess?" He asks, his pupils grow bigger as he continues to slowly pump into me. I nod my head; words are lost upon me right now. That single nod is his undoing.

He grips my legs under my thighs to open my legs wider, and he starts pounding into me, hard, and fast.

I take one of my hands, run it over my breasts, down my stomach and to where our bodies join.

The slight touch to the bundle of nerves I find swollen and soaked, sends a wave of pleasure to the bottom of my spine and I grind harder onto his cock, needing him deeper, needing him like I need the air in my lungs.

"You feel absolutely divine, princess," his voice is strained. "Ahhh, fuck yes, look how well you take my cock." His words send another wave of pleasure through my veins, and I could die right now and be at peace with that, knowing this was how I spent my last moments.

In an instant, he pulls out of me, and I cry in protest. He releases a low chuckle, "don't worry, princess, I just want to worship you from every angle." My thighs clench at his declaration.

He bends me over, pressing my chest to the ledge of the pool. He slides his cock back inside me from behind, and I can't help the pulsing throb that clenches my walls around him.

"Oh fuck yes, pincess, you're perfection, you were made for me," he coos into my ear, his warm breath sending goosebumps over my flesh, despite the heat from the spring and the sex.

"Rory, please," I need to come, the pressure is too much, I've never felt this aroused before.

My plea sets him off in the best way. He grabs my arms from behind and pulls me up so he's holding one of mine in each of his. Using the leverage to impale me as hard and deeply as possible.

"Yes, Rory, don't stop," I scream.

"Come on this cock, princess. Now." He commands.

And I happily obey.

My walls begin to clench around him as I chase my climax to its peak. The intense friction of his cock against my engorged nerves sends me over the edge and I come hard, my muscles squeezing around him for dear life. My vision explodes and fades to black as I feel his hot release fill me up.

"Hmm, Anastasia, fuck you're squeezing me so tight," hunched over, Rory's front is plastered to my back and he's huffing out breaths into my neck, having released my hands to fold his arms around me while he came.

The aftermath is tender, the water lapping against us, mimicking the serenity of this moment, and soothing our heated skin. We stay entwined, reluctant to break this connection that feels like it goes beyond flesh and bone. Two souls colliding and becoming one in the heart of the wilderness.

Holding me in his arms like this is the safest I've ever felt, and I don't want this moment to end.

We get out of the hot springs after what seems like ages, the cold night chill stinging our skin. Dressing quickly, we ready the horses to head back to the castle and I'm recalling what I've learned on this night. Strength doesn't just come from swinging a sword of landing a punch. It comes from knowing when to rest, when to heal and when to welcome the presence of another tortured soul to aid in the healing process.

After mounting our horses, I catch Rory's eye and a smile plays on my lips. Rory has shown me a different kind of strength tonight, and maybe that's the secret to surviving this war; balancing the violence, with moments of peace, so we don't lose ourselves during battle.

369 - *Ruins and Shadows*

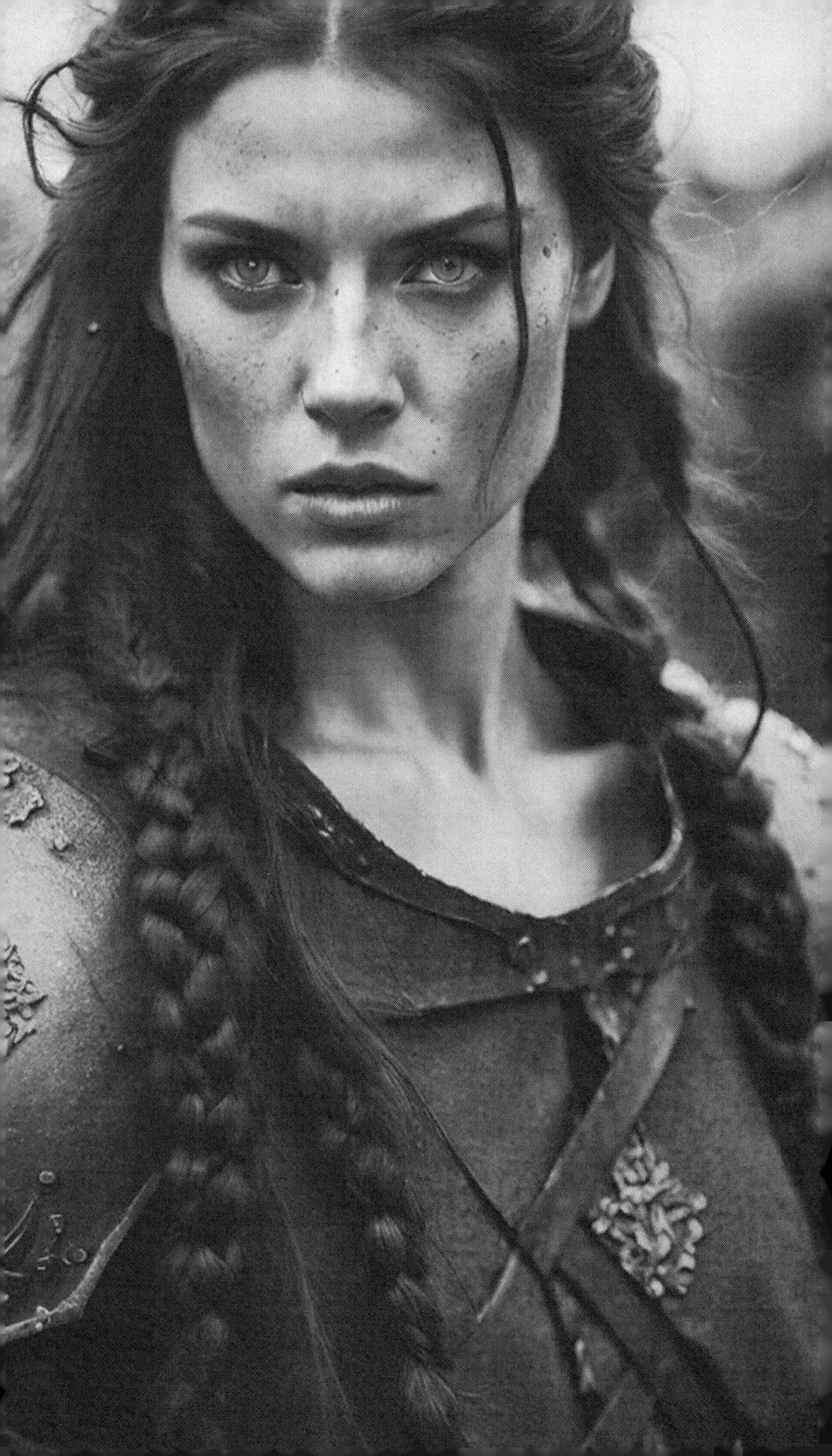

Chapter 29

Anastasia

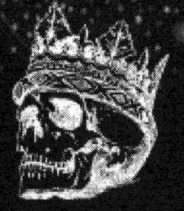

I meet Rory out on the balcony overlooking the courtyard, and he's already dressed for battle, his expression grim but determined. He looks every bit the leader he is, and it's a sight that both comforts and terrifies me. I give my armor a final adjustment before walking to his side.

The walk back from the hot springs was quiet, a rare moment of peace. The snow started falling, large, fluffy flakes around us and it just added to the serenity I was feeling from our passionate love making.

My skin still tingles from where the water caressed it, and where Rory's lips kissed and licked, and I flush at the memory.

Rory meets my eyes, silently telling me he understands my reddening face. His expression quickly turns from desire, to one of concern and something I can only describe as regret.

I understand the unspoken words, because I feel them too, regret and sadness that our peaceful, solitary moment together had to end. And, what if that was all we will ever have? Because it's time for war.

He turns to face the crowd that has gathered—the soldiers, the servants, everyone who calls this castle home.

"People of the court," Rory begins, his voice carrying over the murmurs of the crowd. "The soldiers from our enemy kingdom are upon us, it is time to defend our land."

I'm trying to hold onto the calm as I watch him speak, his words painting the picture of the battle to come.

"We must make haste," he continues addressing the court, urgency clear in his tone. "Look around at the faces of your fellow soldiers and find courage in each other so we can stand together to overcome this tide that seeks to drown us."

As Rory's speech comes to an end, the crowd erupts into a united, energetic applause, and I look out at the expressions, to see faces harden in resolve, statures stand taller and prouder—they believe him.

With the crowd cheering their chorus of determined shouts, and clanging their weapons and shields, Rory takes my elbow and directs me back into the castle.

Once inside he cups my face in his hands, "Anastasia," he whispers, eyes pleading with mine, "stay here, please," I can barely register his words before a shadow sweeps overhead, cold and menacing. "They're here," he says.

His body tenses beside me, and I brace myself for whatever he'll say next. "Stay in the castle, I need to keep you safe." He's practically begging me, my brow furrows in confusion. "What? Are you mad? I've been training for this!" I say, raising my voice in anger.

Rory's eyes flick behind me and I turn to see servants and soldiers rushing about the corridors, barricading doors and securing last minute hiding places for the woman and children.

Loud banging can be heard from the grounds just beyond the castle, the clashing of swords on shields, a battle chorus announcing the approaching army.

I turn back to Rory, his eyes flicking rapidly between mine. I reach up and grip his cheek, a touch meant to comfort, "don't ask me to stay behind, these people need me," my words soft, and gentle. "I need you," he says, choking on the last word, pulling my wrists and wrapping our hands together between us as he presses his forehead to mine.

The sounds of violence and steel are getting louder, closer. He lets out a strained sigh and stares me into my soul like he's trying to commit every detail of my face to memory. "Be careful, princess," he says, his voice low and strained.

I press my lips to his, unwrap our hands and throw my arms around his neck. I kiss him like it's our last, tender and sweet but deep and passionate. Separating myself from him, I look at him in his glistening emeralds, and turn to dash away, joining the mass of bodies heading to the front gates.

The battle unfolds like a dance of death and destruction, with screams and the roar of flames filling my ears.

I fight with everything I've got, the training that Rory and I went through together driving my every move. I see him out of the corner of my eye, a force of nature cutting down anyone who dares to challenge him. Using shadows in unison to grab enemy soldiers, and throwing them into the trees, breaking necks and spines from the force.

The world is full of fire and blood, and I can barely catch my breath. There's no time to think, only to react—to keep swinging, to keep moving, to keep alive. I fight my way to him, and then we're back-to-back, a team in chaos.

As we push forward, the enemy just keeps coming, wave after relentless wave. I don't know how long we fight for, but the sun begins to dip low on the horizon, staining the sky with the same red that coats our blades. It's an endless cycle, this dance of war, and I wonder if we'll make it out with our lives and our souls intact.

As I slice through the battlefield, my sword singing a deadly tune against throats, the chaos around me is like a dark symphony. The ground beneath my boots is sodden with blood, slippery with the remnants of lives cut short. I am in the thick of war, and every sweep of my blade carves a path through the enemy. Tainting the beautiful, pure snow with crimson.

From the corner of my eye, I glimpse Rory, a figure of shadows and power. He's fighting like a god, his darkness ripping spines from men as though they were no firmer than stalks of wheat.

The shadows, like ink spilled across sunlight, weave amongst the soldiers, creating monsters that fight alongside us, turning the tide in our favor. There's a poetry to his savagery, a beauty in the way he commands the darkness to aid our cause.

Each life I take is a weight upon my soul, a scream in the quiet moments that will surely come. But I push forward, driven by a purpose I can no longer ignore. This is about survival, about the people who have put their trust in me.

My eyes meet Rory's across the battlefield, a silent conversation. I see the acknowledgment of my strength; of the partnership we've forged from our training sessions.

As I drive my sword into another foe, I feel a rush of adrenaline that's tinged with sorrow. Each drop of blood spilled feels like a step closer to peace.

I leap forward, catching an enemy off guard, my dagger finding the gap in his armor as his eyes widen in shock and then dim forever.

The battle's been raging for hours, and every bone in my body is screaming for a break. I'm holding my own, fighting alongside Rory, and the people, swinging my sword with a kind of ferocity that surprises me, but fuck I'm tired.

I make it back to the castle, pulling away from the front lines to catch my breath and gulp down some water. I have not had a moment to myself since this chaos erupted, and it feels strange to be alone, even for just a second. As I lean against the cool stone wall, I take a deep swig from the flask, the liquid chilled and sweet against my parched throat.

Closing my eyes, I pour some of the cold water over my face, soothing the heated skin and washing the sweat away. Then, I'm aware I am not alone any longer. A shadow creeps over me, thick and oozing like ink spilling across parchment. It swallows me whole, and for a moment, I'm blind, gasping, panic scratching at my chest.

Then it's gone, the shadows lift, and I'm staggering, caught off balance—not at the castle, but in my room. Confusion ties my brain into knots as I try to make sense of what just happened.

Did I imagine the whole thing? Before I can sort through the fog in my mind however, the door bursts open.

It's Rory, looking like he's been chasing ghosts, his eyes wide and fierce. "Anastasia," he says, and there's relief mixed with something else—something urgent—in his voice as he comes barreling towards me.

He stops short before me. His chest heaving, and I can see the flecks of battle still clinging to him—the blood and dirt marking him as a warrior.

"Rory... what's going on?" I ask, my voice steady even though my heart's doing a mad dance in my chest. "I was just—"

"No time," he cuts me off, and my gut twists with a sudden dread, he takes my face in his hands, his fingers gentle but firm. His lips find mine, and the room disappears.

A shiver runs through me when his lips stray to my jaw, then down my neck. He bites at my skin, and I gasp, torn between wanting to push him away and pulling him closer. Every part of me feels on fire when his rough fingers explore, tracing a protective circle between my legs.

"Rory," I protest weakly, "we can't—there's a war—"

But he hushes me, taking my pants off, his voice low and resolute. "I'm here with you, Anastasia, but I'm fighting for us with every shadow I summon at the same time. Let me have this, another taste of you, right now."

The sensuality of it overwhelms me, the pleasure mixed with the pain of his rough touch. He takes me to the wall, lifting me with ease.

My legs wrap around him, and everything else fades away when he plunges himself all the way to the hilt. "Oh fuck," I gasp, I'm lost in the rhythm of us, the raw connection that we can't escape.

As he presses his body further into me, his voice is a low growl, delivering a chilling confession. "I've just split open the bellies of our enemies," he says, his breath hot against my ear even as our bodies remain locked together. I moan loudly, and he licks his way from my ear to my mouth. "Strung them up by their organs, decorating the evergreens for the holiday season."

He pulls all the way out and freezes. "Rory," I protest, and I grip him with my thighs trying to get him moving again. With his cock impaling me to the wall, he slams both hands on either side of head, flat against the stone. "I killed them all...for you," he whispers into my ear, and I can't help when my wall clench around him in response.

Immediately he grips my hips with both hands, digging his fingers into my flesh, and I feel the tip of his rock-hard length pressing on my entrance. I close my eyes and gasp. My breath hitches, and my skin is speckled with goosebumps from the fluttering this man does to my core.

"Ohh, you like that?" he purrs his voice rough and raspy, "you like when I spread this pussy open with my cock?" The sensation is too much and I'm riding the edge of something explosive, and so is he. There's a wildness in his eyes that tells me he's not just with me, he's also somewhere out there on the battlefield, a man split between two worlds.

My back pressed against the wall, the rough stones digging into my skin through the thin fabric of my shirt. His body slams into mine, hard and unyielding, and I gasp, the sensation raw and powerful.

This battle is of a different kind, savage and desperate. His teeth graze my neck, and I arch into him, my fingers digging into his shoulders. "Fuck I love this pussy, princess," he praises. There's no gentleness, no hesitation—only the primal need to claim and be claimed.

Rory's iron grip moves to my wrists, pinning them to the stone above my head. Our eyes lock, intense and unflinching, and then he thrusts into me, deep and full. A guttural moan tears from my throat, the sensations overwhelming, almost too much.

We move together, a frenzy of limbs and insatiable hunger. The sound of our ragged breaths fills my ears, punctuated by the slap of skin on skin as he pounds into me. There's nowhere to hide, no space for secrets—just the naked truth of our raw, unbridled passion.

I bite down on his lip, tasting blood, and he groans, the sound vibrating through me. The pain is sweet, a sharp contrast to the heat building within. Our bodies are slick with sweat, slipping against each other as we spiral toward a cataclysmic release.

Every thrust is a promise, every bite and kiss and lick a vow. The world outside might be falling apart, but here, we're creating a universe that's all our own—a universe where only our pleasure and our power exist.

I can feel the pressure mounting, coiling tighter and tighter until I'm on the brink. Rory senses it, and his movements become more deliberate, more focused. He's chasing his pleasure, driven by the same desperate need to escape into the oblivion of ecstasy and take me with him.

Then we hit the peak together and dive over the other side, sending an explosion of sensation that obliterates everything else. I scream, my body convulsing around him, and Rory follows, his own cry mingling with mine as he finds his release.

We collapse against the wall, a heap of spent limbs and heaving chests. The sounds of battle are a distant rumble now, irrelevant and far away. For a moment, we just breathe, our sweat cooling in the drafty room.

Finally, Rory lifts his head, his eyes searching mine. There's a question there, a silent inquiry into what this means for us—for our tangled past and uncertain future.

With a heavy breath, I disentangle myself from Rory's embrace and straighten my clothes. The battle outside waits for our return.

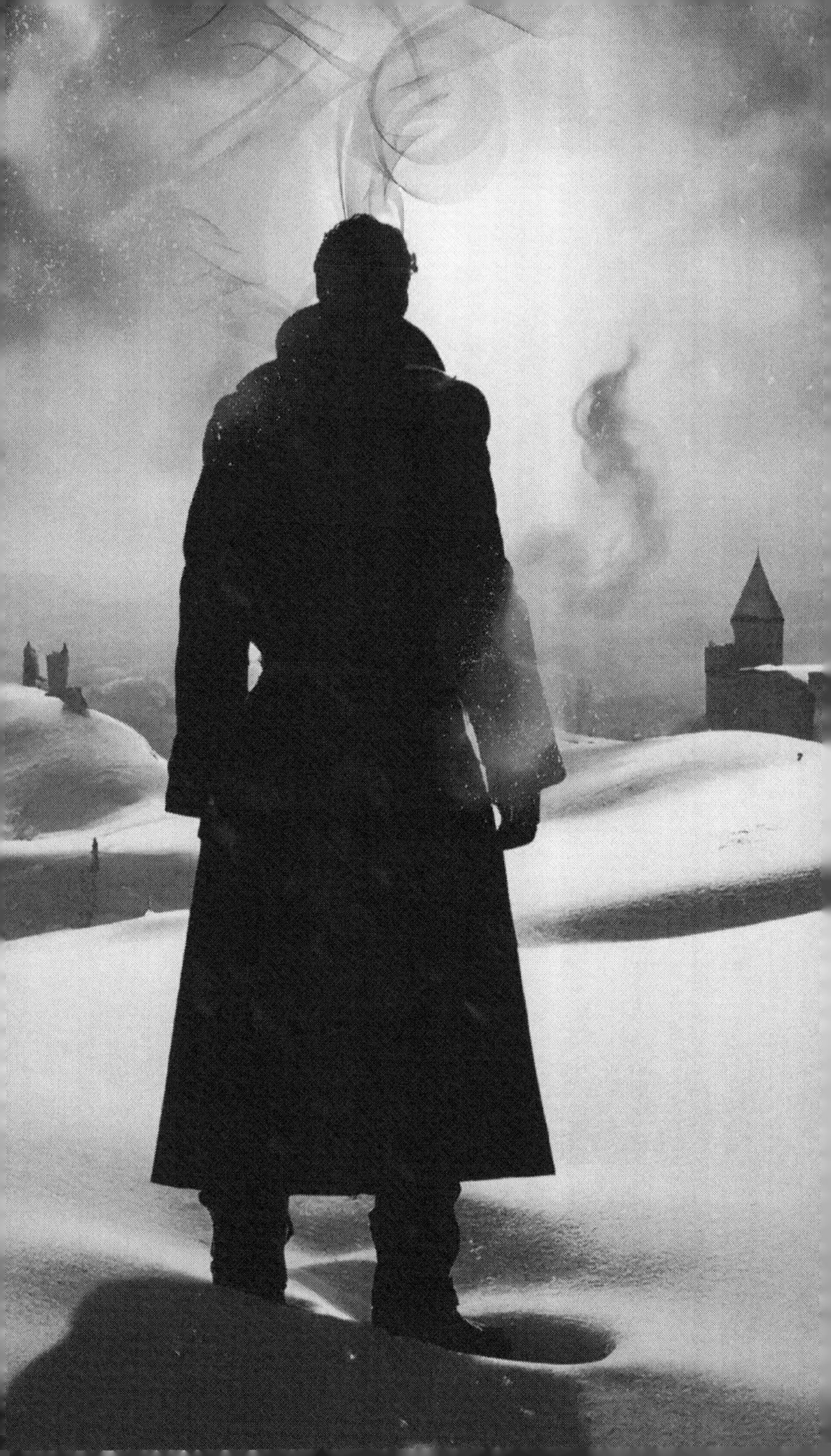

Chapter 30

Anastasia

Everything's a blur of noise and smoke as I stand in the middle of the war-torn field, heart pounding in my chest. The world is all chaos and cries, but then I hear it—a familiar voice.

It cuts through the clamor like a knife, and I freeze. A rush of memories floods in my mind; *Vitriev. The boy who laughed with me in the sun, the man who guarded my nights. My friend, my ally, my love.*

"Anastasia!" Vitriev calls again, and I turn, searching through the haze. I see his silhouette and everything around me disappears.

What the fuck is going on?!

"Vitriev?" My voice is trembling as I step toward him. The next thing I know, his arms are around me, and I'm pulled against his chest. "I've got you," he says, and it's all too much.

I'm overwhelmed by the scent of him, the feel of him. I'm lost in the flashbacks of us.

Running through fields dotted with blooming flowers, fighting back-to-back every day for years while he trained me in combat, the tender moments in the safety of darkness, where he made love to me.

"I thought you were dead. Rory... he told me—" I can't finish the sentence. The confusion is like a thick fog, clouding my mind.

Vitriev pulls back, his eyes searching mine. "Rory has poisoned your mind with his lies, Anastasia. I'm here to show you the truth." He takes my hands, and everything is a blur. I don't stop him when he guides me to the trees lining the battlefield, I don't stop when he unties a horse from one of the branches and ushers me to mount behind him, and I don't stop him when he grabs the reigns, gives them a tug and directs the horse in the opposite direction, away from the waging war.

The world spins and my vision blurs with unshed tears, and when it rights itself again, we're in a camp, enemy flags snapping in the wind. I'm shaking, but I'm unsure if it's due to the cold, or the sting of betrayal.

Vitriev's face is hardened, but not unkind. "Anastasia, you must remember who you are, who Rory's really is," he says, his voice firm but gentle. He guides me into a tent, and it feels like entering another world. "Sit," he commands softly, and I do, my legs no longer able to support the weight of all this.

Vitriev kneels before me, taking my hands in his. I startle, pulling my hands away, but he presses harder, imprisoning them in his own. "Rory Rasputin is a monster, Anastasia, you have to remember some truth to that," he pleads. "He is *not* a monster. He saved my life, and..." I stumble over my words, my breathing becoming shallow, "He loves me!" I cry out. My heart is pounding in my ribcage, and I don't know what to do with myself. I just want to rip my hands away and run to Rory's protective embrace.

"He murdered your entire family. He cured your brother Alexei, gave him back to you, and then took him away again, just because he could. He hunted you for years Anastasia, so he could kidnap you and imprison you for this very purpose, to poison you, to make you forget, so he could bend and weave a tale of his own making. He doesn't love you; he is incapable of feeling anything even close to love." A pang of betrayal mixes with the dawning truth and Vitriev's eyes hold a sorrow that twists something inside me.

All this time, Rory—the man who's held me captive, who's been my enemy—is not the man I thought? The realization hits me like a punch, staggering me.

"And you, Vitriev? What about all the time we spent together?" My voice breaks. "I never stopped loving you, but you need to see the whole picture. I was dying in the village where he found you. An old man approached me and made a deal with me, to live, to save you."

I'm shaking, tears threatening to spill. The world I knew is shattered, replaced by this new, conflicting reality where nothing and no one is what they seem. It's all too much for me to handle.

Vitriev's gaze is steady, filled with an unspeakable pain. "Remember who you are, Anastasia. You are the sole heir to the throne. You are the queen. And the deed has already been done. You were crowned during your incarceration in the castle."

I rub my forehead with one hand and wipe away my tears with the back of the other. "I don't know what to say," his eyes tell me of years we've shared together, a bond we share, but I only feel pain, uncertainty and betrayal.

"I know Rory has done terrible things, yet... if there's truth in what you say..." I trail off, lost in the mess of my thoughts. I take a deep breath, the fighter in me rising above the confusion. "I'll need time to think, to sort through the truth and lies."

Vitriev stands and offers me his hand. "Take all the time you need. I'll be here, just sleep, rest." He helps me down onto a cot, and then sleep consumes me.

I know something is wrong before I even open my eyes. There's a tightness around my wrists and ankles, a biting pain that makes my skin crawl. My heart starts racing like I'm running from something fierce, and when I finally dare to open my eyes—shit.

"What the fuck," I breathe out, taking in the dimly lit tent and the ropes digging into my skin. Panic claws my throat. My wrists are tied to the foot of the makeshift bed, and so are my ankles, forcing me into an uncomfortable position.

How did I manage to stay asleep while someone was fucking tying me up? I tug hard, but the ropes don't budge, a cruel reminder of my helpless state.

Who did this, Rory? I'm still so confused, barely emerging from a far-from-restful sleep. Images of reality, images of what really happened, came back to me in the night.

Rory, standing over my family, covered in their blood. The chaotic twister of shadows and darkness swirling around him, his beautiful green eyes that have become my favorite color, glaring right into my soul. Running and training for over a decade so I could one day have my vengeance.

How can I go back? How can I forget the love I now have for the reaper with stunning orbs my favorite shade?

Lost in the recollection of thoughts in my mind, I didn't notice the old man standing at the entrance to my tent. His eyes, black as the starless sky and a grin sliced across his face, like spilled ink, with his black teeth and gums. He looks like he doesn't belong in this world. He just looks wrong, and it turns my stomach.

"Enjoying your stay?" he cackles, each word dripping with malice.

Glaring at him I feel a ball of fury forming in my gut. "Who the hell are you?" I demanded, already scheming ways to break free and wipe that smug look off his creepy face.

He chuckles, moving closer until I can see the wicked gleam in his eyes. "Does it matter? You're here with us now, my dear."

Us?

I'm in the enemy camp, and I'm strung up like a damn tapestry. Images of Rory and Vitriev flash in my mind. They must be out their minds with worry if they aren't already on their way to rescue me. I'm not sure which one I'd want to see first.

I force myself to breathe, to think like the warrior I was trained to be. As the old man has his back to me, his laughter still vibrates in the air, I try loosening the ropes. My hands, slick with sweat, slipped against the rough fibers. It's going to take all my cunning and strength to get out of these restraints, it doesn't help the fibers of rope are scratchy and rough, leaving rope burns on my skin, raw and sore.

My mind is constantly cycling through the information and emotions, over and over, it's never ending and it's pushing me into madness.

As my frustration continues to grow, the repetitive cadence of footsteps filters in through the tent opening. Vitriev steps into the tent. My heart thumps and I feel a wave of tension release from my shoulders, "Vitriev!" I exhaled, the relief in my voice thick as honey. He's here to rescue me.

"You came! I knew you would—" I rush to say but the look on his face stops the words on my tongue. It's not the friendly, reassuring smile I expected. Instead, it's a hard, unreadable expression. Like ants invading a fallen apple, a jittery itch crawls up my spine, forcing my body to shiver in response.

The decrepit old man stands to the side, his eyes bright, watching us. "Well done, Vitriev," he croaks, his voice like gravel being crushed underfoot. "You've played your part perfectly."

A chill run through me, freezing the blood in my veins. "What's going on?" My voice is barely a whisper, fear tightening its grip around my throat.

Vitriev doesn't answer right away. Instead, he begins pacing like a cornered animal, his face twisted into an ugly snarl. "That *creature*," he nods at the old man, "showed me... things. Images of you with *him*—loving *him*, being with *him*."

Creature? What the fuck?

I shake my head, trying to understand, to deny. "No, Vitriev, you've got it all wrong—"

"Shut up!" His outburst echos in the small space. "You, *my* Anastasia, with that... that fucking monster!" His face morphs into a look of pure disgust, and I want to scream that it's all lies. Only, I can't, because then that would be a lie.

Looking at the boy I grew up with, I can see that his eyes are no longer the eyes of my childhood friend. He's been corrupted beyond repair and now I only see emptiness.

"I made a deal," he hisses, his voice low and menacing. "To fucking save *YOU!* I was dying...you fucking left me dying!" I flinch at his words, "The Domovoi appeared, and I begged him to heal me so I could go after you, even though you *LEFT ME*!" His eyes are boring into my very soul, "You made a fool out of me, you bitch!"

"I don't understand that thing said you played your part well...how could you—?" The betrayal tastes bitter on my tongue as I try to digest this new information.

"I didn't have a fucking choice," he spits the words at me, and the Domovoi chuckles, a sound mimicking grinding stone. "Indeed, he has been most... cooperative," it spews, and I can see it's dead blackened teeth and I think I'm going to vomit.

Vitriev continues his rant, "After we agreed to the deal, this thing," he gestures to the Domovoi with his thumb, "decided to break the news to me that you were in fact already safe and sound, *fucking* Rasputin." I narrow my eyes at him as he continues his recount, "So with that plan having been a complete failure, the Domovoi offered me immense power, in exchange for helping him win this war and acquire the throne, by means of *you.*

My mind raced, trying to piece it together. It was Vitriev all along. All this war, all this suffering—it was his doing, just to gain power?

I glare at them both, my heart broken, my spirit seething with anger. "You won't get away with this," I vow, my voice firm despite my fear. "I will not be your puppet, Vitriev."

"But you will." He laughs, leaning his face over me, I take advantage of his proximity and spit right in his face, with all the force I can muster. He recoils, the amusement wiped from his face as I intended.

"You fucking whore." He yells in my face, the vein in his forehead pulsing with every current of rage.

"What's that plan, Vitriev? Keep me captive where? In the castle, marry me for the throne and then what? Give it to the Domovoi?" I ask, lacing my words with venom.

"Not the castle, a small cage." He states simply, the amusement returning to his face. "Marry you, have my way with you, and....I know...scratch those fucking freckles off your face," he threatens, slowly pulling a knife out from under his sleeve.

"Once crowned king, I'll kill you slowly, Ana, and I'll be granted immortality and unimaginable power," he says my name in a voice that almost sounds like *my* Vitriev and my eyes fill with tears.

"When you die," the Domovoi says, regarding us from the corner of tent, "your bloodline will be completely erased from existence, the Romonov empire will have fallen and the power I have been chasing will finally be mine." Then he's gone, leaving behind a cloud of smoke.

Vitriev turns to leave the tent. At the entrance, he pauses. "I loved you." He says, his words, although not sad, they're filled with something heavy, like resentment. Then he's gone.

I loved you too, I want to say, because I did. Only, I don't think I ever truly knew the real Vitriev. Maybe growing up in poverty as he had blackened his soul to desire all the things, he never had so deeply that it's poisoned who he was.

As I lay here alone, and restrained, the only thought constantly resurfacing is that of Rory, I hope he's okay.

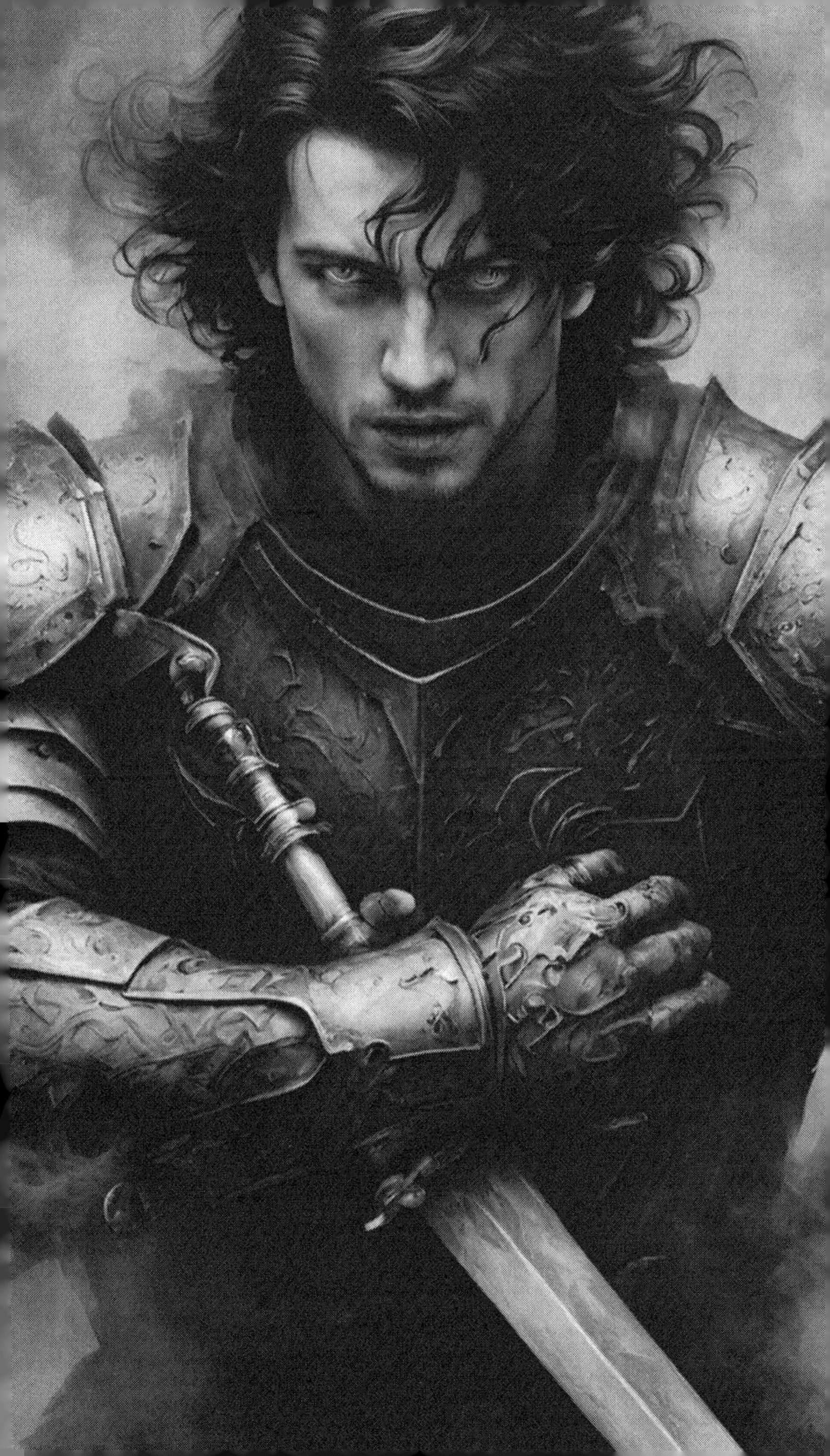

Chapter 31

Rory

    Anger burns in my chest, hot and wild as I storm through the castle. "Anastasia!" My voice echoes off the walls, a desperate and furious call. I can't find her—she's gone, and the panic in me grows with every empty room I search. Yesterday, the enemy soldiers retreated and haven't come back yet. Probably regaining strength to attack again tomorrow.

    I move like a man possessed, my boots thundering through the halls until I go outside. I've already searched everywhere, but I'll check every room over and over if it means finding a clue to where she's gone.

Every dead body I pass, I look for her face, but she's not there. I can't lose her, fuck. I turn over another body, and my breath hitches—no, not her. The relief is short-lived, swallowed by the growing fury.

I refuse to entertain the thought that I might never see her again. She's mine. She's strong, a warrior, the woman who survived me all these years. She can't just disappear; she can't leave me with this gaping hole where she should be.

"Anastasia!" I scream into the chaos, her name a prayer and a curse. My eyes scour the horizon, searching for a sign—anything.

Then, it hits me—the silence of her absence is more terrifying than the thunder of war. I've fought battles for centuries, but this, this search for the woman who haunts my every thought, is a torment like no other.

My mind races, every memory of her piercing like shards of glass. The way she moves in battle, fierce and graceful. The way her eyes spark with challenge when she's with me, the way her lips part when...

Fuck.

No. Focus.

I catch a glimpse of a man, crawling on the ground, my movements automatic, I catch the hem of his bloody shirt to lift him and turn his body so he's facing me. "Tell me where she is!" I roar at him as he falls on his back. His gaze, terrified. "I don't know... don't know what..." I growl louder. Fuck, this man is useless, dying and useless.

I let him go and start walking again, grabbing my hair with both hands. I can't stop—won't stop—until I find her. Because the truth is, without Anastasia, victory is empty. I need her by my side. My heart seems to have come alive again. And I hate it. I hate the way my eyes are tearing up because she isn't here. I hate the thunder of my heart when I'm uncertain of her safety, the gnawing, stabbing pain in my chest when I don't know where she is. I love her, and I hate it but, I'll fucking take it

The battlefield stretches on, a vast expanse of dying and dead corpses and red snow. I stand there, panting, steam coming out of my nose and mouth.

Think Rory.

I look to the skies, the last light of day casting long shadows over the land. "Anastasia," I whisper, the fury giving way to a rising dread. "Please, be alive."

The night falls with no sign of her, and I'm left with the echo of my own cries. She's nowhere, and the emptiness engulfs me.

I killed mercilessly for her, and I'll do it again. For Anastasia, I'd tear the world apart.

As the moon rises, a cold companion to my despair, I realize the hunt is far from over. I'll find her, or I'll die trying. Because she is my battle to fight for, my war to win.

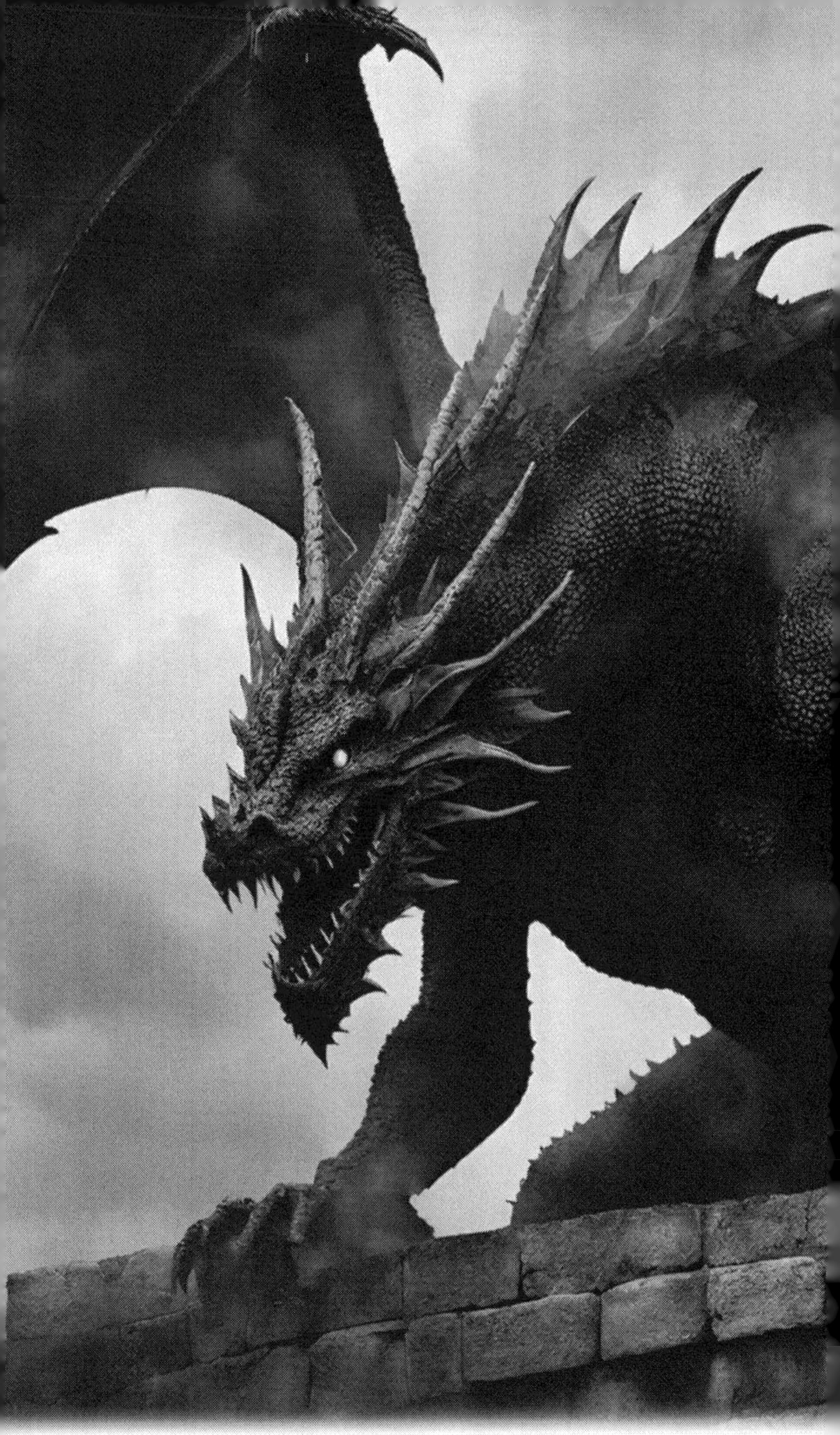

Chapter 32

Anastasia

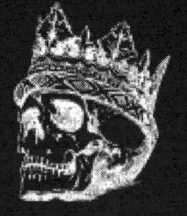

I can't shake off the confusion and the pain. My mind swimming with truths I don't want to accept. Rory—as much as he haunts my dreams—is the villain of my past. And Vitriev, my rock, the one I fled to, and the boy I loved... now, are both the monsters of my present.

I continue trying to loosen my restraints, my gaze fixed on the pointed ceiling of the tent. I analyze its fabric, yellowed by the sun but dark and heavy, clearly due to the weight of the snow that keeps falling.

My head jerks toward the entrance when I hear someone untying the knots keeping the fabric closed.

Vitriev steps inside, and I let out a sigh, turning my gaze on the wood supporting my new prison.

The fresh betrayal burns in my chest, but I can't afford to show him weakness. I need to be strong, to find a way out of this. My mind running fast with ideas, suddenly, I feel my left shoe fall to the ground, making a small thud. I angle my head towards Vitriev to see if he noticed. Slowly, I bend my knee and realize that my leg can now slip out of the rope.

Excited with this new progress at escape, I continue my arm movements, more quickly to free one hand as well. The pain is excruciating, the sensation of the rope rubbing against my already bleeding skin is a constant burn.

He steps closer, and I instinctively grith my teeth together. "You know Anastasia, even when you looked at me as just your close friend, I wanted you." he says, his eyes glinting with something dark. He still hasn't noticed my partial escape from the restraints.

He tries to kiss me, and I turn my head away, repulsed by what he's become. "Vitriev, don't." I order, enriching my voice with all the strength I have.

The rejection has his demeanor shifting from sleazy to dangerous and he grabs me, but because I'm still tied to the bed, I can only jiggle around to try to fight against his strength.

Panic sets in as I realize he's trying to force himself on me. "No!" I scream, struggling against his grip. Still trying to make sure he doesn't realize I'm now free on one foot and one hand.

I manage to lower my free hand without him noticing, too busy trying to tear at my pants, Reaching the seam of his back pocket. There, the little dagger. Gripping it quickly and I swing my arm and stab Vitriev in the cheek with a roar.

He howls in pain, releasing me for just enough time to use my hand and the knife to free myself completely and make a run for it.

I dash through the tent, my heart pounding, gasping for air. I don't get far. Two men grab me before I can escape the camp.

My arms are seized by rough hands, dragging me back as I kick and scream.

Vitriev appears again, and I expect to see him wounded, bleeding. But nothing—his cheek is unnaturally healed, not even a scar in sight. It's as if my attack never happened. He laughs at my confusion, and my stomach drops.

"A little secret," he says casually, wiping a non-existent drop of blood from his face. "Domovoi magic."

The mention of the Domovoi makes my blood turn cold. And sure enough, the dark creature materializes next to Vitriev, its eerie eyes fixed on me.

"Bad girl," the Domovoi speaks in a voice that feels like crawling shadows. "You can't escape. You're the key to the throne. And once Vitriev is king," the creature continues with a snarl, "you'll be disposed of, and I'll finally have all the kings on this continent under my control."

Just as I'm about to spit my retort back, the entire camp slumps over, hands covering their heads and ears as a giant, black dragon lands with a deafening snarl, separating Vitriev and the Domovoi, from myself.

Terror grips me, but I catch sight of its eyes, green, Rory! He's raining down destruction on the camp, roaring his fury, and setting everything on fire. Burning down the enemy in a fire that burns as hot as the passion we share.

He came for me. Despite everything, he still came to rescue me.

Enemies scream, running chaotically as he burns everything in his path. Quickly, the men holding me down on the cold ground are gone, but the madness creates a stampede, and I get pushed to the ground.

I try to adjust my gaze to the light reflecting on the snow, blinding me. Once back to my feet, my eyes focus, I no longer see the cursed old man. *Shit.*

Rory tears through the camp, killing everything in his way. Dead bodies falling from the sky, fire and blood everywhere.

A heavy sense of foreboding settles over me, even as I watch the dragon's fire cleanse the camp of my captors.

Rory and I have some things to figure out, a discussion needs to be had, and I truly don't know what I'm going to say.

413 - *Ruins and Shadows*

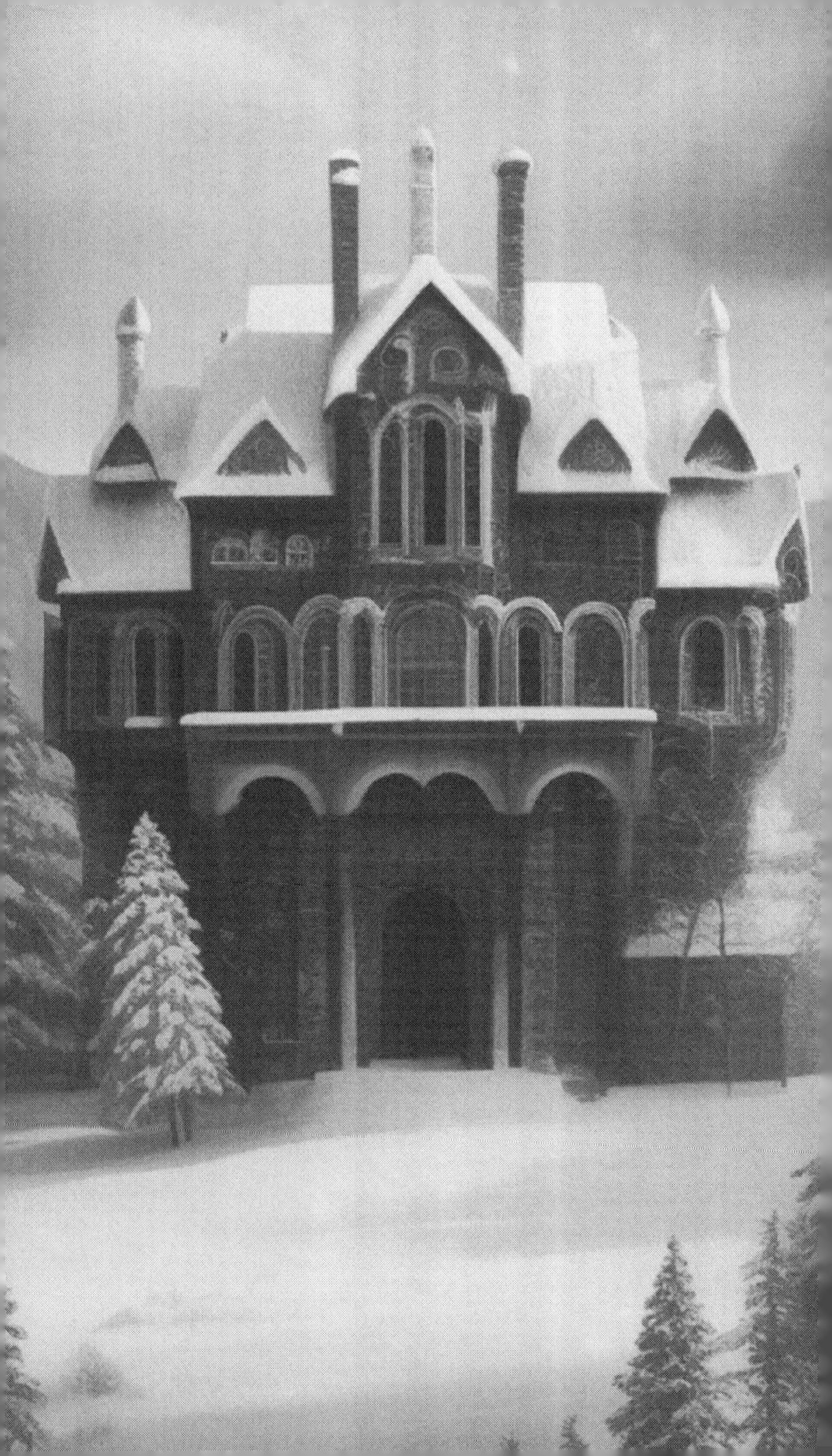

Chapter 33

Anastasia

All around me, people lay lifeless. Rory...as a dragon... is fucking terrifying. Flames and fury and... he fucking slaughtered everyone. This entire camp is the scene of a horrible massacre.

Vitriev, is kneeling on the ground, hurt but alive. For now.

Rory shifts back to his human form, his eyes on me. And I am completely in shock. He had told me that the shadows were part of him, that he controlled them, but not that he was the fucking shadows...?

He stalks towards me, his jaw muscles clenching as he speaks each word, carefully and deliberately. "I have spent four hundred years searching for you. I've stopped so many hearts; I'm not sure that I have one anymore. The only time I feel anything is when I'm by your side. So, if you think, even for a second, that I'll let you go again, now that I have you, you are mistaken, princess." he says, his voice heavy with pain.

He quickens his pace to me, surrounded by smoke, and I stand up. Unable to hold back anymore, I burst into tears.

In the comforting arms of Rory, I look down at Vitriev, my heart pounding. The pain of his traitorous betrayal cuts deeper than any blade. He looks up at me, his eyes begging for mercy.

I can't. I won't.

I take the dagger from Rory's belt, my hands steady as steel. One quick motion, right through his heart. That's the only way to end the curse, the only way to make death final.

Vitriev's eyes go wide, and then... nothing. He's gone. I feel the tears, hot and relentless, streaming down my face.

Rory doesn't say a word. Instead, he shifts back into a dragon– this giant, magnificent, terrifying black creature. Nudging me gently with his head, signaling for me to climb on, I'm too numb to argue or to fight. So, I just do.

We fly through the grey day, and it's freezing. Below us, the world is a blur of wind and snow, life is going on, people are probably cheering about the news of the enemy soldiers vanishing.

Rory's wings beat the air and looking around I realize we're somewhere unfamiliar to me.

Finally, we land in a dense forest and the area looks like it's from an entirely different world. It's isolated, no towns in sight, the forest is quiet, and the wind is less strong. A thick carpet of snow surrounds a cottage—no more like a beautiful mansion.

The white walls and the beauty of its surroundings is soothing. My emotions boil over while Rory lowers his head and I'm able to gently slide off, landing softly in the snow.

Almost immediately upon landing, a swirl of smoke lifts my hair, and I turn back around to face Rory, the handsome man I am now so accustomed to seeing.

The cold bites at my skin, but it's nothing compared to the fire burning in my belly. I'm mad, fuming mad, and I don't bother to hide it from him.

I'm screaming at him, hitting him with closed fists. I want to kill him. I want to hurt him like he's hurt me, like he's hurt everything I ever loved. He stands still and he lets me rage all my aggression out on him.

Before I can spit out the venom on the tip of my tongue, he suddenly grabs me, his fingers digging into my arms like a man clutching at salvation.

It catches me off guard, the raw need in his touch. "Fuck, I missed this." And then his lips crash against mine like the world's coming to an end.

It's a reckless, wild kiss that consumes all thought, all reason. I'm lost in the feel of him, the taste of him. Our breath mingles, hot and desperate, as we kiss like there's no tomorrow.

It's not sweet or gentle; it's fueled by anger and need, a clash of lips and teeth in a battle of wills.

We stumble into the house, a tangle of limbs and heavy breaths. This isn't love making; it's something darker, something raw. It's hatred and desire wrapped up in pure passion, and I hate myself for wanting it just as badly as he does.

My mind screams that this is wrong, that I should hate him for everything he's done. But my body doesn't listen. It betrays me, like everything else in my life.

Arching into him, I feel the hardness of him on my

lower belly. "Never again, princess." He murmurs against my open mouth, a moan escaping.

He bites my lower lips, almost tearing the skin. "I should clean myself first." I manage to say, between two breaths.

He pushes me against a wall, his hands on my shoulders, and steps back just enough for his eyes to meet mine. "Do I look like I give a fuck? I'll fuck you now. Wash you and fuck you again." He purred, eyes burning on me, his hands lowering slowly until it reaches the top of my soiled, shredded shirt.

In one movement he tears it off and I gasp, my breasts now freely bouncing in front of him, he growls low, and it sends a pulse of pleasure to my already swollen clit.

The room is filled with the sound of our harsh breaths. We move together, mouth merged, with a fierce, almost brutal rhythm, each desperate to prove something, to take something, to feel something other than the pain and betrayal that's tormented us.

He grabs my thighs between his hands and lifts me off the ground again, pressing my core against his hard cock.

Shamelessly, I grind hard, chasing the release I crave so much right now. His mouth moves to my earlobe, taking it between his teeth. "Fuck, Anastasia, the feel of your body pressed against mine. It's the closest to heaven I'll ever be." His words push me even closer to the edge of orgasm and I moan in his hair.

As if I weigh nothing, he moves, walking through halls and rooms I don't bother caring to see at the moment. My eyes are closed, as I revel in the touch, taste and feel of us tangled together.

Then I'm falling into the soft luxurious fabrics on a bed and before I have the chance to realize what's happening, where I am, and what color the sheets are, Rory is above me, kneeling between my legs, his gaze burning a hole through my morals.

Suddenly, I'm self-conscious again. "I really should clean myself up." I hug myself, trying to hide the mud, and blood and whatever other dirt is soiling my flesh.

"Arms above your head, princess." His voice is threatening, hoarse, and authoritative, and I comply quietly. "If you mention the dirt covering you again, I'll tie you to this bed and gag you with a towel."

And just like that, I feel loved. He grabs the hem of his black shirt and pulls it over his head, tossing it somewhere in the room. We don't take our eyes off each other. And the warmth in my entire body completely consumes me.

His movements are slow, sensual, and so masculine, probably not even realizing it. I bite my lower lip, paying special attention as his hands go to his pants, removing them.

His hard cock springs free in front of me, a bead of pre-cum on the tip of it. "Do you like watching me, Anastasia?" His voice draws my attention to his face once again, and I nod. "You are such a beautiful girl. My golden freckled princess," he purrs.

He takes his hard length in his hand and starts stroking himself on top of my pulsing pussy, still covered by my filthy pants. "You want me to touch myself for you?" He asks, his voice cutting through with pleasure, the sight of his abs contracting with every wrist movement, the strength with which he grips his cock, and the way he tilts his head back, his eyes closed, and he moans making my core pulse even more.

Involuntarily, I try to close my thighs, applying pressure to relieve myself. He lowers his head, opens his eyes, and catches my hips moving. He stops touching himself, smirks mischievously, and brings his face above mine. "Such a needy, girl. Do you see what you've done to me?"

Without missing a beat, he grips my pants and rips them off. Tossing them somewhere in the room with his own clothing. His mouth on mine, teeth clashing, passion devouring us.

He guides his cock between my thighs, rubbing it on my slit. Up, and down. Again.

Again.

Again.

And again.

I moan so hard; my own ears start to ring in my head. "Fuck, baby. You I feel so good." His voice emerges in a groan of pleasure. I open my mouth against his to try to respond, but in one thrust, he's in me, entirely.

I grip his back with my nails, marking him, leaving scratches and imprints. Each stroke penetrates me more deeply, the sound of skin against skin surrounding us completely until I feel my insides contract, tingles starting to build in my belly and coming up to my nape. "Come for me, milk me, baby." That's my undoing and my orgasm explodes around him. Contracting and sucking his cock for everything I can get out of it.

He jerks one last time inside me and I feel the rope of cum coating the inside of my pussy.

The storm inside us finally quietens to a dull roar, we're left breathless, staring into each other's eyes, wondering what the hell just happened.

We lie there, a mess of limbs and ragged breaths, and I whisper against his lips, "I wanted to kill you." I say, against his chest.

He runs a hand through my hair. "I know. Now, let me wash you while we speak." I lift my head and look at him with a questioning expression. "Fuck, I love this nose," he says, smiling softly and bopping the tip of my nose playfully. "What?" I question.

"When you're thinking, your nose does a little wiggle dance," he admits casually. I smile back at him and rest my head again on him, hiding my childish smile.

Did he really catch that? All this time with Vitriev, he never saw that. But Rory saw me.

"Come on, let me take you to the bathtub and conjure some hot water, I'll take care of you."

I have so much to say, so much to ask. Maybe even stab him somewhere, *he will heal anyway.*

For now, a hot soak in a bath sounds heavenly.

He walks me into a bathing room with a large freestanding bronze bathtub in the center, the ambiance is comforting and peaceful.

Waving his hand towards the tub, steam appears, rising into the air, fogging the windows and the mirror. I face him, his big green eyes in mine, I run my fingers over his stubbled beard. "We'll find a way to beat this, Rory." He nods, his eyes searching mine for something, maybe for the same hope I'm clinging to. "Together," he agrees.

We end up tangled in the hot water, staring at the ceiling, I can feel the rise and fall of his breathing against my back. He wanted to talk, but we find ourselves too comfortable in this silence. Behind me he's stroking my arms in a gentle caress up and down.

I turn my head to look at Rory, his face a mixture of his own inner conflicts. And I realize then, that he possesses more humanity than he believes.

I see the suffering of a past I do not yet know the details of, and I hate that I can see the misery and pain on his face and that I can feel it, and I hate how sad it makes me to see him war with himself constantly. Sometimes, the line between man and monster gets blurry, I need him, both the man...and the monster.

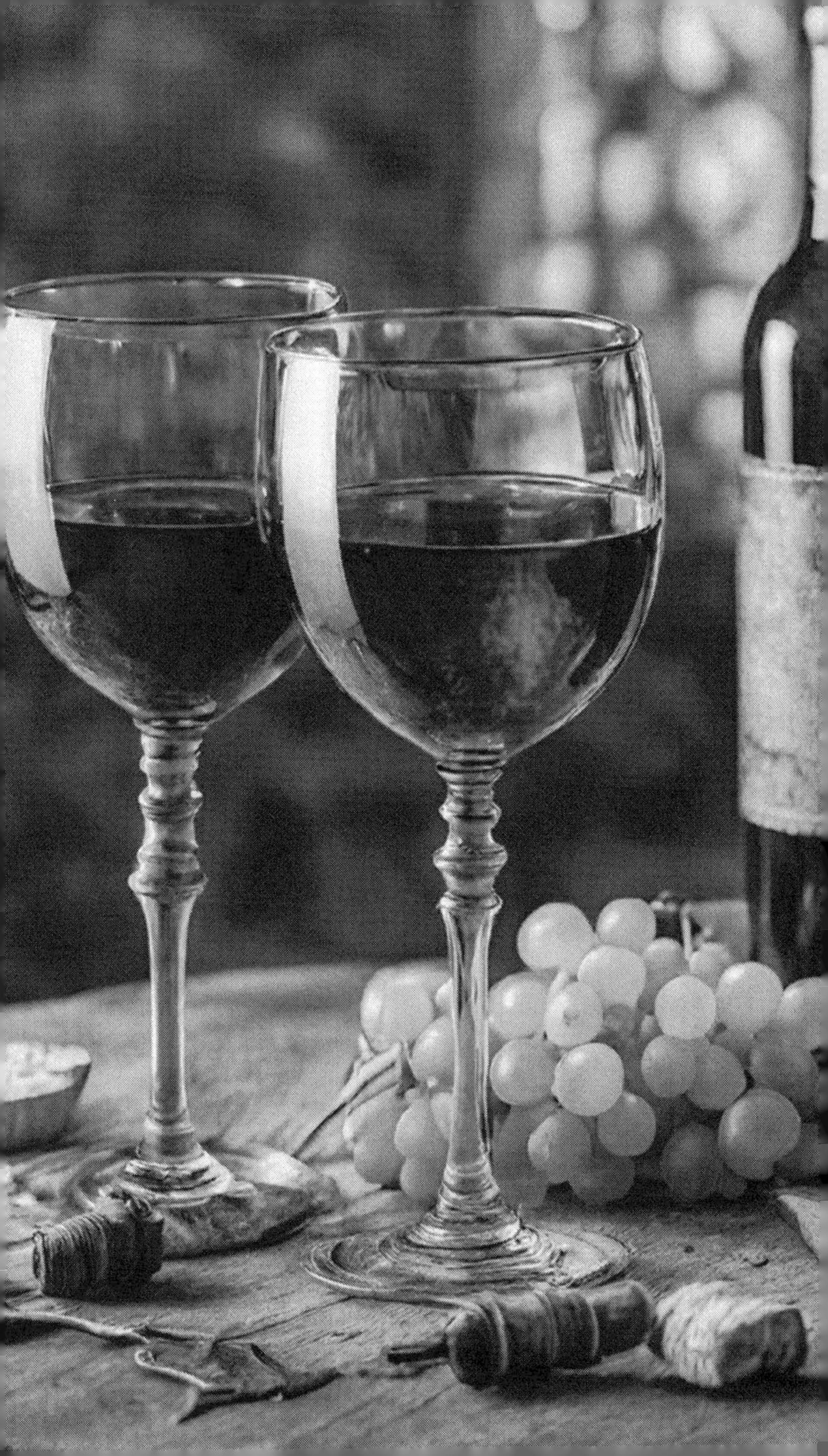

Chapter 34

Anastasia

Sunlight spills through the windows of Rory's secret house, slicing through the stillness of the morning. I wake up alone, the other side of the bed cold, the sheets untouched.

Sitting up, I push away the tangle of dreams that cling like cobwebs. My mind's a battlefield and waking up without Rory only tightens the knots in my chest.

Looking around the room, I take in the sight before me. It's large, majestic, yet simple at the same time. A fireplace faces the bed, adorned with large stones.

The fire blazes, warming my face. The walls are white, like the snow falling outside the large windows. I'm in a four-poster dark wooden bed with cream silk sheets.

I get out of bed and cling to a big wolf fur decorating an old chair in the corner, then start walking lightly towards the door that leads to the rest of the house.

I find him in the kitchen, staring into space with a cup of untouched tea in his hands. The sight of him looking so broken chips away at my heart.

"Good morning," I say, my voice a careful mix of worry and warmth. "You're up early."

He doesn't turn to look at me, his voice flat. "I couldn't sleep."

I take a seat across from him at the table, my eyes on his face. "Rory," I start, gentle but insistent, "what's going on?"

He sets the cup down with a clatter, finally meeting my gaze. "The Domovoi," he says, and the weight in those two words is enough to make me lean in closer.

"Son of a bitch. What about it?"

Sighing, Rory looks down, his fingers tracing the wood grain of the table. "It wants me to... to kill you," he confesses, and the words knock the air right out of me.

My heart jackhammers. "But you won't, right?"

"I can't," he says, his eyes flashing with something like fear. "It's given me an ultimatum—kill you myself or I get to witness your horrible suffering and then watch you die a death, damning your soul."

I swallow hard, a cold dread curling in my stomach. "So, what, you're just going to let it damn you?"

"No," he exhales, the edges of his eyes creasing. "I prefer you to kill me. I would rather face oblivion than cause you harm." The room spins a little. "What?! No, are you fucking bent? I'm not killing you Rory, I can't," tears are streaming down my face.

Rory's jaw tightens. "I can't live knowing I'm supposed to kill you. I won't."

He rises from his chair and walks towards me. I look at him, trying to understand what he's up to. He grabs the handle of a dagger at his belt and extends it in my direction. "Swift, strong and straight through, princess," His voice is low, sad, and completely different from the one I know and love.

I take the blade from him and send it flying across the room. "I can't!" I yell. "We'll find another way." I say, my voice lacking confidence, and full of desperation.

Tears roll down my cheeks and he leans down, resting his head against my forehead. "I've tried for 400 years, princess. We can't just—" I press my finger to his lips. "Shh, Rory, look at me." I demand, and he does. "We will find a solution together, whatever it takes." There's a long, loaded silence as Rory stares at me, raw and unguarded.

His hands grip my arms as if he's afraid I'll vanish again. "I can't kill you, Anastasia," he repeats, a desperate plea in his eyes, his eyes getting shiny with unshed tears.

I grab his face, making him focus on me. "And you won't have to."

We cling to each other, "we'll find a way," I whisper against his lips, more a vow than a promise.

Rory nods, his eyes searching mine. "Together," he agrees. Heat starts spreading through his pupils and before either of us says a word, he lifts me onto the kitchen table. It creaks under my weight as he lays me back, and I feel the sudden chill of the cold wood on my skin.

He lowers himself between my thighs. The hunger in his eyes could devour me whole, and fuck, I would let him.

His hands, those traitorously gentle beasts, trail up my legs, pushing the fur I was wearing aside with an urgency that echoes the pounding of my heart. "You're mine," he grunts, and his voice is nothing but raw, primal claim. It makes my entire body shiver with trepidation and excitement. I strain against him, the promise of his mouth so close to where I need him most. "Then prove it," I dare him back, my words a breathless invitation.

Rory's lips graze over me, a wicked tease. His breath is hot, and every exhale is like a spark along my pussy. "You are so wet I can see it glistening like the fucking diamond your pussy is. Perfect."

When he finally puts his mouth on me, it's a shockwave. His tongue is relentless, delving deep, and I can't help but cry out. He is marking me, claiming me with every flick and swirl.

His fingers aren't idle either; they move inside me, curving in a way that has me feral for every touch, bucking my hips trying to increase the friction, "Rory!" It's all I can manage, a plea, a curse, a prayer.

He looks up at me, his face glistening with my wetness. "You like that?" he taunts before biting gently on my clit, just enough to have me seeing stars and making the table shake on its weak legs.

I'm close, so damn close, the pleasure coiling tight, ready to snap. "Don't stop, don't you dare—" But my words end in a scream as he works me over the edge, my orgasm hitting me like thunder.

At the same moment, the table decides to give out, legs breaking with a crash that sends us both tumbling onto the floor.

I'm laughing, a wild, free sound that I barely recognize as my own, and Rory, he's laughing too the sound so sincere, so beautiful that my eyes fill with tears.

"Princess," he says, still breathless, still laughing, "you owe me a new table." He grins, that cocky, shameless grin. "Only if you promise to break it in with me," I respond.

I pull him down for a rough, messy kiss, our laughter mingling with the taste of each other. This is us—wild, reckless, and real. I wouldn't have it any other way.

The air is chilly, sending shivers down my body as I stretch my legs, the snow crunching under my boots with every flex. I'm out in the woods behind the house, stealing some time for myself.

After the table incident, with Rory, things got a bit too quiet for my taste. I needed to get my blood pumping again, find my center, calm myself. Killing Vitriev —that's a thought I shove deep down, not ready to face it head-on just yet, and when it tried to surface, I needed to get away.

I'm swinging through my drills, punching, and kicking' at trees, when the rustle of footsteps comes up behind me.

Rory strolls over, and I can't help a huff of surprise. "You decide to join the party?" I call out, skidding to a stop with my fists still in the air.

He raises an eyebrow, something like amusement flickering in those deep eyes. "It's hardly a party without me, don't you think, princess?" His voice calm.

My chest tightens, but I bat the sensation away. "Well, I am not the one who ran off to sulk in his fancy tub," I shoot back, heat rising in my cheeks.

Rory steps closer, "I propose something else," he murmurs, close enough now that I can see the flecks of silver in his eyes. "A walk. With me."

I give him a once-over, skeptically. "A walk? What are we courting now?" I tease.

He just grins, the kind that's all charm and no bad intentions.

Rory leads the way, and it's clear he knows these paths like they're written in the lines of his hands—every root, every branch, a part of a map he's drawn a thousand times over in his mind.

Rory's voice breaks the silence, a hint of vulnerability threading through his usual stoic tone. "There was someone once," he starts, the memories flickering in his dark eyes. "Her name was Lily. She was afraid of monsters." He pauses, his gaze distant. "Monsters from stories and legends. I always told her they didn't exist. But sometimes, she was still afraid. So, I promised her that I would always protect her." As he speaks, it becomes clear that this isn't just a casual conversation. This is Rory Rasputin, peeling back the curtain to reveal the haunting fragments of a life steeped in legend, exposing the raw wounds he's carried beneath the cloak of enigma and enchantment.

"Every twisted vine around here," he says, stopping to touch a gnarled tree trunk, "carries a memory of mine. Of a time before I became... this." He gestures to himself, an ironic twist to his lips.

We keep walking until the woods open to a clearing, and Rory's voice fades, leaving us with just the silence and the secrets that hang between us, as heavy as the cloak he usually wears. "This was Lily's favorite lake to swim with me." He murmurs.

He doesn't waste any time. "Anastasia," his voice is heavy, weighted with a sorrow that's palpable even to me, "there are things you need to know, things about me, about my family." He's silent for a beat, and the forest seems to hold its breath with him.

I feel the unease roll off him in waves, the internal battle he's waging. His next words come out harshly, as if they're being torn from him. "Over four centuries ago, I did something unforgivable," he confesses. The words hang between us, a dark cloud obscuring the remnants of sunlight filtering through the trees.

He tells me about his family, the way he was forced to kill them himself after being lied to.

How he traveled the world after, trying to find something, something he lost.

About the Domovoi, that demanded debts paid in blood and obedience. All the horrible murders over the centuries he had commited, in the Domovoi's name.

"I did it because... because of a vision, a dream that haunted me through the endless years," Rory continues, his voice almost broken with the weight of centuries of regret. "I couldn't see her face and, her laugh was my only solace in the dark." His eyes flash to mine, unraveling me in ways I'm still reluctant to explore. "I thought... about her, I wanted to find her."

My heart clenches painfully, a mix of horror and sympathy. His admission crashes into me with the force of a winter storm—that his pursuit to find this dream-woman is what kept him tethered to life.

"I killed your family, Anastasia. I never wanted to... I had no choice. Even the people in the village where I found you. The Domovoi wanted me to kill them. I tried to let the women and children escape but—" His eyes are tormented oceans, dark and fathomless. "You were to be next, but I couldn't, I couldn't—" He breaks off, agony written in every line of his face.

My mind reels, grappling with the gravity of his confession. Betrayal, grief, and an unspoken understanding mingle like poison in my veins. He watches me, waiting for condemnation, for horror, for rejection. But what can I say? What can I do?

Because, even if I loathe myself. I love him.

"It's you." He speaks. I look at him with confusion, the sound of birds singing, and the thump of snow piles falling from branches, "the woman, Anastasia, It's you."

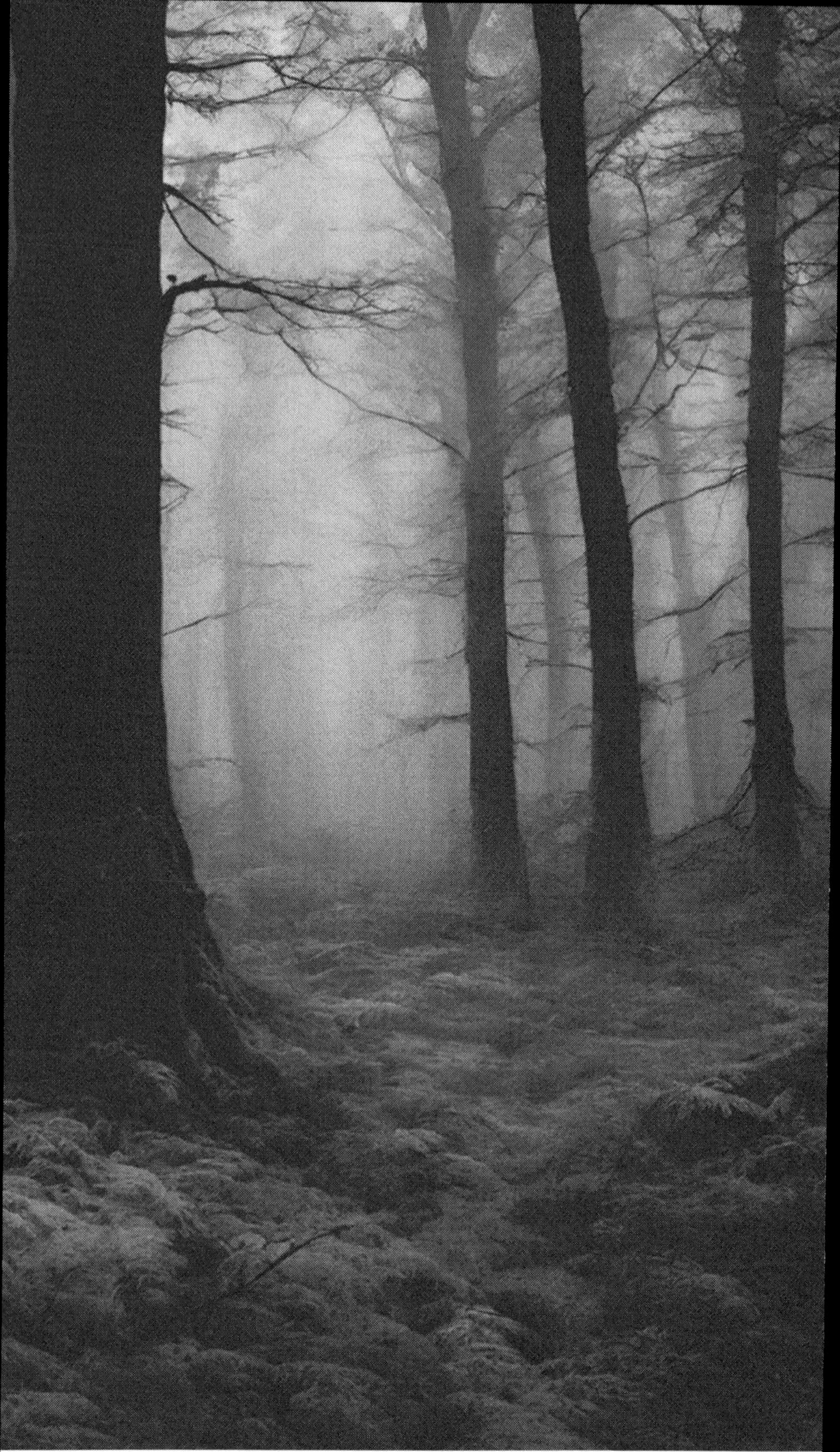

Chapter 35

Rory

My heartbeat syncs with the steady drum of boots against the forest floor. Anastasia and I, we have been walking without a word for hours, both lost in our own thoughts.

I decided to give her some space after my confession to her, and while I was searching through some of my father's old belongings, I found a book about mythical creatures, and it's become a beacon for us. A narrow chance to tackle the curse and get rid of this Domovoi bastard.

She's got this quiet determination about her, like she's ready to walk through hell itself to find answers.

We're searching for a mage, tucked away in the heart of these woods, or so the legends from the book claim. A mage with the sort of power and knowledge to perform miracles. It's a long shot, but hell, it's the only fucking thing we have left.

The dense canopy blots out most of the sky, but we press on, guided by the faintest hints of twilight that sneak through the leaves.

I steal a glance at Anastasia, see how the trees throw their shadows across her face, dancing with the fire in her eyes and the gold on her nose.

Finally, she breaks the silence. "You think this mage can really help us?" Her voice's a half-whisper, barely louder than the rustle of leaves.

I nod, feeling the familiar itch of uncertainty. "It's what the book pointed to. It has to mean something."

Anastasia looks up from the pages, trapping me in the steel of her gaze. "We end this, Rory. No matter what it takes." Her words are a bandage on my heart, I feel it echo through the very depths of me.

We make camp as night falls, a makeshift shelter of branches and leaves. The forest around us is teeming with life, but it's like we're in a bubble of our own.

I catch her eyeing me as I send shadows to start a fire. It's a look that says she sees me—the man, not just the beast or the shadows I command. "Could you just transform into a horse and take us there quickly? Damn, even a giant bird maybe?" She grunts, tossing a branch onto the fire. Anastasia snorts, her laugh bright against the dark. "Unfortunately, it doesn't work that way, princess." I chuckle my response.

The night is long, filled with the noises of the unseen. Together, we've shattered darkness before. And together, we'll do it again. The mage in the woods may have answers, but it's the strength in Anastasia's resolve that gives me hope.

At first light we journey into the heart of the forest, each step is a step closer to the end, to freedom, to a future we dare to carve out from the clutches of the past. And with each step, I feel the weight of the years lifting, the shadows receding.

These woods are quieter than a secret, and I swear even the trees are holding their breath as we shuffle through the underbrush.

A branch snaps somewhere to our left, and we both freeze. "Be ready," I whisper, taking a fighting stance. My hand on my sword, ready to swing at whatever's lurking out there.

Expecting a deadly creature, I'm surprised to see that it's a witch—well, three of them to be exact. They slink out from behind the trees, their eyes gleaming like cat's eyes in the dark.

"Rory Rasputin, you seek us," the first witch croaks, her voice creaky like an old door. "Why?" She croaks.

I step forward, chin high, like I'm about to bargain with the devil himself. "We seek knowledge on the Domovoi," I say, my voice clear.

The second witch snickers, sounding like nails on a chalkboard. "Oh, the Domovoi, is it? And what's in it for us if we help you, eh?"

"We offer a truce," Anastasia says. "Protection from others who would harm you for your craft, I'll make your existence valid for the kingdom. You won't need to stay hidden in the woods any longer."

The witches huddle together, whispering and hissing like snakes in a pit.

They break apart, and the third witch, who's been quiet this whole time, nods. "It is known that the Domovoi fears the bone of a righteous man," she says, her voice smooth as silk. "Find such a bone, and you hold power over the creature."

A righteous man? How in the fuck are we supposed to find that? I glance at Anastasia, but she's already nodding like this makes all the sense in the world.

"Thank you," she says, bowing slightly. The witches cackle, melting back into the darkness from which they came.

As we walk back, she turns to me. "So, any idea where we'll find a bone of a righteous man?" She asks, my thoughts already racing through legends and history.

I wrap my arm around her shoulders, and for a moment, she allows herself to lean on me. "We'll find it, princess," I assure her."

After the marathon trek back to my house with Anastasia, she needs a hot bath, the poor thing. Eight hours on foot is a punishing ordeal even for the strongest, and while she's a warrior through and through, she's had a rough time of late.

Her body is pulled taut with tension, and I see the weariness etched into her face. We step inside the house, the silence wraps around us like a blanket. "Anastasia," I say, turning to her, "why don't you go and soak in the bath? I've already sent hot water up."

She looks at me, her blue eyes searching mine for a moment, and then she nods. "I'd like that, Rory. Thank you." Watching her trudge up the stairs, I can practically hear every bone in her body crying out for relief.

There's a heaviness to her footsteps that wasn't there before, and it nudges at my conscience. I should have found a faster way to get her home.

I follow her up the stairs and pause at the bathroom door. The sound of water lapping against the sides of the tub filters out into the hallway, and I know she's already submerged in the soothing warmth when I reach the doorframe.

I push open the door and step inside. The room is shrouded in steam, and the scent of lavender hits me, calming and arousing all at once. She's in the tub, her skin glowing in the soft candlelight, and my breath catches in my throat. She's beautiful, so bloody exsquisite it hurts.

"Would you like to join me?" she asks without looking at me, her voice laced with sensuality and I'm fucking hard now.

My heart thumps in response, desire pooling low in my belly. "I'd like nothing more," I confess, my voice dropping to a husky whisper. "But there's something I need to do first. I promise I won't be long."

She pouts, and I have to force myself not to give in to the temptation she presents. "Hurry back, please," she says, and there's a promise in those three words that sends my blood rushing southwards.

I lean down and claim her lips with mine. Her hands snake around my neck, and I can feel the tension in her body dissipate, even if it's just for the length of our kiss.

"I'll be as quick as I can," I assure her as I pull away, the reluctance heavy in my chest. I turn and walk to the doorway when she calls after me, "don't be too long, Rory. I might start without you," her eyes, dance with a dark promise.

I groan, *oh fucking hell.*

With one last look, I leave the room and close the door behind me. I need to deal with the matter at hand quickly because the truth of it is, I want nothing more than to sink into that bath with her and fuck those pretty lips.

The forest is cold; it's a strange kind of silence that hangs over the snow-carpeted ground.

I walk through it, my breath misting in the frigid air. It's quiet, but my mind is loud—chaotic even.

The witches' words haunt me, a macabre riddle that leads me into the heart of frostbitten damn woods. They spoke of a bone of a righteous man, a weapon against the unseen forces that hounded us.

Feet crunching on the crusty snow, I find the spot—a clearing that's more a scar on the earth than anything serene. This is where I laid him to rest, the man whose righteousness was never in doubt.

My father.

The thought of what I'm about to do churns in my gut. The idea is disgusting, a sacrilege, but necessity is a cruel master.

I stand there, looking at the unassuming mound, apologizing silently for the desecration I'm poised to commit. No man could claim more goodness in his heart, in his deeds—no man I've ever known.

He was the mold I was cast from, the example I failed to replicate. A father, a leader, a guiding star extinguished too soon. And now, his rest I must unsettle to combat the creeping evil that threatens my life and the cause of the end of his.

My powers gather, shadows coiling around my fingers like serpents obedient to their master. I unleash them on the ground, commanding them to sear away the snow, to reveal the earth underneath. Steam rises, an eerie mist, as the snow vanishes, leaving behind bare, dark soil.

I focus deeper, calling on the shadows once more. They slip through the soil like ink in water, a spreading darkness that delves into the earth. I force myself to watch, force myself to bear witness as the grave is disturbed, as the resting place of a man revered is opened before me.

I can feel the tears before I acknowledge them—a betrayal of my stoic facade. They spill over, hot and unchecked, tracing paths down my cold cheeks. "I'm sorry," I whisper brokenly to the bones that now lay exposed to the harsh elements. It's a desecration of his memory, and legacy.

But it's for the greater good—a good he would have understood. I must believe that.

The femur is strongest, they say, and I find myself reaching down, fingers trembling as they brush against the remains of the man, I admired above all. With one last apology hanging in the air, I snap the bone. The sound is gruesome—a loud crack that fractures the silence and by it the last remnants of my composure.

Tears burn, but there's no time for grief. I clutch the bone tightly, the fracture a physical echo of the crack running through my heart. I need to leave, to return before suspicion finds me amongst the dead. Every step back towards the house is a step weighed with guilt, with sorrow.

My heart is heavy, burdened not just by the act of violation I've committed against my father's memory, but by a deep-seated fear. It's the fear that, despite our efforts, despite the righteousness of the bone clutched in my hand, the darkness may still consume us all.

The shadows follow me, trailing like mournful specters, as I carry with me the weight of my deed, the hope of salvation, and a bone that might just tip the scales in our favor.

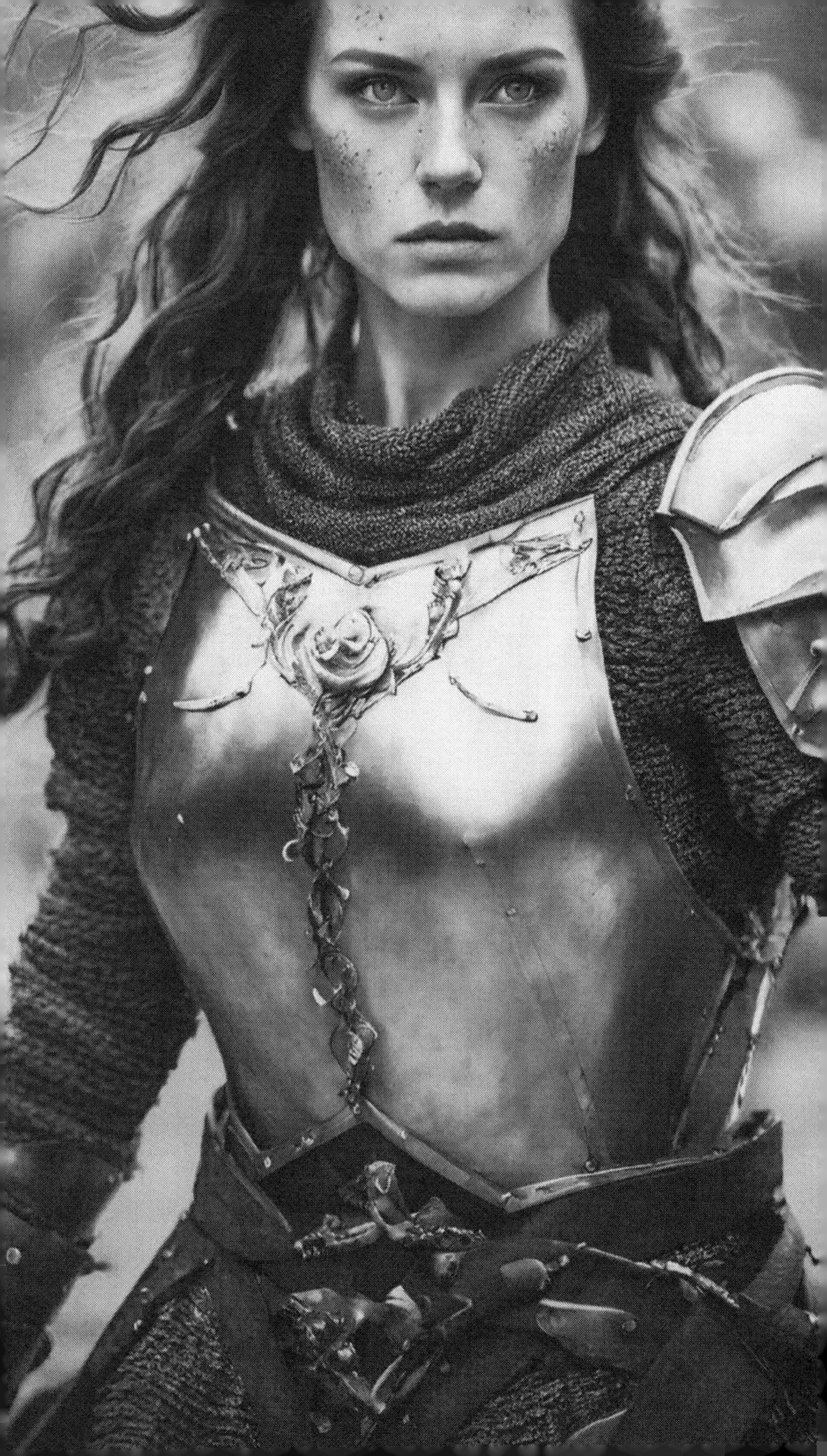

Chapter 36

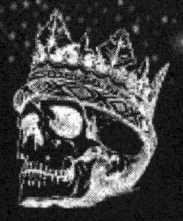

Anastasia

I steel myself, shoulders squared, as Rory and I armor up. The weight of the metal feels familiar. Today is the day we settle this.

My fingers fumble with the straps, nerves raw as I glance at Rory. His face is a mask of resolve, but I can see the shadows of doubt lurking in his eyes. "Rory," I begin, my voice steady despite the quake I feel inside. "I have an idea."

He meets my gaze, and I'm struck by the fierce loyalty I find there, a stark contrast to his usual brooding intensity. "What is it?" he asks.

I draw a deep breath. It's now or never. "We'll give the Domovoi what it wants. The blood of all the Romanov's," I say, the words tasting like iron on my tongue.

Rory stiffens, the armor plates clinking softly. "You mean—" He adds, pointing a finger in my direction.

"Yes," I interrupt, before he can voice anything. "I'll make a cut on my arm, enough for blood to be spilled. Then, you'll send your shadows to the Domovoi, show it the proof, a message that it's finally over."

His jaw clenches, and I see the battle raging within him, the urge to protect versus the necessity of our plan.

"But you'll be hurt—" he protests, a whisper of vulnerability breaking through his usually impassive demeanor and my heart swells once more.

I shake my head, the decision made, my resolve like tempered steel. "It's either that or we lose everything. I'll be fine, you know I've had worse," I say, trying to inject a note of playfulness.

Rory's hand trembles as he takes the blade from me, his eyes haunted. He knows, as well as I do, that this is our best shot. But the thought of intentionally drawing my blood, even for our ruse, visibly torments him.

"I'm so sorry for everything I did." I choose to ignore this comment. Because I have already made my decision about him.

As the sharp edge presses against my skin, I brace for the sting. It's a small sacrifice, a drop in the ocean of blood spilled in this ancient battle.

The crimson beads swiftly, a stark contrast against the white snow beneath our boots.

"Go," I urge, my heart hammering. "Send your shadows, and let's end this."

With a heavy heart, Rory nods, his magic flaring to life. The tendrils of darkness reach for the offered blood, obedient to their master's silent command.

They swirl around my arm, a macabre dance of fate, before darting off into the forest, carrying our hopes with them.

For a heartbeat, we stand there together, a pair against the world. The silence grows heavy, and I look in his green orbs.

"Hopefully, he'll think his threat worked," I murmur, more to myself than to Rory.

Rory's hand finds mine, a grip that speaks of shared burdens and unspoken trust. "It will work, Anastasia. It must, and if not, I'll fucking find a way out of the void, find you wherever you are, and keep you with me." He voices our shared desperation.

We watch as the shadows disappear. The fate of the Romanov dynasty rests on a bleeding arm and a treacherous shadow. There's nothing left to do but wait to see if the Domovoi bites the bait we've so carefully laid out.

Our gambit has been played, the board set, and now, as the cold seeps into my bones, I can't help but hope that it's enough. Rory stands beside me, his body language betraying the internal conflict that rages within him, but his presence is a silent vow—we're in this together, in death or in life.

The world slows to a crawl, like we're caught in one of those dreams where you can't move fast enough. Rory and I stand across from the Domovoi as he appears.

"You think you can scare us with your threats?" I taunt the creature, my hand gripping the hilt of my sword tightly. The blade isn't just steel and edge—it's got the bone of a righteous man woven into its very core.

When Rory came back home last night, he joined me in the bath. I was expecting a man full of desire, but what arrived was a broken man. I immediately got out of the bath, naked and dripping, and I held him in my arms. He explained to me what he had just done. And I cried with him, showering him with my kisses, and then we made love, I would have done anything to ease his burdens in that moment. Hell, I will do anything for this man.

The Domovoi growls, a sound that makes the hairs on the back of my neck stand up. "Foolish girl," it hisses. "You know not the powers you meddle with."

Rory's beside me, a solid presence that steadies my racing heart. "We're ending this, Domovoi," he declares, his voice a cold promise. "Your reign over me is done."

The creature cackles, sending chills down my spine. "Bold words for a man who once cowered before me."

But Rory doesn't flinch. Instead, he nods at me, and we charge forward as one. The battle that follows is a blur—a symphony of steel clashing, magic sparking, and roars echoing in the vast chamber.

The Domovoi's fast, but we're faster. It's like all our past fights—against each other, against the world—has led us to this moment.

I swing my sword, and the Domovoi recoils as the blade sings with the power of truth and justice. There's a flash of light so bright it's blinding, and when it fades, the creature is stumbling back, weakened.

But the pain in my chest is sharp; I look quickly. He touched me with his magic, and I'm bleeding profusely, in the unprotected area on the side of my armor near my armpit.

Rory steps forward, his hand glowing with an otherworldly light. "This is for every life you've stolen," he snarls, and thrusts his hand into the Domovoi's chest with the other half of his father's femur bone.

The scream that tears from the creature's throat is one of rage and pain. It's like the very air is being sucked out of the space. And then, with a final shudder, the Domovoi collapses to the ground, nothing more than a heap of shadows.

Rory's gaze flickers to where the dead Domovoi lays—a pile of ashes and broken curses. The beast once thought immortal, now nothing more than a whisper fading into nothingness. Its demise, our victory—bittersweet as the ash that stains my gloves.

It's over—the command of generations, the weight of Rory's past falls apart like the frail body of the Domovoi before us. The forest is heavy with the stench of burnt magic and fear turned to ash.

I watch Rory, his shoulders hunched as if he's holding the sky from crashing down upon us.

The power that streamed through his veins, the dark energy, seeps out like mist. It leaves him raw, a man sculpted by centuries of torment, shorn of his immortality.

He's mortal. Vulnerable. His chest heaves, each breath an unspoken question, each exhale a chain breaking free.

Rory staggers, his knees buckling as the enormity of it all crashes into him. I lunge forward, my arms wrap around his waist, my grip fierce. "I've got you," I whisper, my voice thick with emotion.

His hand grips mine, a lifeline in the chaos of freedom. "Anastasia," he breathes out, and there's a tremor in his voice that cuts through me. He looks at me, really looks at me, with eyes that have seen the rise and fall of entire worlds. "What have we done?"

I pull him close, our armor clinking—a chorus to our survival. "We've taken back our lives," I say, my heart pounding a triumph that scares me.

And then it happens.

"We did it," Rory murmurs, his voice echoing with disbelief. The power that once thrummed in his blood evaporates into the morning air, leaving a silence that's louder than any war cry.

Then, ever so slowly, he starts to crumble, his body giving way to the exhaustion, and the relief. I catch him, my own strength waning but enough to ground us both. We sink to the floor, a tangle of limbs and heaving breaths, the burden of ages dissipating into the dust motes dancing in sunlight.

I look at Rory, his chest heaving, his eyes wide with disbelief. "It's over," he gasps. "It's really over."

"Yeah," I say, laughing despite myself. "It is."

We rest there for what feels like forever, just breathing. Then Rory's gaze softens, and he presses me harder against him. I step into his embrace, my heart swelling with a mix of relief and something sweeter, tender.

"You're mortal now," I whisper against his chest, and I can feel his heartbeat, strong and steady.

"I am," he says, and there's wonder in his voice.

Snowflakes swirl in a lazy dance, settling on the cold ground around us. Each breath forms a cloud in the air, a fleeting wisp of life against the stark silence. Rory's close enough that I can feel the heat emanating from his body, a silent reassurance that's both comforting and unnerving.

Without warning, his hand finds my face, rough and warm. It's grounding, a connection that steadies the tremble in my bones. I appreciate the gesture, but it's his mouth, so close to mine, that steals my focus.

His lips part slightly, and I catch the scent of him—wood smoke and frost. My eyes flutter shut as he leans in, and then his lips are on mine, a touch as soft as the snow falling around us.

The kiss deepens, warming me from within. Rory's arms encircle me, pulling me on top of him, and I melt, my thoughts scattering like the flakes upon the wind.

It's madness, and yet, there's nowhere else I'd rather be. The feel of him under my palms, the taste of him eclipsing the chill, the heat of his skin through the layers—God, it's intoxicating.

As the kiss burns hotter, I become more aware of a spreading coldness, seeping into my veins, turning my blood to ice. Rapidly, the chill turns to pain, sharp and deep. With a hiss, I pull back, and the world tilts on its axis.

Rory's face blanches, horror replacing the desire I saw just a moment ago. His eyes drop, and there, staining the snow between us, is a stark blossom of crimson. The sight of my own blood is surreal. It's seeping through my armor, a wound unseen but deeply felt.

Panic grips Rory, and his hands flutter over me, helpless, desperate. "Anastasia," he says, voice cracking, "Don't leave me, please hold on."

The world loses its colors, and I'm floating, the snow and Rory's cries now distant. I can't seem to draw enough air; my chest is tight, my body numbing.

As I slip down to the ground, the last thing I feel is the warmth of his hands, frantically trying to stem the tide of red that's slowly pulling me into darkness. "DON'T YOU FUCKING DIE!" He yells in my face, but I smile.

"I love you Rory."

"Princess, NO! Please. I LOVE YOU!"

And then, I feel nothing but the cold embrace of the dark as I fall away from the world, away from Rory.

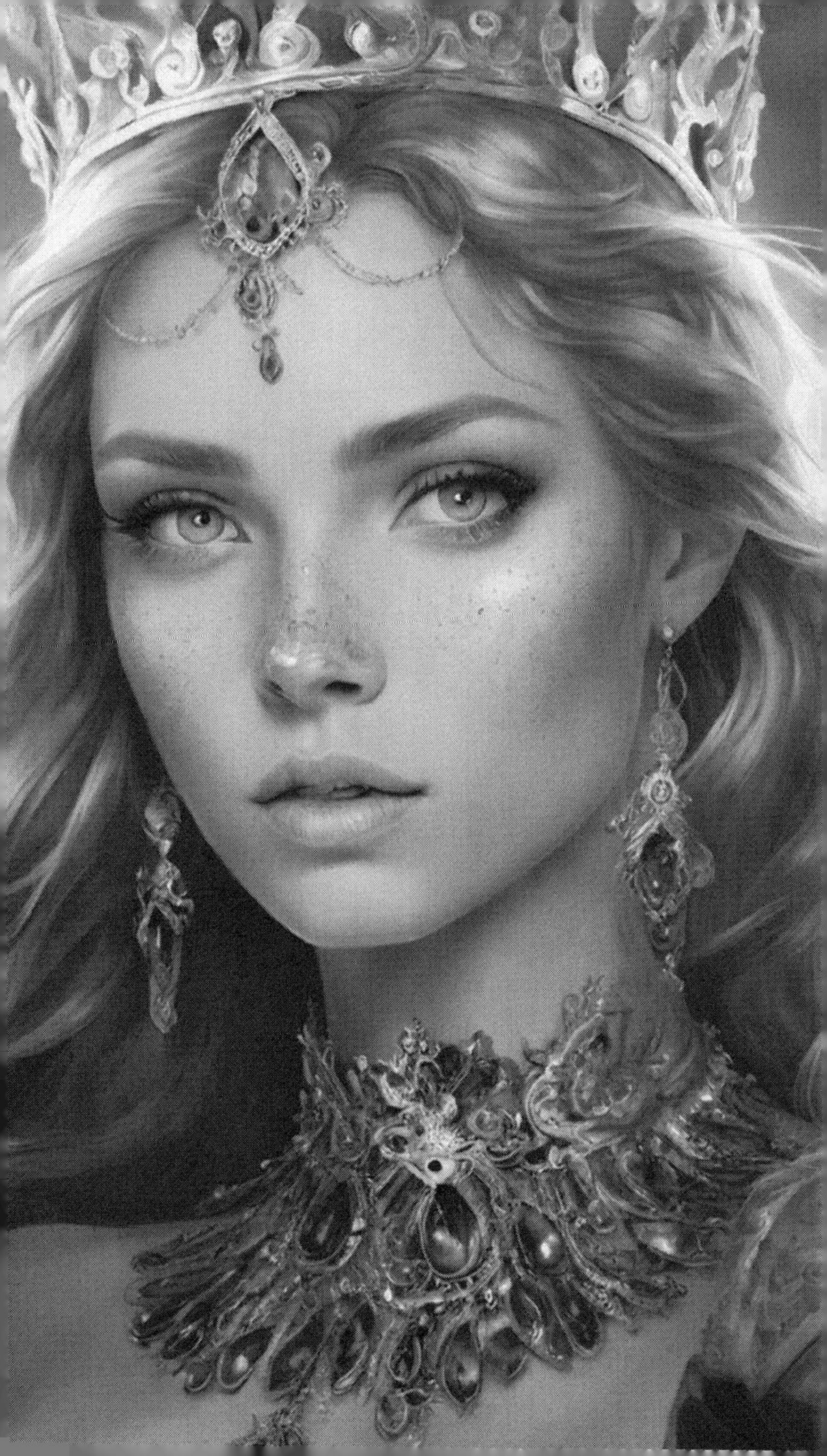

1 month after

My mind wanders back to that night, waking up in Rory's bed in the castle, surrounded by people fussing over me like a broken doll. My head was pounding, my body aching, but the worry in their eyes told me I was lucky to be alive.

Rory's face was tight with concern, sprinting to my side the moment he realized I was awake. After what happened in the woods, I feel blessed that he has saved me in more way than he could know.

I'd been out for days, they said. But now, I am, eyes wide open and staring at the future.

Four days after I came back from the brink of death, the change in the air was as clear as the sky after a storm.

No more secrets, no more shadows. It was time for change — a new era. It was time to choose our own paths, Rory and I, paths that would take us far from thrones and crowns and the echoing halls of power.

I remember watching them, the people, gathering in the square, their faces a mix of hope and desperation. They'd been through too much pain, too many wars, all of it clinging to the stones of the kingdom like stubborn moss.

And by some silent, mutual agreement, Rory and I knew we couldn't be part of that anymore. Our hands had been too deeply dipped in the blood and sorrow that stained these lands.

We organized a big ceremony, and I stood there by Rory's side. Beautiful gowns and jewels, we passed the crowns. There were cheers, the clang of bells, and the flutter of banners — the birth cries of a new chapter for a battered nation.

We decided to let the court and all the inhabitants decide their new ruler, fair and square, voices counting more than bloodlines or birthrights.

It was strange, watching them take those first trembling steps towards self-rule. After all, wasn't that what we'd always feared? Yet there I was, smiling through it all, because maybe they could do better than us. Maybe they could heal the wounds we'd left behind.

As we turned away from it all, Rory's hand found mine, his fingers gripping tight like he was afraid I'd slip away. Maybe he was right to worry. But as we walked away from the kingdom, from the past that had claimed so much of our souls, I thought about that farm, the animals, the quiet life that awaited us.

We were no longer the rulers, the cursed, or the haunted. Just Anastasia and Rory, two people with a chance to write a new story, one without battles or bloodshed, one with mornings filled with animal calls and days ending with his body wrapped around mine after our love making.

Holding my cup of herbal tea, looking out the window of the house, thinking about how different life is now. No more running, no more fighting, no more curses. Just me, Rory, and the peace we fought so hard to find.

"Anastasia?" Rory's voice pulls me back to this moment. He's got that look in his eye that says he's been thinking deep thoughts again.

"Mhm?" I answer, not yet ready to look away from the world outside.

He comes up behind me, his warmth a welcome presence. "Are you happy here?" he asks, quietly, like he's almost afraid of my answer.

I finally turn, meeting those eyes that have seen far too much. "Of course I am," I say, and I mean it. "This is our new start, right?"

Rory nods, a smile breaking through the seriousness, making him look like a new man, a free man. "No more escaping me?"

"No more battles to fight," I respond, feeling the weight of that truth settle between us.

We've lived lifetimes of hurt, but here, in this small, sturdy house, we find a different kind of strength. It's the kind that comes from quiet mornings and simple days, the kind that heals old wounds.

I take another sip of my tea, feeling the peace of our new home seep into my bones. Rory squeezes my body, and we stand there, together, looking out at the life we chose—a life without fear.

It's a strange feeling, to not be on the edge all the time. Not to worry about Rory turning into some kind of monster, about kingdoms crumbling down, about friends turning into enemies. It's quiet here, and the quiet's good.

"I think we did it, Rory," I whisper, a small smile playing on my lips. "We left it all behind."

His hand finds mine, his fingers threading through. "We did, Anastasia. We're safe here, and we're free. And I love you, for all this life and all the next."

The sun's setting now, painting the sky in colors of fire and hope. It's peaceful, and I let out a long breath, feeling like I'm letting go of the last pieces of a world that has no place here. This is our life now, no looking back.

We might not know what the future holds, but that's okay. For the first time, it feels like the future's ours to make, without any curses or ghosts from our past dictating the way.

I finish my tea and set the cup down, deciding that maybe it's time to head outside, feel the ground under my feet, remind myself that this—this quiet, this peace, this simple, beautiful life—it's real. And it's ours.

476 - *Ruins and Shadows*

About the author

Step into the world of Maryse Marullo, who explores the haunting beauty of love in the shadows. Hailing from the landscapes of Canada. Maryse is an author who thrives on the edges of passion and darkness, crafting narratives that delve into the depths of the human heart. She's addicted to dark, taboo, and forbidden romance.

Follow her on TikTok and IG for updates on upcoming releases and a glimpse into the mind behind the captivating tales of dark romance. https://beacons.ai/authormarysemarullo

By the same author

- **Say Sorry (A second chance romance novella)**
- **StepPsycho-Tangled hearts, Twisted fates Duet#1 (A dark-forbidden romance)**

Made in the USA
Coppell, TX
25 February 2024